D0953499

The Witch of
Painted Sorrows

Center Point
Large Print

Also by M. J. Rose and available from
Center Point Large Print:

The Collector of Dying Breaths
Seduction
The Book of Lost Fragrances

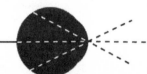

**This Large Print Book carries the
Seal of Approval of N.A.V.H.**

The Witch of Painted Sorrows

M. J. ROSE

CENTER POINT LARGE PRINT
THORNDIKE, MAINE

This Center Point Large Print edition
is published in the year 2015 by arrangement with
Atria Books, a division of Simon & Schuster, Inc.

The text of this Large Print edition is unabridged.
In other aspects, this book may vary
from the original edition.
Printed in the United States of America on permanent paper.
Set in 16-point Times New Roman type.

ISBN: 978-1-62899-609-8

Library of Congress Cataloging-in-Publication Data

Rose, M. J., 1953–
The witch of painted sorrows / M. J. Rose. — Center Point Large Print
edition.
pages cm
Summary: "A gothic novel set in 1890s Paris that captures the erotic
awakening of a young American socialite who flees her dangerous
husband only to be held captive to dark temptation"—Provided by
publisher.
ISBN 978-1-62899-609-8 (library binding : alk. paper)
1. Witches—Fiction. 2. Spirit possession—Fiction.
3. Paris (France)—History—1870–1940—Fiction.
4. Large type books. I. Title.
PS3568.O76386W58 2015b
813′.54—dc23

2015012208

My fifteenth book to Simon Lipskar,
who has been my friend and had my back for
fifteen years, for which I will be forever grateful.

"What makes night within us
may leave stars."

—VICTOR HUGO,
NINETY-THREE

Chapter 1

PARIS, FRANCE
APRIL 1894

I did not cause the madness, the deaths, or the rest of the tragedies any more than I painted the paintings. I had help, her help. Or perhaps I should say she forced her help on me. And so this story—which began with me fleeing my home in order to escape my husband and might very well end tomorrow, in a duel, in the Bois de Boulogne at dawn—is as much hers as mine. Or in fact more hers than mine. For she is the fountainhead. The fascination. She is *La Lune*. Woman of moon dreams, of legends and of nightmares. Who took me from the light and into the darkness. Who imprisoned me and set me free.

Or is it the other way around?

"Your questions," my father always said to me, "will be your saving grace. A curious mind is the most important attribute any man or woman can possess. Now if you can just temper your impulsiveness . . ."

If I had a curious mind, I'd inherited it from him. And he'd nurtured it. Philippe Salome was on the board of New York City's Metropolitan Museum of Art and helped found the American

Museum of Natural History, whose cornerstone was laid on my fifth birthday.

I remember sitting atop my father's shoulders that day, watching the groundbreaking ceremony and thinking the whole celebration was for me. He called it "our museum," didn't he? And for much of my life I thought it actually did belong to us, along with our mansion on Fifth Avenue and our summerhouse in Newport. Until it was gone, I understood so little about wealth and the price you pay for it. But isn't that always the way?

Our museum's vast halls and endless exhibit rooms fascinated me as much as they did my father—which pleased him, I could tell. We'd meander through exhibits, my small hand in his large one, and he'd keep me spellbound with stories about items on display. I'd ask for more, always *just one more,* and he'd laugh and tease: "My Sandrine, does your capacity for stories know no bounds?"

But it pleased him, and he'd always tell me another.

I especially loved the stories he told me about the gems and fate and destiny always ending them by saying: "You will make your own fate, Sandrine, I'm sure of it."

Was my father right? Do we make our own destiny? I think back now to the stepping-stones that I've walked to reach this moment in time.

Were the incidents of my making? Or were they my fate?

The most difficult steps I took were after certain people died. No deaths were caused by me, but at the same time, none would have occurred were it not for me.

So many deaths. The first was on the morning of my fifteenth birthday, when I saw a boy beaten and tragically die because of our harmless kisses. The next was the night almost ten years later, when I heard the prelude to my father's death and learned the truth about Benjamin, my husband. And then there were more. Each was an ending that, ironically, became a new beginning for me.

The one thing I am now sure of is that if there is such a thing as destiny, it is a result of our passion, be that for money, power, or love. Passion, for better or worse. It can keep a soul alive even if all that survives is a shimmering. I've even seen it. I've been bathed in it. I've been changed by it.

Four months ago I snuck into Paris on a wet, chilly January night like a criminal, hiding my face in my shawl, taking extra care to be sure I wasn't followed.

I stood on the stoop of my grandmother's house and lifted the hand-shaped bronze door knocker and let it drop. The sound of the metal echoed inside. Her home was on a lane blocked off from rue des Saints-Pères by wide wooden double doors. Maison de la Lune, as it was called, was one of a half dozen four-story mid-eighteenth-century stone houses that shared a courtyard that backed up onto rue du Dragon. Hidden clusters like this were a common configuration in Paris. These small enclaves offered privacy and quiet from the busy city. Usually the porte cochère was locked and one had to ring for the concierge, but I'd found the heavy doors ajar and hadn't had to wait for service.

I let the door knocker fall again. Light from a street lamp glinted off the golden metal. It was a strange object. Usually on these things the bronze hand's palm faced the door. But this one was palm out, almost warning the visitor to reconsider requesting entrance.

I was anxious and impatient. I'd been cautious on my journey from New York to Southampton and kept to my cabin. I'd left a letter telling Benjamin I'd gone to visit friends in Virginia and assumed that once he returned and read it, it would be at least a week before he'd realize all was not what it seemed. One thing I had known for certain—he would never look for me in France. It would be inconceivable to Benjamin that any wife of his could cross the ocean alone.

Or so I assured myself until my husband's banking associate, William Lenox, spotted me on board. When he expressed surprise I was traveling by myself, I concocted a story but was worried he didn't believe me. My only consolation was that we had docked in England and I had since crossed the channel into France. So even if Benjamin did come looking, he wouldn't know where I'd gone.

That very first night in Paris, as I waited for my grandmother's maid to open the door, I knew I had to stop thinking of what I had run away from. So I re-focused on the house I stood before and as I did, felt an overwhelming sense of belonging, of being welcome. Here I would be safe.

Once again I lifted the door knocker that had so obsessed me ten years before when I'd visited as a fifteen-year-old. The engravings on the finely modeled female palm included etched stars, phases of the moon, planets, and other archaic symbols. When I'd asked about it once, my grandmother had said it was older than the house, but she didn't know how old exactly or what the ciphers meant.

After standing at the door for a few moments without gaining entry, I lifted the hand and let it drop again. Where was the maid? Grand-mère, one of Paris's celebrated courtesans, hosted lavish salons on Tuesday, Thursday, and many Saturday evenings, and at this time of day was usually upstairs, preparing her toilette: dusting poudre de riz on her face and décolletage, screwing in her *opale de feu* earrings, and wrapping her signature rope of the same blazing orange stones around her neck. The strand of opal beads was famous. It had belonged to a Russian empress and was known as Les Incendies. The stones were the same color as my grandmother's hair and the highlights in her topaz eyes. She was known by that name— L'Incendie, they called her, The Fire.

We had the same color eyes, but mine almost never flashed like hers. When I was growing up, I kept checking in the mirror, hoping the opal sparks that I only saw occasionally would intensify. I wanted to be just like her, but my father said it was just as well my eyes weren't on fire because it wasn't only her coloring that had inspired her name but also her temper, and that wasn't a thing to covet.

It wasn't until I was fifteen years old and witnessed it myself that I understood what he'd meant.

I let the hand of fate fall again. Even if Grand-mère was upstairs and couldn't hear the knocking, the maid would be downstairs, organizing the refreshments for the evening. I'd seen her so many nights, polishing away last smudges on the silver, holding the Baccarat glasses over a pot of steaming water and then wiping them clean to make sure they gleamed.

Certainly Bernadette, if it was still Bernadette, should have heard the knocker, but I had been waiting more than five minutes, and no one had arrived to let me in. Dusk had descended. The air had grown cold, and now it was beginning to rain.

Fat, heavy drops dripped onto my hat and into my eyes. And I had no umbrella. That's when I did what I should have done from the start—I stepped back and looked up at the house.

The darkened windows set into the limestone facade indicated there were no fires burning and no lamps lit inside. My grandmother was not in residence. And neither, it appeared, was her staff. I almost wished the concierge had needed to open the porte cochère for me; he might have been able to tell me where my grandmother was.

For days now I had managed to keep my sanity only by thinking of this moment. All I had to do, I kept telling myself, was find my way here, and then together, my grandmother and I could mourn my father and her son, and she would help me figure out what I should do now that I had run away from New York City.

If she wasn't here, where was I to go? I had other family in Paris, but I had no idea where they lived. I'd only met them here, at my grandmother's house, when I'd visited ten years previously. I had no friends in the city.

The rain was soaking through my clothes. I needed to find shelter. But where? A restaurant or café? Was there one nearby? Or should I try and find a hotel? Which way should I go to get a carriage? Was it even safe to walk alone here at night?

What choice did I have?

Picking up my suitcase, I turned, but before I could even step into the courtyard, I saw an advancing figure. A bedraggled-looking man wearing torn and filthy brown pants and an overcoat that had huge, bulging pockets, staggered toward me. Every step he took rang out on the stones.

He's just a beggar who intends no harm, I told myself. *He's just looking for scraps of food, for a treasure in the garbage he'd be able to sell.*

But what if I was wrong? Alone with him in the darkening courtyard, where could I go? In my skirt and heeled boots, could I even outrun him?

He was so close now I could see the grime on his face and hands. Smell his putrid odor. From the way he was eyeing me and my luggage, there was no doubt he was planning something. If he tried to grab my suitcase, I couldn't fight him off. At least a foot taller than me, he was also broad-shouldered and thickset. It was my fault—I hadn't stopped to ensure the porte cochère was locked behind me.

I fumbled in my bag for my keys. Little did it matter they were to our Fifth Avenue mansion in New York City. The familiar feel of them brought on a wave of sadness, but I fought it off. My immediate situation required acting quickly.

Jangling the keys, I pretended to use them, all the while feeling his eyes on my back.

Holding my breath, I waited to hear his retreating footsteps. But there was no such sound.

So I called out, as if to my grandmother's maid, that it was all right, I would get the door myself.

I knew the beggar understood me. Even though I'd grown up in America, my father had taught me to speak French with an accent as good as any local's.

When I still didn't hear the stranger's retreating footsteps, I called again to Bernadette that she should tell my husband or the houseman to come down, that the lock was stuck and I needed help with the suitcase.

Finally, from behind, I heard a sound. At last. The tramp was leaving. But no! I was wrong. He was laughing. And coming closer.

"There's no one home," he called out.

With my hand still on the doorknob, I half turned. "Get away from here before you get in trouble."

"Everyone who lives here has been gone for over a week."

"You're wrong. They are all home. Someone is coming now, so you should leave while you can."

The beggar laughed again. "Moved out. Saw them myself. The fancy madame and her maid and her manservant. Valises and boxes galore."

"You are mistaken. They are all here upstairs, and my husband—"

"You may have a husband. And he very well might have been here . . . so very many women's husbands come here . . . but if yours was here, he's long gone."

17

He took another step and reached out for my suitcase. At the same time leering at me with an expression that suggested he might decide to take more than my luggage.

I was frozen, unable to move, to run, to scream, or to make any effort at all to help myself. My shoulder pushed against the door as I twisted the doorknob, willing it to somehow magically open and give me entry. I might as well have been standing in front of a stone fortress. I was trapped. Powerless again.

And then something changed. I felt a surge of anger. A refusal to accept what seemed so inevitable.

"Get away from me," I shouted as if my words were a weapon.

The vagabond laughed at me, knowing better.

Indeed, nothing should have suggested that my words were a force to be reckoned with except my sense that they were. I let go of the doorknob, shouted at him again to leave, and when he didn't, outrage and anger and frustration all mixed together, and from a place that I didn't know I possessed, determination and fearlessness rose up. I pushed the man away from me.

"No!" I shouted. And again, *"No!"* in a voice that was unrecognizable to me.

Something inside me refused to accept what was happening.

The surprise attack sent the stranger sprawling,

and he slid down the steps into the gutter. I hadn't known he was carrying a knife until I saw it fall from his hand onto the cobblestones. It lay there next to him, glinting in the street lamp's light. Rushing, I grabbed it just before he did.

And then I felt the man's fingers wrap around my ankle and grip it tightly.

No!

I kicked free. And then kicked again, the toe of my boot making contact with his nose, or his chin or his cheek—I couldn't see, but I heard a sickening crack.

He let out a primitive howl far louder than my own shouts. Blood began to trickle from his nose. He writhed in pain.

Who was I? I did not know the woman capable of this. What were the limits of her abilities? I only knew that she was fighting for her life, and that unlike me she thought her life was worth fighting for.

"You whore," the man bellowed as he began to rise up. He was looking at me so differently now. Before he'd appraised me as if I were a prize waiting to be claimed. Now I deserved punishing. It was there in his expression of fear mixed with hatred.

"Give me back my knife!"

"Don't come any closer to me or I'll use it," I shouted back. My father had taught me how to use a pistol, but for me a knife had no use other than cutting the chicken or beef on my plate.

But I sensed this new woman I'd become knew how to wield one.

Suddenly the door of the mansion next to my grandmother's was flung open, and a man rushed out, yelling as he ran down his steps. He brandished a pistol.

"Who is there? What is going on?"

The would-be thief cast one glance toward the newcomer and his weapon and took off. In seconds all that remained of him was an echo of his wooden shoes clattering as he ran away.

The knife fell from my hand with a clang as the energy drained out of my body, and I sank to my knees.

"Are you hurt?" the man asked in an impossibly familiar voice.

Slowly, I lifted my head and looked at him. It had been ten years since I'd been in Paris, but my grandmother's next-door neighbor had hardly changed. If there was more gray in his hair, I couldn't see it in the dim light.

"Professor Ferre?"

"*Mais oui*," he said, surprised and confused as to how I might know him.

In those same ten years, I had changed. Grown from a hopeful young girl of fifteen to an aggrieved twenty-five-year-old woman.

"It's Sandrine."

"Sandrine! Oh my. Are you hurt?"

"Yes."

"Where? How?"

"My foot. My ankle is twisted, that's all . . . but I . . . I . . ."

"You are in shock. Come, let me help you inside. My wife will get you some dry clothes. We'll take a look at your foot."

I looked down, almost surprised to see my dress and shawl were completely soaked through.

"But my grandmother, where is she?"

"Come inside first. You need dry clothes and a glass of wine. I will explain."

He put his arm around me and started to walk me away from my grandmother's house toward his own.

"My luggage," I said.

"I'll come right back and get it," he said. "That man is gone. It's safe for a few moments. This normally never happens. The porte cochère is kept locked when the concierge goes out. That fool must be drunk again."

We walked down the few steps from one front door and up the few steps to the other. All the buildings here had been built at the same time, and had similar layouts inside. But whereas the vestibule in my grandmother's house was ornate and lavish, the inside of the professor's house was elegant and subdued. I had been here before, all those years ago, and like the owner, it did not seem to have changed.

He sat me in a velvet, deep-cushioned chair in the parlor despite my dripping clothes and called up to his wife, who, hearing the racket, was already halfway down the stairs.

Madame Ferre was dressed in a camel silk afternoon dress with cream lace at the throat and wrists, and her once glorious chestnut hair was shot through with gray. But she was still lovely, with warm brown eyes that my grandmother said showed how guileless she was.

"You can always tell how wicked a woman's life has been by the light in her eyes, Sandrine," she used to tell me, and then she'd look into my eyes and say: "I see good, only good, in your honeyed eyes, *mon ange*. Stay like that, Sandrine. Don't become like me. Don't light any fires . . . Too easily the flames leap out to lick and burn you." And then she'd smile in that coy way she had and kiss me lightly on my forehead as if blessing me.

But I never quite believed her because, as much as she admired women like Madame Ferre and my mother, I knew Grand-mère regarded their lives as boring.

"What is all the racket about, Louis? I didn't know you—" And then, seeing me, Madame Ferre stopped talking.

"It's Eva's granddaughter, Sandrine," the professor told his wife.

"Of course it is," she said as she took me in

her arms and began to fuss over me, pulling the sodden shawl off my shoulders and brushing my wet hair off my face. "You poor child, soaked to the bone. What on earth happened?"

Her kindness, the warmth of their home with the flickering fire in the hearth, and all of its familiarity brought me close to tears, but I held back. It would not do to cry in front of these two people.

"Are you all right?" she asked.

I nodded.

"Henri must be at the café again," the professor said. "We need to do something about him. He left the porte cochère open, and that beggar who has been hanging around all week came after her. I need to go get her luggage before some other malcontent makes off with it."

"What did he do to you, dear?" Madame Ferre asked in a low voice once her husband had left the room.

"He only grabbed my foot. I twisted my ankle getting loose." I was still shivering, half from cold, half from shock. How had I been able to fight that man off? I'd never done anything like that before.

"You are freezing and can catch your death this way," Madame Ferre said as she helped me to my feet. "You need a warm bath and dry clothes."

My ankle gave way under me, but she had me by the elbow and kept me standing upright. "Can you hobble upstairs with me? How bad is the pain?"

I tested it. "As long as I'm careful, it's all right," I said. I wanted the bath she was offering more than I cared about the twinges.

I allowed myself to be escorted up the staircase and into the bathroom, where I sat and watched as Madame Ferre drew a bath for me, loaded it with salts, and then helped me out of my clothes.

While I soaked, she left to get me some of her things to wear, and when she came back ten minutes later, her arms full of clothes, I realized I'd fallen asleep in the warm water, which was now growing chilly.

Madame Ferre opened a large bathsheet and held it up as I stepped out of the tub. Then, wrapping me in the towel's softness, she proceeded to rub me dry.

Her motherly kindness was very welcome but also awkward to accept.

The Ferres had three sons and a daughter. When I was fifteen, my parents took me on a tour of the continent and, when they went off to Russia, where my father had business, left me to stay in Paris with my grandmother. During that spring I met all the Ferre children. Their youngest son, Leon, was eighteen and a sculpture student at the École des Beaux-Arts. We became fast friends.

Many afternoons, Leon and I would go to the Louvre, where, as part of his schoolwork, he was modeling a copy of a sculpture by Canova of Cupid reviving Psyche, who lay unconscious on rocks. The artist had captured the moment just before the winged god kissed Psyche awake.

The eroticism in the marble masterpiece fueled the growing attraction between us. For hours at a time I would sit and watch Leon model, awed by his talent, stirred by— What was it?

What is it ever that ignites that first spark? All I knew was that I was sure there would never be anyone like him in my life again, and I wanted to soak up every minute with him that I could.

Sometimes I'd imagine feigning a faint so that Leon would stop his work . . . come to me . . . bend over me and touch me with his lips, reviving me the way Cupid was reviving Psyche. Oh, how I fantasized about his kisses.

At first my grandmother assumed our friendship was charming and innocent, but as the weeks passed, she suspected our growing passion and began to spy on us. When her suspicions were confirmed, she went to his parents.

We were forbidden to see each other alone after that, which only made us more determined.

I bribed one of my grandmother's maids, Marie, to sleep in another servant girl's room. Marie's window, which was large enough for a man to crawl through, faced a narrow alley that our house and Leon's shared. That night, after midnight, he sneaked out and came to me through the window.

We met three more times that way. On the third night Grand-mère found us.

I was naked, and Leon was wearing his shirt. We were wrapped in each other's arms, kissing, when my grandmother pulled us apart. Ignoring me, she grabbed Leon by the arm, dragging him out of our house and to his own front door. I wrapped myself in a blanket and ran after them, crying, begging my grandmother not to say anything to his parents, that it was my fault, not his.

When the professor came to the door and saw Grand-mère, eyes ablaze, holding his practically nude son, he understood exactly what had happened.

Saying nothing, he reached out and slapped Leon.

Leon accepted the blow. His head fell forward. He began to gasp for air. Within moments he dropped to his knees on the stone cold steps as he desperately tried to breathe. And then Leon fell, still gasping, onto his side.

I screamed and ran forward, but my grandmother stopped me from going to him. She held me in her arms, held me as if just holding me was going to make everything all right, but it didn't.

The professor raced inside—to get his son's medicine, as it turned out—but by the time he returned minutes later, there was nothing he could do.

Leon died of an asthma attack in his father's

arms. He died while I stood there, helpless, watching in horror.

I don't remember what I did after that, but I've been told I was ill for days: burning up with a fever and delirious. All I could think was that if Leon hadn't been with me, if we hadn't sneaked off, he would never have died. It was my fault. It was because of my passion, my hunger, my joy of being with him, of wanting more of him touching my breasts and whispering behind my ear . . . It was my fault for wanting to feel his lips bruising mine, for wanting to taste his sweet mouth . . . for craving the sensations building inside of me that I'd never felt before and that were so glorious . . . feelings I couldn't get enough of. It was my fault because I wanted his fingers teasing me . . . touching me where he shouldn't . . . making my heart quicken . . . making magic. It was my fault for not wanting to be a girl anymore but to come to life as a woman as I lay under him. It was that desire in me, those needs, that killed the first boy I'd ever kissed . . . those cravings that were responsible for the first man I'd ever loved dying.

I vowed never to allow myself those feelings again. There was no good to come of them. In my delirium I saw myself as a succubus, one of those demon women I'd read about in the mythology books my father gave me. Evil beings I'd had nightmares about.

Now, ten years later, there I was, naked in Leon's mother's boudoir, and she was pulling a silken chemise over the same skin that her son had pressed his lips to.

How had her husband been able to abide bringing me into their home? How could they not hate me? How could Leon's mother and father show me such kindness?

"There," she said as she buttoned a dress up in the back. The fabric smelled of a fine, expensive perfume, and I felt cosseted and safer here than I had felt in weeks.

"Madame Ferre, can you tell me where my grandmother is? Why is the house dark? Why are the servants all gone? She never travels this time of year. Is she . . ." I was afraid to even say the words out loud. "Is she all right?" My voice broke as I asked.

My father was dead. I'd left my husband. And if Grand-mère was gone . . .

"She's fine, Sandrine," Madame Ferre said. "Your grandmother is planning a renovation. She's taken an apartment not far from here so she can supervise the work. Come, finish getting dressed, and I'll get you something to eat, and then we'll take you to her."

"There's no need to do that, Bridgitte." I recognized the rich honey-toned voice and spun around.

There was my grandmother in all of her glory.

Blazing orange hair, fire opals at her ears and around her throat. A burnt-orange silk dress with black lace trim swirling around her.

I expected her to greet me the same way she used to when she visited me in New York, with open arms and joy, but the woman standing in the doorway was frowning.

"Sandrine, didn't I tell you never to come back to Paris? This city is poison for you." Her voice was tense and tight. "Why didn't you listen?"

And in those last four words I heard something I'd never heard in her voice before—fear.

Chapter 2

Professor Ferre carried my luggage. It was peculiar leaving the one mansion and not going next door to the other. The farther we walked away from my grandmother's house, the more I found myself longing to go back. As if there were a magnetic force pulling me.

It must be that it was my father's house, I thought. Because it was where he grew up, I wanted to stay there and be close to my memories of him.

Our destination was only a few blocks away, on rue de la Chaise. Inside the porte cochère was a smaller courtyard, where a classic six-story apartment building stood, its four stone steps leading up to wooden double doors ornately carved with garlands of flowers and fruits.

"But why are you living here? What's wrong with your house?" I asked my grandmother.

"I have rented three floors here. The public rooms on this floor, bedrooms upstairs and servants' quarters on the top," Grand-mère said as she ushered me in and then turned and thanked the professor for helping with my luggage.

Indeed, at first glance the apartment was beautiful. There were gilded egg-and-dart moldings on the door, an elegant parquet floor, and tall ceilings. The parlor was filled with items I recognized from the mansion, but instead of these knickknacks making the suite of rooms more familiar, they only heightened the displacement I felt.

"But why are you here instead of Maison de la Lune?"

"All in time," my grandmother said with a smile on her face but a harshness in her voice. "First we need to discuss why *you* are here."

From the windows I could see a view of a charming garden, but it was not the same one where Leon and I had sat and fed the pigeons and stolen kisses when dusk fell, the shadows lengthening and dark enough to hide us. And there was no bell tower attached to the back of this building like the abandoned sixteenth-century leftover that rose out of the back of La Lune like a mystical shrine to the past. I was never allowed inside, but my bedroom in La Lune had faced the stone tower, and I used to make up stories about the princess walled up inside who was waiting to be freed. Sometimes at night, I thought I heard the ancient bells ringing softly, whispering to the stars, even though my grandmother told me the bells were long rusted and ruined.

"We'll have chocolat chaud, Alice," my grandmother told her maid, who'd come to help us get settled.

"Isn't Bernadette still with you?" I asked.

"No, she married a widower who owns a restaurant in Marseille. I get letters from her all the time. She's doing well and has two little girls." Grand-mère smiled. "She lets them draw on the envelopes."

All of my grandmother's servants stayed in touch with her. She was more than fair to them, and they never forgot her. My grandmother may have been a sensualist and a businesswoman, but it was her streak of kindness and her genuine interest in people that endeared her to her friends, those in her employ, and the men she entertained.

When I'd lived with her and commented on how the help seemed so much more informal with her that ours was with us in New York, she admonished me for having haut monde mores and being a snob.

"I have more in common with them than with your mother, *mon ange*," she told me. "After all, I'm not a fancy married lady, but just another working girl, toiling every day for my bread and milk." And then she'd laugh. That throaty laugh—like her dramatic maquillage, unusual jewels, and voluptuous clothes—had always made her seem so exotic to me and did still. My grandmother inspired awe. She was like a rare jungle orchid.

My mother, on the other hand, was more like a bouquet of pretty pale pink roses in a Renoir still life. She wasn't interested in the things my father and I were. She didn't like to visit museums or talk about architecture or literature or esoteric philosophies. She preferred gossip to going to the opera or ballet, a visit with the dressmaker to a visit to the museum, an afternoon tea with the ladies to a spirited discussion about a recent gothic novel.

I loved her because she was my beautiful mother, and to be in her presence was to be treated to the scents of lilies and violets, to the sight of cornflower-blue eyes and skin as lustrous as pearls. I loved her, not because of how she thought or the things she said but because she cared for me and showered me with affection. But beneath her attentions I always thought she was uncomfortable around me. Once, as she brushed my hair off my face, she said, "How did I ever give birth to such a serious, dark little girl?" Unspoken was the rest of the sentence: . . . *when I'm so light, so frivolous.*

From her I'd learned what would be expected of me. To marry well and raise a family. To create an oasis of calm in my home, to love and support my husband and be a good mother to my children. Now it seemed I'd never follow the example she'd set.

Alice, who had riotous blond curls and a strong chin, brought in a tray of fine china cups and the silver *chocolat chaud* pot, with its long spout and horizontal ebony handle. There was also a plate of delicate golden madeleines dusted with powdered sugar.

"There is so much to say," Grand-mère began as she poured me some of the aromatic brew. "But first, nourishment." She handed me a fragile cup and saucer. I waited until she poured for herself, and then I took the first heady sip. Of all the things that meant Paris and my grandmother to me, it was our afternoon ritual of sharing this melted chocolate drink, so unlike that thin American cocoa, and talking over what I'd done that day.

Thinking of how different this conversation was going to be brought tears to my eyes. I blinked them back, but she saw and, reaching up her sleeve, withdrew a black lace handkerchief with her initials embroidered in fire orange, handing it to me.

Like the fire opals she wore, these black hand-kerchiefs, scented with her perfume, were part of her signature. Dabbing at my eyes, I smelled that amazing fragrance that no one wore but my grandmother: roses and lily of the valley with a hint of vanilla and spicy pepper and some magical ingredient that smoothed it out and ignited it. The scent had been created for her by the great perfumer Monsieur L'Etoile, whom Grand-mère called a "dear friend." She called each man who visited her salon a "dear friend"—or, as she said, *"mon cher ami."* L'Etoile had named the scent after her, calling it L'Incendie, and promised he'd never sell it to anyone else during her lifetime.

"When did you last eat?" my grandmother asked.

I had to think. "I had breakfast on the boat. A soft-boiled egg and toast."

"That was practically yesterday. You are too thin, besides. I know how upset you must be, but you still have to rail against the fates, Sandrine. Never give in to sorrow. It doesn't do your heart or your complexion any good."

I smiled.

"So you know about Papa?"

I had come to Paris assuming I would have to be the one to tell her, but it appeared I'd be spared that horror.

"I received a telegram," she said. "But there is still so much I don't understand that I am going to need you to explain. Why didn't you contact me? Why did you leave so soon after the funeral? Where is your husband?"

"I wanted to send you a telegram. I wrote it a dozen times. But in the end I couldn't tell you the news that way. Once I knew I would be coming, I thought I'd tell you when I got here. Who sent you the news?"

My father had no family but me in America, and I couldn't imagine who would have known to contact Grand-mère.

"Your father's lawyer, Monsieur Lissauer. He is

the only person outside of you and your mother whom your father ever told about me and the only one who would know to get in touch."

I had not understood that Grand-mère was different from my friends' grandmothers until the summer I turned thirteen and she spent the season with us in Newport.

One night she came down to dinner wearing a pearl necklace that wrapped around her throat twice and yet still reached her waist.

Even though my mother had beautiful jewels, I'd never seen anything like Grand-mère's pearls. Lustrous against her navy silk gown, they looked like tiny moons stolen out of a midnight sky.

She saw me staring and asked if I liked them. When I said I did, she took them off and hung the rope around my neck, telling me they were mine to wear while she was visiting.

"Oh, thank you," I said as I touched the pearls, exploring their smooth surface with my fingertips. "When I grow up, I will have a necklace just like this and never take it off," I whispered.

"Hopefully you'll be given it as a gift and not have to work for it," my mother said a bit haughtily.

My grandmother smiled sadly at her daughter-in-law. "My dear, there's no such thing as not having to work for it, even if you are a respectably married woman of leisure."

Later I asked my father what my mother had

meant and why Grand-mère had seemed insulted.

"Your grandmother," my father explained, "is an independent businesswoman with a razor-sharp mind who has made a career for herself in the art of giving pleasure. Not everyone in America finds it a respectable profession, but in France, in Paris, she's something of a celebrity."

He didn't use the word "courtesan" to describe her, but over time I came to understand that Grand-mère was a high-ranking member of France's famous demimonde, one of the great grand *horizontales*. Thanks to certain wealthy gentlemen, these women lived in opulent apartments, wore the most stylish clothes and mesmerizing jewels, attended and turned heads at the theater, the ballet, and the opera, and frequented the finest restaurants and nightclubs. Even their names evoked fantasy: La Belle Otero, La Paiva, and the Countess di Castiglione.

Like my grandmother, some of these women had been brought up by mothers who were in the profession and trained their daughters to follow in their silk-slippered footsteps. Others started out as singers, dancers, or actresses.

Courtesans were not prostitutes who sold their bodies for money to buy a meal, but freethinking intellectuals who spun cocoons of sensuality and created an oasis of pleasure and escape for wealthy, powerful men. They seduced not just with their bodies but also with their wit and charm, and in return were paid handsomely for their companionship. Many had longstanding arrange-ments with their benefactors. My grand-mother had been with my father's father for more than fifteen years, until his death, and since then had been the companion to an Italian count for more than two decades.

My father was not ashamed of his mother, but when he left Paris at eighteen to go to college in America, she had insisted he keep her a secret. To all the world he was the son of a French banker and his wife. It was true that Papa's father had been a well-respected financier. But Albert Salome had never married my grandmother. Men like Salome never married courtesans.

The banking scion had loved his illegitimate son and given him his name. He not only mentored him and sent him to Harvard University, but after my father graduated, Albert opened a branch of the Salome bank in New York City for his son to run.

Shortly after that, my father met and fell in love with my mother. Even though she was Jewish and her father was also in banking, I think my French father fell in love with her because she was so different from him. Born in Manhattan, Henrietta was part of a big boisterous family, was light and lovely and my father said, had absolutely no secrets at all.

But he had many, the most grievous being my

38

grandmother's identity. Philippe Salome's mother, so the story went, died when the boy was only ten years old. Who was the femme fatale with the burning eyes and orange hair who came to visit our family in New York every few years? An eccentric and distant cousin. If she caused tongues to wag and gossip to fly, so be it. After all, one couldn't be responsible for *everyone* in one's family.

"We lost someone so special, didn't we, *mon ange?*" my grandmother said sadly, bringing my thoughts back to the more recent past.

My eyes filled. I had not really wept yet, not let out the full range of my grief. While the tears had come often in those long, lonely hours after my father's death, then during the service and after in my cabin on the boat, I always fought them back. I needed to be vigilant and protect myself, not give in to my sorrow, until I was safe.

And now that I was, I couldn't hold back.

My grandmother sat beside me on the settee, took me in her arms, held me to her chest, and let me shed my tears. Only when I was spent and finished did I realize she'd been crying along with me and that her tears had wet the curls on my forehead.

"You'll let me stay here, won't you?" I asked.

"With me, yes, of course, *mon ange*, for a time. But I wish you hadn't come . . . I would have traveled to New York." After a moment she disentangled herself. "Now tell me, why didn't you ask me to come to be with you? That's always been the way we've visited."

"I'll explain all that, but first, did Mr. Lissauer say anything about me in the telegram? Did he ask if I was here?"

"No, why should he?"

"So you didn't tell him I was coming?"

"How could I? I didn't know you were coming."

"You can't tell him. Not him and not anyone."

She looked at me with some confusion. "The Ferres know you are here, *mon ange*. What is this about?"

"Do the Ferres know my married name? They have always known me as Sandrine Verlaine. Did you tell them I married?"

Growing up in New York, I had been Sandrine Salome, but when I'd spent time with my grandmother in Paris when I was fifteen, I'd been Sandrine Verlaine. She'd had me use her last name, instead of my father's, to protect the secret and the Salome family out of respect to her lover.

"I'm sure I mentioned that you'd married, but I doubt I would have mentioned your husband's last name."

"Then don't. Not to them or anyone. I want to go back to being Sandrine Verlaine. That is the name I booked passage under."

"But this makes no sense. Why?"

"I don't want anyone to be able to find me. And

no one in New York looking for me would know that name."

"To find you? Are you hiding? Won't your husband try to find you? Doesn't he know where I live?"

I took a breath. "My husband," I said, "is the reason I've left. It's my husband who I don't want to find me."

"What do you mean, Sandrine? Surely there's nothing wrong with your marriage?"

I could see worry mixed with the sadness in her eyes. The time had come to tell my grandmother about the terrible thing that had happened to her family.

Chapter 3

We'd all had dinner together. It was a cold and silent affair. My father and Benjamin had been fighting before we dined and had brought their chilliness to the table. Any semblance of civility was, I guessed, for my behalf. As soon as dinner was done, my father told Benjamin he wanted to talk to him in the library.

I went into the parlor and was reading some book or other when I heard their raised voices. I could only pick up an occasional phrase, but from the tenor of his voice, it was clear my father was furious. Benjamin and I had been married for four years and had always lived with my father in his Fifth Avenue mansion. In all that time, I'd never heard my father talk to my husband, his protégé and junior partner, in that tone of voice.

At one point I heard him accuse Benjamin of being a thief. At another of dishonoring his name.

"But you were my partner, you were like a son to me," I heard my father scream. My father never screamed. What was going on?

After more than thirty minutes, I heard my father shout out my own name. Thinking he was calling me, I went running. I came to the threshold of the library. The door had never been properly shut and remained open a bit. I stepped inside the shadowed antechamber lined with books. Neither man noticed me as I stood in the shadowed alcove and stared.

My father was holding a pistol pointed at Benjamin.

"I trusted you with my daughter!"

"Go ahead and shoot me. How will that protect Sandrine? What kind of life will she have then? Spending her days visiting her broken old father in prison? Embarrassed and humiliated. Ostracized. Is that the life you envisioned for her?" Benjamin said. I couldn't see his face, but I could hear the smile in his voice. He was taunting my father. "Every loan and transfer form has your name on it, not mine, Philippe. I've left instructions that in case of my death the whole packet of incriminating evidence will be sent to the police. You will be the villain of this piece."

"But they are forgeries."

"No one will be able to prove that. You've let me sign too many legitimate contracts with your name over the years."

"You organized this whole deceit behind my back while living in my house, with my daughter? You gambled like a fool and then borrowed against reserves to pay off your own debts? You stole from me? You used my trust and largesse to put our bank in jeopardy? How could I have been so blind?"

My father noticed me then. He looked right at

me. I'd never seen my father embarrassed before. Never in my life. In that moment he was so ashamed that he could barely hold my gaze. I stepped farther into the room.

"What's going on?" I asked. When my father didn't answer, I turned to my husband. "Benjamin? What is going on? What is this? What is Papa talking about?"

Benjamin took me by the arm. "This isn't something you need to be part of, Sandrine."

"He's right," my father echoed in a broken voice. "Please go, Sandrine."

Benjamin led me out of the room, and like a fool I went. I shouldn't have. Had I stayed and demanded to be told all the details of the crisis, I might have made my father see there was another way. Some other solution. Hadn't he taught me there's always another way? But I didn't stay. I went off with Benjamin, leaving my father to suffer his long night alone.

The next morning Papa didn't come down to breakfast. I asked his valet to see if he was all right.

Sometime during the night, my father, who was so fastidious, who was so impeccable, had shot himself in the mouth and left behind a bloody mess so horrific that even when I demanded to see his body, I couldn't stand to be in the room for more than a few moments.

Before I left, I picked up his pistol. It was cold,

and I shivered as I slipped it into my pocket. Of all my father's personal effects, this was the only one I took from his bedroom. I was still married to Benjamin, and I now knew I might need to protect myself one day.

The note his valet found next to his body, when they moved him, had my name on it.

My dearest Sandrine,

There was no other way but this cowardly exit. Leaving you is the hardest thing I have ever done, but this is the best solution. I am not guilty of what Benjamin would have claimed, but I would never be able to prove it. The shame of what you would have to live with is more than I can bear. At least this way, you are protected. Say I was ill and could not bear the pain. Even though the illness is of my soul, not my body, it is true.

With all of my love to you forever,
Your devoted Papa

By the time I finished telling my grandmother the story, I was standing by the fireplace, and she was still seated on the settee. Across the room, our eyes met and held.

Hers sparkled with unshed tears.

"*Mon ange*," she said in a hoarse, whispery voice that reminded me of burnt sugar. She held

45

out her arms. I went to her and, for the second time that evening, took refuge there, smelling her fiery, spicy perfume and face powder and feeling no less sad but much safer.

It was only after a few moments that I noticed she was shaking.

"What is it?" I asked.

She shook her head. "My poor Philippe."

Now I was not the one taking solace but giving it.

Chapter 4

My life in my grandmother's apartments on the rue de la Chaise took on a routine that was rather comforting in its sameness. We both needed to mourn before we could begin the process of healing, and we mourned together. Our days moved slowly and with less social interaction than was typical of life in Paris. Especially for a woman of my grandmother's ilk.

In the mornings we would breakfast in our separate bedrooms on trays and then attend to our toilettes. At ten we met in the sitting room, where Grand-mère would write letters, go over the household matters with her housekeeper, receive the seamstress or the milliner, and make arrangements for upcoming assignations, dinners, and salons. Regardless of the recent tragedy, Grand-mère could not afford to ignore her business.

While she saw to running her household, I read the morning papers. At home, my father and I had read them together, stopping often to discuss this article or that. The world was still reeling from the 1893 financial crisis, and there were often items about failed banking institutions in the press. Indeed, at the end of my second week in Paris, there was an article about the Salome Bank of New York. Since it had ties to one of France's greatest financial institutions, I shouldn't have been surprised to see it, but it startled me nonetheless.

The Salome Bank of New York, I read, had merged with another institution and was now to be called the Salome and Tarcher Bank of New York.

So Benjamin had found the backing he'd gone to California to secure. Now he would have the funds he needed to replenish those he'd stolen to pay off his debts. Desperate, he'd left the day after my father's funeral, and the lack of respect his haste showed astounded me. But the money markets never stop for any one man, Benjamin said, and his business was urgent. I'd argued until I realized his being gone would give me an opportunity to take a trip of my own.

It had not been a love match. Benjamin had been dashing and smart and was my father's protégé. My father regarded him as a young man of substance. And I, who had somehow grown into womanhood eschewing the idea of romantic love, certain I would be better off avoiding it, was relieved to have the matter of my marital status over with.

Had my father not died, I could have accepted and stayed in a marriage without passion. But I could not remain with a brute who had my father's blood on his hands.

The day after Benjamin left for San Francisco, I ran away in the opposite direction.

● ● ●

Most afternoons, after lunching together, Grand-mère and I would take a walk regardless of the temperature. She believed in braving the chilly air and moving briskly through the Luxembourg Gardens or the Tuileries or just walking by the Seine. Exercise, she told me, kept the body strong and the mind clear. Even rain didn't keep us from our constitutional. On those days we took the carriage to the Louvre or Bon Marché, the extraordinary department store where Grand-mère was filling in my wardrobe. Not wanting to alert my household staff to the length of my planned stay, I'd taken only what I'd required for a short trip to Virginia. There were all kinds of clothes and accessories I needed that I didn't have with me. After only two weeks, under my grand-mother's tutelage, I already looked more French than American.

Usually after our walk we'd stop at Angelina's for hot chocolate if we were on the Rive Droite or at Café de Flore for coffee if we were on the Gauche. Often, as we sipped our beverages, Grand-mère reminisced about raising my father in a Paris that had changed so much since then. She talked easily with me about her past, even telling me about men she'd known and who had been in love with her. Listening to her and getting caught up in her stories, I understood where my father had gotten his tale-spinning talent.

The only subject that would make my grand-mother grow quiet was when I tried to get her to talk about her beautiful house on rue des Saints-Pères. I dreamed about it almost every night . . . strange dreams that were dark and complicated. Visions of ghostlike women wandering through the halls, weeping. I wanted to tell my grand-mother about them, but she was so uncomfortable when I raised the subject of the house. She'd always say the same thing—that old houses had many problems, and hers needed extensive renovations, so she'd shut it down to do the work.

Her rush to change the subject made me wonder why discussing the house unsettled her so, but she never gave me a clue.

On Tuesdays, Thursdays, and most Saturdays, our routine included a light supper together at seven, and then at eight I'd retire to my room when my grandmother's business life began.

Her job required her to be coiffed, perfumed, and manicured, to dress in the height of fashion, to make her salons entertaining fantasy retreats serving up only the finest foods and wines, along with witty repartee and delightful music. All of this took time and effort. Visits with hairdressers, dressmakers, hatmakers, masseuses, and other purveyors took up hours every day. The salons usually commenced around nine and ended by one or two in the morning, but my grandmother prepared all week. Other nights we dined later, sometimes with a friend or two of hers and sometimes by ourselves.

During her soirees, I was glad to remain upstairs, away from the men, the music, and the noise, hiding in the pale yellow bedroom where I would try to read. I was finally making headway through *The Picture of Dorian Gray*, a book I'd brought from home and tried but failed to read on the ship. I'd been too disturbed. I wasn't sure if it was the novel's foreboding tone that mirrored my mood or the fact that this was the last book my father had read before his death. Once I fell under its spell, Mr. Wilde's story absorbed me and, for a short time, allowed me to stop thinking about everything that had happened to me and worry instead about what was happening to his characters. The novel was a dark, disturbing tale that excited me and made me afraid at the same time.

My father had left annotations and marginalia in the pages that were not always welcome. Sometimes they made me feel closer to him; other times they caused me great sorrow, especially when I found something of particular interest and grasped anew, with a fresh stab of grief, that I couldn't just get up and go find him so we could discuss what he'd written.

The Picture of Dorian Gray was reported to be salacious, but my father said he thought I'd like it because it proposed some fascinating theories about the power of art.

My father and I both loved art; he'd nurtured that love in me. I could get lost in a painting, become mesmerized by a fine piece of sculpture. Like him, beauty astounded me. Talent awed me. The magic of art—the transformative powers, the luscious hues, textures, patterns—it all absorbed me. I was fascinated by the way an artist took something he saw and then turned it into a personal statement. I loved seeing the world translated by these great poets of color and line.

When I was thirteen, wanting to please my father, I'd taken up painting in school. But I could never put down on canvas what I saw so clearly in my mind and was always frustrated. My teacher said that I had real talent and showed great promise but needed to learn to be more patient.

One afternoon my mother found me in tears over a muddy watercolor and asked why I was so upset. I told her it was because I'd wanted to make Papa something that he would love as much as the paintings in the museums and on our walls at home.

After she'd soothed me, she brought my father in, showed him what I'd done, and told him what I'd said.

He tried to point out how good the painting was. No matter what he said, I objected that it was not good enough and that my effort was not great enough to create the kind of gift I wanted to present to him.

"But Sandrine, you are my gift—don't you know you are the treasure? You don't have to become something you aren't to please me."

But it was not just because the book was about a painter that my father gave me *The Picture of Dorian Gray*. He'd told me the occult aspects of the tale had stirred his imagination, and he was interested in discussing those with me, too. For a self-proclaimed rationalist, he found arcane and esoteric knowledge surprisingly fascinating and studied it with great interest. He wasn't alone. From France to Russia to America, the occult was experiencing a major revival.

My father believed it was a reaction to rationalism, materialism, and the exciting but frightening scientific discoveries being reported almost daily. Explorers returning from the Far East with stories of strange lands and mystical customs also fueled everyone's imagination. My father had funded several of those expeditions, as well as others, to find the fabled Hermetic books based on the ancient pagan prophet's esoteric teachings. Our library was full of books of ancient lore and magick mysticism and the forbidden. For my father it was also personal; he once told me that he believed his mother was something of a psychic, although she protested vociferously.

At the end of the second week of my stay in Paris, Grand-mère changed the routine. When I came downstairs at ten, she was already dressed in her street clothes and preparing to leave. When I asked where she was going, she told me she was meeting an old friend who needed some advice and added she would be back in time for our lunch.

Indeed she was, and since it was raining, we went to the Louvre.

I had grown up in museums, but even compared to New York's august Metropolitan Museum of Art, the Louvre was so large as to be almost overwhelming.

"As with all wonderful things in life except jewels, it's best to avoid gluttony when visiting here," my grandmother said as we entered the ancient palace.

"When we went to the Metropolitan, Papa and I would always pick one small section, take it in, absorb it, and then leave. He always said moderation makes for finer appreciation."

She smiled. "He learned that from me, *mon ange*." But it was a sad smile, and I turned away so she wouldn't see the tears that had sprung to my eyes. Her grief always triggered my own.

We wandered through the Denon wing, on the first floor, heading to room thirteen. "One of my favorite paintings is here," my grandmother said as we entered, and she headed to a relatively small-sized, brightly colored painting of a voluptuous nude female and muscular male.

"This is Tiepolo's marvelous *Apollo and Daphne*. It's so lush and imaginative, don't you think?" she asked.

Before I could inspect it, I was distracted by two men in blue smocks, each standing at easels in front of a dark, muted painting.

I inched closer. They were copying a complicated and disturbing tableau. I strained to see its name.

THE WITCH OF ENDOR
SALVATOR ROSA, 1668(?)

Stepping back, I studied the original, eight-foot tall vision of horror. The central figure, according to the legend beside the painting, was the spirit of Samuel, called forth by the witch to speak to Saul, who had come to her for advice.

Shrouded in a white hooded robe, the spirit was illuminated by a frenzied fire. Behind him his guards look stricken. And no wonder—the scene was filled with terrifying creatures, owls with supernaturally bright eyes, bloody horse heads, and bat-winged skeletons. The witch herself was a wrinkled old crone, repulsive and offensive. My reaction to her was one of anger, though I didn't know why.

As I turned to step back so I could examine the

foreboding work from a greater distance, one of the painters caught my eye and smiled at me.

"Impressive, isn't it?" he asked.

At that moment an older man came into the gallery.

"Are you talking or painting, Gaston?" The man, who appeared to be in his sixties, had piercing brown eyes, and there was something very gentle about him. I watched as he stood behind Gaston's canvas for a moment, inspecting the work. Then he pointed to the masterpiece on the wall.

"Look at the life in that painting. The way Saul cowers. You can feel his fear of the specter and of the witch. That's what you need to put into your effort. That fear. Have you ever seen a witch? A ghost? In the dark? At night? Been afraid?"

My grandmother had come up beside me. Taking my arm, she walked me toward the exit of the salon. "I'm suddenly in great need of an espresso. There's a lovely café here. Let's go."

Before we crossed the threshold, I looked back at the painter and his teacher, still talking, the teacher gesturing to the painting on the wall. The student appeared to be listening with all of his soul. I could see how he was trying to soak up every bit of knowledge the teacher was offering. Something about the moment struck me and stayed with me, and as I fell asleep that night, it was the painting teacher's voice I heard, telling his student to put his fear into his painting.

How easy it would be, I thought as I drifted off to sleep, to be able to take all of my fear and put it into a painting. To rid myself of it like that. I wondered if it worked. If you could paint yourself sane.

The next morning my grandmother left the apartment early again but was back for lunch. The following day, Wednesday, our routine resumed. On Thursday, for the third time that week, she left at ten.

I'm not sure why I did what I did that day. Perhaps the sinister goings-on in *The Picture of Dorian Gray* were affecting my thinking. But I had become certain Grand-mère was hiding something. When she told me she was going on one of these excursions, she always looked away from me slightly.

Papa had the same affectation whenever he was telling me something not quite true.

That Thursday morning, I grabbed my overcoat and followed her out. I'd never tried to trail anyone before, but I'd read enough of the very popular Sherlock Holmes books—one of Papa's favorite characters in literature—to know the basics.

Keep a good distance between you and the suspect.

Stay close to the buildings.

Watch for the subject's sudden movements.

Hang back in the shadows if the suspect turns.

Papa appreciated Holmes's deductive reasoning, and we often read the stories at the same time so we could try our hand at outguessing the master detective. My father was far better at it than I was.

Sometimes on the street, we'd follow the careful rules of observation Holmes engaged in, and we'd spot something—a curious scuff on someone's shoes, an umbrella with a strange nick in the handle, a woman with a parcel of unusual proportions—and guess what might be behind these oddities.

By the time I reached the corner of our block, Grand-mère had turned right and was almost to the next corner. I watched her cross the street and turn right again. I followed, but by the time I got to the next corner, she was gone. How had she managed to disappear so quickly? I looked left. There was no one in sight with Grand-mère's rust-colored coat. I glanced in the opposite direction, but there was no one to the right either—or was there? Did I see a flounce of her dress turning into the rue des Saints-Pères?

I ran for a few yards and reached rue des Saints-Pères in time to see her stop in front of our family home, Maison de la Lune. The house that she'd moved out of and closed down. What was Grand-mère doing here? And why lie to me about it? Why invent a friend who needed advice, or an appointment with a hairdresser or glove maker, if she was just going home?

It was then I noticed a man step out of the shadows beside the porte cochère. He was quite tall and towered over her as he bent to kiss her hand. His profile was to me, so when he rose, I could not see his face, but his hair was dark, like the color of a raven's wing. His long fingers curled around the portfolio case he was handling with ease. His black coat was stylishly cut. When he moved, it was with an effortless grace. He looked like the kind of man my father would have said was comfortable in his own skin.

Together, the man and my grandmother stepped inside the courtyard, and the street doors shut after them.

They might be inside for a long time. Should I leave? It was a cloudy day with a chill in the air. There wasn't any point in waiting, was there? What would seeing them exit tell me? What did I want to know?

I turned and started to walk away when I experienced a moment of dizziness. I put my hand on the wall of the building and stood still for a moment. I was facing the Maison de la Lune again. Looking at her walls, her steps, her windows. I wanted to be inside her, enclosed within her walls, sitting on the green velvet couches in the parlor and looking at the colors the lovely stained glass windows cast on the floor.

Maison de la Lune was the palace of my dreams. The elusive magical enclave that I'd never stopped thinking of since I'd left it when I was fifteen.

The *hôtel particulier*, as houses like Maison de la Lune were called, dated back to the mid-eighteenth century and was a type very popular in Paris. Built by noblemen as retreats, most were constructed around an inner courtyard and boasted lavish and well-manicured gardens. Ours was on the smaller side, and half of it had been turned into an indoor orangerie with a fountain, hothouse orange trees, and orchids.

While I was still deciding whether to leave or to stay, the porte cochère opened, and my grandmother came out. Alone. I waited, but the gentleman didn't follow. How odd. Why was she leaving him inside?

Without glancing around, my grandmother walked toward the corner and turned north. Probably, she was going home.

Grand-mère had been vague about why she'd shut down the house. She'd said there were ancient pipes and structural damage, and to stay there was dangerous . . . that repairs were costly, and finding the right people to work on it, who wouldn't take advantage of her financially, would take time. She said she was too distracted with my father's death to see to it now.

I didn't find it strange she would be restoring this old house. It was her lie that interested me.

Now that I had started telling them, I was more aware of other people's.

As soon as my grandmother was out of sight, I ran across the street, hoping the heavy door still took a long time to shut and lock. I was in luck and managed to slip through before the door closed.

Once inside the courtyard, I walked up to the house. Standing in front of it, I looked up at its limestone facade. What was Grand-mère hiding here? Why had she lied?

I had an overwhelming sense of belonging here, of being welcome. The same sense I'd had two weeks before, standing in the rain when I first arrived.

I lifted the bronze hand of fate and let it drop. The knocker should have been cold—it was, after all, a cloudy winter day—but instead it was warm to the touch.

Behind me, I heard footsteps and glanced around. A man and a woman whom I didn't recognize were heading my way. There were six separate houses inside the courtyard, and even though there were often people coming and going, it wasn't smart for me to be standing here. What if the Ferres saw me? They might say something to my grandmother, and then she'd know I'd followed her. I had two choices: either walk away so that it appeared I'd been visiting someone, or—

I lifted the knocker again and let it drop. A few

moments passed. I heard footsteps, and then the door opened.

At my back I felt an odd little gentle push of wind, as if even the winter breeze knew where I belonged and wanted to help me inside.

I took a step forward.

"Yes?" A man was looking at me curiously.

I once read that there can be meetings between kindred spirits with whom you are so simpatico, your blood and your bones know it before you do. You come upon someone, and your very chemistry alters. You shift. Realign. Your senses become alert to sights and sounds and scents that eluded you just moments before.

"Can I help you?" was what he said, but I heard something far more complicated, a kind of harmony of chords and tones that resonated within me, and I was confused.

I could smell his scent: a mixture of amber, honey, and apples mixed with his own skin's oils and the brisk winter air. Something deep inside me responded to the fragrance. I felt as if I could lose myself in it. Wrap it around me like a cashmere shawl and be forever warmed.

I did not even slightly understand the rush of sensations I was feeling. I'd never experienced this before. If I had understood what actually was happening, I might have turned and run, or so I'd like to believe. If I had, everything would be so different now. But we don't have the ability to retravel time and change our decisions. I knew then and know still that no matter what the price, I never wanted to stop peering into those clear evergreen eyes and inhaling that heady scent. It did not occur to me to turn and leave. I wanted to be right where I was, to go inside and revisit the house I had never stopped dreaming of for the last ten years.

"Is my grandmother here?" I asked. It was the one question I knew would allow me entry.

"Who is your grandmother?"

There was everything ordinary about this meeting and everything extraordinary about it at the same time. I felt as if I were in one of Jane Austen's novels, which my father had always made a little bit of fun of me for reading over and over.

The stranger was waiting for an answer. I needed to act normal if I wanted him to let me inside.

"My grandmother is Eva Verlaine."

"You just missed her."

"She said to meet her here." My first lie of the day. I often counted them. A good day had one lie or less. A bad day had four or five.

"But she just left."

I lifted the chatelaine I wore on my neck that included a gold watch. A gift from my father. Glancing at it, I said, "She said to arrive at eleven."

He was leaning on the door with an attitude of

insouciance that I didn't like but at the same time was drawn to. "She didn't mention it to me."

"Perhaps she's coming back to meet me."

"When she left, she didn't mention it."

"Should she have? Wouldn't it have been strange for her to have told you her plans?" I challenged.

"Do you want to come in?" He smiled despite my tone. And then he bowed and performed a bit of a flourish with his hands as if offering entry. "I shouldn't be asking that—after all, it is your house, isn't it?"

How to describe his voice? What words to use to explain a sound? I felt his voice. Fingers rubbing moss. Smoke curling. Wood worn and smoothed over time. His voice had darkness in it that hovered close to the ground, like a mist hanging over a lake deep in a forest at dusk. A bolt of sea-green velvet. A sensation as much as a series of sounds. It reverberated inside me.

When I look back on that meeting now, I think I fell in love in that moment.

He was waiting for me to answer, peering at me intently as if trying to understand my hesitation.

"Yes, I'll come in. I'm certain she's coming back to meet me here."

As I stepped over the threshold, I wondered who he was to her. A lover here for an assignation? No, he was too young. My grandmother was still an attractive woman, but too seasoned for a young man. He had something of the poet in his eyes and sensitive lips. Had he taken her for his muse? Several famous courtesans had written books about their lives. I'd read one: *Mémoires de Cora Pearl*. Had my grandmother decided to tell her story? Was this man her biographer? Or maybe he was a painter. I remembered there were portraits of women in our family hanging on the wall going up the staircase. I used to love looking at those strange paintings, all done, it appeared, by the same artist. Except that would have been impossible. They covered centuries, from the first painting of La Lune herself, from 1609, to Grandmère's aunt painted in 1832.

What if she'd sold the house to this man? Maybe that's why he was hesitant about letting me in. I wasn't sure about my grandmother's finances. Perhaps she was no longer the mistress of the count who filled her coffers and gave her enough jewels to open a shop. Every time she'd visited us in New York, she had more treasures to show us. Maybe she had decided to sell the mansion and lead a simpler lifestyle and had not yet wanted to tell me.

I walked up the steps as if it was totally natural for me to act the mistress of the manse. And without my grandmother in residence, I might as well be.

As I stepped into the foyer, I felt an overwhelming sense of finally being where I belonged. I hadn't been inside since I was fifteen, but this house had been alive in my memory all this time. I felt as if the marble floor itself was elated to feel my weight. As if the antique mirrors on the walls were delighted to be filled with my image.

Was it my imagination, or did the Limoges china vases' shine intensify, did the silver flower bowls gleam brighter, did the crystals in the chandelier twinkle more? It seemed as if all the inanimate objects recognized me and glowed in welcome, pleased that someone who loved them had returned to notice them and pay them homage again.

"Am I keeping you?" I asked, thinking that this way I might discover what he was doing here.

Another smile, slightly secretive, as if he knew something but was waiting until I figured it out. "It's quite all right."

Could he be taking lessons in lovemaking? I hadn't thought of that before, but my grand-mother had told me of similar arrangements. Sometimes shy young men employed women like my grand-mother to teach them to be bolder or educate them in the subtleties of seduction so they might be better able to please themselves and their lovers. Sometimes fathers made the arrange-ments, other times older brothers.

I didn't want this to be the case with him, but my mind was wild with the possibility of it. I could not stop myself from imagining my grandmother sitting beside him on the settee, stroking his face, brushing the dark waves of hair off his forehead, and whispering instructions to him.

He was speaking, and I had missed the first few words.

"I'm sorry?"

"I do have a certain amount of work to get done, but I was going to make myself coffee before I began. Would you care for some?"

"The kitchen is in working order?"

"Yes, why wouldn't it be?" he asked.

I shook my head. Of course my grandmother knew how to lie. "I must have misunderstood," I told him. "I thought my grandmother had said that there were certain repairs the house needed."

I followed him into the kitchen. Nothing here looked broken, outdated, or amiss.

There was a pot of water boiling on the stove and an apparatus beside it that I had never seen. Nothing like the percolator we had at home, this was a tall glass cylinder. The man put ground coffee in the bottom, then poured the water on top of it and placed a silver disc attached to a plunger on top of the water.

"Now we wait," he said. "Have a seat. Or should you be inviting me to have a seat?"

I sat at the marble-topped table where I had sat so many mornings, a young girl drinking milk and eating *pain au chocolat* that my grandmother's cook had just taken out of the oven.

He sat down and looked at me. It was, I'm sure,

meant to be an uncomplicated glance, but his eyes—dark forest-green eyes—lingered too long on my lips. His fingers moved to his watch fob, and I saw him finger a heavy gold ring. "Forgive me," he said suddenly. "My name is Julien. Julien Duplessi."

"Mine is Sandrine Verlaine."

"Mademoiselle Verlaine," he said, and bowed his head slightly, dark waves of hair falling forward.

I liked how that sounded in French. Mademoiselle Verlaine . . . not Madame Asch. My new name without Benjamin's surname attached . . . I knew women who had divorced, but none had returned to her maiden name. Was there a court procedure for such a thing?

The smell of the coffee permeated the kitchen. Monsieur Duplessi got up and attended to the process. He pressed the plunger down and then poured the steaming beverage into two of my grandmother's china cups. I'd never seen their pattern outside of this house: a white background with a dark midnight-blue band encircling the rim, inside of which a galaxy of silver stars and moons danced. Created by Limoges for the Maison de la Lune.

Opening a paper bag, Julien removed three buttery croissants and placed them on a plate. The mixed scents of the coffee and the baked goods made my mouth water. Had my grandmother brought these for him? No, she'd left our apartment and come straight here. Had Monsieur Duplessi stopped for them? What kind of guest was he that he felt so at home here, he brought food with him?

Noticing me eyeing the croissants, he pushed the plate toward me. "Please, help yourself. I can always go and get more if I get hungry. There is an excellent bakery just a few doors down." He paused and then added, "But of course you know that."

"So you plan to stay the day?" I asked.

"Yes, of course. Every day for several weeks. It's going to take quite a while." He looked pleased at the thought.

"I imagine it will," I said even though I had no idea what he was talking about and less of an idea how to ask.

But for the moment it didn't matter. Nothing did. Not that I was alone here with a stranger, in the kitchen of all places. Or that we were so informally sitting across from each other. Not that my grandmother might in fact return—though I doubted it. None of that mattered because for the first time in two weeks the ache of my recent loss receded. I felt as if I was where I wanted to be. In this house, be it in the kitchen or the parlor. Just here in this house in Paris.

And even odder, I wanted to be here with this stranger. Breathing in the same air. Observing him. Listening to his low, sultry voice, which warmed me through. I watched him put his lips on the rim of the cup and then, as he was taking a sip, look up and find my eyes on him. He didn't smile. Didn't respond. And he didn't look away. Oh yes, I wanted to be here feeling the sweet and sharp sting of— What was it that I was feeling?

I vaguely remembered it from that long-ago spring I'd spent in Paris when I was fifteen. Leon Ferre had stirred me like this. It had been as much about the clandestine aspects of being with a boy for the first time, hiding from my grandmother and doing what was forbidden, as it had been about him, but it was real. I used to ache to touch him and have him touch me. For that brief time, ten years ago, I had been fully awake, and then, after the tragedy of him dying, I had gone back to sleep.

Now, many dreams and terrible nightmares later, my mind was tricking me. Teasing me into thinking I might be able to feel. But I couldn't. My body would never respond.

First love, my mother had called my infatuation with Leon when she and my father stopped in Paris on the way from Russia to Algiers. She'd smiled and smoothed down my hair and kissed me on the forehead. "Enjoy it, darling."

Hearing her, my grandmother had frowned. "Love? Don't put any stock in it. Marry well, Sandrine. Not often and never for love. That is the only way you'll be happy. For the women in our family, love is a curse, not a blessing."

Chapter 5

After drinking Monsieur Duplessi's coffee and eating one of his croissants, I left Maison de la Lune without looking around as I'd wished to and without discovering what Monsieur Duplessi was doing there.

I needed to hurry back to the rented apartment before too much time passed. My grandmother would surely have returned, found me absent, and begun to worry as it was the first time I'd gone out without her.

As I shut the front door behind me, I whispered to Maison de la Lune that I'd return. Walking down the steps to the sidewalk, I wondered why I'd begun to think of the house as a living entity. Was it because I missed my father so much and he'd grown up there? Because I'd spent time there as a child and it was familiar to me as few things were anymore? Or was it because so much had happened to me in such a short time that I was slightly mad with grief?

On the walk from our ancient family home back to the apartment on rue de la Chaise, I worked out the small lie that I would tell my grandmother to excuse my absence. I'd say I hadn't been able to shake a nightmare, and with her gone, I decided taking a walk might help.

As I'd expected, she had returned, but she was preoccupied with the dressmaker who was there pinning a new frock and accepted my explanation of needing fresh air without reservation.

That afternoon, the rain started as Grand-mère and I went out for our daily excursion. We spent the afternoon at the Louvre in the dusty Egyptian wing. It had fascinated me as a girl, and I found it just as compelling now. People in that ancient civilization had spent so much time and effort preparing for the journey to the afterlife. Did all those ablutions make death easier to bear?

"Would you like to visit Egypt one day?" my grandmother asked.

We were standing in front of the sarcophagus of Madja. The whitewashed outer coffin was highly decorated with a painting of the dead woman wearing a blue-and-yellow wig and an elaborate gold, carnelian, and lapis lazuli necklace. Her large, kohl-rimmed eyes and placid expression suggested an acceptance of death as something inevitable, perhaps even enviable.

"I'd love to," I answered. "It must be very exotic. We used to visit the Egyptian rooms at the Metropolitan at home, and when we were in London, Papa took me to the British Museum and showed me the Rosetta Stone and explained how it was the key to finally understanding the entire cryptic Egyptian writing system. Did you know he was learning how to read hieroglyphics?"

"Maybe we should visit Egypt," my grand-mother said. "Paris is so cold and dreary this winter. Exceptionally so."

The chance to visit Luxor and Alexandria and sail down the Nile should have excited me but instead filled me with dread. "Leave Paris?"

Grand-mère turned and gave me a sad smile. "I suppose you've had too much change too quickly, *mon ange?*"

As I nodded, I felt threatening tears spring to my eyes.

"But you know you can't stay in Paris indefinitely," she added.

"Why not?" I hadn't expected this.

"You have a home and a husband in New York. A life there. You are young and beautiful." She reached out and smoothed my auburn hair. While it wasn't as fiery as hers, it had her reddish highlights. "You want to have children, don't you?"

"Not with Benjamin, no!" I shook my head. "I'm never going back to him. I want to divorce him."

"I would imagine you do. Sandrine, I think it best to tell you that I received a telegram from your father's lawyer yesterday."

"Mr. Lissauer? What did he say?"

"Your husband returned from his business trip to find you'd gone to visit friends in Virginia. When a week passed and you still weren't home, he made inquiries and discovered you'd never

73

been in Richmond. He is distraught and anxious about your safety. Knowing how close you and your father were, he reached out to Monsieur Lissauer to see if he had heard from you or had any information."

I began to tremble. "Please don't telegraph him back. Don't tell Mr. Lissauer you know where I am."

"I trust him, *mon ange*. Maybe he can help?"

"Don't tell anyone, please. Promise." My voice was shrill and despairing. People were looking over at us.

"All right. Perhaps it's too soon to talk of these things." She took my arm, and we walked away from the sarcophagus. "Let's go have some chocolat chaud at Angelina's. And perhaps a pastry."

My grandmother's news about Benjamin kept me up almost all night. Restless despite the comfortable bed and soft pillows, my mind turned over all my actions during those days before my departure. Had I been sloppy in my haste and left behind any clues as to where I was going? Had anyone other than William Lenox seen me? Was William back from his trip yet? It seemed unlikely, but if he was and had told Benjamin he'd seen me on the ship to England, was there any way someone could have tracked my journey from Southampton to Calais? Could I even be certain Benjamin didn't know of my grand-mother's existence? It was supposed to be a tightly guarded secret, but what if my father had taken Benjamin into his confidence? Perhaps he'd decided it was a part of our family history his son-in-law should know. Wouldn't my father have told me if he'd done that?

Finally I reassured myself that if Benjamin did know where I was, surely he wouldn't be *trying* to find me but would already be here, demanding I return home with him.

By the time the night gave way to a pale dawn, I had convinced myself that, at least for the time being, I was safe here in Paris with my grandmother, and I allowed my mind to turn to thoughts of another man. I began to wonder about Julien Duplessi. Who was he, and why had he been left alone at my grandmother's house? And why was I so curious about him?

Early the next morning, as I drank my tea in my bedroom, I heard my grandmother leave the apartment. It was not even ten o'clock.

Hurrying downstairs, I looked out the window in time to see her turn at the corner, heading, it appeared, toward rue des Saints-Pères and Maison de la Lune.

Little more than an hour later she returned, surprised to find me reading in the sitting room instead of in my bedroom.

"Good morning," she said. "Are you feeling

all right, Sandrine? It's early for you to be downstairs."

I nodded. "Fine, thank you. And early for you to go out," I said, wanting so much for her to tell me where she'd been.

"I needed some things from the pharmacy, and there was no one to send. Once I was out, I thought I'd stop to have tea at Ladurée and bring you some macarons."

She held out the pale green-and-gold box. Taking them, I thanked her. They had always been my favorite, and a wash of memories came over me of when I'd been here as a young girl. I kissed her. The scent of the cold winter morning on her skin made me think of Maison de la Lune again. Was she telling me the truth, or had she returned to the house and then gone to the patisserie to hide her real reason for leaving so early again?

Grand-mère went upstairs to her room, and I remained where I was, reading, or trying to. Why didn't I just ask her?

I found my grandmother in her bedroom, sitting at her vanity, her jewel boxes open before her.

Seeing me, she gave me one of her most inviting smiles. Grand-mère was an expert at the art of expression, claiming it was always more seductive to speak with the lips or the eyes than with words.

Before I had a chance to ask my question, she told me that she was being taken to lunch today by her *dear friend* who was in town and that she would be gone for most of the day.

There was no question what kind of *dear friend* he was. I'd been living with my grandmother for almost a month now and knew the difference between how she dressed on an ordinary day versus a day with an assignation. Today's visitor was clearly even more special than the others.

"Who? Is it the count?"

I had wondered why her benefactor had not visited once since I'd been in Paris but had been loath to ask in case I was bringing up a sensitive topic.

Grand-mère smiled. "Yes. Now help me pick out my opals," she said, patting the space beside her on the silk-covered bench.

Count Gregorio Carrara of Bergamo, Italy, spent most of his time overseeing his family's marble business. I had met him ten years ago and remembered how much older he was than my grandmother. But from how nervously she prepared, I sensed he was still a demanding lover, and I worried for her.

"Yes, the count has been away but is back in Paris." She pulled out an opal choker: four rows of the fiery beads with a diamond-and-emerald clasp. She held it up to her throat and looked at me. I nodded.

"After a certain age," she said, "a neck full of jewels is the best camouflage."

"For what?"

"Sad skin that is no longer taut." Her voice was tinged with melancholy, but only for a moment. "Close it for me, Sandrine."

As I snapped the clasp, she laughed. "At least," she said, examining the effect in the mirror, "his eyesight isn't as good as it used to be and he doesn't see my lines and wrinkles."

"But you don't look your age, not at all."

And she didn't. My grandmother was sixty-six years old, but her skin was creamy and still quite firm. Her hair still thick and lustrous. Her hands were graceful and almost without age spots. Her *opal de feu* eyes were wide and sparkled, filled with all kinds of secrets.

"I don't see any of the imperfections you do," I said.

"Do you want to know my beauty secret, *mon ange*?"

"Of course."

"Spend lavishly on creams. Wash your hair with henna at the first sign of gray. Never spend one minute thinking about what you do not have. And most importantly, indulge in everything but love."

She looked at me, waiting for some response, but I didn't have one. I had so little experience with love.

"Love," she said emphatically, "is heartbreak. Now, pick something for yourself that you'd like from all these trinkets."

The box she offered was brimming with jewels. Hardly trinkets. I knew, because she was quite open about how she made her living, that these were all gifts from lovers over the years. As she'd gotten older, she hadn't needed to sell her treasures like so many women of her kind because Albert Salome had given her several properties that provided her with an income large enough that she would always be comfortable.

I picked through the necklaces and rings. Inspected earrings and bracelets. There were ropes of creamy pearls and . . . I lifted out a strand of black iridescent pearls from the South Seas. Holding them up to my neck, I looked in the mirror.

Grand-mère shook her head. "The color doesn't suit you. But my fire opals will. They'll pick up the highlights in your hair and the glints in your eyes that are like mine."

"No, they're your signature stones," I said, and kept searching through the emeralds, sapphires, aquamarines, amethysts, and diamonds. Every stone but the one that I loved the best.

"You have no rubies," I finally said.

She shook her head. "I don't fancy them. Do you?"

"I love them." I held out my left hand. On my ring finger was an oval ruby surrounded with diamonds. "I never take it off."

My grandmother took my hand in hers and

looked down at the ring that had once belonged to her mother. My father had given it to Benjamin to give to me when we'd become betrothed. I would have left it in New York, as I had my wedding ring, but it had never symbolized my marriage to me. It was a family heirloom that I treasured.

"Papa told me you once said every ruby is a frozen drop of human blood preserved forever as a jewel, and that if we could unlock the secret of how to turn it back into blood, we would have the key to immortality."

My grandmother seemed to shrink into herself. "I never told him that."

"Who did?"

She shook her head. "I wouldn't know," she said emphatically.

"Then why did he tell me you said it?"

"I don't know," she insisted, but there was something in how she turned away from me, almost imperceptibly, that alerted me. She was lying. She knew exactly where my father had heard it, but for some reason wanted to keep that from me.

"You haven't chosen anything," she said, scooping up a handful of gleaming jewels and sorting through them herself. "Earrings, perhaps, since you didn't bring any with you?" Picking out a pair of turquoise-and-diamond earrings, she held them up to my face. Each smooth stone was the size of a hazelnut and surrounded by a halo of pink diamonds that sparkled in the morning sunlight.

"It's believed by the ancients that turquoise can draw evil to itself and away from the person wearing it." She held them out. "I think these will do."

"So you know a lot about stones and their properties, too?" I asked as I screwed in the first earring.

"A bit. Why?"

"Papa loved studying gems and stones. He once told me how Renaissance painters made their own paints by grinding stones: turquoise, lapis, ochre, malachite, and then took me to the museum to show me the masterworks that had been painted with stones."

"The two of you spent a lot of time together, didn't you?"

I nodded.

"He was a wonderful father to you. And a wonderful son to me."

Grand-mère's eyes closed for a single second, and I saw her eyelashes quiver against her cheeks. Then she shook her mane of glorious sunset hair and forced some gaiety into her voice. "So what will you do today? I think you should get out of the apartment even though it's drizzling. No moping around. The time for that is over."

"Yes," I said. "You're right. I think I'll take myself off to the dusty Louvre."

This made her smile.

But I was lying. I wasn't thinking about going to

the museum but rather visiting the Maison de la Lune. If Monsieur Duplessi was there again today, he'd let me in, and I wanted to walk around the house, wanted to see all the rooms that were still so vivid in my memory. I wanted to surround myself with La Lune's treasures.

Chapter 6

Getting up my courage, I asked, "Monsieur Duplessi, what is it you are doing here exactly?"

We were once again in the kitchen, eating his croissants and drinking the bitter coffee he'd brewed for us.

"Haven't you asked your grandmother that?"

I could see he was confused by my question.

"No."

"And why is that?"

"She is too upset to speak of this house." It was true: whenever I brought up La Lune, she'd become uncomfortable. I guessed that since she had raised my father here, the memories were bittersweet and too painful.

"But she doesn't seem upset when she's here," he offered with a slightly sly smile, as if he was half teasing, half challenging.

His hair had fallen onto his face, and I found myself wanting to reach out and feel its silkiness. I stared down at my hands as if they belonged to a stranger. I had never given a single thought to touching my husband's hair.

"Mademoiselle?" Julien was looking at me, waiting for a response.

"Perhaps you don't understand Grand-mère well enough to judge whether she's happy or unhappy.

Exactly how do you know her?" I asked, finally.

"I'm an architect," he said, and I noticed that he lifted up his head a little when he said it. "She hired me."

"So you are renovating the house?"

"Yes. Didn't she tell you?"

"She did, but what are you doing here every day without any workers?"

"I'm making an inventory. If we are to turn the mansion into a museum, I need to know what items will be displayed and how to show them off and how much room will be needed for the different exhibitions so I can plan accordingly."

I felt cold. Certainly I had not heard him correctly. A museum? "But she lives here. This is our home."

He shrugged. "She never revealed her reasons to me. All I know is there's more than enough here to make for a fine jewel of a museum. There are over thirty pieces of sculpture. Eighty paintings, some that rival anything in the Louvre. An excellent selection of china dating from as early as 1700. Your family's holdings are a treasure trove of objets d'art going back to the 1600s. It's astonishing."

"But she's going to live here after you're done, correct?"

"I am so sorry to distress you." He was looking at me tenderly. "But no, our conversations would suggest not. We've discussed using the second-floor bedrooms as galleries devoted to the art of seduction. Your grandmother has collected antique clothes and accessories used in the courtesan's art, which will fascinate visitors."

I gripped the edge of the table. Felt the chilly marble on my fingertips. A shiver ran through me. I could not allow this house to be turned into a museum . . . could not allow strangers to walk through the doors and examine the things that belonged to us . . . belonged to me.

I pulled myself up and walked out of the kitchen, down the hallway and out into the grand foyer, with its glass-domed ceiling. I then moved into the drawing room, where I stood and gazed around the most excessive and elaborate room in the house.

It was a riot of golds, reds, scarlets, purples, peacock feathers, ferns, palms, and orchids. From the turquoise and lapis tiles around the fireplace to the exotic Indian carpet to the ebony monkeys with ruby eyes holding up gold bananas outfitted with candles, the room was a marvel of opulence, style, and wit. How could she open it up to strangers?

I was unaware that Monsieur Duplessi had followed me until he spoke.

"She says she wants to call it the Museum of the Grand Horizontals. Quite an avant-garde concept, don't you agree? A flirting museum. Centuries of artwork collected by France's most revered courtesans."

The cold I had experienced before intensified. Taking a step away from the sudden draft, I felt cobwebs brush against my face and hands. No, this had been my father's home, too, and one of the places I could feel close to him. He had eaten breakfast at the kitchen table every morning, munching on hot pastries the cook had just taken out of the oven. I glanced over at the grand staircase. He'd gone sliding down that banister, and been spanked for it—more often, he'd said, than he could count. I knew he'd found hiding places under the piano in the music room, inside a giant brass vase in the smoking room, and under the four-poster bed in Little Red Riding Hood's chamber—some of the bedrooms in the house were named for fantasy or fairy-tale characters that might incite a gentleman's imagination. Other bedrooms were designed to evoke a particular exotic time period or place. I had yet to go searching for the little things my father had told me he'd stashed away: marbles, a frog skeleton, broken pottery he'd found digging in the gardens that he was sure dated back to Roman times. If this house was taken apart, it could not become my refuge.

"Are you all right? You look pale. I should not have said anything." He was standing beside me and had taken my arm as if he was prepared to keep me standing if I became faint.

"I'll be fine, thank you." I looked into his face,

and he returned my glance. The moment lasted one beat longer than was appropriate. I looked away first, but even when I did, he didn't take his hand off my arm, and my skin felt hot where he was touching me.

The freezing air was gone now. The atmosphere around me had returned to normal. In fact, there was the faint odor of violets in the air. How was that possible? It was the dead of winter. Perhaps there was a bowl of potpourri in a corner somewhere, perfuming the room. There was almost gaiety in the atmosphere. As if the house itself was pleased.

But that was impossible. A house didn't have emotions or personality. I was simply overwrought, as my grandmother had been telling me since I'd arrived in Paris. And for good reason. Losing my father would have been bad enough, but *how* I lost him—that my husband had ruined my father, had in effect killed him by destroying his ability to salvage his reputation if he turned Benjamin in—was enough to test anyone's sanity.

"Are you sure you are fine?"

"Yes." Of course I wasn't, but I couldn't share how I felt with someone I barely knew. Fury filled me. How dare my grandmother make a decision like this without me. Maison de la Lune was my birthright. She had inherited it; she had not built it. Not created it. It was not hers to destroy.

My eyes rested on an Ingres painting of a harem

of sensual, naked women at a Turkish bath that hung above the fireplace. This one was far more evocative and erotic than the similar painting of the same scene in the Louvre. Heat rose up my neck, and I knew I was blushing. To be examining these with Monsieur Duplessi right beside me was brazen, and yet I didn't turn away as I would have imagined.

It was one thing for the men who attended my grandmother's evening salons and visited with her to see these rooms, but to have tourists walking through the house and gaping at our treasures?

All around me the house seemed to be reaching out and asking for help. I had to get to her heart and comfort her, reassure her that I would not allow this to happen.

Suddenly I was sure this emergency was what had brought me back to Paris. After all, I could have taken refuge with my Aunt, my mother's sister, and her husband, who lived in Chicago and with whom I had spent so much more time. No, of course not. It was not my wild and irrepressible grandmother, who had always flitted in and out of my life on a whiff of L'Etoile's bespoke fragrance, who had brought me here. It was the house, this living thing, that had called me back so that I might save her.

I began to run. Back out into the grand foyer. Up the sweeping stairs to the second floor. Up to the third floor. Down a long hallway past rooms used by servants. At the end of the hallway was another staircase that led to the attic. The pathway through the stored trunks and furniture seemed to circle in on itself, and I was caught in its coil.

I'd discovered this part of the house when I was fifteen. Remembered coming up here and finding a silk robe in one of the trunks and wearing it downstairs, showing off how I looked, only to have my grandmother fly into a fit of rage. It was the same robe as the women in the portraits wore. A beautiful burnt-orange silk, embroidered with russet and cream flowers and green dragons. My grandmother had ripped it off me. Why had she cared so much that I was wearing it? I couldn't remember now, but she had lectured me adamantly about never venturing into this antique-filled part of the house after that excursion. There was nothing here but old, useless things, she'd said.

"But what about the door?" I'd asked her.

Her face fell at the mention of it. "The door?"

"There are stone steps leading from the attic to a very old wooden door. Why does it look like that? Where does that door go? What's behind it?"

Reluctantly she explained that in the fifteenth century a church had stood on this plot of land. At some point it had been torn down except for its bell tower, and the house had been erected abutting the ancient structure. A structure my grandmother insisted was not safe. It was too old, too fragile to hold the weight of a person. It was empty, she said, and absolutely not a place to explore. "The steps are broken, and you could trip. The bell tower is only scaffolding now. If you even tried to walk there, you would fall right through!"

I had never completely believed her. And now, as I walked up that last flight of steps, I thought about how solid the stones felt. Narrow and steep, yes, but sturdy and strong. Three hundred years of bell ringers had tramped up and down them. Could the tower they led to be any less well constructed?

At last I came to the door. It was not even as wide as my outstretched arms, but every inch was carved with the most extraordinary tiny bas-reliefs, each one intricately detailing events similar to etchings I'd seen in my father's alchemy books. In the center of this whole amalgam of magick and religion was a facsimile of the same bronze hand from the front door downstairs. But here the hand was flat, not three-dimensional, and in its very center was a keyhole.

I was out of breath. I'd run all this way to stand here, in front of this strange door. Why? My grandmother had told me it had been locked since she was a little girl and that no one had ever discovered the key.

"This is astonishing," Monsieur Duplessi exclaimed as he examined the door. "Where are we?"

I hadn't even known he'd been following me,

but I was glad. It felt right to have him here with me.

I explained what my grandmother had told me about this part of the house. He agreed that it looked sturdy, noting that often these old structures made of stone in the Middle Ages withstood time better than most of our modern buildings would.

"Let's see what's here, shall we?" And without waiting for my answer, he reached out and tried the knob.

Of course it didn't turn.

For no reason that made any sense, for certainly he was stronger than I was, I reached out and tried the handle after he had. The most peculiar thing happened. Without any great effort, without pushing or pulling, the door opened for me.

"But it was locked," he said incredulously.

Together we stepped into a large circular stone room. In its center was a spiral staircase. Looking up into it was like gazing into a seashell, a perfect nautilus spiral leading up and up and up. At its summit was the bell chamber itself beneath a pitched roof crisscrossed with wooden beams, and hanging from those beams were three large brass bells.

Long ruby-red velvet cords, frayed and faded, dangled from the bells all the way to where we were standing. At the end of each was a hand-sized sandbag covered with iridescent muslin.

Smells assaulted me: dust, mold, years and years of stale air, and something familiar that I couldn't identify. As I stood there, looking around, taking in the sights and odors, I heard something. Listened harder.

"Do you hear that?" I asked Monsieur Duplessi.

He listened for a moment. "No, what is it?"

I shook my head. How to tell him I thought I heard tears being shed? Tears can't be heard. They are silent as they slide down a cheek. Except I was, I *was,* hearing the silken slip of them. I was listening to someone's broken heart.

But whose? There was no one here but Monsieur Duplessi and me.

As I looked around, trying to pinpoint the sound, I noticed different-sized shapes shrouded in sheets.

Monsieur Duplessi saw them, too, and pulled off one of the coverings. "Look at these," he said as he revealed a stack of paintings.

"Look at the walls," I said, pointing. "Beneath all that dust it looks like all the walls are decorated with frescoes."

"It's clearly an artist's studio," Monsieur Duplessi said as he opened the doors to a cabinet filled with dusty bottles and jars of brushes and a tall stack of wooden palettes.

I walked closer, ran my finger over one bottle and then another, bringing bright red pigment to light in one and verdant emerald in another.

How long since anyone had touched these things?

"Your grandmother isn't a painter, is she?"

I shook my head.

"Perhaps she was renting it out to an artist?"

"I don't think anyone has been here in a long, long time. Since before . . . since before she was born."

"How do you know?" he asked.

I shrugged. "I can smell the centuries, can't you?"

He sniffed the air.

"Your grandmother never even mentioned this part of the maison existed," Monsieur Duplessi said.

I was listening to him, but at the same time thinking that I had to let fresh air into the studio. It wanted to breathe.

Long iron rods hung against the walls. Approaching one, I began to twist it. The shutters covering the windows that were cut into the stone high in the tower began to open. With a final creak, a whoosh of fresh air poured in.

I opened the next window, and then the next, until all six were open and the room was filled with light and cool air.

Gently I took hold of one of the sandbags, pulled the crimson cord, and held my breath as the first bell let out a lovely peal. I pulled the second cord. Then the last. The sounds were pure and deep but ominous, too. A glorious warning rising up to the heavens. Beautiful and portentous, like snow falling on a dark lake on a moonless night.

I shivered. Something in the room shifted and altered.

I looked at Monsieur Duplessi. "Do you feel that?"

"What?" He didn't seem surprised by my question. The expression on his face suggested he might have felt what I felt, but first wanted to hear what I thought it was before he acknowledged it.

"As if . . . someone just flew in . . ."

"Or maybe flew out. Certain cultures used bells to chase away unwanted spirits and negative energies, especially from a place of worship."

The bell's last reverberations surrounded us, embracing us in a final melancholy echo.

"Do you believe in unwanted spirits?" I asked.

He had a faraway look in his eyes. "I don't believe in spirits, wanted or unwanted, but fascination in the occult and the supernatural has exploded, and we hear about such things all the time. A few years ago more than forty thousand occultists attended a Congrès Spirite et Spiritualiste here in Paris. On the one hand it's a phenomena. On the other, it's nothing new. There have been mystics and Freemasons in France since the 1700s, but interest does seem to be greater than ever."

"Do you think there's a tangible reason?"

"I've read it's not unusual for people to become

overly superstitious and nervous at the end of a century—perhaps that's all there is to it. Or perhaps we are experiencing a backlash against positivism, naturalism, and secularism. It's possible the occult movement has escalated because we are searching for answers that we can't find through science, reason, and facts. Sometimes I think this preoccupation with the supernatural demonstrates the real tensions wrestling for the soul of France."

From his expression and the tone in his voice, even I, who didn't know him well, knew that all this was troubling him.

"Let's see what is under this dirt." I picked up a rag and swiped the wall. "Aren't you supposed to be here inspecting the rooms and making an inventory? This is definitely something that should be included in the museum."

As I spoke, I felt a burst of chill air blow through the windows. It seemed to reach down, as if it had arms, and press against me, almost as if it were trying to communicate.

"Yes, let's see what we have," he said as he grabbed another rag and began helping dust off the murals.

Under the layers of grime brilliant colors appeared, fresh and vibrant as if the fresco had been painted just weeks ago. The painting was High Renaissance, lush, evocative, colorful, and extremely eroticized, even more so than the

Ingres, and I was embarrassed to be looking at it with a man I didn't know.

"It's the story of a woman . . . and a man with wings . . . ," I said.

"It appears to be an illustration of the myth of Psyche and Cupid," Monsieur Duplessi said in a faraway voice, as if transfixed by the beautiful and strange allegory we were uncovering.

"I think you're right."

Cupid had strong limbs, penetrating eyes, and was well endowed. Psyche was voluptuous and sensual. I could almost feel how soft her skin was, how seductive the perfume was that she was wearing.

We made our way around the room, revealing more of the story, until we eventually found the spot where, in a darkened bedroom, the artist had painted the doomed lovers in a deep embrace, coupling.

I was riveted to the lovers' scene. I'd never known any desire that strong in my life.

"I wonder why the style changes here . . . and here," Monsieur Duplessi said, in what I was sure was an effort to distract us, practically strangers, from the intimate nature of the paintings them-selves.

We had reached the corner of the room where two tall objects loomed. Covered, it was impos-sible to guess what they might be. Pulling the sheet off the first, I exposed an easel holding a painting, its back to me. There was a brush on the shelf with dried ruby-red paint on its bristles. I picked it up. Holding it, I knew I'd found what I was looking for. I had no doubt. Here, right here, was the heart of the house.

I pulled off the other covering, revealing a second identical easel. Also with a painting on it, also with its back to the room.

Something occurred to me. I looked down at the tarp that had been protecting the first easel and then the second. There should have been more dust on them. There was dust everywhere else. How could these items have been spared the detritus of the years when everything else in the studio had not?

With trembling hands, I turned the canvas on the second easel around. I was staring at a portrait of a nude woman seated in front of an easel just like this one, in this room. She held a paintbrush. On its tip was ruby paint. Behind her was an untouched, clean canvas. This woman resembled Psyche in the mural, but here she wasn't playing a part.

This was her, who she was, her very self naked for the viewer to examine.

There was a mixture of expressions on the woman's face. Pleasure and pain at the same time. I'd certainly read enough about romantic entanglements to understand I was looking at a portrait of passionate longing.

When I'd been fifteen and thought I'd been falling in love with Leon, I had felt a child's version of this, hadn't I?

I remembered that last night again . . . my grandmother finding us, calling me ungrateful and willful as she dragged us apart and pulled Leon out of the servant's room. I remembered how I had followed, running behind them, crying. And then that one terrible blow that had set off an asthma attack that sent Leon to his knees and finally to his death.

I'd gotten so sick afterward that my parents had been summoned from Morocco. And I remembered, too, listening to my grandmother talking in hushed tones to my father outside my bedroom.

"You have to protect her from love," my grandmother warned.

I lay in bed, weeping, hiding under the covers, cowering and confused, delirious with fever, hearing the phrase like some verse repeated in a song.

Protect her from love. Protect her from love.

As if love were a disease that would destroy me.

My parents and I left for London once I recovered and spent several weeks seeing the sights and taking tea and visiting museums. Sometimes at night, when I was supposed to be asleep in the adjoining room of the suite, I overheard hushed and worried conversations between my parents.

What were the secrets they talked of?

It was all very vague until a letter arrived from my grandmother that I wasn't supposed to read, but did.

> Love is dangerous for Verlaine women. It leads to heartbreak. It leads to tragedy. We are too passionate, and it is like a poison for us. Don't let it rule Sandrine's life or it will ruin her. Teach her to rise above her instincts; marry her off to a man who will not incite or excite her but make her feel safe and calm. She can have a grand life, but it needs be a certain kind of life.

"There are initials here," Monsieur Duplessi called out.

He had made his way around the room and finished wiping off the mural. It was still fairly dirty, but the whole myth was clear and beautifully rendered.

" 'CCLI,' " he called out.

I repeated them. Shook my head. "I don't recognize them, do you? But that could be the date: CCLI is two hundred and fifty one in Roman numerals."

"I might do some research at the library at the École des Beaux-Arts."

"Look at what I found." I pointed to the second easel, then walked around to the first and turned its painting around.

"It's the same man who's Cupid in the mural," I said.

"But he's a cartoon in the mural scenes compared to this."

It is one thing to be with a man when you view a painting of a nude woman. We are inured to the female nude, even if she is flirtatious or lascivious as painted by Rubens. Or voluptuous as painted by Renoir. She is still within the norm of what polite society sees as *art*. But it is quite another to be alone in a medieval tower with a stranger whose eyes seem to see through you while you're looking at an erotic painting of a nude male.

I couldn't stop gazing at the canvas. Who was the sitter? Who had captured him so feverishly?

The man was painted with passion that informed every stroke. He was not handsome—his nose appeared broken; a scar ran through his right eyebrow; his lips were too full and almost mean; his eyes were dark and hooded. Mysterious and driven, he was all energy, all excitement: a hungry satyr.

He was not only naked but also slightly erect. He appeared so real that I wouldn't have been surprised had he stepped out of the canvas and I'd discovered it was one of those tableaus so popular at parties in the States, where hostesses have models pose as great paintings for the guests' amusement.

I felt heat coming off me in waves and wondered if Monsieur Duplessi sensed it.

"Interesting . . ." Duplessi mused as he moved closer to the easel and me. So close I could feel his breath on the back of my neck. "The styles of these two portraits are the same. He's created a dramatic effect using chiaroscuro—those heavy contrasts between dark and light—to achieve three-dimensional volume, hasn't he?"

He stepped back. Looked at the woman's portrait. "How do you think they compare?"

I studied one and then the other. "I think he's more sure of himself painting the woman—bolder perhaps?"

"And there's a sense of urgency in the woman's portrait. As though every time the artist worked on it, he'd rush to finish his work for the day so he could bed the model."

Obviously Monsieur Duplessi was less embarrassed to be standing here with me than I was with him. And also more comfortable talking about what men and women did together than I was. And why shouldn't he be? I was the granddaughter of one of the most famous courtesans in Paris. Who would guess at how naïve and unsophisticated I was when it came to matters of the heart and the bedroom?

I began describing the male portrait. "This one is painted more adoringly, as if the painter was lingering over each stroke, luxuriating in each curve and contour of the male form. As if she was loath to finish it."

"Why do you say that?" Monsieur Duplessi asked.

"What?"

"That the painting of the man was done by a woman? I assumed the same painter painted both." He gestured to the murals. "That one man painted everything here."

I shook my head. "I don't know."

Monsieur Duplessi inspected the portrait of the female.

"There are initials here, the first two that are on the mural. 'CC.'" He walked around to the portrait of the male nude. "You may be onto something. There are initials here, too—the last two in the mural—'LI.'"

I walked over and inspected what he was looking at. Stared at it. The initials had a circle painted around them, and it seemed there was some kind of serpent or dragon's head on the circle. "Not 'LI.' That's an *L*. It's 'LL.'"

"Could be," he said, peering at it.

I felt his wool jacket sleeve brush against my hand as he came close, and a rush of feeling began to flutter and gather inside me.

So intense and foreign was the experience, for a moment I thought for sure I was going to be unwell. And then I almost laughed as I comprehended that my reaction was anything but illness coming on.

"You are right," he said. "CC and LL. Two painters sharing this studio . . . when? How long ago? This is a marvelous find. It could even be an important find." His excitement was palpable and infectious.

"There's a lesser-known Renaissance painter named Cherubino Cellini. I saw his work in the Louvre one day when I visited with my grandmother. It was a very dramatic painting of Judith beheading Holofernes, and I remember commenting on it. The model he'd used for Judith had oddly reminded me of my grandmother. She didn't think it was much of a compliment."

I turned to inspect the wall art. "Now that I think about it, this style matches the painting in the museum. And both use mythological themes. It was quite fashionable at the time, especially in Italy."

"You're well versed in art history," Monsieur Duplessi said.

"My father collects"—I corrected myself—"*collected* art and gave me the unofficial job of curating for him. Some of the happiest times I've had were visiting galleries with him and buying art. Supposedly an ancestor of mine was—" I broke off. Of course. How could I not have put it all together?

"Listen, I know who LL is . . . I'm certain of it. One of my ancestors was a woman named Lunette Lumière. La Lune. This was her house."

"Was she a painter?"

I shook my head. "I don't know . . . She was a well-known courtesan, and there was a legend that she was the lover of a famous painter."

"Surely these both could have been painted by the same man, and he put her initials on his self-portrait and his initials on hers. But that doesn't really make sense. One painting is CC alone. The other is LL alone. Only the mural has both initials. Maybe they both painted the mural, and this is a portrait of La Lune painted by Cellini, and this is a portrait of Cellini painted by La Lune?"

"Let's look at the rest of them." I began to unstack the paintings that were against the far wall. One after another after another, I turned them face out. Each was of either him or her. All nudes or only slightly draped. Those of the woman were all signed "CC." Those of the man, all signed "LL."

The heat in the room seemed to grow more intense and oppressive as more and more of the erotic studies were exposed. We organized them with all the paintings of him leaning against one wall . . . staring at all those of her leaning against the other wall.

I looked from the portraits to Monsieur Duplessi. As he intently studied the artwork, I imagined him turning, walking to me, undressing me, and lying down with me on the daybed.

I glanced over at it now—not meaning to, but involuntarily staring at its silk coverlet and overstuffed pillows. Strangely there was no visible dust there either. Had it blown off when we opened the windows?

Then a sense of unreality came over me.

I was seeing myself there with Monsieur Duplessi, our bodies as naked as those of the man and the woman in the paintings on the easels. Our bodies intertwined. My hair fanned out on the pillow. His fingers gripping my shoulder.

Suddenly, I was embarrassed to look at the architect for fear he would see what was on my face, in my eyes. I did not understand what was happening. I had been married for almost four years and had never imagined an erotic scene, not even in my dreams.

But Monsieur Duplessi was not looking at me. Not paying any attention to me at all, in fact. He was bent over the paintings, intently examining one after the other. And then suddenly, he did turn. Quickly. And caught me looking at him. Our eyes locked for a moment.

No, this was unfair. My mind was mocking me. My body wasn't capable of enjoying the idea of lovemaking.

I flew out of the room, down the steps. Going dangerously fast on the narrow, slippery risers. Behind me Monsieur Duplessi's footfalls followed.

"Sandrine! Stop! What is it?" His voice echoed, and it sounded as if he was calling out in this moment and in moments past.

I didn't notice that I had gone from being Mademoiselle Verlaine to Sandrine. I just ran and ran, trying to escape my shame. But he was faster and caught up to me just as I tripped down two steps and was heading toward a nasty spill.

He grabbed me and pulled me back, kept me from falling.

I was out of breath, panting.

We were both covered in dust, rivulets of perspiration dripping down our faces. What a fright I must have looked!

"What are you doing? Are you mad? You can't take these stairs so fast! You could kill yourself! What were you running away from?"

I shook my head. Even if I had wanted to explain, I was too out of breath to talk.

"I wanted to show you the most extraordinary thing," he panted.

"What?" I asked, forgetting myself for the moment.

"The paintings all are dated."

"Yes, I noticed the dates . . . They were mostly 1606 and 1607."

"But there were some that were later, Sandrine. Some were dated the mid-1700s. Some even in the early and mid-1800s."

"There were?"

"Yes. But what was even stranger is there's one dated this year, and there are two dated in the future."

Chapter 7

"I'd like to know something about our family history," I said to my grandmother the following night at dinner. It was her birthday, and we were dining at Le Grand Véfour, a fine restaurant tucked away in a corner of the Palais Royal. From our table we could look out at the elaborate gardens in the courtyard, the *cour d'honneur*, which was surrounded on all four sides by the palace once occupied by Cardinal Richelieu and his court. As we alighted from her carriage, Grand-mère had told me that the restaurant was more than a hundred years old and that Napoleon had often dined there with Josephine.

"Our family history?" Grand-mère asked as she watched the sommelier fill the crystal flutes with champagne. "We come from a long line of courtesans dating back to the 1500s. Cultured, lovely women born into a life that offered little escape."

"Tell me more about them. Who was the first?"

"Why are you asking about this?"

"There's so much history in Paris. All around us, everywhere we go. It's made me curious. Tell me about La Lune."

She looked at me strangely with an expression

that I couldn't quite read. But clearly she wasn't pleased.

"Why bring her up specifically?"

"She's part of my heritage."

"There are more interesting things to discuss. Such as which operas we will be going to see this winter and how we are going to introduce you to society. Are we going to say you are married or unmarried? And if married, why are you using the name Verlaine?"

"I have no interest in being introduced to society."

"You are pouting, and it's not flattering. We do need to discuss the question of your marital status and your plans."

The main dining room of Le Grand Véfour was decorated in an eighteenth-century Italianate style, with red velvet banquettes, crystal chandeliers, and tall mirrors framed in gold, flanked with delicate neoclassical paintings under glass of women with baskets of flowers. Roses and stucco garlands graced the *boiserie* ceiling, where more women, as well as paintings of fish and game and flowers, filled in every space. Lovely and busy decorations that gave the restaurant a timeless quality. In the mirrored wall behind my grandmother, I glanced at my own reflection. Was I pouting?

But I didn't see my own face glance back at me. The face of the woman in the paintings in the stone tower was superimposed over my own. I shivered. The ghostly image was at once beautiful but also deeply disturbing. Who was she? Why was she haunting me? And why was the tower shut off like that?

"I really would like to hear about La Lune. What reason could there be for not telling me about her?"

Rather than answer, my grandmother lifted the crystal champagne glass and brought it to her lips.

We were seated beside the windows, which were as tall as the mirrors and faced the gardens. Snow began sprinkling the trees and flower beds with a fine white powder that reminded me of the dust in the artist's studio that Monsieur Duplessi and I had found.

"Why don't you want to talk about her?" I asked.

"It's all legend and myth and not very pleasant."

The sommelier arrived with the bottle of Bordeaux my grandmother had ordered and poured the ruby wine. The waiter arrived with our first course. Placing china bowls in front of us, he ladled out spoonfuls of lobster bisque. Once the waiter had filled the bowls three-quarters full, he sprinkled lightly toasted croutons on the top and wished us Bon appétit.

I tasted my soup. Fragrant and flavorful, the bisque offered the essence of the sea mollified by luscious cream.

"I need to talk about her," I said.

My grandmother lifted the spoon to her mouth, then dipped it in the soup again.

The sounds of the restaurant made the silence between us all the louder. All around, silverware clinked, glasses tinkled, conversations flowed, guests laughed, waiters recited specials. Only at our table was there such quiet.

There we were, two women, both wearing black silk mourning dresses, while around us were women bedecked in jewel-toned gowns, fanciful lace and ribbons, rich velvets and shimmering satins. My grandmother followed my glance.

"Yes, we've had enough black," she declared, as if she'd been reading my mind. "On your birthday you get a wish, don't you? Mine is that we stop being so very sad." She finished off her soup. "None of this moping will bring your father back. Besides," she said as she laid her spoon down, "I knew my son, you knew your father. He would most certainly not approve of us languishing."

She was right about that. My father took great pleasure from life. But would changing the color of the silks we wore make us miss him any less?

"Papa," I said, tying in the last conversation with the previous one, "told me that you knew much more of the story about her than he did. That she was a woman of grand passions."

"About who?" my grandmother asked.

I knew that she was pretending not to know who I was asking about.

"La Lune."

"Oh, Sandrine, really. What is there to discuss? She lived over three hundred years ago. She was a very successful courtesan who inspired a few poets and painters and dabbled in painting herself."

"Did she marry?"

"We don't know."

"Did she have children?"

"Yes. She had a son who became an actor and two daughters who continued in their mother's footsteps, or so the story goes. It seems many of the male children in our family go on to become quite respectable, but the women . . ." She shook her head.

"Are you saying that you aren't respectable?"

"Well, I'm not a duchess living in a château, am I?" Grand-mère laughed. It was such a wonderful sound. Not a light laugh like crystals tinkling, but a rich, seductive laugh that came from her throat and was tinged with a voluptuousness that, suddenly that night, for the first time, made me envious.

"Papa always said that he could hear your whole personality in your laughter. He said it was all there—your joie de vivre, your refusal to allow life's troubles to weigh you down. And in the lower notes, he could sense your indefatigable determination."

Tears sparkled in my grandmother's eyes for a moment.

"Will it always be like this?" I asked. "Will remembering Papa, even happily, always make me sad . . ."

"No, the sadness will soften, its edges will become less rough. In time missing him will be the way you love him." She reached across the table and took my hand. Her skin felt like velvet. "You've lost a lot. Your mother when you were seventeen and needed her the most, and now your father, and in a way your husband. You speak of him so little, *mon ange*. We should, you know."

"I'll make a deal with you. I'll answer all your questions about Benjamin and why I am afraid of him coming after me if you tell me what you are hiding about La Lune."

She shook her head. "I'm not hiding anything. So much time has passed, she's nothing but a fairy tale."

The waiter approached and refilled our wine-glasses.

"All right. If you want to hear about Benjamin, tell me the fairy tale. It's been a while since I heard one, and I might quite like it."

"So stubborn, just like your Papa, aren't you? And he was so like his father. I wish Albert were still alive so you could spend time with him while you are here. He would be delighted by you."

"Was he your favorite? Did you love him?"

She shook her head. "I loved only my son. It's

112

best for our kind never to fall in love and become vulnerable. But I liked his father more than most. Albert was a good friend to me. He taught me about money and how to invest it. And he took care of our son. I have much to thank him for." She raised her glass to the long-gone lover and took a hearty sip.

Before I could pressure her to tell me about La Lune, two waiters arrived with identical silver domes. One was placed in front of each of us, and then at the same time, with great ceremony, the lids were lifted off. The aromas and perfumes rose up. We had both ordered capon with truffle sauce, and for a few moments we admired our beautifully appointed plates before we began to eat.

"My husband is a very cruel man," I said finally.

"Clearly, from what you've told me, he is certainly a ruthless businessman. Do you mean he is also cruel to you?"

I nodded.

"In bed?" my grandmother asked.

I was startled by her bold question for a moment, but only a moment. She was L'Incendie. Making love was her occupation. Matters of the bedroom were not a subject of embarrassment to her.

"In all ways."

Since we were seated beside the window, there was no one to my right, and to my left was a party of six, busy conversing and not listening to us, but still I was uncomfortable talking about this at dinner.

"What were his particular persuasions?"

"He is . . . He was very rough—" I broke off. I'd never spoken of what went on between us to anyone.

"*Mon ange*, there is nothing that a man can want that I have not heard of and probably done for him. You don't have to be coy with me. Did he hit you?"

"No, no."

"Did he ask you to perform uncommon acts?"

"I'm not sure I'd know what is uncommon, but I don't think so."

"What then?"

"He was violent and quick. It was always very painful, and he didn't care. Sometimes I thought he even enjoyed my pain."

"It was always like this?"

I nodded. It would have been difficult answering her questions if we were at home, but it was especially so in a public place. Despite my discomfort she pursued the topic.

Leaning forward, she asked, sotto voce, "Did he ever pleasure you?"

"No."

"Never?"

"No. I said no. Not ever."

"How long did he take when he made love?"

"Do you we need to discuss this here?"

"I find that sometimes lovely surroundings, wonderful food, and amazing wine make it easier to deal with the unpleasantries."

"But the more you ask, the more I have to picture him, to remember him, his stench of cigars and whiskey . . ." I was feeling Benjamin's large, strong hands squeezing my breasts and his fleshy mouth slobbering over me as he shoved himself in between my legs.

"How long did he take?"

"Two or three minutes."

"Always? From the very beginning, *mon ange?*"

"Yes," I whispered. "He told me there was something wrong with me on our honeymoon, and he seemed never to forgive me for it."

"What do you mean something wrong with you?"

"With how I couldn't respond," I whispered.

"Did he tell you that you were frigid?"

The word shocked me. Especially said out loud in a fine restaurant. "Yes." I drained my wineglass. Felt the warmth flood me. The worst part of it had been said. There was some relief in that.

"I knew it was not a love match, but I never suspected that it was so unsatisfying and hurtful. Based on your description of his performance, you can't assume there's anything at all wrong with you."

"But I am sure. I know it. I can feel it."

"No, lovemaking with a callous brute is never

pleasurable." She looked at me and smiled sweetly. "Until you've taken a gentle lover, you can't know how responsive you are. No woman is incapable of pleasure, but some must be taught. Now, eat a bit more. You're too thin to be healthy." She put another pat of butter on my bread plate. "I promise, there's nothing wrong with you. The women in our family aren't made frigid."

I knew she was mistaken. I'd bought illicit books and tried to do things to myself, and I'd failed to coax my body out of its frozen state. But rather than argue I took a forkful of the delicious food and put it in my mouth.

We ate in silence for a few moments more, and I allowed the sounds of the restaurant to lull me into thinking that this was an ordinary night, with a grandmother and granddaughter having a delightful dinner in one of Paris's most famous restaurants.

"You have only told me a sketch of what happened in New York. Are you certain of what you heard between your husband and father?"

"That Benjamin gave Papa no choice? That it was shame either way?"

She nodded.

"Certain that I heard the conversation, yes."

I again described walking into my father's study and seeing him pointing the gun at Benjamin and then hearing what was said. I was calm in recounting the events of the night and how the next morning I had sent the valet to my father's room, and the poor man returned to tell us why my father was not yet at the breakfast table. But when it came to describing the scene of her son's death for my grandmother, I could not continue.

Our dinners had grown cold. The waiter removed the plates, and my grandmother ordered us cognacs and coffees without asking me if I wanted one.

"For money," she said in a sad faraway voice. "All for money." Her eyes filled with tears, but only for a moment. I had seen her eyes fill like this before, and I marveled at how she could blink away her grief so efficiently.

"Did you know Benjamin was gambling?" she asked.

"Papa had only just told me."

"Your father was such a good judge of character. I wonder why he never saw through Benjamin?"

I shrugged.

"I think . . . ," Grand-mère said as the idea occurred to her, "that he didn't want to believe he could have been so wrong about someone and doomed you to such a life all because of—" She broke off.

One waiter approached with the crystal balloons of brandy and the fine china cups for coffee. Another approached with a plate of pastel-colored petit fours and chocolate bonbons.

"Because of what?" I asked.

While I waited for her to resume explaining, I put one of the chocolates in my mouth. It was darkly suggestive, slightly bitter and lushly sweet all at the same time.

"Because I warned your father so often and so vociferously that love is dangerous for Verlaine women. It leads to heartbreak and tragedy. We are too passionate, and it is a poison for us. I told him to marry you off to someone who would take care of you and be good to you, but someone whom you wouldn't fall in love with. Philippe made fun of my superstitions, but in the end he listened to me, didn't he? Or at least he tried to."

I remembered the letter she'd written to my parents after the tragedy with Leon that terrible spring. She'd used almost the same words.

"A family curse? That's preposterous."

She trained her fiery opal eyes on me; her gaze was intense. "No, no, it's not," my grandmother said.

I bit down on the bonbon so hard that my teeth pierced the inside of my cheek, and the taste of blood ruined the chocolate.

"Sandrine, quick." Suddenly my grandmother was standing, shouting at me. "Turn this way, come with me, run." As I stood, she grabbed my arm and pulled me away from the table just as I heard an ear-shattering crash.

Cold air poured in.

I looked back. We were a dozen feet away from

our table, which was now covered in fragments of glass glittering in the candlelight. It was all over our plates. Our seats. We would have been showered by the sharp splinters if Grand-mère hadn't pulled me away.

"Don't stop," she shouted.

A man—either a diner or a waiter—screamed: "It's the anarchists!"

"It's a bomb!" another man yelled.

My grandmother kept moving us farther away from the gaping, wounded window. In the pandemonium around us, people pushed over chairs and tables, breaking china and glass as they rushed to get out of the path of what they expected to come.

"It is all right, Messieurs, Mesdames," the restaurant manager was shouting over the din. "All is fine. It was only a rock. Not a bomb. Not a bomb. Please, everyone. No reason to panic. Brandy for everyone. Take your seats. Please, everyone, please, there's no reason to panic."

The guests were becoming aware of what he was saying.

"Not a bomb."

"A rock? Someone threw a rock?"

"Why?"

People gathered around the manager, peppering him with questions.

"Not a bomb. Just a rock with a note wrapped around it." He held it up.

Beside me, my grandmother, who was holding my arm, leaned very close and whispered in my ear: "I was warning you just when it happened, wasn't I? Telling you that we're cursed. Just at that moment. You see? Just as I was about to tell you that love is what *she* wants and what you can never give her."

But I wasn't thinking about the curse. Wasn't wondering who *she* was. My grandmother had grabbed me and told me to get up moments *before* the window smashed. How had she known what was about to happen?

Chapter 8

I didn't dream of angry mobs or bombings or men destroying beautiful things. For the second night in a row, ever since I'd discovered the hidden studio in the bell tower at Maison de la Lune, I dreamed that I was a painter. I saw my canvases: dark and mysterious visions of winged creatures and women with bloodred lips and fiery auburn hair. And while I slept, I was happy—happier than I could ever remember being.

I woke the morning after the incident at Le Grand Véfour determined to do something about my dreams. After all, I was in Paris. The mecca of artists from all over the world. The home of Ingres, and David, Poussin, Millet, Georges de La Tour, and more. And now the very capital of impressionism and symbolism.

The finest art school was only blocks from our apartment. Of course I would take lessons. Just because I'd failed during my one try at school didn't mean I couldn't learn. Besides, now that the count was back in residence in Paris, my grandmother was too busy for us to spend every afternoon together. Certainly, I could occupy my time reading or visiting museums on my own . . . or I could try my hand at creating something.

When I went downstairs that morning, my

grandmother was readying to leave—to visit her milliner, she said, and then meet the count for a shopping excursion.

"What will you do today?" she asked me with a little nervous catch in her throat. I knew she was worried about me.

I could have told her, but I held back. I wanted to find out what the requirements were to attend art school and then surprise her with how enterprising I was. While I was sure she'd be delighted that I had decided to do something with my time, I wasn't sure she'd embrace my choice. My father had said she had many superstitions about women in our family; one was about them going into the arts. I'd never thought much about it before, but it made me even more hesitant to tell her my plans until they were a *fait accompli.*

I left shortly after she did. The day was cold, and carriages crowded the streets. People were moving more quickly than normal; horses snorted white breaths as they pulled their cabs. Heading north toward rue de Grenelle, I made a left onto rue Saint-Guillaume, a right onto rue Perronet, and then a left onto rue des Saints-Pères. The school was around the corner. I had made a mistake choosing this route. It took me right past my grandmother's house.

As I looked, I saw her emerging through the Maison de la Lune porte cochère. With her was Monsieur Duplessi.

I prayed he wouldn't notice me, or if he did, not let on that I'd visited the house, met her architect, disobeyed her wishes.

Once they were safely out of sight and headed in the opposite direction, toward Boulevard Saint-Germain, I proceeded to the river and my destination, the École des Beaux-Arts.

Leon had been attending the École, and I'd often accompanied him on his walks to school in the morning. It was a hallowed place to someone who revered art.

The imposing school took up much of the block, and for a moment I was overwhelmed with memories of being that fifteen-year-old girl, so impressed she knew a boy who was studying here.

Then the memories were replaced by intimidation. What made me think I was good enough to attend this institution? I had taken painting classes and shown talent, but not enough to attend the École des Beaux-Arts.

For hundreds of years, France's most famous artists had studied here—Delacroix, Géricault, Fragonard—and the modern masters, too: Monet, Degas, Renoir, Moreau, and so many more. There was no more august art institution in the world. Two dreams for two consecutive nights, and suddenly I thought I belonged here?

But I did. I was certain of it.

A crowd clogged the large wrought-iron gates. All manner of men and women and even children were gathered. Marching up to a guard, I asked where I might go to talk to someone in admissions to the school. He regarded me with an odd glance but gave me directions.

Hurried and determined students—wearing smocks and coats, long hair, most with whiskers, carrying boxes of paints or rolls of architectural drawings—crisscrossed the courtyard beyond the gates. I walked among them, my heart beating fast. I was mesmerized by the activity and the architecture. Inside the building the floors were marble. Gleaming gilt columns held up the high ceiling. The walls were covered in paintings. Sculptures loomed. I imagined all the great artists who had stood here and gone through this very process.

After encountering some trouble following the directions, I eventually navigated the last long hallway, which smelled of tobacco and turpentine, and found the office I was searching for.

The clerk behind the desk, a dour-faced man with skin as gray as his hair and beard, asked if he could help me. I explained I wanted to apply.

"But this is not the correct office," he said with a sigh as if he answered this question far too many times a day and had no time for it anymore.

"But I asked at the gate."

"Why didn't you stay at the gate with the others until it was time?"

"Others?"

"Didn't you see the other models?"

I had, but what did they have to do with me?

"Ah, no," I said. "I'm not here to apply for the position of model. I wanted to find out about applying to the school. I want to study painting."

He shook his head and looked at me with disdain. "We don't accept students in the middle of the semester, but Mademoiselle, even if we did, women cannot study at the École."

"I don't understand."

"What don't you understand? It's quite simple. We don't have female students."

At the Art Students League in New York City, men and women studied together. Was it really possible that here in Paris women could not attend the École? There were so many fine female painters in Paris—Mary Cassatt, Berthe Morisot, Eva Gonzalès. Did none of them attend classes here? Did none of them teach here?

He must have taken pity on me, for he gave me a half-smile and said, "There are many good painters who take female students at their ateliers. I can offer some names." He glanced at my empty hands and frowned. "But of course, you cannot just appear and ask to join without a portfolio. You will need to show your work."

It was a gray, chilly day, the clouds hung low over Paris, and I had nowhere to go. Restless, I walked by the Seine. Just being inside the school had intensified my desire to paint. I could still smell the turpentine and feel the energy of those students. I didn't want to give up. I wanted to study there. I felt, as odd as it was, as if my future happiness depended on it. But what choice did I have? If I wanted to study, it would have to be privately. And I did want to study.

Even on that cold morning, walking by the river, I was already seeing the world around me differently, the way a painter would see it. Breaking the sky up into patches of colors, I noticed impressions of light and shadow. I examined the people who walked by as forms, and the negative shapes between them jumped out as spaces to be dealt with.

You will need to show your work.

But I had no work. I remembered that sad little watercolor I had tried to paint for my father when I was younger. That had been a pastime, not a passion. Now I felt the desire to stand in front of a canvas and explore the world through the stroke of a brush oozing color.

I did not go back to the apartment on rue de la Chaise but rather to Maison de la Lune. Maybe there were paints in the tower studio that I could use and try to do something good enough to get me admitted into one of those ateliers the clerk had told me about.

As I let the hand of fate drop on the outside of the door, I remembered that I had seen Monsieur

Duplessi leave with my grandmother earlier. He wouldn't be here. Disappointed, I was just turning to leave when I heard the door open behind me.

"Oh, hello," he said.

I turned. He was smiling.

"I'm so glad you're here," he said, almost out of breath, clearly not in the slightest surprised that I had appeared without prearrangement.

"Why? What is it? What's wrong?"

"We left the door to the tower studio unlocked, did we not?"

I nodded.

"I went back just a little while ago to take inventory, and it was locked again. But no one has been here but me."

I'd followed him inside, and we were standing in the foyer.

"Are you chilled? I can make you some coffee. It's about time for me to take a break."

It was almost as if this was his house and I was the visitor. I said I would like some, and as we walked to the kitchen, I offered a suggestion: "Maybe my grandmother locked it. She comes in the morning to let you in, doesn't she?"

"Yes, but she doesn't usually go upstairs."

I wondered if my grandmother had found out—or somehow sensed—that I'd been in the attic and had come earlier than Monsieur Duplessi specifically to relock the door. She had that uncanny skill—her *capacité*, my father had called it—to know things that had happened or would be happening without being told. Like in the restaurant when she'd told me to get up just before the rock had been thrown through the window.

When I'd asked my father more about her *capacité*, he'd laughed and said legend had it she had some witch's blood in her and that must be how she could foretell the future.

But what if she knew I'd found the studio? What would she do? My grandmother seemed so determined not to tell me about La Lune—surely the studio was La Lune's world.

"Did you tell her I've been here?" I asked.

"No, I honored your request, but still don't understand why you'd want to keep it a secret."

"Was she already here this morning when you arrived?" I asked.

"No, I was first, and was quite uncomfortable waiting in the rain, if you must know, so as soon as she did arrive, we went to the locksmith and had a key made for me. She said she finds it tedious to have to come just to let me in, and that I shouldn't plan on seeing her until I've finished taking inventory and am having the plans drawn up."

"Perhaps the key to the front door will work on the bell tower studio."

He poured the hot water over the coffee grounds, and a marvelous aroma filled the kitchen.

"I doubt it. The front door is a double-acting pin tumbler lock, which was only invented about a hundred years ago. The lock on the tower door dates back at least a hundred years before that and is much simpler."

"How do you know that?"

"I'm an architect and trained to notice details."

When we were done with our coffee, I suggested we try the door with the key anyway. As we walked through the empty mansion, he told me that he'd hoped I'd be back today even before he discovered the locked door.

"Why is that?"

He seemed surprised by my question, as if it were normal for him to hope I'd return. After a moment, he said, "I enjoyed your company. And I was worried about you. You seemed so upset yesterday when you left."

"I was frightened."

"Because of the dates on the paintings?"

"Yes, the dates were disturbing, but . . ." I couldn't finish. How could I explain that what had scared me away were the feelings he'd stirred in me?

"Was it something I said?" He'd stopped just as we were about to ascend the main staircase and turned to me. "I hope I didn't offend you in some manner."

In the hours since I'd been here, I hadn't quite been able to remember the shade of his eyes. They were more black than green, the color of evergreen trees in a thick forest. How would you mix up the right colors and hues on canvas to capture their gleam? I'd been wrong about the slant of his cheekbones, too. They were more exaggerated than I'd recalled. The hollows beneath them, deeper. The desire to paint him overwhelmed me. I understood neither its scope nor its persistence.

I shook my head. "No, it was nothing you said."

Continuing up the grand staircase, we passed the gallery of family portraits.

"This is an odd collection of paintings, isn't it?" Monsieur Duplessi asked.

"It's funny how you can see something all the time and never really focus on it," I said. "I've never spent much time looking at them. They were all courtesans. Did you know that? Is that why you think it's an odd collection?"

We'd stopped and were examining them.

"No, not at all. It's that, looking at the dates on the plaques, it's clear they span centuries, but all of them seem to be painted by the same hand. I wonder if someone re-created older portraits. And how do you think they became damaged in the same way?" he asked.

"Damaged?"

He pointed to first one and then the next.

"I'd gotten so used to them, I forgot how they must look to someone seeing them anew."

The damage was indeed curious. Each of the ladies' lips were unfinished and pale, with bits of bare canvas showing through.

"When I was a little girl," I told him, "I always thought it was because they'd been kissed too many times."

He laughed, and his eyes became less black and more green. "How charming. You must have been quite a precocious little girl who got into all kinds of trouble."

I had a sudden image of Leon and myself in the servants' quarters and felt my cheeks flush. I ducked my head down and continued up the stairs, past Monsieur Duplessi, hoping he would not notice my embarrassment.

Even before we reached the tower's heavy wooden door, I recognized the same aroma I'd sniffed at the École earlier that day. It was an artist's scent: oil paints, turpentine, and linseed oil mixed with the same scent of violets I'd smelled downstairs the other day. How could the smell of the paints and old flowers still be vital after so many years?

We reached the top of the steps and stood facing the large carved door.

"Why don't you just try the key anyway?" I asked.

He did but the lock didn't release.

"Let me try," I said. The metal door handle was icy, and as I held it with my left hand, I inserted the key with my right and jiggled it.

I felt the pins move.

"It's opening," I said.

What I didn't say was that, as I held it, the doorknob was warming. Perhaps it was simply a sensitive metal responding to my body temperature. But it was a very odd sensation.

"I don't understand. I just did that," Monsieur Duplessi said.

"Maybe . . ." I didn't know what to say. He had; I'd watched him. But the door had not opened for him. Only for me.

"Well anyway, now we know the same key works on both doors," I said, and handed it back to him as I stepped inside the room. "The locksmith must have been asked to create a lock for the front door that used the same basic configuration as this one, but more complicated. Is that possible?"

Monsieur Duplessi followed me in. "I suppose so. Possible but not logical."

"And you prefer logic?"

"I'm an architect."

"You're also an artist," I said. "I think that sometimes art defies logic."

"You may be right, but in architecture logic is important or the buildings we build wouldn't remain upright."

I opened the louvers and let in the light and the fresh air.

"There is something different about it here today," I said.

"So you believe your grandmother did come up here since we visited?"

"I'm not sure. Does it feel different to you?"

"I'm not sure I understand what you mean."

I didn't know how to explain it, but the room seemed to have come alive since we had been here. As if it wasn't holding its breath anymore.

"I wanted to inventory the canvases. What was your reason for wanting to come back here?" Monsieur Duplessi asked.

"I've decided to take art lessons while I am in Paris, but to be admitted, I need to show samples." I took a jar off a shelf and opened it. Inside was the most gorgeous blue color, like the whole evening sky turned into powder. "I hoped I could use these supplies to paint some samples."

Cabinets were filled with dozens of bottles of pigments and oils. Canvases stacked against one another covered the lower half of the wall. Containers held paintbrushes in every size.

"Surely everything I need is here. If I only knew how to mix paints." I wanted to laugh and cry at the same time.

"Monsieur Sennelier's store is not far from here. He has premixed paint in tubes. All the artists buy from him. I can walk you over and introduce you."

But how could I buy anything? I'd spent most of the little money I'd brought with me from America and couldn't use credit in a store where I was not yet known. I could ask my grandmother for some spending money—but that could mean

I'd have to tell her about my plan. I didn't know why but was sure she'd be against my taking lessons.

I dropped down on the bed, my excitement and enthusiasm evaporating. I put my head in my hands. My plan suddenly seemed impossible.

Monsieur Duplessi pulled up a chair and sat opposite me.

"What is wrong?"

"My father always said that I was curious and impulsive. One trait would help more than it harmed. The other would do exactly the opposite."

"And which is it that is bothering you now? Your curiosity or your impulsiveness?"

His eyes were lively, and he seemed interested in my dilemma. I didn't mind explaining about the money and the other issues.

"So I haven't really thought everything through. And there are so many obstacles in my path. Even if I could get the money, what I want is to study at the École, but they don't take women. I know I can take private classes, but I don't want to. I have to be at the École."

I knew I sounded like a petulant child.

"Why does that matter so much to you?"

"I don't know. But it does. I just have a sense . . ."

I stopped, afraid for the moment to reveal what I was thinking.

"What kind of sense?"

"Do you believe in destiny?"

An uncomfortable worry appeared in his eyes.

"I'm not certain. Perhaps I do but wish I did not."

I laughed. "A strange answer."

"Some of my clients put great faith in things like destiny, and we've had our share of disagreements over it."

"My father and I used to talk about fate as a philosophical construct, my father coming down against predeterminism, although it fascinated him. I agreed and, until coming to Paris, never sensed that anything that was happening to me was predestined."

"But since you've come to Paris?"

"I feel as if I'm following a path that is somehow inevitable. Do you think that's possible?"

"I'm not much of a believer in religion, the mysterious, or the esoteric. It makes me uncomfortable to think there are other forces operating that we have no control over. I can accept nature as a force I can't control, but psychics, séances, and ghosts?" He shook his head. "I don't even believe in God, which is not a stance as revolutionary here in France as I believe it is in America. I think that's why I like architecture. It's A plus B equals C. It's all based on the laws of physics and engineering. One draws up plans, purchases wood, stone, tiles . . . mixes the concrete and the plaster . . . hires the men to build it, and voilà."

"But there's inspiration, isn't there?"

"Ah, yes, divine inspiration." He laughed. "No, inspiration isn't magic; it's discipline. If you develop your powers of observation, ideas are all around you. Really studying just one tree can inspire my designs for an entire house, inside and out."

I was still seated on the daybed, and Monsieur Duplessi was still in the chair he'd pulled up, facing me. Behind him was an old mirror spotted with mercury. When I glanced into it, he was all I could see, sitting there, his back in the mirror. I wasn't visible at all; his form obscured me. So it looked as if he were all alone, a man alone in the tower.

I knew how I could attend the École.

I got up off the bed, ran over to the north wall, and began riffling through the stacks of paintings.

"What are you looking for?" he asked.

"You studied at the École, didn't you?"

"Yes, yes, I did."

"Do you know anyone there who might make an exception and let someone in even though the new session has started?"

"I know many people there, yes. But you can't study there, Mademoiselle Verlaine."

"I'm a woman, I know. But I have a plan."

I continued sifting through the canvases. I needed ones that were not too finished. That someone might believe had been painted by a student. I was searching for early portraits of the man painted by LL before her style was fully developed, when she still wasn't very proficient.

I lined that side of the room with a half dozen portraits of the man I believed was Cherubino—painted, I thought, by the courtesan La Lune. After brushing the dust off my skirts, I stepped back and examined them. Monsieur Duplessi joined me.

"What are you going to do with these paintings?"

"The student you are going to introduce to the admissions office is going to present them as samples."

"Even if you could convince them to accept you, what will happen when you start to paint and can't reach this level of accomplishment?" He pointed to the portraits. "Do you know how to paint at all?"

"I took both drawing and painting at finishing school. My teachers always told me I had talent, but I was too impatient . . . until now."

"But can you come close to this level of achievement? My credibility is at stake. Introducing you to these men is serious business."

"I will not embarrass you, I promise."

I don't know why I was so certain that I would rise to the challenge and be a quick study, but I was.

Monsieur Duplessi was still looking at me skeptically.

"Please don't worry. I have a plan."

"So you said."

"We're going to tell them I broke my wrist and my fingers in a horseback riding accident last spring and that I am learning all over again. That this is how I had been painting and need to relearn." The fiction came so easily.

"But there's another problem, no?" he asked, pointing to the paintings.

I examined them, unsure of what he meant. And then felt a flush creep up my neck and reach my cheeks. Yes, there was a problem. The paintings were far too sensual. La Lune had painted Cherubino Cellini with lust. It was layered into her glazes. It saturated her colors. And I was going to be applying as a man.

Aware of Monsieur Duplessi's presence close to me, I was overwhelmed with the desire to turn and look at him. I refrained, but he turned away from the paintings and in my direction. Then I faced him. I almost took a step toward him, but couldn't.

"What are you afraid of?" he whispered.

How had he known, even before I had, that I was afraid? And why *was* I afraid?

I wanted to draw him. To capture his elegant long neck, the graceful slope of his shoulders, his hair falling in curls over his forehead, his right eyebrow arching just a hint and making him look slightly devilish. He was so long and lithe, bending toward me just a hint, like a willow reaching toward a lake. I wanted to learn his face so that I could paint it and have it with me forever. So that from this moment on, whenever I was lonely or lost, I could gaze at the portrait and remember how he was looking at me and know that, for a moment, a man who was this exquisite had wanted me.

But why did wanting to paint him frighten me?

Because it wasn't all I wanted. I wanted him to touch me, but was afraid that if he did, I would feel nothing, the way I felt nothing when my husband touched me. I didn't need more proof that I was incapable of passion. I had years of it.

The daybed was behind us. The pillows on it smelled fresh and sweet, as if they'd been scented that morning. I imagined us falling against them. I'd open his shirt buttons. Feel his warm flesh on my fingers. He would touch his lips to mine.

Maybe I had changed. After all, I'd never felt desire like this for Benjamin. And before him, there had only been Leon, and I'd been too young and really only playing at being grown up to know what I'd felt.

I knelt down on the floor and began to search for less suggestive canvases, looking through a new cache of paintings stored in wooden slats— to protect them, I assumed, so they wouldn't lean against each other while drying. There were several I could use, studies of Cherubino in more formal poses. I was about to stand up when I noticed there was a cupboard behind the storage unit.

I swung out the slats and opened the door to a cubbyhole.

Inside was a tumble of fabrics: silks and velvets, chiffons and lace twisted into one another. And beneath them was a pile of drawings on thick yellowed paper.

I withdrew a handful of the sketches and examined them. All were of the same man and same woman from the paintings. But these were even more intimate. How uninhibited they had been to draw each other as they were undressing, as they were becoming aroused, as they touched themselves. If the drawings weren't so beautiful, they would have been lewd and indecent—and possibly would have landed the artists in jail on morals charges. And since they were hidden away like this, the artists must have known that.

"What did you find?" Monsieur Duplessi crouched beside me. The sunlight coming through the windows cast a shadow from his thick, dark eyelashes onto his cheeks. "May I see?"

It was far easier to show him than explain. "Please, do."

He fanned through them. "Well . . . these are certainly evocative." His voice sounded thick and heavy, like a long drip of honey.

Starting at the beginning, he examined them one by one, and I looked over his shoulder. Seeing them for the second time, I noticed what else was on the pages, other than the nudes.

In the corners were odd-looking symbols.

"Do you know what those are?" I asked Monsieur Duplessi as I pointed.

"Yes, do you?"

"I believe so. My father was interested in all the esoteric sciences and collected ancient books on subjects from alchemy to astrology. These look like ancient magick and Hermetic symbols. I think this one is satanic." I looked at him. "What are they doing here?"

Chapter 9

As we left the studio, I carried one canvas and Monsieur Duplessi the two others that I thought would serve my purposes. After making the trek down the dangerous staircase, made even more so by our encumbrances, we returned to the main part of the house.

I excused myself to wash up.

A few minutes later, emerging relatively dust and dirt free, I found Monsieur Duplessi in the kitchen, opening a bottle of wine.

"I thought some fortification was necessary if I'm going to figure out how to get you into Les Beaux-Arts."

"So you will help?"

"After the help you've given me, I have no choice, do I?"

"What help have I given you?"

"Let's go sit down and I'll explain in situ, so to speak."

We took the bottle and glasses into the fantasy drawing room at the front of the house and sat on opposite couches, facing each other.

"Everything here is amazing . . ." He gestured around the room. "The antiques and artwork are as opulent and wonderful, as one would expect. But the treasures in the bell tower are a remarkable find. The artist's studio might make designing the museum more challenging, but potentially adds so much interest that I'm bound to get more recognition for the project."

"I'm glad for you." I sipped the Bordeaux out of a crystal glass that had belonged to my grandmother's mother.

"You seem disconsolate."

"I'm sure you're a wonderful architect and that you'll do an amazing job and the critical acclaim will propel your career. It's just not what the house wants. She doesn't want to be on public display."

"She?"

I stood, began to pace. I had barely articulated to myself what I sensed about this ancient building—how was I going to explain it to Monsieur Duplessi?

"In theory, as an architect, can you accept that a house might be a living thing?" I asked.

"Of course, it's made of organic materials: wood, stone, plaster, and cement. It moves imperceptibly in strong wind, swells in extreme dampness, shrinks back in the heat."

I nodded. "And might that be more complex? Could a house be inhabited by the soul of the one it once belonged to?"

"Now you're treading into territory where I have to shake my head. Ancient souls and ghosts? No. I told you before, I have friends who dabble in the occult. I've done work for them. I'm afraid none have been able to convince me of forces and powers from beyond the grave."

"I never would have thought I could be convinced . . . In fact, I'm not yet convinced, but I do feel as if this house is a living thing. And that she would be upset . . ." I stopped to search for the word. "That it would be sacrilegious to let strangers traipse through here, gawking at what was bought and paid for with . . . with women's bodies." I had shocked myself, but it was true.

Everything in this house had been bought with the money given to my ancestors by their lovers and consorts in exchange for sexual ministrations.

"To put this house on display would be like going about undressed in public. We'd be baring the breasts of each woman who made the best of what she had and engaged in the profession into which she had been born."

"That's an extraordinary way of describing what I thought of as making a display of all the beautiful things here that no one has ever seen but the handful of men who've visited your grandmother's soirees over the years," he said. "Come look at this the way a stranger would."

Standing up, wineglass in hand, Monsieur Duplessi walked out of the room into the hallway and then the grand salon. I followed.

"Stand here." He pointed to the center of the room. "Now turn around slowly. Really look at where you are."

As if looking through a stranger's eyes, I examined the grandly decorated, great, and gilded room. I had never spent much time here as a child and hadn't ventured in here during my previous visit.

An almost full-size marble sculpture of Diana wearing her crescent-moon headpiece stood on a pedestal between the windows. Someone had draped a double string of gray pearls around her neck, and they hung there still.

I walked over to them and fingered them. Were they real? If they were, they were quite valuable. Suddenly, I was seized with an idea. I spun around, examining the room. There were so many precious objects here—surely no one would notice if I borrowed one or two and pawned them. Just for a short time. Just until I could arrange to get some of my own money from America.

Could I do this? Did I dare remove something that didn't belong to me from my grandmother's house? Such a brash idea was so uncharacteristic of me, but so was my sudden determination to attend art school and my daydreams about taking a stranger as a lover.

Monsieur Duplessi was gesturing to a painting that hung over the couch and talking, but I'd missed what he said.

"Excuse me?"

"I was just saying this Georges de la Tour might

be my favorite painting in the whole house," he said.

"It's always been one of my favorites, too."

I turned back to the room with purpose. Like in Ali Baba's cave of mystery and delight, every corner was filled with wonders, curious oddities, fanciful amusements and riches, all gleaming and shining. Did I really dare borrow one of these treasures?

We all belong to you, they seemed to be whispering. *Take whatever you need.*

I began my search. A collection of Japanese netsukes of men and women in erotic poses graced one table. Silver repoussé vases filled with iridescent peacock feathers were tucked in corners. On the mantel were a half dozen birds' nests made from spun silver, each holding eggs carved out of semiprecious stones. On the top of the grand Bösendorfer piano was a collection of tiny enamel- and jewel-framed miniatures of women's eyes or breasts painted on ivory.

Everything was too out in the open. Any one of these items might be missed. I wandered over to a pair of six-foot-tall glass-and-wood break-fronts flanking either side of the fireplace. Each of these elegant vitrines had four shelves. The cabinet on the right was filled with flowers and plants, the one on the left with animals, all of them exquisitely carved from crystal and gemstones. What duke or lord or banker or vintner had given them to which of my illustrious ancestors? Every piece was worth a small fortune, and there were more than thirty.

Yes, one of these would do.

I opened the jeweled zoo vitrine.

"You seem to have a knack for opening locks in this house. How did you do that?" Monsieur Duplessi asked. He pulled a set of keys out of his pocket. "Your grandmother gave me these so I could open those cabinets and take inventory."

I shrugged. "Perhaps she forgot to lock them."

"Perhaps," he said, but he didn't sound convinced.

On the top shelf was an onyx panther with sapphire eyes, a turquoise-and-coral fish, and a pair of agate owls with onyx eyes. Behind the one on the right, I noticed a glimmer of green. Pushing aside the bird, hidden behind it, I found a small jade frog with ruby eyes.

"Perhaps you should turn around," I said to Monsieur Duplessi. "I don't want to implicate you in my crime."

"What crime?"

"If I told you, I'd be implicating you, wouldn't I?" I joked as, with trembling fingers, I picked up the frog and slipped it in my pocket.

Had Monsieur Duplessi been watching? Even if he had, I'd been quick, and he was halfway across the room, sitting on the couch; he couldn't have seen what I'd done.

As I was about to close the vitrine, a light glinting off an amethyst-and-ruby parrot on the bottom shelf caught my eye. Was another object hidden there, too?

Reaching in, I dug my fingers behind the shelf and found an opening in the back of the cabinet. Inside I felt cold metal, a smooth surface . . . I grabbed and, with a little effort, pried out a ring. It was very old, its gold shank worn down by wear so thin it looked as if it might snap if I just touched it wrong. Its bezel held a black cameo surrounded by a halo of tiny rubies. The carving detailed a cherub, with his bow and arrows slung on his back between his wings.

"Look what I found," I said as I slipped it on my ring finger, which it covered from the base almost to the knuckle.

Monsieur Duplessi joined me at the cabinet.

"I think this was a man's ring." I showed it to him. "Don't you?"

He took my hand to look. The contact shocked me and shot through me and startled me all at the same time. I had been handled by men before—but this was more than my skin being touched; it was as if my very soul were being pierced.

"Yes, a man's ring," he said. "And I would guess it's very, very old. The rubies are cut in a style that suggests it dates back to the Renaissance."

I left it on, liking its heft, and reached back

inside. This time I fished out a pair of emerald-and-diamond earrings.

There was still more that had slipped down in the cubbyhole—or been secreted away in this perhaps intentional hiding place. I pulled out a wide bracelet that matched the earrings and then a ring that completed the set.

I reached back in. There was only one item left, harder to extricate because it was all the way at the bottom of the cavity, and I had to stretch my fingers to grab hold of it.

I had it and pulled it out. I'd rescued half a dozen rubies the size of large walnuts carved into rosettes, strung on a platinum chain. A clasp of a dragon with ruby eyes, his tail in his mouth, operated in a toggle fashion. It was like the circle around the "LL" in the paintings in the studio, and it reminded me of something, but I couldn't quite find it in my memory.

I held the necklace up, and the light caught the facets, and the jewels glinted. "It looks familiar, but I can't figure out why."

"It's the necklace that all the women in the portraits are wearing," Monsieur Duplessi said.

I shivered. He was right. How had I not recognized it right away? In my hand, between my fingers, the jewels began to vibrate slightly. Almost as if they were coming to life. But that was impossible. It had to be my hand that was causing the sensation. Not the necklace.

I walked over to a large gilt-framed mirror and held the piece up to my throat. The rubies had an inner glow, like coals that had been burning for a long time, and strangely they felt instantly warm against my skin, not cool the way jewelry usually feels when you first put it on.

I tried to open the clasp, but my fingers shook so much I couldn't manage.

"Let me help you."

Monsieur Duplessi stood behind me. I saw him in the mirror, his black hair curling over his forehead as he bent to focus on the clasp. His lips, the same dark wine color of the stones around my neck, pursed in effort.

His breath heated the back of my neck. As he closed the clasp, its metallic click sounded almost like a murmur, as if the necklace was relieved to once again be worn.

Monsieur Duplessi remained standing behind me a moment longer than necessary. I felt the heat coming off his body and imagined what would happen if I turned around and kissed him. I had never done anything so spontaneous with any man. I was astonished I could even imagine it. I'd only known him for two days. Certainly the woman who had left New York three weeks ago could never have even thought anything so bold. But everything about her and the city where she lived and the tragedy she'd endured seemed far in the past.

I turned. We were only inches apart. His eyes were burning black-green, and a slight smile played on his lips. He waited and watched.

I don't know for certain, but I believe that I moved toward him first. After all, he wasn't the type of gentleman to take liberties unless he was sure the attention was wanted.

The kiss was a revelation. An embrace to get drunk on. It sent me into a spill of overwhelming sensation. Behind my closed eyes, I saw my blood in a rainbow of reds. All the shades of ruby from every jewel that had ever been mined. I felt the pressure of his lips as if he were branding me for life and believed that when he pulled back my lips would be burned. This was something to be afraid of and give yourself over to. To worry that it would end and that it wouldn't.

I could hear my heart beating, or was it his heart beating? I felt a hunger that was more animal than human. I wanted to taste more of him, to feel his fingers on my skin, to feel his skin with my fingers.

He ended the kiss. The air in the room cooled and assaulted me. He stepped back, looking at me, curious, examining me. I should have lowered my eyes. Been demure, ashamed even. I barely knew this man, and yet I did neither of those things.

"Why did you stop?" I asked. Words that could not have been mine. Words that I could never have imagined uttering the day before this day. Or even the hour before this hour. Where was this forwardness coming from? Who was I?

"I do not want to take advantage of you, Mademoiselle Verlaine."

"Sandrine, my name is Sandrine."

He gave me one of his dazzling smiles. "And mine is Julien."

"What a pleasure to meet you, Julien."

He bowed, took my hand, pressed his lips to it, and then brought my hand up and held it in both of his. For a moment he just stood there, holding my hand and looking at me, as if he was trying to see through me.

"You were not taking advantage of me," I answered his question from a few moments before. "And to complete the introductions, I am not 'Mademoiselle.' I am married."

He was taken aback. I saw shock but also relief on his face. After all, a virgin can be a certain kind of trouble a married woman cannot.

"Are you married, Julien?"

"No, affianced."

Had he said it with some reluctance, or was that my imagination?

"How lovely."

He nodded but didn't offer any information.

"Is it a love match?" I asked brazenly.

He didn't answer, and his face offered no clue as to what his response might be. Finally he said: "My situation is complicated."

"What situation isn't complicated? My grandmother says it is the grand complications of life that keep her in diamonds and pearls."

"Your grandmother is a wise and witty woman."

"She's also very secretive. She still has not told me anything about hiring you and this decision of hers to turn La Lune into a museum."

"I wish I could give you some insight, but she hasn't shared any of her secrets with me."

"I thought when I came here the first day that perhaps you were a new lover."

He shook his head. "I've never had the pleasure."

"Which pleases me."

"And why is that?" he teased.

"It would make me quite uncomfortable to take my grandmother's lover as my own."

Again I had astonished myself and, from the expression on Julien's face, astonished him as well.

"I'm sure your husband wouldn't like that either."

"My husband and I are separated," I said, lowering my eyes.

"I'm sorry."

"He's not a kind man." I wanted to tell him at least part of the truth. I lifted my face. "But that is in the past. I've come to Paris to start over."

"Let me help you. Tell me what you are planning."

"I don't want to get you in trouble with my grandmother."

"You mean if she were to notice that a jade frog is missing from the cabinet?"

"I asked you not to look. If Grand-mère thought you took it, she would—"

He put his hand up and touched my cheek. "Don't worry about me, Sandrine. Are you in trouble? Tell me why you took it. What are you planning?"

How could I make him understand how deep my need was to study painting, to begin my life anew? What would he think of me?

Julien leaned down and kissed me, letting me know without a word that he didn't need to understand, that he wasn't there to judge; he just wanted to help.

"Any way I can, Sandrine."

"Can you find a place where I can pawn the little frog? If I am going to attend Les Beaux-Arts, I need money for supplies and clothes, and I can't ask my grandmother."

"Of course I'll help you. I told you that, but you do realize it will all be for naught. Les Beaux-Arts doesn't accept women."

"You mean they haven't yet accepted a woman, don't you?"

"You're going to challenge centuries of tradition? How?"

I didn't want to tell Julien; I wanted to show him. As long as he didn't know what to expect, his reaction would be a true test of whether I could actualize my idea or was just dreaming.

Chapter 10

"All right then, we'll go to my aunt's," Julien said. "Get your hat, bring the jade frog."

I was astonished. "But why your aunt's? Does she buy jewels?"

He laughed. "It's an expression we use here in Paris. 'My aunt's' is what we call the Crédit Municipal, the pawnshop owned and operated by the government. It's the only one in Paris and has been for over a hundred years, since individual pawnshops were outlawed for overcharging interest."

While we'd been inside, a light snow had begun falling, and rue des Saints-Pères was dusted with white. Standing on the steps of Maison de la Lune, I imagined we were inside a snow globe, two small figures in a dark fairy tale, about to set off on a dangerous adventure.

And it was dangerous. If my grandmother knew that I had taken an objet d'art out of the maison, she would be furious. And probably even angrier if she knew the reason.

There were no carriages to be had, so we began to walk. I didn't mind; Paris looked so lovely under the mother-of-pearl sky, and so quiet. Everyone seemed to be inside due to the weather except for us.

We reached the corner, and he took my arm. "It's slippery here." When we reached the other side, he didn't let go, and I was glad.

"You can really see the shapes of the buildings when you aren't distracted by the materials they are made of," Julien said as we turned onto Boulevard Saint-Germain.

"Are any of these yours? Can I see something you've built?"

"No, not here. I've done nothing on so grand a street. We would have to go out of our way."

"Would you mind?"

He looked surprised by my request.

"There's one just three blocks out in this direction, and once there we might find a carriage. Are you interested in architecture?"

"Very much. My father and I would often watch construction going on in New York."

"Your father seems like a most unusual man."

For a moment I couldn't speak for missing him. "He was. For one thing he was a perennial student. He craved knowledge and studied constantly. In addition to the arts, he was interested in mystical teachings and was working on a paper that traced connections and showed the similarities between different esoteric philosophies."

Julien laughed. "He sounds like a Renaissance man. That was a wonderful period for thinkers. Many men of the time were quite enlightened in the way they treated women."

"I think my father would have supported me if I'd chosen the life of an artist. Even if he'd had to contend with my grandmother's protestations."

"Why would she have objected?"

"My father told me she was superstitious about Verlaine women becoming too involved in the arts."

"So she knew there was an artist in your family?"

"Now that we've found the studio, I guess she must have, but at the time when I asked my father about it, he didn't know why she felt that way."

"So you always wanted to be an artist?"

"No, not seriously, not before I came to Paris. I was happy being my father's companion in his pursuits. Going to museums and galleries with him, attending auctions, growing his art collection. He involved me when he built his bank on Wall Street. Together we met all the architects he considered, and afterward we pored over their plans and discussed their philosophies. Do you have a philosophy, Monsieur Duplessi?"

"Julien," he corrected me.

"Yes, Julien." For a moment I felt almost giddy to be walking down a Paris street in the snow, arm in arm with such an interesting man. Even though it was cold out, I welcomed the weather. The icy flakes stinging my cheeks were helping me wake after a long-dormant existence.

"Do I have a philosophy?" He hesitated for a moment, and I wondered if I had asked a naïve question. Then he smiled. "An architect who does not have a philosophy is just a draftsman."

"What is yours?"

He gestured to the buildings we were walking past. "These are outdated masks. There's nothing here not borrowed from other ages. There's nothing new and certainly nothing noble about adapting styles from Byzantium and medieval times and slapping them onto our present-day buildings. I'm not seduced by the past.

"I believe in the unique. Like the architect Viollet-le-Duc, my eyes are looking toward the future. Architectural forms for our times. I supposed you could say I'm tired of being mired in tradition and sick of the commonplace. Why build an ordinary building when you can create one that is unique? I strive for a structure that has harmony, logic, and will appeal to our love of beauty."

I couldn't help but think how much my father would have liked Julien Duplessi and his radical ideas. "Yes, yes, I agree. How many of these amazing buildings have you erected?"

"I haven't had many commissions yet. Mostly I do the kind of interior work I am doing for your grandmother. But I'm hoping that when people see what I've done, even though it's extreme, a few will be drawn to them." He pointed to a building on the corner. "Look at how wrong that is. If you are going to use stone, then it needs to be treated like stone. Glass, on the other hand, should not be treated like stone but like glass. Iron and cast iron have a beauty that shouldn't be hidden, and by exposing them, you can allow in so much more light. And is there anything more important than light? Bay windows, glass roofs, wide-open vistas. And why do ornaments that have nothing to do with the form of the building show up all over it like a woman wearing far too much jewelry? It's time to reject the flower and seize the stem. Today's design needs to be about line! Nature is a living thing. I want my buildings to live in nature."

We had reached the corner of rue de Rennes. Julien stopped and turned to face the direction we'd just come from. He gestured to the buildings we'd passed. His face was animated, his voice filled with passion. "None of them have any life. They are boxes with cutouts. But come look at number 76."

We turned onto de Rennes.

I hoped Julien's building would indeed be unique. That the structure would live up to the promise of the man. He'd set himself a lofty goal. Papa and I had often talked about how duplicative and unoriginal most artists' creations were. Paintings that were really imitations of other paintings, music that was nothing more than a rehash of what had come before, novels that were plots borrowed from other plots.

We walked by one ordinary building and then

another until Julien stopped in front of what was indeed a unique structure. It was small and scrunched in between two others, neither remarkable. But number 76 was like a tree growing out of the sidewalk. The upward movement of its lines carried the eye to the sky. It was a force of nature, indeed a living thing.

Beside me I could feel Julien waiting to hear what I thought.

"This is astonishing. It's beautiful. I've never seen anything like it. What is this style called?"

"Some of us are calling it the new art, Art Nouveau. Sinuous lines and whiplash curves, first inspired by botanical studies of the German biologist Ernst Heinrich Haeckel and the marvelous Japanese art prints that Edgar Degas, Mary Cassatt, Paul Gauguin, Vincent van Gogh, and Henri de Toulouse-Lautrec have embraced and incorporated into their work. Art Nouveau is our reaction to the academic art and architecture of the last century. It's taking off all over Europe, and it's encompassing everything. Furniture, art, architecture, jewelry, even book design."

"Art Nouveau," I repeated. Liking how it sounded, sinewy and rounded like the style itself.

Even the lettering on the sign above the door was free and spacious and curving. I read the words it spelled out: *Librairie du Merveilleux*.

"The Marvelous Library?" I asked Julien. "What amazing books do they sell here? Is there

160

more of your design? Can we look inside?"

I was already at the door. Even the handle was a surprise. Like a branch it arched and had a grace to it that captured my imagination.

Bells chimed as I opened the door, and two men sitting at a table turned around. Two ordinary businessmen poring over a large map.

"Hello, Julien," the older, gray-haired man said. "I'll be with you shortly."

"No rush, Dujols. I just wanted to show Mademoiselle Verlaine around your library."

This was not a store, not a library; it was a cave of wonders, its secrets waiting to be explored. One wall undulated in a series of alcoves outfitted with chairs and tables designed in the same curving, sumptuous style as the building itself. Exotic-looking brass and stained glass sconces emitted dappled golden light in unusual patterns. The windows were bowed and had their own landscape. The books that were piled everywhere were, I thought, the only visible straight lines.

"Did you design everything here? The furniture and the lamps, too?"

"Yes. And I had it built by my uncle's furniture factory in Nancy, where I grew up. My other uncle, who has a fine glassmaking studio, did the lamp shades and windows to specifications."

"It's all marvelous. Just like its name."

I spun around. Shelves lined the other two walls. On some were candles, braziers, and alembics that suggested alchemical experiments, but the majority were filled to capacity with books. I began to read the spines, but then turned again and noticed the west wall. Painted from the floor to ceiling was an open book, its pages yellowed and fragile, filled with ancient text that was near impossible to read. I went closer to inspect it.

"How curious."

"Monsieur Dujols"—Julien nodded at the man still engaged with his customer—"is a publisher. This isn't just a store, but a meeting place for artists and writers interested in psychic and spiritual worlds. Paris is overrun with them. There are followers of theosophy, the Last Pagans, Swedenborgians, Eclectic Buddhists, Luciferians, Gnostics, Satanists, Rosicrucians. Yes, Paris is overrun with them, and of course there are rumors of dark things that go on. Some of it quite gruesome." He shook his head. "Black magick, white magick . . . it's quite the fashion, and you'd be surprised how many people of note are involved."

"Really? My father would find it all most curious." I bit my bottom lip to distract myself from the onslaught of emotion I felt and focused my attention on the magical, mystical, astrological symbols painted on the walls. Some I'd seen before in my father's books, and others were identical to the ones that we'd just found on the drawings in the studio.

"Everything in the store, from the messages and

symbols in the mural to the wall hangings, was chosen by Dujols to evoke and stir thoughts of the ancients' knowledge, mystery, and wisdom. To open the mind, he says, and help usher in a new age of enlightenment."

"Well, that doesn't sound like a bad thing," I said.

"No, of course not. It's a noble goal."

"Except?"

He smiled and lowered his voice. "There's just a lot about it that's not rational."

"Ah, yes." I nodded.

I had learned something about Julien that I hadn't known before.

A red silk sash caught my eye. It was hanging in one corner, embroidered with Hebraic letters that looked familiar. Above that was a carved wooden winged sphinx. I saw first one and then another and then dozens more paintings and etchings of serpents, dragons, and snakes grasping or biting their tails so that they formed circles. Some of the creatures had wings, some vicious teeth. More familiar images.

"Look." I pointed it out to Julien. "That's the same type of circle that was around the painter's initials in my grandmother's house. And on the clasp on the necklace. They are all similar—a dragon biting his tail. Did you recognize it when you saw it at the house?"

He nodded.

"But you didn't say anything."

"I assumed the painter was drawn to it because of the address. The church was situated on rue du Dragon."

I was still taking in more and more amazing sights. There was a huge embroidered wall hanging of a zodiacal wheel, each sign done in another gem-like color of the rainbow. There were papyrus scrolls of hieroglyphics similar to those I'd seen in the Metropolitan Museum of Art's Egyptian wing.

On either side of the door was a mural of symbols painted in bronze, silver, and gold. Yes, there was the ankh that my father had told me symbolized life, and others that looked familiar but that I couldn't identify.

"Do you know what this one means?" I pointed to a five-foot-long drawing that glowed in the lamplight like a beacon.

"Yes. That's the Monas Hieroglyphica. Designed by John Dee in the sixteenth century as part of his mystical symbolic language. It's the emblem of the philosopher's stone."

"Alchemy?" I asked.

"Yes. It's a wonderful design that actually encompasses seven others." He pointed them out. "This *V* is the sign of Aries, for fire. The cross represents the four elements. The circle with the dot in the middle is the symbol of the sun. And the sliver on top is the lunar crescent."

"What is that one?" I pointed to another symbol that incorporated one form I was familiar with—a six-sided Jewish star.

"The Sigil of Ameth. It has the name of God and the angels inscribed on it. Also used by Dr. Dee."

I asked about the rest, curious about them all.

Julien knew what most of them were and what they stood for.

"You know so much about all of this. Are you a student of these ancient arts, too?"

"No, but in order to direct the painters and sculptors I hired, I needed to understand what everything we were representing meant."

I heard the door shut. The proprietor had just escorted his customer out. He bustled over to us with a quick step.

"Julien! How good to see you." The owner embraced him.

Julien introduced us. "Pierre Dujols, this is Mademoiselle Verlaine."

The gray-haired publisher took my hand and bent over it.

"Beware, Mademoiselle, Dujols is something of a showman. Don't be taken in by everything he says."

"Monsieur Dujols, how nice to meet you."

"Yes, yes, you as well. Are you by any chance related to the Madame Verlaine who lives on rue des Saints-Pères?"

"Yes, she's my grandmother."

"A charming woman," he said.

I wondered if that was his way of telling me he visited her salon, but of course I didn't ask.

"And are you also a student of occult disciplines? A believer?" he asked.

Was my grandmother? Wasn't that what he

166

was implying? But my grandmother had never mentioned the occult to me.

When I didn't respond right away, he asked, "Or are you more like my friend Julien here, a skeptic to the core and just here to see his handiwork?"

His gestures were exaggerated, almost as if he were on a stage, performing for us, but in a totally engaging way.

"I did ask to see something he'd built, yes, but I also have some interest in esoteric knowledge, though I'm afraid I'm not the student my father was."

"Oh, was he? Did he favor one school of thought over another? Was he a Mason by chance?"

"No. His focus was on the Kabala, but as fascinated as he was by secret societies and hidden knowledge, he was interested only as a scholar."

"I have quite a few ancient artifacts and rare books a Kabalistic scholar would find fascinating. Would you like me to show you around a bit?"

"Yes, please."

Did Julien look dismayed? I couldn't be sure.

"Dujols is quite the spellbinder," Julien said as if answering my unspoken question. "If you let him, he'll keep you all day and we won't make our prior commitment."

"Don't worry, Julien. I have an appointment myself in a little while." He smiled at me and then pulled out a heavy leather-bound book. "This is one of my prized possessions, an extremely rare fourteenth-century manuscript of a major work of Jewish mysticism called the Sepher Yetzirah. The Book of Formation. Do you know it?"

"Yes, my father had a copy, but not nearly this old." I bent over the tome, and when I looked up to ask Monsieur Dujols a question, I caught him staring at my neck with consternation.

When he saw that I'd noticed, he glanced away. "Can I offer either of you coffee?"

"Why were you looking at my necklace?" Even though such boldness wasn't done, I wanted to know.

"It's most unusual," he said. "I was just admiring it."

But he was lying. I could tell. Something about the ruby necklace disturbed the man. I looked at Julien, and his eyes told me he knew it, too.

"What is it, Dujols? Why be coy? What is it about Mademoiselle Verlaine's necklace?"

"The rubies appear to be cinquefoils. Five-petal roses."

"Yes?" Julien asked.

"You didn't recognize the symbol?"

"I'm a neophyte when it comes to all this—you know that. Knowledge doesn't equal interest," Julien said.

"What is the significance of a five-petal rose?" I asked.

"It's an ancient Hermetic symbol that signifies closed lips, sexual secrets, and hidden messages.

Queen Elizabeth's spymaster used one on his seal. The cinquefoil's association with the worship of the Great Goddess in ancient times spilled over to worship of Mary in Christianity. You can see it on many Gothic churches here and in England."

I fingered one of the flowers, feeling the petals on each of the round discs as he described them. I knew it was my fingers trembling, but it really felt as if the necklace itself was vibrating, almost humming against my skin.

But he wasn't finished. "And the clasp is a gold Ouroboros. The symbol of eternal return and rebirth. Of a life that exists with so much force and power that it cannot be extinguished."

Chills ran up my back. His words resonated within me. I knew these things but hadn't been aware that I'd known them. How was it possible for them to be familiar to me but at the same time something I'd neither read nor heard before? Had my father told me about them when I'd only half been paying attention and I'd forgotten?

"One of the things so fascinating about the Ouroboros is how many cultures used it in some form or another. From ancient Egyptians, to alchemists, to heretics. Where did you find such an unusual piece?" he asked.

"It's a family heirloom," I told him.

"Yes, yes, of course. It would have to be," he said.

The bell rang out as the front door opened, and

two gentlemen entered before I could ask him what he meant.

Dujols looked over, and they greeted him. "Are we early?" one asked.

"No, no, not at all," Dujols said to them.

The two men walked to the back of the library and took a seat in one of the alcoves.

"I'm sorry," Dujols said to us. "My appointment."

"That's quite all right, we did just drop by," Julien said.

Dujols ushered us to the door. "Please just drop by again whenever it suits you." He bowed to me. "And if you have any more family treasures, Mademoiselle, please feel free to bring them with you. The original owner of that necklace probably possessed other pieces of Hermetic interest. There is, after all, the legend of the mystical treasure hidden in your grandmother's house."

"What legend is that?" I asked.

"You don't know of it?"

"Clearly she doesn't, Dujols, or she wouldn't have asked. Enough of your theatrics. What's the legend?"

Dujols glanced over at his visitors, who were examining the book I'd been looking at and seemed quite preoccupied.

"All throughout recorded time there have been allusions to a special drink that imparted immortality. From ancient Greek references to ambrosia that only gods were allowed to imbibe, to Egyptian stories of Thoth and Hermes Trismegistus drinking liquid gold in order to live forever, to Sumerian and Hindu texts mentioning a similar elixir. Have you heard of the philosopher's stone?"

I nodded. "Of course, it was mentioned frequently in the books my father studied."

"It has always been said alchemists coveted it for its promise of turning metal to gold, but that wasn't their true objective. No, it wasn't riches they were after. The gold created from those metals was claimed to be the major component of the beverage that bestowed immortality to those who drank it. Some writings suggest the philosopher's stone itself was the main ingredient of the drink. But a fifteenth-century master, Bernard Trevisan, claimed he knew the recipe for this miraculous liqueur and that submerging the stone in mercurial water was the key to what Cagliostro called the Elixir of Life.

"The ancients claimed this rare fluid cured diseases, could repair skin and organs, and kept one looking young forever. If a dead body was embalmed with the ambrosia, it was said, it would remain uncorrupted forever. Even the Bible references the potion and warns against men partaking of it."

He paused, fascinated with his own tale.

"And how does all this connect to my family?" I asked.

"Have you really never heard of 'The Witch of Rue Dragon'?" Dujols's tone was incredulous.

Shivers ran up my arms and down my back. I'd never consciously heard references to a witch, but at the same time I was not surprised. Had the phrase been whispered in the shadows when I was young and the adults thought I wasn't listening? Or perhaps I'd been sleeping and they had spoken of her as they left my nursery, and the memory had left an impression on me like a footprint in the snow.

"The witch, was she called La Lune?" I guessed.

Dujols nodded. "Yes, yes, the sixteenth-century courtesan who learned alchemy in Prague and brought her secrets back to Paris with her. Brought them to her home, which sat on the property where your grandmother's house now sits. It was said La Lune lived to be over one hundred and fifty years old but remained young and beautiful and as fresh as a rose because she had discovered what so many before her had been searching for."

"The elixir?" I asked.

Dujols nodded.

"What happened to the formula?" Julien asked.

"We know part of it, but it means nothing to us. 'Make of the blood, a stone. Make of a stone, a powder. Make of a powder, life everlasting.' But how to use that? How to interpret it? Lost to us. Forever lost to us," Dujols said.

I was having a déjà vu. Or had I heard that phrase before? *Make of the blood, a stone. Make of a stone, a powder. Make of a powder, life everlasting.* But where? In what context?

Dujols was still talking: "All we have is a legend that La Lune, fearing she would one day be struck by old age and become forgetful, hid the recipe somewhere safe. And when she did become old finally, and needed it, she couldn't remember where she'd hid it." He shook his head. "Perhaps, Mademoiselle Verlaine, you will be the one to unearth it somewhere in your grandmother's fine house. If you do, I am at your service to aid you in creating La Lune's magick."

After we left the shop, as we walked to the corner to search for a carriage, I asked Julien if he found the occult distasteful. I'd sensed his impatience when Dujols was talking about the Elixir of Life.

"I don't want to insult the memory of your father, but yes, a bit. I think it's a waste of time," Julien said.

"Oh, he wouldn't feel insulted. My father loved debate. Especially on topics that captivated him. And secret and forbidden knowledge did. The Kabala explains the relationship between the eternal and mysterious. At its heart is the human effort to define the nature of life and the universe. He wanted to understand that— the 'un-understandable,' he called it."

"It does sound a bit as if your father was a mystic, you know."

I laughed. "Are you picturing a man with a long beard, wearing robes and disappearing into trances? No, he was a banker and art collector who also happened to be interested in arcane knowledge."

Julien managed to hail a carriage, and our conversation halted while we climbed in and he gave the driver the address of the Crédit Municipal.

"So *was* he a mystic?" Julien asked.

I laughed again. "He was curious. And I with him. He hosted symposiums at our house attended by many of the leading thinkers, writers, mathematicians, art historians, and philosophers, even some who were zealots."

"All that searching for the un-understandable?"

"I think at its heart was the recurring dream my father suffered. He'd always been curious as to its meaning, but after I began to have the same dream, he became determined to decipher it."

"You shared the same dream?"

I nodded.

"How curious. What was his dream, do you mind telling me?"

"Not at all. It began with him sitting in a tree on some kind of a platform and looking down at the ground at a barren rosebush. As he watched, the bush blossomed, and in the center of each flower was a woman's face—the same woman every time—but no one he'd ever met.

174

"In the dream she spoke to him, giving him instructions, but he could never hear her from his perch. He'd climb down to try and catch her whisper, except the closer he got, the fainter her voice became. The woman, he told me, was very beautiful, with long reddish-brown hair and eyes almost the same fiery color. That she looked something like me did not escape him in the dream. When he was close enough that he could finally look into her eyes, he saw a reflection in her pupils. A full scene of that same woman drawing stars on the floor of a darkened dirty cell, weeping as she worked.

"My father was never able to decipher what she said or understand what she was doing other than to know she was trying to pass on some secret information to him in that drawing. He knew some of the words, he said, but they made no sense.

"The more he studied, he told me, the more he became convinced she was doing what he said the Kabalists called *tikkun olam*. I think he said it meant 'repairing the world,' and that Jews believed it was every human being's duty."

"What an extraordinary dream," Julien said. "No wonder it preoccupied him. And no wonder he told you about it."

"He didn't. When I was about ten, I drew a picture of the bush, full of roses, each with a face in its center. When he asked me about it, I told him I'd seen it in my dream."

175

"How many times have you had the dream?"

"About half a dozen. My father had it more often and was determined to understand what it meant, and although he never did, it led him into some very dark and dangerous places, as well as some exalted ones."

I looked out the window at the ordinary street scene. Talking about my father had made me sorrowful, and I was glad that we had reached our destination and that this conversation was at its close.

"Could you hear what the woman in your dreams said?" Julien asked.

"I don't really know. When I try to remember, all that happens is that in my mind I see white light mixed with the colors of the rainbow."

"You try to remember words and see colors?"

"Yes, I know it makes no sense."

"Dujols says there are so many mysteries that we have yet to explore. I suppose he's right."

"Didn't you think he was right before?"

"In theory, yes, but it's what I've seen since you came to the house. How did you open the door to the artist's studio?"

"I'm sure I don't know."

"Are you familiar with Debussy, the musician?" Julien asked.

I shook my head.

"He and Erik Satie are creating music that fits the world you're talking about. They believe that there are symbols in sounds as well. They are often at Dujols's."

We had arrived at rue des Francs-Bourgeois. The carriage stopped in front of an imposing building where a long line suggested pawning was quite popular in Paris.

"I'm not sure why, but I didn't imagine there would be so many well-dressed people here," I said to Julien as we got on the end of the line.

"Pawning is practically a national pastime. Victor Hugo used to come here when he was short of cash. Auguste Rodin often had to hock his tools. Artists and musicians and writers are frequently in and out of trouble and visit their 'aunt' for help. There are stories of women who bring their mattresses in the morning, use the money to buy potatoes in bulk in the market, proceed to sell them for a profit, and come back at the end of the day to redeem their mattresses and start the whole process again the next week."

The line snaked from the street, through a large stone courtyard and into the building itself. Half of Paris must have been there that day. I saw women wearing large hats and elaborate costumes walk in with jewels and exit without them. A fancy gentleman carried a violin case. An old woman, an ornate and ugly painting. A couple struggled with an oversize garish gold clock. The courtyard teemed with activity as those on line talked to others behind and in front of them, and a street vendor hawked roasted chestnuts.

The man behind us had a rococo chair that he kept picking up, moving, and then putting down again as the line progressed. Behind him, an elderly couple each lugged a sack of books. The man in front of us pulled a large Louis Vuitton trunk on a trolley. It was the same luggage my grandmother used, and I felt a pang of remorse that I was here without her knowledge. But my excitement was enough to dispel it. The whole of the Paris art world waited for me.

Inside we finally sat down at a worn wooden desk opposite a dour-faced bureaucrat who eyed my offering, carefully examining the frog with a jeweler's loupe.

The sum he offered was adequate, but not what I'd hoped for.

"Can you give us any more?" I asked.

His eyes lighted on my necklace.

"That should bring in quite a bit more. If those are real, they are very large rubies."

I put my hand up to my throat and touched the rosettes. Why not? I would be able to come back and retrieve all these things as soon as I figured out how to get some of my money from my father's banker in New York.

Reaching behind my neck, I tried to open the clasp to the necklace, but the mechanism wouldn't release. I tried again, but it didn't budge. The stones felt warmer, almost as if they were heating up as I touched them. Almost as if I might get burned.

"Julien? Can you help me?" I turned to him.

"There seems to be something wrong with the clasp. I can't get it open."

"What's going on there? We are waiting—you can get undressed at home," a man behind us shouted.

Raucous laughter.

"Is there a holdup? They're closing soon, and we all want our money," a woman said.

"It's all right," I told Julien. "This will be enough for a while, and we can always come back."

As the bureaucrat wrote out the slip we were to take to the cashier, my fingers worked the clasp. I no longer was intent on pawning it, but it seemed odd that it was stuck.

Back in a carriage on our way to a clothing store, my fingers crept to my neck again, and this time I unlocked the necklace without any trouble at all. My neck felt suddenly bare and exposed, and I reclasped it. But the mystery remained. Neither of us had been able to unlock it while we were inside the Crédit Municipal. And now it was incredibly easy. How was that possible?

Chapter 11

With the count being in town for an extended stay, my grandmother's days and nights were busy and preoccupied. The next morning, when she invited me to her room for our usual pot of chocolate, I walked into a flurry of activity. As the maid did up Grand-mère's hair, she gave the housekeeper instructions for that evening's salon.

"Caviar . . . there must be enough caviar. And oysters. The count loves oysters. Do we have enough champagne?"

I had been concerned about what kind of excuse to make up for my going out without her that day, and had concocted a lie about a friend of mine from New York being in Paris. But before I had a chance to offer it up, my grandmother made her apologies for not being able to spend the day with me.

"I need to visit the dressmaker and the hairdresser and then meet the count at Cartier." She was looking at me in the mirror, not facing me directly. "He wants to buy me an anniversary gift." She smiled, and her fire opal eyes lit up.

"How exciting. Do you know what it's going to be?"

"He said it is to be something of my choosing."

The maid pulled Grand-mère's hair too tight, and for a moment the smile left her face. "Alice, do be careful." Her eyes returned to mine. "I wish you would let me put some makeup on you and bring out the warm tones in your hair and the red in your lips. You're so pale, Sandrine." And with that she applied another dusting of powder to her own face. "What will you do to keep yourself occupied today?"

I told her about my made-up friend.

"Oh, wonderful. Will she be in Paris long?"

"Quite long, I think. Perhaps the whole winter."

"You'll have to bring her around for tea."

"I will, of course," I said, hoping that my grandmother would be too busy with the count to remember about the invitation.

"What is her name?"

"Eloise Bedford." I named one of the girls I'd gone to finishing school with.

"Is her family French?"

"No. Her father works for the government and has been posted here." I assumed that would keep Eloise and her family off Grand-mère's invitation list. She found government officials boring and preferred filling her salon with artists, writers, musicians, and dilettantes.

"Government men don't make good lovers," she said. "They are too obsessed with proving their power, and too often they prove it with force. I pity Madame Bedford."

• • •

Two hours later I was looking at myself in a very different mirror in one of the fantasy boudoirs in the Maison de la Lune.

Julien had left me alone to undress. I'd taken off all my clothes and removed the ruby necklace. But I felt strange without it around my neck. Diminished somehow, and even though it was impossible, weaker and less capable, as if it were some ancient talisman created to give me strength and power.

I put it back on, covering it up first with undergarments and then a shirt and finally the cravat I'd bought the day before. I finished dressing just as Julien knocked on the door.

"Are you decent?" he asked.

"Yes, come in," I said as I slipped on a black suit jacket, "and meet the newest applicant to École des Beaux-Arts."

Julien stood on the threshold and examined me in the mirror. For a few moments he didn't say a word but just stared. I watched him trying to make sense of the illusion that stood before him.

It was difficult even for me. Not only did I look different, but I felt different, too. These clothes were unlike anything I'd ever worn. The fabrics were heavier and rougher than my frocks, but from the first step I took in the pants, I adored the freedom the masculine garb allowed. There was also another benefit to my costume, a comforting one: if Benjamin did manage to trace me to Paris, dressed like this, I'd be that much more difficult to spot.

"I don't know what I'm seeing. Or not seeing," Julien said. "You aren't there."

I knew what he meant. I was looking in the mirror, too, and *I* wasn't there. A young man I didn't know was looking back at me. My costume concealed the most obvious female curves. The wig I had bought at the theatrical supply store hid my soft auburn curls, and this darker brown hair hung loose to my shoulders. A mustache, also purchased there, was glued to my upper lip. A pair of spectacles completed the transformation. There were traces of my face left: the jut of the chin my father called impish, the lips that were almost too full to belong to a man.

But if you weren't searching for Sandrine, you'd never see her, never recognize her. I was missing. And that was as it should be, for *I* wasn't applying for admission to the École; Monsieur Verlaine was.

I took off the wig.

"What are you doing?" Julien asked. "It's perfect the way it is."

I picked up some scissors and cut my hair scandalously short, with the curls reaching just as far as my shoulders, the length only men wore theirs.

"The wig is too uncomfortable. This will work just as well."

183

"Your voice?" he asked. "Sandrine, how are you disguising your voice?"

"When we put on plays at school, some of us had to take on the male roles. Since I'm tall, I got more than my share. To create the illusion we really were men, our teacher taught us to how to speak from our diaphragms in a lower register. Most of us couldn't fool anyone, but my voice is deep to begin with, so it was easier for me. All that practice, according to your response, seems to have paid off, yes?"

With Julien accompanying me, I had no trouble being shown to the admissions director's office at the École des Beaux-Arts. Julien introduced me as Monsieur Verlaine, and Monsieur Girraud didn't give my appearance a second glance. He welcomed me and proceeded to rifle through my portfolio. At first he hurried, but then he slowed and really examined the drawings and paintings.

As he did, I tried not to think about the painters who taught here and how much I wanted to study with them. Especially the symbolist Moreau. He would know how to help me invoke the visions that I had been seeing both waking and sleeping since coming to Paris.

"Where have you studied?" Girraud asked.

"In New York City at the Art Students League," I said, speaking in my best mock male voice, naming the institution that I had walked by dozens of times without much interest.

"These do indeed show promise and skill. A certain force that is unusual. There's no doubt you have talent, but you would be coming in halfway through the year, and all our classes are full. A stumbling block, you see?"

"It would be a favor to me, Girraud, for you to consider making an exception," Julien said. "Since his accident, Monsieur Verlaine has been disconsolate." He gestured to my hand, which I'd wrapped in a linen bandage, suggesting a calamity.

Julien continued: "It was my idea for him to come and get his hand back in practice, and I would feel terrible for having encouraged him to apply if you were to dismiss the request so rapidly."

Girraud closed the portfolio. "All right. I won't make the decision on my own. Let's show your work to Monsieur Moreau."

I was more than pleased he'd mentioned the one teacher I'd wanted most of all. As we set off, the three of us down the august hallways of one of the greatest art schools in the world, I thought of my father and how much he'd appreciate this scene. And how excited he'd be for me, knowing I was about to meet and speak with a painter whose work we'd both admired. Moreau was the best-known symbolist of the time. He concentrated on religious, historical, and mystical mythical subjects, the kind that appealed to my father and to me. A Moreau painting of Leda and the Swan was hanging in our Fifth Avenue home in my own bedroom. For my twenty-first birthday my father had given me a choice of a painting done by any living artist, and I'd chosen Moreau. Now I was going to be given the chance to meet him, and I hoped I could convince him to take me under his painterly wing.

My hands were trembling, and the portfolio shook.

"Moreau has stirred a lot of controversy," Girraud said as we turned a corner. "He treats historical art tradition as a mystery religion or cult of the dead, and his poetic interpretations have tried critics' souls. There is still much discussion over his theoretical approaches to subject matter, but as a teacher he is committed to his students' mastery of the human form, as we all are, and seems to have quite a gift for bringing out what is best in each student as opposed to pushing them into a uniform style."

We'd reached an enormous room covered by a glass roof supported by an ornate metal structure. The walls were painted in a wonderful Pompeii red-orange. Light poured into the grand space and illuminated the terra-cotta floor tiles so that they appeared to be on fire.

More than a dozen rows of plaster casts of famous sculptures created aisles. I counted six full-size horses, eight Greek and Roman warriors, a dozen gods and goddesses, several copies of treasures from the Louvre like *Winged Victory*, and too many academic plasters to count.

The room was so beautiful and overwhelming that at first I didn't notice a group of men at the far end, each standing in front of his own easel, painting from life. The nude on the raised platform was posed like Diana, goddess of the hunt, whose visage was all over Maison de la Lune. The artists were so quiet they might have passed for more of the sculptures if only their hands had been still.

An older man with a heavy white beard and a dark, rumpled suit stood beside one of the students, pointing to his canvas and speaking in a quiet voice.

He looked familiar, but at first I wasn't sure why. It wasn't until we approached and I could hear his voice that I realized I had seen this very man in the Louvre, talking in a similar way to a student who was copying the Witch of Endor painting by Rosa.

"Monsieur Moreau?" Girraud said, interrupting.

Moreau turned, excused himself from his student, and came over to our small group. Introductions were made.

After hearing Girraud's explanation for the interruption, Moreau looked at me with deeply penetrating brown eyes. I could see sadness there.

He, too, had loved someone who had died. Two people. Recently. His mother and a lover.

I felt a trickle of perspiration travel down my back. How did I know that?

"Any artist who studies with me walks a difficult path. Are you sure you are prepared to embark upon it?" he asked.

My throat was so dry, the words came out as a croak. "Yes, yes, I am."

I'd spent so much time visiting galleries and museums with my father, never dreaming of creating art, just happy to be enjoying it. Now he was gone, and all that mattered to me was learning how to paint. As if my very existence depended on it.

"Then let me see what you have," he said kindly.

I offered my portfolio with a hand that still trembled. Everything depended on what this one man thought.

Moreau studied La Lune's work even more carefully than Girraud had. He examined the first drawing for a long time. Then the next. Scrutinizing a third, he stroked his beard while Girraud explained about my hand. Only after Moreau had studied the canvases, did he turn his gaze to me.

Did he somehow know that I hadn't painted them? No, that was impossible. Then what was it? What was he trying so hard to figure out?

"There is a lot you need to address. For instance,

here"—he pointed to the thigh section of a seated nude in one of the drawings—"the articulation is awkward. From your sketches I can see that you know your anatomy, which is good. Nudes are part of the academic repertoire. But your technique is a bit tentative and sometimes lazy. Your composition is interesting. You have a solid classical sensibility but no unique style. You need to be developing one that is wholly your own. How long have you been studying?"

"Five years, Monsieur."

"Where?"

"In New York City."

Moreau once more returned his attention to the canvases.

Julien glanced at me. I met his gaze. His expression was curious. Was he warning me about something? I couldn't read his face well enough to know.

"Where do your interests lie?" Moreau asked.

Until he asked, I would not have had an answer, but there it was. "I'm interested, like you, in allegorical work."

"Really? You want to paint *l'art épique*?"

I nodded.

"And not just to flatter me so I make this decision in your favor?" He laughed, and we all joined in, although my laugh was so nervous it sounded more like a squeak.

"Yes." Even though I was making this up as I

went, I was telling the truth. "My father and I were both fascinated with mythology, legends, and fantasies. The imagination, my father believed, was humanity's most powerful force. Our ability, he said, to create is what makes us great."

It was true. It was what he believed—even though, I thought, he didn't himself create anything other than a larger fortune than he'd started out with.

"So you want to peruse symbolism?" Moreau asked.

"Soft lights and pretty women are best left to the impressionists," I said with a stridency that surprised even me. "I am interested in the search for the eternal truths in our ancient stories."

Had I gone too far? I wasn't trying to flatter him. These answers came unbidden from some deep wellspring of intention inside of me. But now I was afraid he would think I was just being politic.

As if reading my thoughts, he said, "I should wonder at the authenticity of your comments, but I think I believe you. I sense a passion in you. An almost frightening passion."

A chill passed through me.

Moreau looked from me to Girraud. "I think I can find room in my class." He turned back to me. "We meet on Saturdays and Wednesdays."

I sputtered out a thank-you that I repeated twice, but he brushed my gratitude off with a gesture. "When there are no classes, I expect you to visit

190

the Louvre along with my other students and copy the Old Masters like Poussin, Raphael, Rembrandt, Titian, and Watteau. One must learn the techniques of others before one strikes out on his own. Don't waste your time with the moderns in the Luxembourg. There's time for that. Only when you know all the rules can you begin to break them and find your own style, and that is the goal. Not to turn into one of these boring copyists, but to become an artist with a vision. I'm not an easy teacher, Monsieur Verlaine. If you don't prove yourself, I will ask you to leave . . . If you do, I will invite you to join me at my studio on Sunday mornings where I offer more extensive critiques than I give in the atelier and to spend some afternoons painting alongside me."

I thanked him. I was elated. I had been admitted to the finest art school in the world. I glanced over at Julien. He smiled back at me, clearly pleased that he had been able to help me.

"Excuse me," I said, still imitating a man's speech patterns and tone.

Girraud and Moreau both turned.

"I need to tell you both something, if you could spare just a few more minutes."

I felt strange. Cold and warm at the same time. I smelled those faraway violets again, but this time they made me slightly nauseated.

"I need to explain who I am." I was looking at Monsieur Moreau, but I could see Julien's face, too, and I could read the apprehension there.

I was feeling the same fear he was. Part of me watched the scene from a distance, terrified, horrified. Another part of me wanted to laugh with delight at what I was about to do.

"I can't attend the École like this," I said as I reached up and pulled at the mustache, took off my hat, and shook out my hair. As I loosened the cravat, my fingers trembled.

"What are you doing?" Julien whispered as an appalled look contorted his face. "You are ruining the disguise."

Julien had told me he and the admissions director were friends, having met when Julien attended the École, and that the director had proved himself a rebel who challenged the institution into readying itself for the upcoming new century. I was about to give him a chance to prove just how forward thinking he really was.

Both Moreau and Girraud watched in shock as I revealed myself to be a woman.

"*Mon Dieu*," Moreau said, "I had no idea."

Without shame, Monsieur Girraud examined my face. "I didn't know. I saw . . . but . . ." He was flustered and confused, trying to make sense of the optical illusion that appeared before him.

Monsieur Moreau put his hand up to his chin as he, too, peered at me. Despite his obvious shock, I detected a bit of delight in his eyes.

"We have a policy," Girraud said finally, and

then turned to Julien. "We have a policy," he repeated.

"You *had* a policy," I said in my normal voice. "It's 1894, Monsieur Girraud. In America art schools accept women."

Julien took up the challenge. "You always talk about the future, Girraud. Now is your chance to do something about it. Break with tradition."

"I'll fit in," I said, imploring him. "I'll keep my hair cut short, dress like this. I won't be a distraction but just another student."

"I could never allow such a thing," the admissions officer said as he shook his head vehemently.

"Why not?" I asked.

"You can't make a change like that without consulting the directors, the professors—there are so many people who I would need to discuss this with." Vexed, he threw up his hands.

"Really?" Julien smiled at his friend. "Is there an actual written rule about female students? I understood it was just another archaic assumption. Why not do it, Girraud? You both looked at her work, and you accepted her."

"Her work does indeed show promise and skill." Girraud glanced over at Moreau for affirmation.

The painter nodded. "Mademoiselle Verlaine—" He looked at me. "Is it still Verlaine?"

I nodded. "It is."

"Mademoiselle Verlaine exhibits a certain force and passion that is unusual in either a man or a woman," Moreau finished.

"There's no doubt you have talent, Mademoiselle Verlaine," Girraud said. "But we have a policy. Most of our fine painters offer private classes. Even Moreau does sometimes. Perhaps you would consider—"

"I don't want to take private lessons. I belong here," I cut him off.

"But why?"

"I know how much easier it would be to accept convention and take private lessons, but it won't be the same. This is the greatest art school in the world. Nothing else will do."

Moreau glanced from my face to my clothes and back to my face. "As long as your presence doesn't turn my class into a circus, I have no objection." He turned to the director. "Girraud, it's high time we joined the modern world. Let's take this on."

"But can we manage the attention the decision will get?" Girraud was shaking his head in worry.

"You and Moreau will be heroes," I said. "You will make history."

Girraud was thinking it through, and when I saw excitement replace the concern in his eyes, I knew that I, Sandrine Verlaine, would be the very first woman to attend the École des Beaux-Arts.

Chapter 12

Outside on the street, I took a deep breath. Beneath the heavy jacket my shirt was soaked in perspiration, and my portfolio felt extremely heavy in my hand. As I shifted it, Julien tried to take it from me, but I resisted.

"What excuse do I have to give it to you? I need to be able to carry my own weight now, literally."

"How's this for an excuse? You broke your wrist, remember? You don't need to put extra weight on it."

I smiled and conceded. It was a relief to hand it off.

"Where are we going?" I asked.

"To that café."

He pointed to the corner of rue de Seine and rue Jacques-Callot at a canopied café appropriately named La Palette.

It was a short walk, and we found a table by the window. Everywhere I looked, the walls were covered with paintings and drawings of palettes. I even spotted some actual three-dimensional ones signed by the artists who'd used them.

"Students frequent this place. It's inexpensive and convenient, and the owner is an artist himself," Julien explained. "Sometimes if you're low on money, he'll trade you some food and drink for a palette. He thinks one day some of them will be priceless. And he's probably right."

The waiter arrived, and before I could order the coffee I so badly wanted, Julien ordered a bottle of their best champagne.

When I looked at him questioningly, he just smiled but didn't say anything until the waiter arrived back with a bottle of Jarretière and two flutes.

"Messieurs, voilà," the waiter said.

He'd thought I was a man. How much the eye is fooled and sees what it wants to see.

The waiter worked the neck until the cork escaped with a festive *pop*. He poured the golden sparkling wine almost to overflowing.

Once he was gone, Julien raised his glass to me. "I've never seen anyone quite like you," he said. "You're fabulous, Sandrine."

I felt his words inside of me, and their pull was instantaneous and urgent. I bowed, hiding my flushed cheeks.

"A toast to the first woman ever admitted to the École des Beaux-Arts. Even if you are a bit of a hybrid." He leaned back in his chair and peered at me. "You're extraordinary. A woman without fear!"

"Oh, I'm afraid." I laughed.

"Of what?"

"Of what is going to happen when I actually start to paint and I'm found out as a fraud."

I was afraid of other things, too. I was thinking of my husband. While I may have succeeded in running away and hiding behind my grandmother's name for now, my fear that Benjamin would eventually find me was always on a low simmer in the back of my mind. I knew him, and if he was intent on ferreting me out, he would. Benjamin never accepted failure. My father's suicide was proof of that.

But it would not do to tell Julien any of those other fears now. Except for one. "And I'm a little afraid of you."

He reached for my hand. Saw something out of the corner of his eye and retracted it. "Your dressing like this is going to take some getting used to. Those people over there clearly think you're a young man and I'm a lech. And even in Paris, that raises eyebrows."

"Other than them thinking you are a lech, I think I like people mistaking me for a man. It's very liberating to be sitting here and not have anyone paying attention to me, going out of their way for me. Treating me differently."

Through the window, I saw students from the École walking down the street, carrying sketchpads and with knapsacks on their backs. Behind them was a couple in their twenties, strolling arm in arm. They appeared very attentive to each other, and I continued watching as they entered the café and sat down fairly close to us.

Their demeanor was so very different than ours, with the gentleman being so solicitous of his female companion, and she being so flirtatious, looking at him from under her eyelashes.

Julien and I were playing none of those games now. By taking off my female clothes, I'd altered how we spoke to and interacted with each other.

"I should like to meet your fiancée," I said.

"You would? Why?"

"I'm curious what kind of woman you've chosen to marry."

"Most women don't come out and say things like that."

"I know, but most women don't steal family jewels to pawn so they can become libertines and attend the École des Beaux-Arts."

"That's true."

"I want to see if she's worthy of you."

Julien blushed. I laughed.

"It won't matter, though," he said solemnly as an afterthought. "I'm engaged to her. There's no turning back."

"You make it sound like an obligation."

"Isn't marriage a series of obligations?"

"Mine was. But does it have to be? I know her father was your professor at the academy and took you into his firm and gave you a start, but does he demand you marry his daughter in payment?"

"No, there was no price. She had her choice of

suitors. Charlotte Cingal is a brilliant opera singer, a star and my greatest supporter." Julien picked up his champagne glass and drained it. "I have great affection for her."

"My grandmother has great affection for her terrier, Mou-Mou."

"How cruel and sarcastic you are without the encumbrances of lace and satin. I might prefer the more demure Sandrine to the outspoken one."

"Really?"

"I'm not quite sure," he said, more seriously than I liked.

"Well, I'll finish my thought regardless. You have great passion, Julien, and so many dreams—"

"Yes, and I'm going to make them all come true."

"With her father Monsieur Cingal's help?"

"Of course. He is my mentor. Like a father to me." Julien's hand had moved to his watch fob, and I noticed he was fingering that heavy gold ring again. "What of it?" he asked.

I shrugged. "You aren't marrying her family, you know. You are marrying her. You deserve a marriage of passion as well. Not one of obligation and convenience."

"Said with such disdain. Did you and your husband have a different sort of marriage?"

"No, which is why I can speak this way. My marriage was disastrous."

"But we are in France, not America. And

Charlotte is marvelous. As for passion, how often does passion outlast the first year or two of marriage?"

"Why not strive to have one of the unions where it does?"

"You are romanticizing marriage. We don't do that in my country. Romance is its own phenomenon. In France a husband and wife have more freedom inside a union than you do in America. There are not the same constrictions here. Not the same outrage over dalliances."

"Dalliances? You think you'll be satisfied by that?"

He poured more champagne. "When the time comes, why not? Most men are. Why do you think I'm any different?"

"In truth, I don't know."

After finishing the champagne, we walked down the street, turned left, and walked two blocks to 3 Quai Voltaire. The green-and-gold sign on the front of the building read simply: *Sennelier*.

Julien opened the door, and I walked into a swirl of colors and smells. Men in white smocks waited on customers, showing them pencils, pigments, brushes, pastels, watercolors, and choices of paper. I swung slowly around in a circle, taking in the world that had just been revealed to me.

My fingers itched to buy the supplies I needed

and to take them back to the house and begin experimenting.

"Monsieur Sennelier, this is Mademoiselle Verlaine. She's going to be studying at the École with Monsieur Moreau."

Like the admissions director's, Sennelier's stare told me he'd thought I was a young man and was surprised to discover my true gender.

"Welcome to my shop, Mademoiselle. We supply Monsieur Moreau and many of his students . . . but did you say the École?" He looked at Julien, who nodded.

"Well, this is something indeed. How amazing! Congratulations, Mademoiselle. This is surely going to be news. I'd be honored to sell you whatever you need."

"I've recently arrived in Paris, and all my supplies were lost in transit, so I need to be totally outfitted."

"But of course," the color merchant said. "A full complement then. Will you be making your own paints, or would you like to buy my special extra-fine oil paints in tubes?"

"Tubes, please."

"Very well," he said. "You're in good company. Messieurs Monet, Matisse, and Gauguin prefer them also. I have been working with them for years now, creating variations on colors to accommodate their work. Are you interested in impressionism?"

"To admire, yes, but I'm more of a symbolist," I said.

"This way please."

As I followed Monsieur Sennelier through his store, I felt my father's spirit with me. Though I wasn't sure he'd approve of my method to getting into the École, I was sure he would be excited by the idea of my attending. We'd spent many afternoons at museums and galleries, inspecting and discussing the work of current-day painters, and now I was on my way to becoming one.

Monsieur Sennelier was waiting. "Mademoiselle? Brushes?"

He led me to an area of shelves filled with a vast and varied assortment of brushes.

I had anticipated my choices would be difficult as I struggled with items I had little familiarity with. I'd learned little at school.

My father was interested in the concept of lives being recycled. Metempsychosis, a concept dating back to Pythagoras, was a popular topic among spiritual circles in New York, especially the Theosophical Society, which my father found interesting. We'd attended some lectures together and discussed the concepts at length. Walking home from one, my father, I recalled, had described me as an "old soul."

He said that one day I'd find my way to creating something beautiful and meaningful because my soul would demand it of me.

I had never understood what he meant. But perhaps I was going to find out.

Sennelier was waiting. "Mademoiselle?"

Nervously, I inspected my choices. There were at least fifty different sizes and shapes of brushes. How many was I supposed to choose? Which were basic and required? Did I want the longer or the shorter handles? I reached out and touched one and then another. Did I want bristle or sable? I read the names of the shapes: flats, filberts, brights, rounds. For one dizzying moment I thought that I could not manage this charade. I even wondered what was propelling me. Why did it matter that I go to the École and learn to paint?

With a tentative hand I took a flat bristle brush with a long handle. Then a long-handled sable filbert. My hesitation was unexpectedly gone. My hand seemed to be moving of its own accord, knowing exactly what I needed.

After I'd chosen a dozen assorted brushes, I chose a palette knife with a smart, round wooden handle.

"Now for the paints," Monsieur Sennelier said as he proudly showed me to another section of the store. "We use the most pure safflower oil and grind the pigments more finely than other merchants. You'll find the distinctive texture more like satin than other brands."

Here were at least one hundred tubes in a rainbow of color selections. Each was affixed with a simple label: a band of black with the block letters *SENNELIER* in white, then a thicker band of the color inside the tube both shown and spelled out, and a third band with the number and other information.

But instead of the panic I expected, there was only a thrill as I reached for the colors that would make up my palette. I chose the basics: titanium white, cadmium yellow, pale orange, red and green, along with quinacridone rose, dioxazine violet, and French ultramarine blue.

The tubes were cool to the touch, and shivers of excitement traveled up my fingers, up my arms. I put each one in the basket Sennelier provided. Using these slithery paints, I would create some-thing magical. Dipping my brushes into the luscious oils, I would bring forth visions that were going to change my life and fulfill the covenant of my heritage.

In my mind, from some unknown place, came unbidden images in shadows. Secrets of light and dark, mysteries and puzzles waited for my brush.

"I'll need these, too." Unable to refrain, I added more of the exotic colors and then more, as if each one held another promise: Chinese orange, cinnabar, cobalt green, Orient lake, Sennelier blue, and baryte green.

I could see the swirls on a palette, a wet brush making daubs on a canvas, images emerging in the penumbra. And strange images they were, all painted in my imagination as I stood in the store.

It was the last image from my father's dream and mine. The scene reflected in the woman's eyes: a dark stone cell, moisture glistening on the mossy rocks, a single crack of light illuminating a woman, woebegone, prostrate on the ground. I could hear her crying. In my mind, she looked up at me. Her face etched with terrible sadness. Her hand on the floor, one finger pointing to something she'd drawn in the grime. A symbol that I recognized—one of those I'd seen in the bookstore I'd gone to with Julien.

When I was in school, we'd done still lifes of flowers and fruit. My father collected masterpieces, favoring impressionism and evocative portraits done by the likes of John Singer Sargent and Whistler. Other than the one Moreau that he'd bought me, nothing he bought was symbolic, nothing as suggestive or evocative, as illustrative or iconographic, as my vision. Nothing like the paintings I suddenly knew I wanted to tackle: forgotten dreams, lost legends, mysterious messages. Was I being influenced by Dujols's bookstore? Or by knowing I would be studying with Moreau, the greatest symbolist artist of the day? He was one of the reasons I'd wanted to study at the École, so that I could work with the one painter I believed could help me along the path I wanted to take. The strange thing was that

I'd never had to mention him to Girraud. He'd chosen Moreau for me.

The very professor I'd been thinking about.

Encumbered by a multitude of packages containing canvas, wooden arms, stretchers, paints, primers, turpentine, oil, and various other tools, Julien and I left the store and took a carriage back to the Maison de la Lune.

We stumbled into the foyer with all of our parcels, and as we did, it felt to me as if the house had eyes and could see what I had brought home and trembled in excitement. It was then, for that first time, that I heard, very soft and low, one sentence, uttered, it seemed, with her lips moving slowly so she would be sure I could understand the archaic French:

I have been waiting so very long. Welcome home at last, my Sandrine.

Chapter 13

I glanced over at Julien. From the way he was stacking the packages, it didn't appear he'd heard the voice. Had it even been real? We'd had a lot of champagne at the café, so perhaps I could blame the sparkling wine for what I'd heard. Or simply an overstimulated imagination. Certainly the day had been momentous and curious. There'd been the odd coincidence of having Girraud suggest Gustave Moreau as my teacher. Then meeting him and realizing I'd seen him before in the Louvre. The exhilaration of being accepted and then the celebration. The strange experience in Sennelier's of my knowing which brushes and paints and supplies to choose without having to be told. Was it really any wonder I was able to imagine that the painter who had lived in this house hundreds of years before would welcome me home?

"Are you all right?" Julien asked. "You look like you've seen—"

I cut him off. "I'm fine. Wonderful. Famished, though."

"I can cure your ills then. Especially if you're thirsty, too. I'll go fetch some things from the kitchen. Don't go anywhere. I'll be right back."

"Where would I go?" I laughed.

He laughed, too, and then, without a word, leaned down and kissed me full on the lips. And I kissed him back.

He broke the embrace and stepped back.

"Forgive my being so forward," he said. "I've wanted to do that all afternoon."

"There's nothing to forgive." I smiled. "I wanted you to do it all afternoon."

Suddenly unsteady on my feet, I took hold of the banister. I didn't recognize myself or the sensations coursing through me, and was at the same time embarrassed and excited by them. And, yes, afraid of them. Here in this house I was someone so very different from the woman I'd been all my adult life.

"Let me get some wine and some cheese. I think there's still some fruit," he said, and left me standing there as if this was his house, not mine.

He returned with the bottle and two of my grandmother's marvelous bloodred Baccarat crystal glasses and a tray of delicious-looking soft cheese, hard bread, and two oranges.

"How did you know where these glasses were?"

"I've been inventorying the house. At this point I think I know where everything is." He gestured to the salon. "Should we take our feast in there?"

"No, let's go back up to the studio." I wanted to be there with the paintings and easels and shelves of dried-out supplies I'd soon be replacing. My desire to create was so intense, I was almost frightened by it.

Once we'd climbed to the hidden bell tower, Julien opened the wine. I removed my jacket and my hat and shook out my hair and then, using the pins I'd left there, put it back up.

"My grandmother will never know that I've cut it," I said as I examined myself in the mirror.

"So you are going back to dressing like a fine lady and keeping your studies a secret when you aren't at school?"

"Yes, for the time being. I'll set up my studio and keep my paints and clothes here. It's close enough to school. I need to find the right way to tell her, and she's quite busy now."

Julien came over to me, handed me a glass of wine, then stood behind me and pulled all the pins out. "While you're here, though, you don't need to be so formal." He ran his fingers through my hair.

In the mirror I watched his face with wonder. I'd never seen a man's lust so clearly etched on his visage. Never watched muscles tighten in desire, nor noticed how lips parted, heard how breath quickened; never known how one's natural scent becomes more exaggerated.

"The wine," I said, pulling back a little and taking a sip. I couldn't let him get too close, couldn't let him touch me again. When he found out that I had no ability to take pleasure from a man, he'd reject me. And I didn't want that to happen yet.

"Yes, the wine," he said.

Stepping away, he picked up his glass and drank from it, never taking his eyes off me.

"What an intriguing picture you make, Sandrine. Half woman, half man. Quite fetching."

"I don't think anyone has ever called me fetching before."

I sat down in one of the wooden chairs, and he pulled his over to be nearer to me.

"Your life has been very different from your grandmother's, hasn't it?"

"It couldn't be more different."

"So she didn't have a great influence on you?"

"Hardly any influence at all. I visited here once, I think I told you, for a season. And she came to stay with us in New York three or four times. But who she is, what she does, was never really discussed. I knew she was younger and more exotic and beautiful than my other grandmother, or my friends' grandmothers, but I didn't really understand that she was a courtesan until shortly before I married."

"You say that with regret."

"Knowing my grandmother better might have been a help to me. Perhaps I would not have been so easily talked into marrying if I was more . . ." I shrugged. "It doesn't matter anymore."

"It does. This isn't the first time that I've seen you come close to explaining your marriage and then retreat."

"It's not a worthwhile conversation."

"If it disturbs you this much, it must be."

I drank some of the deep, tangy wine. "I'm not able to be a proper wife, so I can't really fault Benjamin for not being a proper husband."

"Proper?"

I felt suddenly warm. Taking off my cravat, I laid it on my knee.

Julien was watching me.

"What is it?" I asked.

"You are so much more comfortable than you were when I first met you."

"Well, you were a stranger to me, and you are not one any longer."

"It's more than that."

"What do you mean?"

"When you arrived, you were running away from one thing, and now you are running toward another."

He was right. I felt it inside of me. Unconsciously, I reached up and touched the necklace around my neck, warm against my skin.

"Those rubies become you; they bring out the color of your lips. I'm glad you didn't pawn them."

"How you flatter me, Julien."

"It's what I see."

I felt myself blush. "I'm not quite sure what to do with you."

"What would you like to do with me?"

What I did then was the most shocking thing I had ever done. More surprising than leaving New York, taking an assumed name, lying to people about who I was; more outrageous than stealing treasures to pawn, or dressing so I appeared more like a man than a woman, or applying to the École; even more astonishing than kissing Julien back when he kissed me.

Unbuttoning my blouse, I slipped out of it. Standing, I pulled my camisole over my head. Bare-breasted, I undid my trousers and stepped out of them and the pantaloons I wore under them. Finally naked, I walked over to Julien.

He had remained seated, and now looked up at me, staring at me. Inside, I felt a gathering and pulsing. Our eyes held for a moment, and then I bent over him, my hair falling into his face, and pressed my lips to his. I was the one who exerted pressure, who slid my tongue in between his smooth teeth, who explored his mouth, who gripped his shoulders and did not let up. Could not let up.

Julien reached up and pulled me down, positioning me so that I was sitting on his lap, maneuvering it without our lips coming apart.

"You're shaking," he said softly.

All I could do was nod. Everything I wanted,

everything I had come to Paris to find, even if I hadn't been aware of it, was here in this room. I had to know, was I truly capable of taking hold of it and making it mine?

Julien's long fingers stroked my skin. Each touch set off trembles down the length of my torso. Little licks of flames dancing on my skin. Was it true? Was I feeling what I'd thought I could never feel?

Whispering my name, he moved his lips to my breasts.

I threw back my head, basking in the sensation that I had never known before: dark violet-and-ruby passion, powerful and dangerous and—most of all—delicious.

Reaching for his shirt, I undid the buttons, pulled it off, and started on his undergarments until I reached flesh and then pressed my breasts to his chest. I had rarely been naked with a man. My husband almost always took me while he was still dressed, hard and fast and rough.

This amazing fire I was feeling where our skin touched was more than I'd been able to imagine. My body was awakening. Every inch of flesh was alive. Every bone inside of me reverberated with the want coursing through me.

Julien lifted me up and, still pressed against me, moved to the daybed and laid me down.

"If I was an artist and painted you the way you look now, every man in Paris would desire you.

The expression on your face, in your eyes, is magnificent. You want this as much as I do, don't you?"

I nodded, not sure how to say it, but the feeling I had, odd as it seemed, was that I wanted him more, much more. That I had spent lifetimes wanting him.

"Hurry," I said, suddenly impatient.

He shook his head. "No, no hurrying."

Taking his time, Julien stroked my neck, my arms, my breasts, my stomach, then my thighs. Everywhere but the cleft between my legs. Softly and slowly, so slowly, but never stopping.

Writhing, I tried to move so that his hand would slip to where I wanted it, but he was in control. I arched and moaned. I begged, and even my own begging aroused me. That I *could* beg, that I was capable of wanting anything this much, made the flames rise.

When he lowered his head and placed his lips on my nether parts, I thought I might explode. Suddenly he stopped and waited. I thrust up toward him, and with a smile, he began again until my insides were dancing to a rhythm I had never known before.

He stopped again just as I had ceased being aware of where I was and what was happening. I opened my eyes to see him standing, loosening his pants, and letting them and his undergarments fall to the floor.

I gasped. Julien's sinuous body was as beautiful as any of the paintings or sculptures I'd seen in the Louvre. But those weren't living, breathing, flesh and blood men. I'd never seen a completely naked man before. Certainly never one who was aroused. I'd felt my husband inside of me—quickly and furiously pleasuring himself—but I'd never seen him in those moments and never wanted to. His attentions were just something I had had to endure. Now, I luxuriated in the sight of Julien's naked body.

Slowly, achingly slowly, he lowered himself down on top of me until his whole body was touching my whole body. His lips covered mine, and as he kissed me, he slid inside of me so very, very slowly that I thought I might scream with anticipation. So this was what it felt like to be deeply and perfectly connected. We could not be any more entwined. I was breathing in Julien's breath, and he was breathing in mine. His body filled the space inside of me completely and utterly.

And then he began to move.

Gently, he pulled out and then just as gently slid back inside. Again. And again. I opened my eyes. Looked at his face suffused with desire. His lips thicker. His skin slicked with perspiration. His eyes shut. His concentration all on the few inches of skin where he lay inside me and I enclosed him.

"Now," he whispered to me. He said it again and added my name. "Now, Sandrine." But by then I had lost all sense of who I was or where I was. I was flying through sky; stars were falling around me; I could hear the earth spin and the ocean roar. There was no way I could speak, or even keep thinking. I'd become nothing but sensation.

As everything exploded inside me, while I was still rocking, I thought I smelled the fragrance of roses and burning wood, and I thought I could hear an ever-so-slight hum from the tower's ancient bells, as if our coming together was making them sway in contentment.

Chapter 14

The next few days brought huge changes. Taking my place among Moreau's students at the École, I created quite a stir. News had spread quickly that a woman had been admitted and even though I was dressed the same as all the men, wherever I went heads turned.

After class, I would rush back to Maison de La Lune where Julien would be waiting and we would drink wine and make love. Afterward I'd dress in the clothes my grandmother expected to see me in and return to her apartment on rue de las Chaise.

At the end of the week, I arrived home to two pieces of terrible news. Grand-mère's uncle had died that afternoon, and she had received a telegram from Mr. Lissauer in New York City.

I read it with a shaking hand. Benjamin, the lawyer wrote, had been to visit him again, now demanding information about my father's family, looking for the names of even distant or estranged relatives who I might have turned to for sanctuary. Mr. Lissauer insisted he knew of none. Benjamin swore to do whatever it took to learn my whereabouts and left the lawyer's office much aggrieved.

I was trembling by the time I finished reading it.

Benjamin's presence was suddenly there with us in the room, looming large and threatening. Try as I might, I was not sure I believed Grand-mère when she told me that Monsieur Lissauer would never betray my father's trust in him.

In retrospect, agreeing to go with my grand-mother to her uncle's funeral the next day was a terrible mistake. How did I not realize that the service would sharpen the pain of my father's death? I wasn't thinking clearly. I'd been so disturbed by the telegram, by the knowledge that my husband had stepped up his hunt for me, I was almost childlike in not wanting to leave my grandmother's side.

Temple Emanu-El in New York City, which my family occasionally attended, and which was the most famous and elegant in all of Manhattan, was not as grand as the magnificent synagogue on rue Buffault by half. This house of worship was worthy of royalty. Everywhere was gilt and silver, gas lamps and candles. Everywhere, there was a glow, a shimmer. If God existed, and my father and I had never been certain he did, surely he would visit here and be impressed by the home he was offered.

Upstairs in the women's section of the synagogue, all the mourners reminded me that loss was an inevitable reality. There was no escaping it. There were only ways to push it aside, hide it behind locked doors, but eventually it seeped out, its pain fresh and raw as if it were new.

Buffeted by feelings, I was not sure how I was going to survive the day. Then I remembered Moreau's lecture about capturing not just the shapes and forms but also the emotion of the body. The most difficult lesson, he said, was learning to draw through pain and with pain.

I pulled a small sketchbook out of my reticule and began to draw the face of a woman mourner who sat in such a way I was able to include some of the architectural elements of the temple.

Grand-mère glanced at me. "What are you doing?" On her face was an expression of deep concern. Almost horror, I thought.

"I'm sorry if you think it's rude. But it's so hard to sit here . . . to see all this sadness . . . to think of Papa . . ."

She shook her head. "That's not what I mean," my grandmother said in an annoyed tone of voice. She pointed to my hands.

"I'm just sketching."

"But why?"

"Why not? I've been spending so much time at museums. Everywhere I go there are artists and galleries and talk of this painter and that, and it both interests me and occupies me."

She was staring at my drawing, and I knew what she was seeing. I knew how good I had become. And far too quickly. In class, the studies I was doing were getting better every day. Boring though they might be—I was just painting the model as she or he stood or sat or lay on the platform—my work was improving daily. Moreau didn't question it—he had seen the paintings I'd presented as mine, the nude studies I'd taken from the studio. He expected me to excel as my wrist healed. But Julien had been astonished by my progress when I'd showed him what I had done in class. More than once he had asked me if it was really true that I had not been painting all along and just hid it from him. I assured him that I never had studied seriously. And when he asked how I could explain my ability, I told him I couldn't.

"But if you are doing it here, now, this is no hobby," Grand-mère said.

"What do you mean?" I asked

"You are obsessed, aren't you? I've seen this affliction. I know about it. She—" My grand-mother stopped herself from what she was about to say, paused, and then continued. "No, this is not good for you. I don't like it, Sandrine. It's not healthy."

I was about to argue when the organ music began. I continued sketching, though. Suddenly my pencil was drawing something I wasn't seeing in front of me but imagining. I'd experienced this twice in class. It had made me excited and afraid then and was having the same effect on me now.

Even though this image was coming from my

own mind, it seemed foreign. I was drawing a gaunt creature with large sad eyes, dripping tears that, even though I only had a graphite pencil, I knew were tears of blood. And as I drew, I heard words . . . her ruby-red words flowing . . . flowing like blood . . . as she whispered to me. I understood the words but not their meaning, but I used them as part of the composition, weaving each letter of each word into her long curls, into the fabric of her elaborate skirt.

Finally to love. Finally to end the pain. Finally to find the secrets of my soul.

I was still filling in the garments when my grandmother put one of her gloved hands on the tiny sketchbook, and with her other hand took the pencil from mine and put it in her purse.

"I said enough."

Staring at her, I dared her to look at me so I could show my displeasure, but she did not. I closed my Sennelier sketchbook and put it back inside my silk bag.

As the music filled the cavernous space, it also reverberated inside of me, the chords making my bones and my insides thrum. When Julien was inside of me, I felt like this, and as I sat there on the cushioned pew, I experienced the same surge of excitement his touch engendered. I was alive. I might not have wanted to be, but I was. The cool blood that used to run through my veins was always hot now. A small look, a gesture, was enough to ignite me. And it wasn't just Julien who could spark me. In Moreau's class there were several men who appealed to me. Of course I did not approach them. I tried to keep from even looking at them, but sometimes one would say something or move a certain way, and I'd feel that throb deep inside me and know.

I wondered if it was blasphemous to think such thoughts in shul. Certainly it was brazen.

The cantor ended his song, and the silence alerted me to the rabbi leading us in a prayer, followed by him speaking of the sad occasion that had brought us all there. As his words droned on, staid and expected, I imagined painting this scene: the black-robed, dour rabbi; the upturned faces of the mourners; the shafts of colored light filtering through the stained glass; the glinting silver and gold accoutrements and ornaments.

Moreau was a master at painting this kind of opulence. I didn't want to copy him, though. Nor did he want me to. There were so many students who did nothing but that. Rather, he had been urging me to find my own painterly vocabulary. I hadn't yet, but every day it became clearer to me that, once I learned the language of color and line, shadow and shine, I would paint the mystical world that we live in. The penumbras, the mysteries, the secrets behind the obvious. Everything that lay just beyond sight.

In my lap, my fingers twitched as I imagined

squeezing yellows and browns and greens onto the palette. Dipping my brush into the luxurious colors. Stroking them onto a canvas just waiting for their embrace.

I longed to paint the faces of the mourners with their angels hovering above them and with the ghosts of their dead looking down on them, wanting to comfort them if only they knew the magical pathways to reach them.

The angels and ghosts were recognizable to me, and yet the people in the pews were strangers. How was that possible? I should have at least thought some of them looked familiar since many of us were related.

After the service we climbed into one of the waiting carriages and set off for the cemetery where my great-great uncle would be interred in what Grand-mère told me was the family mausoleum.

The idea of seeing this edifice excited me for some reason, and I sat perched on the edge of my seat in anticipation. With us were two of Grand-mère's cousins, elderly sisters who didn't stop gossiping about family the whole ride. They paid me little heed. They were far more caught up in the drama of how Max had died, in his lover's bed, and the way he had—most fairly, they thought—left his estate. Only enough to his wife for her to subsist. And why? She had been carrying on an *affair de coeur* with a married woman, a famous English writer, and the doctor, for all his brilliance, found his wife's flagrant sexual escapades embarrassing.

"A male lover," one of the cousins said, "wouldn't have bothered Max a bit. But a woman? Well, that implied far too much about him."

As we walked through the rows of graves at the cemetery, I began to see things that could not be there. Or perhaps I was just composing a horror painting in my mind's eye and, because of my grief, believed I was seeing it.

The people beneath the graves, skeletons wearing shrouds, were celebrating our arrival. A burial wasn't a sorrowful occasion for them. Welcoming a loved one to the underworld was a happy event. Most of the ghouls' faces were largely intact; only bits of flesh had rotted away to reveal bone.

One ghoul, who I somehow knew was Max's first wife, even though no one had mentioned he'd been married before, stood apart from the pack. She had lustrous black hair and glowing blue eyes that dripped pearl tears that pooled at her feet as she joyously waited for the father of her babies to join her.

Small children who had died far too early scampered up to her, stealing the pearls, stringing them on sinew they pulled from their bones so they could make wigs of them. Soon all the imps were wearing elaborate hair dressings of pure white or pink-tinged pearls. The scene shone with their glow.

The graveside service was long, and when it was over, I hoped we would leave hastily. I wanted to return home so I could sketch out my vision, but my grandmother insisted we stay so she might introduce me to the rabbi, Jacob Richter, another of my cousins.

"I am so sorry for your recent loss," he said. "Your father and I were very close growing up. I loved him like a brother." Taking my hand, he held it to his chest. For a moment, he gazed into my face as if searching for something.

Then he frowned.

My grandmother never missed an expression, a gesture, a mood, or a fleeting thought that passed over someone's face.

"Is something wrong, Jacob?" she asked.

He ignored her and leaned closer to me. "Have you been well, Sandrine?"

"Well?"

"Since coming to Paris, how have you slept? Have you been having disturbing dreams?"

How did he know? I'd told Julien about the dreams but not that they'd returned.

I backed away a bit so that it seemed the rabbi was pulling me. I let go of his hand and stumbled.

"You're in touch with a troubled spirit, aren't

you?" he asked. "She's showing you her realm. We must find out why."

"No, no . . . I don't know what you mean."

"The dreams you are having may not be yours but hers," he said, in such a low voice I wasn't sure my grandmother could hear him.

I sensed he was trying to be compassionate, but he was frightening me, and I just shook my head. "No, no."

My grandmother spoke. "Since Sandrine's father so recently died, whatever disturbance you sense is her grief."

"Is your father's passing *all* that is troubling you?" he asked me. "Or is there something else?"

"Do the souls here today stay here? Are they trapped here?" I asked the question that had been bothering me.

"What are you talking about, Sandrine? You sound mad," my grandmother exclaimed.

"It's all right, Eva," the rabbi said to her. "Her question makes sense to me." He looked back at me. "You know, it's forbidden for women to study the Kabala."

"I never studied the Kabala. I just want to know if the souls are trapped here."

"Are you saying you haven't read it?"

It was as if a door inside my mind opened and information came flooding in. The way it did when I painted. One moment I would be looking at a white canvas, and the next I would see an entire composition in my mind.

"I haven't read it, no. My father did, and we discussed certain parts, but nothing about what I've seen here today."

"If you would like, we can meet to talk about what is troubling you," he offered.

"Her father died, that's what is troubling her." Grand-mère seemed determined to assign her own meaning and explanation to my conversation with the rabbi.

Ignoring my grandmother, the rabbi continued to hold my gaze. "Have you been finding new interests?"

I said nothing, but my grandmother answered: "She's sketching."

Part of me wanted to laugh. Of all the things I was doing, sketching was the most benign and least radical.

"Are you feeling things with more intensity?" the rabbi continued his questioning.

I didn't answer, but I felt my cheeks flush. Suddenly, standing there in the cemetery in front of the large mausoleum with its lovely stained glass windows, I was actually experiencing Julien's lips on mine, and the gathering and pulsing that was so new to me still, started up deep inside me.

Beside me, my grandmother became even more agitated. "What is it, Jacob? What do all these questions mean? What are you suggesting?"

Ignoring her still, he asked me if I was able to sleep.

I told him I was.

"And when you are awake, are your thoughts your own?"

"What do you mean?" My grandmother's voice was raised. Had anyone from the mourning party still been present, it would have been most embarrassing. "It's not possible, Jacob. These things don't exist."

The rabbi turned to her and put a hand on her shoulder. "It's all right, Eva. I can help her."

She brushed off his hand. "No, this is rubbish. Nonsense. Old-fashioned fairy tales. We are living in an age of science and reason. There are no ghosts. No demons. People are not possessed by spirits from the past."

I stared at her. What was she saying? The rabbi had not mentioned any such thing to me. But that was what his questions meant, wasn't it? And my answers, even if I had not voiced them out loud, suggested they certainly did exist, and I was being haunted by one.

Chapter 15

"The modeling here is heavy, Mademoiselle Verlaine. And too light here."

"Yes, I see."

Monsieur Moreau stood beside me, studying my canvas. Per the assignment, I'd been painting the female nude posing on the podium, but in my composition had positioned her in blue-black darkness. Lurking in the shadows, I'd sketched in some of the angelic creatures I'd seen hovering over the tombstones in the cemetery. One of them, a male with wings, was about to swoop down on her.

"You've lost some of the figure's dimensionality, and she's too flat around the calves and ankles. But I'm pleased to see a style emerging." He stepped back and peered at my painting from another angle. "Yes, it's an interesting and atmospheric vision." He looked away from the canvas to me. "You are impatient, aren't you?"

"Yes, I think I am."

" 'Time's wingèd chariot hurrying near'?" he said, quoting the well-known Andrew Marvell poem. "You're young and have years of painting ahead of you. What is your rush?"

I couldn't tell the maître that I had another life and that I might not be able to remain in Paris for long enough to soak up all the knowledge he had to impart. Just that morning my grandmother had shown me yet another telegram from Mr. Lissauer. This one coming only a week after the last.

According to the lawyer, Benjamin had hired a detective agency to find me. Once again I mentally retraced my steps. Had I left any clues in Southampton? My passage to Calais couldn't have been recorded; I had paid for my ferry ticket with cash, not a bank note, and had not been asked to offer any form of identification. But surely there were people who'd seen me on the boat. Or on the train from Calais to Paris later that day. Would they be able to identify me if shown my portrait?

No, I might not be able to stay and study with Moreau indefinitely. I might not have years of painting ahead of me. Nothing was certain; events were unfolding and changing so rapidly that I couldn't be sure the center, as I knew it, would hold. But I couldn't say that to my teacher, so instead I said: "I am trying to make up for all the time I lost after my accident when I couldn't paint."

"Understandable," Moreau said, "but may I suggest you slow down while in class. Improved technique will lead to refinement of style."

"I'll try, of course."

"If you want to increase our time together, you might think about joining my atelier. Is that something that you would like to do?"

"I would be honored."

Moreau only asked a few students to join him at his studio, and I had only dared to dream I'd be invited into the inner circle that included Desvallières, du Gardier, Matisse, Rouault, and Maxence.

"We meet two nights a week, and the work we do there is a commitment in addition to what we do in our classes here. The address is 14 rue de la Rochefoucauld." He was about to move on. Then turned back. "The Old Masters had a very specific technique using a strong contrast between light and dark to give the illusion of three-dimensionality . . . I see that seventeenth-century chiaroscuro in your work, and I like it. I didn't think they were teaching that at the art school in New York. Very few painters still use it. Is it part of the regular curriculum?"

I was stumped. I had no idea. I had to come up with an answer. He was waiting. "Not usually, no. When I tried to copy techniques I'd seen at the Metropolitan Museum in the Caravaggios my father and I enjoyed so much, my teacher gave me special instruction."

It was a lie. But what else could I have said? I wasn't aware of how I'd learned anything that I was able to do with paints and brushes on canvas. Yes, Cherubino and La Lune had employed chiaroscuro to give their paintings depth, but how could I have learned it from artists who'd been dead for over two centuries?

"You're a very exciting student, Mademoiselle. Your compositions are still slightly awkward, your color sense could be more refined, but your vision is provocative and very curious. You show great promise."

He walked away, and I picked up my brush and continued working on the woman's form. Why was I so afraid of the future? I could write Mr. Lissauer and ask him if there was a way to start divorce proceedings while I remained in France. Regardless of the social stigma, there was no question I needed to end my marriage. If I could sell my father's house in Newport and the mansion on Fifth Avenue, both of which had been left to me directly, I'd have more than enough money to remain in Paris, buy a small house, and have my own studio. Like Mary Cassatt, Sandrine Jeanette Verlaine could be an American painting in Paris. Once I had my own home, I wouldn't need my grandmother's help or even her consent to live my own life the way I wanted.

Our conversations since the funeral the previous week had been stilted. She was convinced I was troubled, hated that I had taken up drawing, was certain I was being affected negatively by being in Paris, and wanted me to consult with her cousin the rabbi.

I refused. Her theories about me were rubbish. I was certain that when I told him, Julien would agree. Being possessed by a demon was a non-sensical concept invited by overactive imaginations. But Julien wasn't there to concur. He'd left the day of my cousin's funeral to travel to his hometown of Nancy to oversee several suites of furniture his uncle was creating for a house on the exclusive Avenue Hoche in the 8th arrondissement.

When the class ended that day, a few of the students whom I had gotten to know invited me to join them at the café around the corner. Since my grandmother would be dining with the count and I'd told her I was spending the evening with my imaginary visitor from America, I was free.

At La Palette our group included Gaston Billet, who was gentle and quiet but painted boldly and with fervor; Maurice Soubrelle, an aesthete and intellectual who frustrated Moreau with questions that our teacher said were better left to critics than creators; and Serge Mouton. I had the hardest time with Serge, who was often lewd and always smelled of beer, but his paintings were glorious and full of colors that made me want to get lost in them. I never could reconcile his personality with his beautiful canvases. He was two different people—the artist who was a marvel and the man who was often appalling and unappealing.

"Lillian's skin today glowed like a peach," Gaston said when we were seated and the wine had been served. He was blond and had pale blue eyes that he blinked a bit too often.

"She's the toast of the art school," Maurice said. He was a bit of a dandy, always dressed better than everyone else, and wore a lemon-scented pomade in his hair. "But very aloof," he added.

Serge laughed. "That's putting it mildly." A big man, he took up more space than anyone else. I was surprised he didn't break the wineglass when he touched it.

It was a strange phenomenon, but when I was dressed in my art school garb, the others weren't circumspect with me the way they would have been had I been in a dress and all the finery that went with it. I was one of them, a fellow artist, and it made me fearless. Freedom, when you've never really known it, is exhilarating. I found it liberating not to wait for someone to help me with doors or offer to carry my packages, and to be able to say anything I pleased without worrying about being considered unladylike.

"Don't worry, when we get to male models, we'll tease you, too, Sandrine," Gaston said.

"Do you prefer them fair or dark?" Serge asked.

"As long as they don't look like you, I'll be happy," I answered.

They laughed.

"You prefer someone handsome then?" Maurice joked at Serge's expense, but he didn't seem to mind.

"Tomas," Gaston said. "That's who she'll like."

"No, she'll go for Alexander," Serge said.

"Why Alexander?" I asked.

Gaston told me: "Serge is attempting humor. Alexander is an ancient man, about eighty, with a long Methuselah beard and a cane."

"I hope Moreau keeps Lillian a bit longer," Maurice said.

"Yes, yes, she's quite an eyeful. But it's clear she's not interested in artists," Serge told me.

"So you've all tried?" I asked.

"We all have," Serge said. "She may look hot, but when it comes to art students, she's a cold fish."

"Maybe it's just that you all have cold hands," I said, and rubbed my palms together as if to start a fire.

After more laughter, more wine, and a plate of cheese, the conversation turned to our work and our teacher.

"You know what the author Huysmans wrote about Moreau, don't you?" Maurice asked me.

I told him I didn't.

"He called him an extraordinary and unique artist and said he was 'a mystic locked up in the middle of Paris in a cell.' And that nothing from everyday life penetrates that cloister." Opening his sketchbook, he riffled through the pages. "I have more of the quote: 'Thrown in ecstasy, he sees the resplendent fairy-like visions, the apotheoses of other times.' "

"Some say he's our greatest living painter," said Gaston. "You'll see if you join the atelier. He has two hundred paintings he's working on at one time." Gaston paused. "He's changed since his wife died."

"They were never married," Maurice corrected.

"No one knows very much about her," Serge said. "But Gaston is right. Since she died, he's become even more obsessed with painting Orpheus and Eurydice."

"How poignant that he keeps painting the story of soul mates over and over," I said.

"There's a rumor that he is part of a secret society," Maurice whispered.

"Who in Paris *isn't* part of a secret society?" Gaston said, and then quaffed what was left of his wine.

"I heard he met with Delacroix when he was younger," Maurice continued. "And Delacroix was linked with the secret Angelic Society made up of artists who received visions of angels who aided them in their art. It's always been rumored Delacroix introduced and inducted Moreau into the society."

"Does the society still exist?" I asked.

"Are you interested in joining?" Gaston asked.

"From the looks of your work you already belong," Serge added under his breath.

I blushed then, which I hated. None of the other students blushed when given compliments. I resolved to accept commendations the way men did. Why did women think they had to be demure when they were praised?

"I could use a little angelic intervention," Serge said, "to help me get into the Salon. I wasn't accepted last year. But with Moreau as my teacher, I have a better chance this year."

"Why does having him as a teacher help?" I asked.

"Because Moreau is on the acceptance committee," Maurice said.

Every student at the École and thousands of artists in Paris—from all over France, in fact—had been working toward the goal of having a painting accepted into the 1894 Salon de la Société des Artistes Français for longer than I had even been in the city. Academic-quality paintings took several months to achieve, and submissions were due at the end of March.

"What did Moreau say about your *esquisse*?" Gaston asked me. "As you might imagine, the advice he gives about a painter's sketch is invaluable."

"I haven't done a sketch to show him. Even if I knew what I wanted to paint, there's just not time. And there are so many restrictions to what the Salon would accept from a woman." I shrugged.

"You're fast, though. At least try," Gaston said. "Moreau encourages us to submit portraits, figure studies, or history paintings. You're excellent with nudes, which take the least amount of time, and a woman can submit a female nude."

Some secret part of me soared hearing him say that. Second-class medals, third-class medals, and honorable mentions were given out, in addition to the most prestigious Prix de Rome, but with over ten thousand paintings being submitted and less than half making the first cut, just being accepted was a feat. What would it be like to achieve that?

"Don't encourage her, Gaston. Less competition for us," Serge said.

Gaston laughed. "You only wish you could compete with her."

We'd reached the end of the bottle of wine, and Serge suggested we move on to a bistro a few blocks away on Saint-Germain that served the best *soupe à l'oignon* in all of Paris.

It was there, a half hour later, just as the waiter was putting our food on the table, that I noticed the door open and a group of three men enter. One of them was Julien. He must have gotten back from his trip.

I watched as the maître d' seated them inside toward the back.

"Do you know them?" Serge asked me.

"One looks familiar, but I'm not sure. Why, do you know them?"

"The gentleman with the gray beard is Monsieur Cingal, the architect. He teaches at the École, so perhaps you recognize him from seeing him there. I don't know who the other two are."

"But of course," I said, and spooned some of the hot, fragrant soup. It was delicious: brown and buttery with a crisp layer of cheese on top that had just the right bite to it.

So that was Cingal, Julien's prospective father-in-law. I glanced over at their table, trying not to bring any attention to myself. Cingal and Julien interacted much like father and son. And why not? Julien had known his father-in-law-to-be for over ten years, first as his student, then his apprentice, and now his partner.

Examining Cingal's features, I tried to imagine them feminized and picture what his daughter would look like. But his nose was too big, his chin too square, and his brow too heavy.

As I ate and talked, I kept casting glances over at Julien's table. I paid less attention to how many times my wineglass was filled than I ought, and before long began to hatch a plan that a more sober soul might not have dared.

Julien had told me his apartment was in one of Monsieur Cingal's buildings and that his mentor and his family resided there also. If I followed them, I might find out where Julien lived. Where *she* lived. And once I knew that, I could return during the day, wait for her, and see her. See what my rival looked like. What she was made of. Learn better how to fight her for what I'd come to realize I wanted to wrest from her grip.

So when Julien and Cingal paid their bill, I threw some coins on the table and told my fellow students that it was time for me to leave and hurried out.

It was foolhardy, I knew. I wasn't even sure where they were going or how they were going to get there. What if they took a carriage, and I was left in some neighborhood I didn't recognize? What if it was unsafe?

But as it turned out, they walked and never left the 6th arrondissement. After crossing Saint-Germain, they strolled down rue de Tournon toward the Luxembourg Gardens and then into the gardens themselves, traversed a diagonal path and exited on rue de Fleurus.

After they crossed the street, the two men proceeded down de Fleurus, stopping in front of number 6, a five-story building with lovely wrought-iron balconies and a slight undulation to the facade. Designed, but not overly so, it was elegant without being grandiose. Julien remained outside while Cingal disappeared inside. I waited a few doors down in the shadow of another building's entrance. There were no gas lamps on my side of the street, only on theirs, and since Julien didn't glance my way, I believed I was safe.

Was this the building where they lived? Why hadn't Julien entered? Where had Cingal gone? I was imagining scenario after scenario when, after a few minutes, Cingal returned, a young woman on his arm.

In the lamplight, I could see her well enough for her countenance to disturb me. She was very lovely, with blond curls, full lips, and a feminine figure, and from the way she tossed her head, she was very used to being the center of attention.

I tried to imagine Julien touching her face the way he had touched mine. Kissing her the way he had kissed me. But I couldn't. It wasn't just because I was jealous. There was an iridescent aura about her that was evil. It made me uneasy and frightened for Julien. And for me.

Just like the creatures hovering above and living below the tombstones in the cemetery, the shimmer, I had no doubt, was real and a manifestation of dimensions never before accessible to me. But it was visible now for some reason I couldn't comprehend.

The rabbi's words echoed in my mind just then. *You're in touch with a troubled spirit, aren't you?* he'd said. *She's showing you her realm. We must find out why.*

A carriage pulled up, and Cingal, his daughter,

and Julien climbed inside. I watched as the horse trotted off, and was left standing on the street by myself. How was I to get back to my grandmother's on my own? Unused to traveling alone in Paris at night, I walked to the corner and hoped that I'd find a carriage as easily as Cingal had. But there wasn't one in sight. And so I began to trace my footsteps, back through the park, back toward rue des Saints-Pères.

There were no other pedestrians in the gardens. The pathways were dark. Figures seemed to lurk in the shadows. The wind rustling through bare branches sounded like footsteps. What was I doing? How foolish to have put myself in the position of being a helpless woman out alone after dark in a park. How would I be able to defend myself if attacked?

I looked straight ahead and kept my pace quick. While I walked, I distracted myself with thinking about Charlotte Cingal and the way she'd tilted her face to look up at Julien. How the light had skimmed her cheekbones and how fine her skin had been. How petite her feet and hands were.

My mother had been small like that, but I took after my father and my grandmother. Taller than most women, my shoulders slightly wider, my hands just a bit bigger.

My father used to say that he was glad that I wasn't fragile, that fragile women never seemed to claim life. And that out of everything, that was what he hoped for me. That I would claim my life. I asked him once if my mother had, and he'd smiled and said she had, but he didn't think it was the kind of life that would satisfy me.

Reflecting on my parents had distracted me further, not from the possible dangers lurking in the park but from a darker danger. But it would do no good pretending. I had to admit what I was thinking, even if it was only to myself.

I'd hated Charlotte Cingal the moment I'd seen her. As the carriage had pulled up, I'd imagined the horse suddenly rearing on his hind legs and coming down with his full force, knocking her to the ground and trampling her.

The vicious and violent image disturbed me. How could I have conjured such a scene in my head? Of course some jealousy was in order—but hatred and murderous rage?

The ugliness of my thoughts embarrassed me. And worried me a bit. I'd never had any kind of malevolent fantasy before. Not toward anyone. Even Benjamin, who had been such a curt and callous husband, had not engendered these kinds of thoughts. Not even when I discovered that he'd driven my father to his death.

From whence had this blackness in me sprung?

I was afraid I knew. And again the rabbi's words came to me: *You're in touch with a troubled spirit, aren't you?* he'd said.

• • •

I had almost reached the rue Bonaparte exit when I realized that I wasn't alone. I couldn't see anyone, but I was certain I'd heard footsteps. I stopped suddenly, spun around, and searched the shadows but saw no one. I began walking again and after a few seconds was sure I heard a twig crack, as if it had been stepped on. Should I turn around again? Or hurry out posthaste? Was someone following me? Had one of Benjamin's detectives found me?

Hastening out of the park, I turned onto rue Bonaparte. Had someone watched to see what direction I'd take? If so, I couldn't lead him directly to my grandmother's apartment, so instead of heading directly toward Saints-Pères, I stopped in a café for an espresso and kept my eyes on the door. It didn't appear anyone had followed me inside, and peering through the windows, I saw no one hiding in wait in any doorways.

Believing I'd lost my pursuer, if indeed I'd had one, I continued on home, imagining what Julien and Charlotte Cingal were doing right then. I saw them in the carriage. Her looking at him from under her eyelashes again. Him taking that tiny hand to help her down.

He had not told me the truth when he'd implied that he wasn't in love with her. Of course he was. He'd only said that it was going to be a marriage of convenience so that I'd welcome him into my bed.

I envisioned the three of them walking into a luxurious restaurant with red velvet banquettes and golden wall sconces and glittering chandeliers that would give her skin an even more irresistible glow. He would not try to resist her. Why should he? She was his. He was going to marry her, and she was going to make him a good French wife. Looking resplendent in her lace and satin and pearls and diamonds. Being oh so good for his business and charming all his clients.

Hadn't I done the same for Papa and Benjamin? It was only since coming to Paris that I had begun to think of that life with such disdain. And why? Because unwittingly my husband had shown me the danger of allowing the pursuit of the dollar to take over your life. Because all the effort I had put into behaving correctly and doing the right thing and being the proper sort of wife and daughter had not protected me. I'd been too dependent on my father and now was unprepared for a life without him. Charlotte Cingal was who I had been. Not who I needed to become. I was going to learn to be on my own, like my grandmother, making my own way, never being dependent on a man again.

But she *was* dependent, wasn't she? Without men how would she live? Where would she be?

As I turned left on rue du Vieux-Colombier, I

began plotting how I might meet Charlotte myself and discover who she really was under those Fragonard-pink cheeks and rose-colored lips. There was something rotten in her soul. I'd sensed it, and I would expose it, and Julien would sour on her like cherries tasted before their season.

The thought was so satisfying, I smiled to myself.

No! It was wrong of me to think this way. Where was this evil coming from? Why did it give me pleasure to indulge in these black thoughts? I had known Julien was engaged when I took him as a lover. Our affair was a temporary passing fancy. I had read enough and had enough female friends to know how these things worked even if I'd never indulged before. One did not take these dalliances seriously.

I opened the door to the porte cochère, crossed the courtyard, and entered my grandmother's apartment.

In the grand parlor, a salon was in full bloom. My grandmother, ablaze with her fire opals and a dress of the same incendiary hue, sat surrounded by admirers. Gentlemen in fine evening clothes lounged as they drank champagne from sparkling crystal flutes or sipped brandy from large glasses engraved with Napoleon's crown. Several young women served drinks or lit cigars, or flitted around the room, flirting. They were either blondes or brunettes; not one had red hair to compete with my grandmother's. The women were clearly sophisti-cated and clever given the way the men hung on their every word. One girl in cobalt lace passed a tray of tidbits around. A gentleman sat at the piano, playing a Debussy etude.

My grandmother looked up as I stepped into the room. With a confused expression, she whispered something to the gentleman to her right, who got up and walked toward me. From across the room, she watched.

I'd never seen my grandmother regard me with such ambivalence, and it disturbed me. Had I made some mistake I wasn't aware of? Had she expected me even though she'd told me that she was busy that night?

In a formal voice, the gentleman said: "Good evening."

"Good evening."

"Can you tell me who it was who invited you?" he asked.

Why was he asking me? Why was he peering at me as if sizing me up?

"Do you have an invitation?" he asked when I didn't answer.

I shook my head. "No."

And then I caught a glimpse of us in the mirror and realized with horror exactly what was wrong. My grandmother hadn't recognized me. Of course she hadn't. Why would she? I had forgotten that I was still dressed in my art school costume. I'd been at the École, then the café, and then had followed Julien. I'd never gone back to La Lune to change into my clothes, into my pretty dress and daintily heeled shoes. I was wearing men's trousers, and my hair fell to my shoulders in easy waves. I had on a hat that cast shadows across my features.

"I would encourage you to leave then, without further ado, to avoid any unpleasantness," the gentleman said as my grandmother continued to watch.

"Yes, yes, I . . ."

The man put his hand on my arm. "Now would be best."

"Yes, of course," I said.

Just before I turned to go, I saw the expression on my grandmother's face change from one of suspicion to one of fear. She'd recognized who I was. But she didn't get up. She didn't stop her friend as his hand tightened on my arm.

"Now would be best," he repeated, and showed me out of my own house.

Chapter 16

"Why were you dressed like a man last night?"

My grandmother sat at the table in the dining room. She didn't look well rested, and I was unsure if it was solely because of me or if something else had occurred.

"I wanted to study painting, and women weren't allowed at the École. So I thought I'd disguise myself as a man and bought these clothes. As it turned out, I applied and was accepted as a woman, but I found I liked dressing like this; it's easier to do everything—from walking through the streets to painting."

Her eyes searched my face as if there were some secret written there she would be able to detect with intense scrutiny.

The maid entered with coffee and a plate of toast, which she placed in front of Grand-mère, and then asked me what I'd like. I said I'd take the same thing. Once she left, my grandmother resumed her inquisition.

"Why do you need to study painting at all? I don't understand. You never cared about painting."

"Why is it such a disturbing idea to you? I've always loved art. Museums have been a refuge and delight for me my whole life."

"Yes, but it's one thing to admire and appreciate

art and another to put on a smock and stand in front of a canvas." She took a bite of her dry toast.

"What about my studying painting could possibly bother you?"

She took another bite and chewed slowly, as if that was going to help her explain.

"Well, for one thing, you are dressing up to do it. Walking about in costume."

"Yes?"

"It's perverse."

"I'm not sure that dressing up like a man in order to study painting is any more perverse than dressing up like a seductress in order to ensnare a man."

She flinched as if she had been slapped, and a few drops of the coffee in the cup in her hand sloshed out and spotted the white linen tablecloth.

"How long has this been going on?" she asked.

"Almost a month."

"Were you going to tell me?"

"Yes."

"Really?"

"Why don't you believe me?"

"Sandrine, you have changed since your first week here."

"Yes, Paris agrees with me."

She shook her head. "I'm not sure that it's all been for the best. You are more secretive, strident, argumentative. You're darker."

"My father died."

"What I'm seeing is not mourning. I know what that is." Reaching over, she put her hand on mine. "Am I wrong to be afraid for you?"

"Yes. I'm enjoying it here. I feel as if I'm becoming the person I was meant to be. Finally."

"What do you mean?" She leaned in closer, her voice stressed. "What exactly do you mean?"

Alice entered with my breakfast. I hadn't realized how hungry I was until she put it down in front of me. Before answering my grandmother, I took a bite. There was the perfect amount of butter melted into the bread, and it was delicious. I took a second bite.

"Sandrine? What do you mean when you say you feel as if you are becoming the person you were meant to be?"

"I'm not sure how to describe it. But living here, painting . . . I simply feel as if I am where I am supposed to be. Doing what I am supposed to be doing."

I took a sip of the steaming coffee laced with cream. Grand-mère's cook was a marvel.

"I have a question for you, too. Why is your house closed up? What are you really doing with Maison de la Lune?" I asked.

"I told you. A renovation. Why?"

"How long will it take?"

"Why?"

"Because I would like to live there instead of

here, and I'd like to know when I might be able to move in."

"You will not live there. Ever." Her voice was strong and loud and raised goose bumps on my arms. "Don't you understand that you shouldn't even be in Paris? It's far too dangerous for you just to be in this city, but certainly you cannot live in that house. You cannot step foot in that house."

Her cheeks were red; her eyes were blazing. She grabbed both my hands in hers. "It's my job to keep you safe. You have to promise to stay away from La Lune."

I wrested my hands away. "What are you talking about? What could be in the house that could put me in danger? You lived there your whole life. My father grew up there. I spent time there when I was fifteen. The only danger I face is if Benjamin finds me."

"The house is closed and will be for some time. There's no question about you living there." She stood.

"I'll find out. I want to know, and I'll find out."

She whirled around, bent down, and slapped me hard on the cheek. I felt the sting of her fingers. The pain where her rings had hit my flesh.

"You will do what I say. I don't care how old you are. You are under my care and protection now, and I will not stand for your insubordination and tone. I am telling you that you will stay away from La Lune."

I laughed. From shock? From anger? The sound was scarlet and strong and nasty. The way a snake might laugh when confronted by a strident mouse.

"Try to control me, old woman. Just try."

"What did you just say to me?" She was staring. Both horror and disgust on her face. She picked up my glass of water and splashed it in my face. "How dare you? Who are you to talk to me like that?"

The water did nothing to deter me. She was a fly on the wall trying to contain me. To control me. And I would not be controlled.

My robe was soaked and uncomfortable. I pulled it open, separating the wet, clinging silk from my skin, mopping the water with a napkin.

"What is that on your neck? What are you wearing?" my grandmother shrieked.

She was pointing to my neck. My hand went to my throat.

"Where did you get that?"

I wasn't sure what to say. To tell her the truth would mean I would have to admit that I had been inside the house. Perhaps the necklace had been hidden in that secret space long enough that even she didn't know that's where it had been.

"It's something Papa gave me." I lied. "Don't you like it?"

"It's the same as the necklace that the women in the portraits are wearing."

I knew full well what she was talking about but feigned innocence. "The portraits?"

"On the staircase in La Lune." She was still frowning as she stared at the necklace. "I haven't seen that since I was a little girl. My mother kept it with her other jewels, and it was the only piece I wasn't allowed to play with."

"Why was that?"

Grand-mère shook her head. "How did your father get it?"

"Perhaps it's not the same one? Maybe he had it made because he remembered it from the portraits and liked it."

"Take it off. Give it to me."

"Why?"

"It doesn't matter why. Take it off, Sandrine. Give it to me."

"Tell me why."

"I said take it off!"

Before I could react, she had her hands on the necklace and was working the clasp.

I tried to pull her hands off.

She swatted my hands away, gave up on the clasp, curled her fingers under one of the rosettes, and pulled hard. The necklace dug into my skin. She pulled harder. The chain didn't break, didn't come apart. How was that possible? She was pulling so hard the pain was extreme. I didn't want to be fighting with her. This was my grandmother. A wave of nausea overwhelmed me for a moment.

I grabbed my grandmother by the wrists and pushed her away. She stumbled but righted herself by taking hold of a chair.

I walked past her and out of the room.

Behind me I heard her shout. "Take it off, Sandrine, take it off." It was a combination of a plea, a prayer, and a threat.

Chapter 17

I was still thinking about my grandmother's behavior and my own, which was so unlike me and which I admit I felt both sad and guilty about, when I arrived at the Louvre to paint with Maître Moreau and a dozen of his students.

"I'm impressed by your technique," Moreau said when he came up behind me. "You said it was a teacher in New York who gave you such a good grounding in Renaissance practices?"

"Yes," I said, hoping he would not ask me for a name.

"At what school did you say?"

"At the Art Students League."

Of course I had never studied there, but as I offered up the lie, I was seeing my teacher. He stood over my shoulder, just out of sight, advising me on how to mix rich pigment with pure oil to get the right transparency in the glaze I was using so as I built the layers, they would create the impression of depth.

He was not handsome but compelling. His nose appeared broken, a scar ran through his right eyebrow separating it, his red lips were too full and almost mean, and his eyes were dark and hooded. He spoke French, but with an Italian accent.

I could see his face so clearly. He was so familiar to me. Who was he? And then I knew. Of course. It was the man in the portraits in the bell tower. The portraits painted by LL. I was imagining *I* had been taught by Cherubino. That *I* had been taught by La Lune's teacher.

When the class ended, I packed up my canvas and paints and returned to the house on rue des Saints-Pères, hoping that Julien would be there waiting for me. I hadn't seen him, other than when I'd shadowed him, since he'd returned from Nancy.

He wasn't at the house, but he'd been there and left a note saying that he'd returned to Paris and would meet me the next day since Moreau didn't teach on Fridays.

Without Julien there, I might as well go back to my grandmother's apartment for dinner. I began to undress in order to change back into my gown. The air in the studio was always chilly if no fire was lit, and I wasn't going to bother to start one. I could maneuver by the light of the candles and then leave.

I removed my jacket, shirt, pants, pantaloons, and stockings. The cold air was refreshing. I stood there naked for a moment but for the rubies around my neck, shimmering in the candlelight.

Suddenly I wanted to paint.

I opened the hidden cabinet, where I'd found La Lune's and Cherubino's drawings, and began to pull out the fabulous fabrics that I had discovered there. I stepped into a long skirt of pearl lace that only partially concealed my naked legs and the V of darkness where they met. The tiny silk vest embroidered with dragons I slipped on came to just beneath my breasts and left my cleavage and part of each nipple exposed. Slippers of silver shot through with ruby threads and gold combs studded with rubies completed the costume.

I stood back and examined my reflection. Since coming to Paris, I had adopted the costume of a male art student. Now I appeared a half-naked siren, a seductress.

I grabbed a canvas from the stack by the wall, one that had been stretched and primed but never painted on, placed it on the easel, opened my box of paints, and prepared my palette.

Ready, I looked from mirror to canvas, mirror to palette. I dipped my brush in burnt ochre, thinned it with some oil so it was translucent, and began.

With broad strokes, I sketched out her figure, standing, staring out at the viewer. Me, and yet someone else, too. I'd never looked like this. Never been a wanton, sexual creature. Never been a woman so determined. With sure strokes, even though I didn't have a model, I roughed out the man behind her. With his arms around her, locked in a sexual embrace. While she stood watching me, it seemed, he was taking her from behind.

Despite the cold studio I began to grow warm

as I felt his hands on my breasts and his thighs against the back of mine and his fingers on my nipples. His voice burned in my ear as he whispered urgent words of lovemaking.

On and on I painted, all the while shuddering as he moved behind me, his hardness asserting itself, determined to find its home.

He sighed. I moaned.

On and on I painted as he grew larger and larger inside me. He slipped out as the brush dipped in the vermilion. As the brush slid across the canvas, he slid back inside. He thrust with every brush-stroke . . . again and again . . . He moved and the brush moved . . . until with a great shudder I felt all the colors on the canvas explode inside me, and I dropped the brush and the palette and sent splatters of paint in a dozen directions.

When my breathing returned to normal, I examined what I'd created in the white-hot heat.

I had thought as I worked that I was painting Julien and myself, but the people in the painting were not us. I had been La Lune painting herself and her lover, Cherubino.

Without taking off her clothes or jewels, I sat on the daybed, staring at the canvas, trying to make some sense of what was happening to me.

I woke up to bright sunshine shining through the openings in the roof of the bell tower. The room, which should have been cold without a fire burning all night, was warm. It only took me a moment more to comprehend that, along with the paints and turpentine and linseed oil, I smelled coffee. And then I understood I was not alone.

Julien was sitting in a chair by the table, drinking a cup of coffee and nibbling a croissant while staring at the portrait I had painted in my heated frenzy.

As I stretched and fully came awake, I remembered I'd never gone home the night before. What had my grandmother thought? Did I care? She had slapped me and thrown water at me. Did I even have to go back? I could just move in here, into this bell tower. Keep selling jewels at the pawnshop until I ran out and then move on to selling the antiques. There was enough silver and china and artwork to last years.

"Good morning, Sandrine." Julien's luxe voice and penetrating eyes made my skin tingle. "You look quite fetching."

I glanced down. I'd forgotten how naked I was with my see-through lace skirt and tiny vest. Trying to be demure, I covered myself with my shawl, got up, and visited the small lavatory inside the tower. I would have preferred to go into the main part of the house for the convenience of the modern plumbing, but it was a long walk in the cold, and if La Lune had been able to live like this for years, certainly I could manage one morning.

When I returned to Julien, he was inspecting the still-wet painting.

"Did you do this yesterday?"

"Last night."

"All night?"

"Until very late, yes. I don't actually know what time I finished."

"It's marvelous. And brave." He turned to me now. "Thinking of you painting it makes me want to—" He broke off, took two steps to where I was standing. He pulled me toward him and kissed me full on the lips.

I had read enough books to know what to call it, but I'd never experienced a swoon before. I truly did not think I was going to be able to remain on my feet. I became that kiss. Became its emotion, its sensation. Everything around me disappeared: the tower room, the painting. There was only the wave of euphoria and the weakness that made me hold on to Julien all the tighter.

Pulling him with me onto the daybed, I undressed him, unashamed in my desire to see him naked. To feel him. There on the rumpled blanket, I took him with a hungry mouth and active hands. And he watched me in wonder until he succumbed to my ministrations, and together we went into the dark purple and red and magenta and orange world of colors and scents and feelings that was inside my mind and behind my eyes and deep in my womb where the explosions caused ripples that left me breathless and panting.

And then I heard it, that faint chiming I'd heard before when we'd made love, the hum of those glorious, ancient bells.

After we had recovered, we set to putting the room back in order, and I told him what had happened with my grandmother and the fight we'd had.

Julien was planning to remain at La Lune that day; he had work to do in the main part of the house. I wanted to stay with him, but he encouraged me to go home to my grandmother's and make peace with her.

"She's a strong, stubborn woman, but she'll get used to the idea of you becoming a painter. Why wouldn't she? She's worked her whole life. Surely she will understand your desire for your own kind of independence. She can't be that superstitious. I've met her."

"I know, but she becomes irrational when it comes to La Lune and me painting, or even me staying here in Paris."

After folding up the clothes I'd worn the night before into neat piles of fabrics, I opened the cabinet to put everything back where I'd found it. Rays of sunlight coming through the oblong windows illuminated the interior, and I noticed that one of the panels was a slightly different color wood.

Reaching out, I touched it. It wobbled.

"Julien, come look. There's something here."

Beside me, he peered into the semidarkness.

"It's empty."

"There." I put his hand on the edge of the hidden panel—surprised I'd been so bold to take his hand. And then I laughed at myself. I had taken so much more in the bed only minutes ago.

"Do you think it might be a hidden compartment?" I asked.

He knocked on it, and we heard a hollow echo. "It appears to be one."

"Do you know how it opens? You're an architect. You must know things like that."

He laughed. "I must? Well, let's see . . ."

Julien pressed on one corner and then the next. Nothing happened. But well-versed in secrets and how to reveal them, he tried another way, and then another. Finally he pressed the panel in the right combination, and it sprang open.

"I can't see much—this goes fairly deep," he said.

I lit a candle, brought it over, and he thrust it inside the cabinet.

We both peered in.

"There's something in there, isn't there?" I said.

Using both hands, Julien reached inside and then, struggling, pulled out a well-wrapped and very large package.

The burgundy silk wrapping appeared expensive, ancient, and musty. It gave off the same odor I'd smelled the first time we'd visited the tower: a lush fragrance that combined ancient air, frankincense, cedar, myrrh, and roses.

Gingerly I pulled the fabric away to reveal a thick book, bound in creamy brown leather. There was no writing on the back cover, so I turned it around to see if there was anything on the front.

Where there had been a title, only tiny fragments of gold were left, as if someone had traced the word's outline with a finger over and over. Nothing was legible any longer.

I opened it to the frontispiece and found the page had been ripped out, and only a ragged edge of it was left near the spine.

What remained was the part of a name, two Roman numerals, and the words *Paris, France*.

The first two complete pages contained three columns of small medieval type in what appeared to be archaic French, for some of the words were foreign to me. There was foxing on the edges, and the thick paper had a landscape to it, little hills and valleys, the way very old manuscripts do.

As I turned to the next set of pages, more of the same mystical, spicy fragrance escaped, almost drugging me. The heady scent added to the mystery of what this ancient volume might be.

"Look," Julien said, pointing to the margin, where tiny handwriting filled the white spaces. Inky scratches faded to a pale brown.

I bent lower and tried to read the inscriptions, but the words were too faint and too small.

"We'll need a magnifier," he said.

"There must be one downstairs."

"If not, I can bring one tomorrow from my office." He turned the page. And I gasped.

Painted over the writing was an illustration of a woman drowning in a pond. The expression on her face was sheer terror. In the margins onlookers watched with horror, except for one creature jumping into the air, wild with enjoyment, his brilliant verdant-green eyes shining with delight. Horns broke through his reddish-brown hair, and he sported a long tail.

Next to the drawing was another notation in the same minute handwriting and same pale ochre ink, but this one was slightly more legible. I read it out loud.

" 'To call upon a ghost, stand in the front of a tomb and call out loud the names of the angels of the first camp, holding in your hand a glass bowl of pure honey mixed with the oil of almond and say: I command you, O Spirit, Ram-bearer dweller of the graves, who sleeps upon the bones of the dead . . .' "

Beside me, Julien Duplessi did not take even one breath until I stopped.

"What kind of book is this?" I asked.

"Have you ever heard of a grimoire?" He answered with another question and with what I thought was a touch of dread in his voice.

Chapter 18

From the back of the carriage, it seemed my grandmother and I had left France and traveled to some other country. Haussmann's remolding of Paris had not extended to the ghetto in the Marais. The cobble streets were narrow, the buildings ancient. Signs in Hebrew identified the various shops. The setting sun glinted off mezuzahs nailed to door frames as if the houses were all catching fire.

Beside me, my grandmother seemed restless, no doubt due to the words we'd exchanged when I'd returned home earlier that afternoon. If she had noticed that I'd not slept in the apartment, she didn't refer to it, but she did sniff the air when I came in. Her nose wrinkled as if she smelled cow dung. She told me I stunk of oil paints and requested I bathe since I was to accompany her to dinner at her cousin the rabbi's house.

"It would be appropriate to wear your new bottle-green satin gown," she'd said. One of the dresses Grand-mère's dressmaker had created for me, it was fancier than my clothes from New York, with its black bows and black lace edging. The accompanying small hat, in the new style so many Parisian women were wearing that season, sported two tiny bunches of velvet grapes, one in green, the other dark purple.

Was she telling me which dress to put on to ensure I didn't wear my art student's costume? I didn't argue—it didn't matter. I'd been too preoccupied with what Julien and I had found to care. Looking back, I think that must have been why I even agreed to accompany her. The discovery of the book in the tower had shocked me. Disturbed me. And confused me.

A grimoire, Julien had explained, was a book of spells. He'd designed a special cabinet for them in Dujols's shop. And knowing that finding one would exacerbate my interest in the strange occurrences happening around me, he wasn't pleased with the discovery.

The grimoire I'd found was handwritten in the margins of a printed book by an entirely different author.

Some of the grimoires Dujols owned, Julien explained, contained remedies for various ailments, charms for manipulating nature and man, rituals for making pacts with the devil, incantations for summoning good or evil—or, like the spell I'd been able to read in the book in the tower, for summoning a ghost.

Dressing up that evening had actually been a pleasant diversion. Luxuriating in a bath of steaming perfumed water, I'd soaped my arms, my legs, my torso, my breasts . . . running my hands over my body, touching all the places Julien had touched and made toll like the bells.

Amazing, how his fingers had the power to inflame me so profoundly. When I touched myself, it took more work and concentration to induce the same feelings. But they did eventually rise to the surface. In this new life I was leading, painting and passion seemed to be going hand in hand. And what a feeling of power they gave me. I was finally becoming the woman who my father had always seemed to believe was inside. I even imagined that he had, in some subtle way, been grooming me for this very life by including me on all the excursions we took together, all the books that he gave me to read.

"My job is to protect you, and I will do that till my dying day. But I am not sure that protecting you will allow you to reach your fullest potential," he'd once told me.

And he was right. I knew I was finally reaching that potential. Knew, too, that he would be proud when I joined the ranks of women painters like Mary Cassatt and Berthe Morisot and my canvases sold in galleries alongside theirs.

But I wouldn't be painting boring mothers whose breasts were full of milk or sniveling children in their pink and pretty clothes. I would be illuminating mysterious and difficult tales from history. Of murder and mayhem, of jealousy and revenge and pain. Spinning stories from pigment so I could warn man of the darkness that hides in every shadow, crack, and corner and that must be respected.

Where were these thoughts coming from? Even there in the bath as they occurred to me, they excited me and my fingers itched to leave, to go back to the bell tower and paint, paint, paint.

"We've arrived," my grandmother said as the carriage pulled up in front of a tall, skinny house sandwiched in between a temple on one side and a Judaic store on the other. Its window was filled with books, cloths, and religious objects, the setting sun's reflection turning the silver candlesticks, menorahs, and goblets to burning embers.

"I thought Jacob's home was next to his synagogue on rue Buffault? Where are we?"

"The funeral was held at that shul there because this one could never fit all the mourners. But here on the rue des Rosiers is where the rabbis in your family have lived and served for over two hundred years."

"Rabbis and courtesans." I laughed. "What an auspicious heritage. Throw in some murderers, and we'd have a perfect novel."

"Show some respect," my grandmother admonished. "And don't arch your eyebrows when I say something."

"You usually have a better sense of humor," I said.

She ignored me and got out of the carriage.

Inside the house Cousin Jacob's wife, Sophia, greeted us warmly, and she and my grandmother chatted as she ushered us into the parlor.

"I'll tell Jacob that you are here. He's in his office, studying. Always studying," she said, and left to get him.

The modest parlor was tidy but overflowing with books: piled on the floor, sitting on chairs, stacked on occasional tables. From where I sat, I could glimpse into the dining room, which was similarly crowded. Clearly my cousin's studies had taken over not just his time but also their living quarters. His wife's attempts with vases of flowers and velvet cushions only went so far in keeping the house looking like a home.

"Eva, Sandrine, welcome," Cousin Jacob said as he entered the room with open arms. First he went to my grandmother and kissed both her cheeks, and then he embraced me.

"Sit, sit." He gestured to where we'd been seated. "I'm so pleased to have you both here."

I sat back down on a different spot and felt something shift beneath me. The horsehair couch was lumpy. The velvet was slightly worn, too. With Jacob came the unpleasant odor of cheap tobacco. My sense of smell was more attenuated lately, and it wasn't always enjoyable to experience the nuances in the air. I suspected it had been brought about because of the oil paints. Or perhaps the turpentine was making me more sensitive.

Suddenly, for no apparent reason, I felt trapped. My cousin's face, which before I had thought kindly, now looked sinister. His eyes were too small. His grin too miserly.

Under Moreau's influence, I had become deft at studying people's faces and seeing what was unique and intriguing in each one.

"Look deeply at everyone and everything if you want to find the magic and mystique of life, the life you want to commit to canvas," Moreau had said to me that very week.

Looking at Jacob Richter, I saw a threat.

"Would you like some wine, Eva?" he asked.

My grandmother said she would. He asked me, and I said yes also.

At the sideboard, he filled up three glasses from a decanter.

After handing us our wine, he toasted. "*L'chaim*," he said, and held up his glass. The gas lamp's glow caught in the crystal cuts, sparkling with what seemed to be abandon. As if the goblet delighted in being so wicked here in the house of a man of God. The thought made me smile.

"What is it, Sandrine?" my grandmother asked. "Something amusing?"

I shook my head and sipped my wine. It was a

fine Bordeaux, and I took several sips in a row. A few minutes passed in idle chitchat about various members of the family, and then we were joined by another man, whom Jacob introduced as Emanuel Zeller, his assistant rabbi.

Zeller took my grandmother's hand, bent over it, and then did the same to me. His lips were warm, and when he looked up at me, I noticed how light green his eyes were. I had three thoughts simultaneously—that he was quite attractive, that I should like to see him naked, and that I should leave the Richter household immediately. Just stand up and walk out and away from this street and this section of Paris and never come back.

I forced myself to make conversation to chase away my overwhelming desire to run.

"Are you from Paris?" I asked Rabbi Zeller.

"Not originally, no, from Lyon," he said. "But I've been here working with Rabbi Richter for ten years now."

"And you came to Paris with your wife?" I leaned toward him. "Or do you not yet have a wife?"

From the corner of my eye, I saw my grandmother frown. Why? I was simply making small talk and being friendly.

"I do have a wife, but I met her here. We've only recently been married." The rabbi smiled.

"How do you find Paris as a newlywed? Isn't it a bit too tempting?"

Cousin Jacob interrupted. "Excuse me." He cleared his throat. "I think now would be an appropriate moment to show you both something." He nodded to my grandmother and myself. "Don't you think, Rabbi Zeller?"

"I do," the younger man said.

Jacob stood and gestured to the parlor door. "This way."

We followed him out of the room and down a hallway filled with bookshelves. The musty smell nauseated me. At the end we went through a door and down a flight of whitewashed stone steps. At the bottom, cold air accosted us as we entered what appeared to be a storage cellar crowded with stacked crates and trunks. On the other side of the room was yet one more door. This one oddly ornate for being underground in a storeroom.

"Here we are," Cousin Jacob said as he opened it.

I stepped into a beautiful, pale aqua and turquoise tiled chamber lit by what seemed to be hundreds of candelabras. The ceiling and floor were covered by mosaics in a rainbow of underwater hues. In the center, a square pool of water glinted in the low lights. The air was warmer, damp, and perfumed with incense.

A mosaic mural decorated the walls. Depicting an oasis in the desert, it featured swaying palm and date trees.

Framing the top edge were Hebraic letters.

העולם אשר קדשנו במצותיו וצונ על הטבילה
ברוך אתה יי אלהינו מלך

Not having been taught the language, I didn't attempt to read them. But impossibly, I knew what they said.

> Blessed are You, God, Majestic Spirit of the Universe, Who makes us holy by embracing us in living waters.

"Where exactly are we?" I asked.

"In the basement of our temple," Cousin Jacob explained as he lit more of the candelabras. "This is the sacred mikvah, a holy and ancient part of our faith where we purify and cleanse ourselves. When a person immerses herself fully in this sacred water, she is on the path to rectifying blemishes to the soul."

I walked around the pool. I noticed a small hole about the size of a lemon on one wall, and on the opposite was what looked like a removable cover. The candlelight reflected off the surface, sparkling like diamonds. It all seemed familiar except I didn't have any memory of seeing anything like this before.

Had my father shown me a similar room in an ancient temple we'd visited on our travels? In Venice when we'd gone to see the Jewish Quarter?

"Sandrine," Cousin Jacob said, interrupting my reverie, "we—your grandmother, Rabbi Zeller and I—want to help you."

Something *was* amiss. I should have fled before when it was possible. There was danger down here for me.

I backed up, away from the pool. I turned, looking for the door. But all the walls were tiled. I couldn't make out the exit. It had to be there. We'd come in through a door. But now it was hidden.

"Your grandmother believes, as do I," Cousin Jacob continued, "that you could benefit greatly from a purification."

I wrapped my arms around my chest and shook my head. I felt as if they were coming for me, as if I were about to be attacked. "No," I said. "I'm not religious. It won't work on me."

"God knows you are a Jew and a member of the tribe of Israel."

"But what do I need to be purified of? I don't understand." I looked from Cousin Jacob to my grandmother, who was standing beside him. She was hard as nails, a businesswoman, in charge, and yet for the last two days, when she had regarded me, it was with fear and trepidation, as if I were a rabid dog that had trapped her in a small room. I saw that fear there now, even more strongly.

"When your father talked to you about the

Kabala, did he tell you about spirits that enter into a susceptible person's soul, their very being, and take over?" Cousin Jacob asked.

"Dybbukim. Yes. What of them? They're just ancient folklore . . . metaphors for immorality."

"We take the holy and mystical books more seriously than that, Sandrine. We believe in these malicious sprits. They are the dislocated souls of the dead, and they can prey on a susceptible person, eventually possessing them and causing them to act on the dead person's behalf. When we met at the funeral, I sensed that such a creature may be preying on you."

"You think that I . . ." I was so stunned I didn't even know the words to use. I turned to my grandmother. "And you believe this nonsense?"

I needn't have asked; I could see it so clearly in her eyes.

"Yes, I believe you might be possessed by a demon—" she said.

I burst out laughing. "This is preposterous."

Without my noticing, while I'd been questioning my grandmother, the two men had closed in on me. The young handsome rabbi and my cousin had moved so close I could smell their stale body odor and garlicky breath.

"You planned this?" I shouted at my grand-mother. "There never was an invitation to dinner. That was a ruse to get me here so you could"—I waved my arms—"enact some ridiculous ritual and cleanse me? Because I'm painting? Because I'm becoming an artist?"

"You aren't yourself, Sandrine," my grandmother said.

"You haven't seen me in years. How do you know who I am?"

"You're brazen and brash and rude and willful."

"That's who I am now. My brute of a husband cheated my father out of his pride and his fortune. My father killed himself. I've changed, of course, but . . ."

"No. One woman arrived in Paris. She was sad and mournful but very much my Sandrine, my granddaughter. But in these weeks you've changed in ways that cannot be explained in any other way than possession. You are Sandrine with another inside of you. It's happened before in our family. There are legends. For generations, certain daughters . . . the susceptible ones who are yearning for love . . . who are capable of love, have been thus afflicted. There's the painting, too. It's a sure sign. That's what she lived for. To love and to paint. That's what she's been waiting for, to find the right host to allow her to do just that, to—"

"This is utter nonsense," I interrupted. "I am myself and no one else, and you are delusional." I smiled at her sadly. "This is so far-fetched. I'm sorry I shocked you with my new outfit, but that's all it is. Let's go home, Grand-mère."

Tears filled her eyes, and I saw her soften. But only for a moment. "No, Sandrine. I know the signs. The painting—"

"I've always loved art."

"La Lune was a painter. A great courtesan. An artist. But she was also a—"

I cut her off again. Whatever she was going to say, I didn't want to hear it. Not here. Not uttered as a curse. "This is absurd."

Cousin Jacob sounded impatient. "If it is absurd, then you cannot object to granting your grand-mother her wish."

"If it's absurd, then I don't have to grant her anything."

But neither Cousin Jacob nor Rabbi Zeller heeded me as they closed their eyes and began their ritual.

"*Baruch ata adonai eloheinu melech ha-olam asher kid-shanu bi-tevilah b'mayyim hayyim . . .*" both men intoned.

I ran from them and my grandmother and over to where, from slight deviations in the mosaics, I was sure the door was. And yes, there was a small recess, and in it was a silver knob.

I turned it, but it was locked.

Panic began to course through me. What were they going to do to me? Would I no longer be able to paint? Would Julien still want to lay with me? That was all that mattered to me, painting and Julien, my whole world.

I had to escape, but how? I turned around. The room felt smaller, and the two rabbis seemed to have grown in stature during my effort to leave. They both appeared taller, broader, more menacing.

Cousin Jacob took a bottle out of the pocket in his jacket. It was smaller than a wine bottle, made of ruby glass, with an elaborate silver overlay on it that glowed in the candlelight. A cork hung from its long neck on a silken cord and rested on its round belly.

The rabbis were still chanting, ceaselessly. My grandmother was standing against the wall, her hand up to her mouth, terror shining in her eyes.

"What are you going to do to me?"

"There is nothing to be afraid of," Cousin Jacob said as he and Zeller approached. "We are not going to hurt you, but here, in this sacred space, the demon is susceptible. So we're going to coax her out of you and trap her." He held up the bottle. "We are going to free you from her."

"There is no demon!" I looked from them back to my grandmother. "Why are you doing this to me?"

"To save you." Her voice was hoarse but strong.

"There is nothing to be afraid of, Sandrine," Cousin Jacob said. "This will all be easier if you go behind that curtain and take off your dress and put on the robe you will find. We want you to be able to go home in dry clothes."

"I will do nothing to aid you in this mockery."

"Sandrine, please," my grandmother pleaded.

"No. This is absurd. A theatrical stunt. How much are you paying these men?"

"Nothing."

"Sandrine," Cousin Jacob said, "we are men of God trying to restore goodness to your soul."

"Yes, I have changed since I've come to Paris," I began begging my grandmother, but included Cousin Jacob in my glance. "But it's been a wonderful change. I've found myself. I am stronger than I have ever been. I am painting, and I'm good at it. I have goals and desires. That's a positive change. Not something to be afraid of."

And, I thought to myself, after so long of thinking I was frozen, I've found Julien and discovered passion . . . scarlet-black feelings pulsing inside of me.

"I won't give up who I am." I crossed my arms on my chest. If they wanted me to go into that pool, they would have to undress me and take me themselves. And as if by some prearrangement they each stepped closer and took one of my arms in a tight grip.

I tried to fight, but there was nothing I could do. They jerked and yanked me toward the pool. I tried to kick, to hurt them so they would let me go, but if I was causing any pain, they ignored it.

"Put me down."

"Sandrine, don't fight them. Do what they suggest," my grandmother cried.

But I kept fighting. For my paintings. For my lover. For myself. Leaning in, I bit Cousin Jacob on the ear. He flinched when my teeth sunk into his flesh. As he moaned, I kicked Rabbi Zeller in the groin. He shouted out as he doubled over. That was my moment. I wrested free only for a second before both of them recovered fast enough to grab me before I got away. Despite all my efforts and all my energy, I was no match for two strong men who, with their fingers squeezing my arms, dragged me into the pool. Within seconds, I found myself standing in icy water up to my thighs. My shoes, my dress, my petticoats soaking, I began to shiver.

Wasting no time, the two rabbis began to pray, a mesmerizing chanting that, despite my efforts to withstand its pull, lulled me with its rhythms.

I had read about mesmerism. Hypnotizing someone into a deep state of relaxation during which time they were susceptible to suggestions was popular as a medicinal treatment. I was certain that's what the rabbis were doing to me, and I could not allow it. But no matter how hard I tried to block out the sound of their voices and concentrate on something else, I couldn't. Their sacred lullaby was softening my resolve. I slipped into a state somewhere between sleep and restfulness and awareness all at the same time.

As the prayers continued, a shaking and tingling took over my body, and then I experienced a bizarre sensation I can only describe as a sexual release, akin to what I'd experienced with Julien, but this was painful, where that had been pleasurable. Like magnets they were drawing this release from me, from between my legs, from inside my womb. It was ragged and ripped. I looked down and saw I was dripping blood into the water.

Cousin Jacob had not lied. All this was happening without either of them touching me there. The power of their voices raised in prayer were doing it.

I felt lighter, as if I were becoming less. As if I were becoming weaker. My senses dulled, too. The room lost some of its shimmer. The blue and green tiles were less intense. The scents faded. A sense of loss and immediate longing took hold of me.

"I have her," Cousin Jacob shouted in triumph, and fumbled, shoving the cork into the bottle.

Zeller lessened his grip and placed an arm around my shoulders.

My grandmother stood nervously at the edge of the pool. "She's bleeding. What is going on? Is she all right? Sandrine, are you all right?"

But I wasn't. I was crying, and I couldn't respond.

"She is fine," Rabbi Zeller answered for me.

But I wasn't. I wanted the colors and the smells and the power and the feelings back.

"Something is wrong here," Cousin Jacob complained as he struggled to fit the cork farther into the neck of the bottle.

Zeller left my side to see what the trouble was.

For the moment no one was focused on me. This was my chance. Despite my heavy, waterlogged dress, despite losing blood and feeling weak, I lunged forward, grabbed the cork, and wrenched it from Cousin Jacob's hand. Instantly I felt a surge of energy. I knew the bleeding had stopped.

I laughed with delight. They could not change me. Even with all their prayers, they could not separate us.

"What's happened?" my grandmother asked nervously.

"Zeller, I've lost it," Cousin Jacob lamented.

"She pulled the cork," Zeller said over and over.

They were all talking on top of one another in a panicked response. I didn't care what they were saying. I was myself again.

Then . . . What was that? More chanting? I put my hands up to my ears to try and drown out the seductive sounds. As long as I didn't listen, I would stay in control. I tried to climb up the steps, but both rabbis, anticipating my move, blocked me.

Zeller positioned himself at my back, took hold

of both my arms, pulled them behind me, and held on while Cousin Jacob pushed the bottle close to my chest.

With one of them in front and the other behind me, the sound of their singsong prayer surrounded me, and despite all my efforts, for the second time, I fell victim to their ministrations, not strong enough to fight their devout entreaties. And once again, though this time with less elation and more trepidation, Cousin Jacob announced he had captured the spirit, and I was left feeling drained of my life force.

"Thank God," my grandmother uttered as Cousin Jacob very cautiously and carefully corked the bottle.

Rabbi Zeller offered to help me out of the pool. I had so little energy left that I accepted his arm and emerged, my skirts dripping, my shoes squishing.

Holding the glass bottle tightly, Cousin Jacob followed. I watched him as he stepped out of the pool, and I noticed that his hand holding the vessel was trembling. At first it was slight, but it became more and more exaggerated.

"Help me, Zeller," Cousin Jacob cried.

Rabbi Zeller ran to his side and tried to take the bottle and help Cousin Jacob at the same time.

"Arghh!" Zeller screamed.

He'd burned his hands touching the container. As he let go, I could see his palms were scarlet.

My grandmother and I watched as the bottle began to vibrate even more violently, dancing in Cousin Jacob's hands. He pulled it closer to his chest, trying to protect it, but the effort appeared too great for him. He broke out in a sweat, beads of moisture forming on his forehead and dripping down his face. His skin turned ashen. He bit through his lip, and a trail of blood marked his chin.

"Release the bottle, the pain will stop," I shouted, not even wondering how I knew, but certain I was right.

Cousin Jacob shook his head. His eyes bored into mine. "I cannot. For your soul's sake, I cannot."

He was in terrible pain now. Tears streamed from his eyes.

The glass glowed brighter, generating a red-tinged aura around the rabbi. Suddenly Cousin Jacob shrieked and let go as he grabbed his chest. From the expression on his face and the sound issuing from his lips, the pain must have been excruciating.

The bottle fell to the tile floor and smashed inside its overlay. Fragments sent rays of the ruby light all around the room, bathing us in its bloody glow while we all watched, helpless, as Cousin Jacob clutched his chest, his heart.

I should have felt remorse. But powers were surging through me again, reuniting with my senses. I saw not the body on the ground but the droplets of water shimmering like diamonds, the otherworldly light shimmering. I smelled not death but the resinous perfume of burning incense. I felt not fear but great strength.

Chapter 19

The night that Cousin Jacob died lasted longer than any I could remember.

My grandmother and I had returned by carriage to the apartment on rue des Saints-Pères. We did not talk in the ride. Grand-mère wept quietly, steadily.

I kept rubbing my wrists, which were red and raw from where the rabbis had tried to hold me. The pain kept me centered there in the carriage; I could focus on it because I could not process what had happened.

A man, a holy man, my blood relation, had just had a heart attack and died. He had died in front of me while he was trying to help me. Could anything be more terrible to witness? To be part of? And yet somewhere inside of me, it was also a relief. How could that be?

I felt terrible for my grandmother's loss and at the same time was furious with her. I didn't understand the conflicting feelings within myself and didn't know how to reconcile them.

As soon as we entered the apartment, she went to the salon, poured herself a large glass of cognac, and took a long sip. I'd followed her, and she turned to me then.

"Do you know what you did?" she asked in a shaking voice.

"I didn't do anything. I couldn't have." I didn't feel as sure as I sounded. Had I somehow been responsible in some way?

"You fought him. What is inside of you fought him."

"You sound crazy," I said. "There is nothing inside of me." Even to me, my voice did not sound certain.

She shook her head, as if refusing to believe what she was hearing, and in a quivering voice told me to be ready by ten in the morning, that I would be attending services with her. And then she told me to go to my room.

In the Jewish religion, we don't wait to bury our dead. The funeral is the day after the death unless that day is the Sabbath. The tragedy at the mikvah had occurred on a Thursday, so the funeral of Rabbi Jacob Richter would take place the next morning.

I didn't want to go back to the cemetery. I was scared of what I would see. I was apprehensive of how my grandmother would treat me. I didn't want to miss a day of painting, but my grandmother was distraught, and I didn't want to upset her even more. I cared about her and was worried for her. She was paler and more fragile than I had ever seen her. There was no way I could get out of attending services without causing a scene, and for Grand-mère's sake I decided to just do what she'd asked.

On Friday morning, dressed and ready in a black dress and small black hat, I waited for my grandmother in the front parlor.

When she came in, she looked me over appraisingly. Like me she wore black, a lace-and-taffeta effort that revealed less of her ample bosom than usual, as was appropriate for the occasion. It was, in fact, the same dress she'd worn to the funeral we'd attended only two weeks before.

"I think you should wear your other black hat. The larger one with the veil. And keep the veil down," Grand-mère said.

"I prefer this."

She shook her head. "Sandrine, it's too provocative. You look like a flirt."

"You would know."

She retreated a bit, as if stung by a blow. "Please change the hat, and also please take off that necklace you insist on wearing all the time. It's not appropriate."

My hand went to my throat to touch the ruby flower garland. I liked how it felt enclosing my neck, and I didn't want to take it off. And yet part of me wanted to please her. I knew she was highly distressed, and I loved her.

"I think this hat is fine."

She reached out, grabbed the hat, and pulled it off my head. The comb holding it down scratched my scalp. While I rubbed the scraped spot, my grandmother ripped my hat apart, threw it on the floor, and stomped on it till it was a misshapen mess.

"Now," she said, "please put on the larger hat with the veil."

Upstairs in my bedroom, I opened the armoire and pulled out the more sedate hat that my grandmother had requested I wear. Then, looking in the mirror, I attended to the damage she'd done to my hair. I could still feel the tenderness of my scalp when my brush touched it.

I had just lifted the netted and plumed confection to my head when, in the mirror, I saw my grandmother at the door.

"What is it?" I turned just in time to watch her slam the door shut. And before I could take a step, I heard the key turn in the lock.

"Grand-mère?" Running to the door, I tried the knob even though I guessed that it wouldn't turn. "What are you doing? Let me out," I shouted through the wooden door that separated us.

"I don't think it's wise for you to come with me after all. I am going to the funeral and then am going to meet with Zeller and the other rabbis about what to do next. The exorcism failed, but we can't give up. You aren't capable of protecting yourself, so I need to protect you. Sandrine, you are all I have left of your father. Even though he thought he was performing the ceremony according to strict Hebrew law, perhaps Cousin Jacob failed to follow some aspect of the procedure. We have to repeat it. I have to find the right men to try again."

"There is nothing to exorcise. You are wrong about me." I pounded on the door, my rage growing with every strike. "You can't keep me locked up like some child!"

"Not like a child, Sandrine. Children are not inherently evil. But the spirit that is possessing you is and always has been."

I heard her skirts rustling as she walked away from the door, leaving me locked in my bedroom.

Rushing to the window, I unlatched it, grasped the frame, and yanked the window open. I would jump. Then I looked down. I couldn't. We were too high. Shouting for help was pointless, too. My room faced the inner courtyard, and the only people who could hear me were the maid and the cook inside our apartment. But perhaps . . . Was it possible? Would my voice carry?

"I need help," I shouted. "I am being held against my will!" My voice echoed off of our own four walls. Even if someone on the street heard my cries, they wouldn't have any clue where they emanated from.

I ran to my locked door and hollered for the housekeeper till my voice was hoarse. She never came. Of course she wouldn't. My grandmother had obviously given her instructions to stay away from my room. And besides, Grand-mère had most probably taken the key.

I collapsed onto my bed. Trapped like an animal. And why? I had not done anything. Cousin Jacob had been sick. That he chose that moment to succumb to his illness was no more my fault than the appearance of the stars at night.

For about a half hour I lay atop the coverlet and felt sorry for myself and fury at my grandmother. I would not be jailed like this. I would take revenge. When she returned, I would leave her, and she'd be sorry. She herself had said I was all that was left. Her only immediate family.

I wouldn't have to bother with a hotel or finding any other place to live. I'd move into the bell tower. I'd get Julien to block it off when he turned the rest of the Maison de la Lune into a museum. He could build me a secret entrance. No one would ever discover me there. Or perhaps I could entice or convince him to break off his engagement and we could live there together. Charlotte and Julien had been affianced before he met me, before he knew that someone could touch his soul. Surely he could not marry her now that we had met.

I was growing bored sitting in the simple room, concocting fantasies about the future.

There was nothing to watch out the windows, and the room offered little distraction. Oh, it was lovely enough, with pale yellow curtains that puddled on the mustard-and-lavender rug and even paler yellow walls trimmed with lavender molding. There were half a dozen prints of various purple flowers framed in gold and hanging on the walls.

Unlike the opulent and fantastical rooms in La Lune, this bedroom was certainly not decorated by my grandmother, but rather by whomever she was renting from. Grand-mère's style was nowhere to be seen.

I already had read the one book in the room, the one I'd brought from home, *The Picture of Dorian Gray*. There were dozens of novels downstairs in the library, but they were out of my reach now. I picked up the Oscar Wilde novel and started to reread it:

> The studio was filled with the rich odor of roses, and when the light summer wind stirred amidst the trees of the garden, there came through the open door the heavy scent of the lilac, or the more delicate perfume of the pink-flowering thorn.

After three chapters, I couldn't keep reading. My father's annotations were like little stabs, and I closed the slim volume. I tried to sleep but was too worked up.

I needed to do something or I might go mad.

That's when I thought of my paints. I pulled the box out from under the bed. Just touching the fine wooden case that I'd bought from Sennelier began to soothe me.

Opening it, I caressed the brushes. Moreau had drummed it into us that we must be rigorous in cleaning our supplies. He said if we showed them respect they would be more willing to do our bidding. My brushes were pristine. My tubes of color were squeezed only from the bottom up. My palette was wiped clean every night.

The siren call of the brushes and the paints was undeniable. I longed for the state of bliss that always settled on me as I swirled the silken colors into one another and dabbed them on the canvas.

I knew I would be fine if I could just paint the hours away, but I had no canvas with me. I looked around the room. Was there anything I could use? No, nothing.

Except . . .

I undressed, since I was used to painting either in my masculine garb in public or wearing nothing but my shift over my naked body when I was in the bell tower. Corsets and stays and petticoats hampered my movements.

Stripped down, I threw on my silk robe, not even bothering to fasten it. Next I removed all the prints from the walls so that I had large, empty surfaces. Then I prepared my palette. Holding it in my right hand, I picked up a brush in my left.

With so much space, my mind was as unencumbered as my body, and I began to paint. I wasn't conscious of making up the story I painted. Rather the story seemed to be whispering to me, begging me to give it life. To commit it to form and figure, color and shadow.

The mural told a saga worthy of an opera, but it was not written by some Italian master. It was a drama worthy of being enacted on the stage but was not a play penned by Molière. No, this was the true and actual story of the making of La Lune. The tale of how my ancestor came to be who she was.

In the first panel, she was a young courtesan entertaining a string of lovers. Lounging on an opulent scarlet velvet daybed, she looked not at the men awaiting her attention but out at me with a challenging expression. We shared fiery reddish-brown hair and almond-shaped topaz eyes. Her mouth was more petulant than mine, and her full lips a darker cranberry.

Like a ripe piece of fruit, she looked ready for the picking.

Outside the door to her bedroom were three older men dressed in bejeweled silks and satins and a fourth, a younger man, dressed in simpler clothes.

In the next four scenes, each man presented her with a gift: the first, six strands of fat pearls; the next, an overflowing casket of gold chains; and the third, an ebony box brimming with diamonds, one having fallen at her feet, glinting in the candlelight.

In the last scene in this sequence the younger man knelt at her feet, holding out a bunch of paintbrushes, like flowers. Her hand was reaching out, about to accept his offering.

This was the man she had chosen. On his jacket was the clue to his identity: a pair of intertwined *C*s embroidered in gold on brown velvet. This was Cherubino Cellini, the great Italian painter whose work hung in museums all over the world, who had met La Lune and asked her to be his muse.

Everything about his face and body and the way he carried himself was sensual. I remembered the feelings I had as I painted his coarse black curls and his bony nose and the scars on his face and hands, and I felt surges of desire that made me want to put down my brushes and touch myself.

I fought the urges and continued painting instead, illustrating the tale of the young woman who accepted Cherubino Cellini, not because he was the wealthiest of those who came to call but because he offered her the one thing the others could not: Access to the world that she wished to belong to. The world forbidden to women. The world of artists.

Cherubino was in Paris on a commission from King Henry to paint a series of frescoes in the

Louvre, and in his search for a model for his Virgin of the Rocks, he visited La Lune. All through art history, prostitutes had modeled for artists and wound up as Virgins and saints. La Lune was not the first and would not be the last woman to pose as the mother of Christ. But she was one of the most provocative.

Initially it was a business arrangement between La Lune and Cherubino. She modeled for him, and he paid her by teaching her to draw. He started with simple things. A wooden cube. An egg. It was difficult because she was impatient and not a good student.

He was falling in love with his paintings of her, and she was falling in love with learning to sketch, but they were not yet lovers.

Once the king saw the first fresco featuring La Lune, he insisted on meeting her and found her so fetching, he took her as his paramour. For her ministrations he bestowed so many gifts on her that she didn't have to take other men to her bed. Not then or for the rest of her life.

In addition to all the jewels he bestowed on her, the king gave La Lune a plot of land that sat between rue des Saints-Pères and rue du Dragon. Once a church had occupied the spot, but now there was a fine house in only slight disrepair that was connected to an abandoned bell tower. She hired an architect to help her restore what would become Maison de la Lune.

Cherubino painted La Lune more than twenty times for the king during the next year, and for every sitting, she received a drawing lesson. That was all.

And then came the day that changed their relationship, when Cherubino walked in on La Lune, who was in her bed, servicing the king.

Cherubino's jealousy was a wild and living force. It took him by surprise and left him defenseless. Soon his paintings of her showed her in suggestive poses. No longer a Madonna or saint, she was now a seductress. Cherubino left one out to dry, and that night the king discovered the erotic painting and, without asking, took it for himself.

When Cherubino found out, he went mad. Screaming and shouting, he demanded that La Lune ask for it back. It was not hers to give away. When she refused, saying she could never ask that of the king, Cherubino stormed out of her rooms and didn't return for days.

After a week without him coming around, La Lune was bereft. Her education was incomplete. She hadn't mastered spatial relationships. She didn't understand perspective. She needed him back.

So La Lune told the king that Cherubino had been approached by the duke of Milan to paint her for his palace and that Cherubino was considering leaving the French court.

It was a lie, of course. But she needed to do

something to force the king into action. She'd correctly guessed that the idea of her face and her body gracing some other royal chamber would disturb him.

The next day Cherubino returned, saying that the king had commissioned a second set of paintings, but only if La Lune was the model. So relieved that he'd returned, La Lune threw her arms around him and kissed him.

Until they touched that first time, neither of them had known they desired each other. La Lune believed she only craved art lessons. Cherubino believed he only wanted a muse.

In a fever, I painted them that afternoon consummating their affair. In one panel La Lune lay under Cherubino's body as he thrust into her and she received him with delight. In another she hovered above him, her breasts grazing his cheeks. I painted him kissing the lips on her face and those between her legs. I painted her wanton expression. The sweat on his forehead. The single bright drop of blood on her lower lip from when she bit herself as she exploded with him inside of her. In my mural were sexual positions I had never known about—never experienced with my husband, nor with Julien.

In my delirium, I not only saw the lovers; I heard what they said, too. Cherubino promised that these embraces were for her alone and that these intimacies would bind them together forever.

Her poses for his private paintings became more lewd. He positioned her with her legs spread and her hand touching her nether parts. He painted her bathed in sweat and writhing with passion. When she saw how provocative the paintings were, how much of her soul he'd captured, she made him promise never to show them to anyone.

"No one will ever see them," he swore. "They are for our own gallery. Just for our pleasure," he told her. "To commemorate for all time the wonder of us."

And it was wondrous. La Lune had taken men to her bed in exchange for payment since she was fourteen years old. She had been well schooled in the art of pleasuring. She knew how to be a lover, a confidante, a model to painters, a muse to poets and writers, and, when necessary, a mother. But she had never craved a man. Never been moved by one.

"I don't just want to know how to draw . . ." she told him one night as they lay in bed, smelling each other's sweat as their skin cooled.

"What do you want?" he asked as he stroked her hair.

She raised up her face and mouthed the words against the pink shell of his ear.

"To learn to paint," she whispered.

"If I teach you, it has to be in secret. Here. Under the stars. With only the bells to know."

"Won't I need a model?"

"I will be your model." He laughed.

Over and over she painted him, laughing with delight as she began to manage his likeness. He would stand behind her and correct her. Sometimes even taking her hand, putting his fingers on hers so she would feel the fluidity of the line, so she could sense how sensuous a movement painting a body should be.

Sometimes when her lover slept, La Lune sketched him, trying to capture the expression on his face while he dreamed. Painting each other was an extension of their lovemaking. They caressed each other all over again with brushes and sensuous oils.

Then came the scene of Cherubino opening a letter with a royal seal. Emperor Rudolf had invited him to Prague, to bring La Lune and create a royal gallery of secret erotic paintings. Gold coins came with the letter, along with a promise of more awaiting them.

It was almost as if the lie La Lune had made up for the king had come true.

"But how did he know about your erotic paintings?" La Lune asked.

"I sent him one as a gift."

"Why would you do that?"

"He is well-known to collect paintings of a suggestive nature. The more explicit and varied, the better. He pays far more for them than your king is paying for my murals."

La Lune hurled her paints at her lover, shouting that he had promised he would never show those paintings to anyone. That he had given her his word.

"So many men have seen you, what does one more matter?" he asked.

She slapped him for insulting her and not understanding, and then collapsed weeping, realizing she had done the unthinkable. Broken the golden rule that her mother had taught her, that her mother before her had taught her: Never fall in love. Do not become vulnerable.

"No man has ever seen me as you have seen me. With emotion on my face!" I was shouting the words. I was feeling the sting of the slap on my fingers. And when Cherubino bent to whisper to her and apologize and cajole her, I felt his lips on my lips, and I felt myself forgive him for what he had done to my ancestor more than three hundred years before.

Chapter 20

My grandmother's scream contained no words. Neither was it the shriek of a woman in pain. It was an inhuman sound containing all that was terrifying about the dark, dreadful about a fire, and sickening about a massacre. The noise made me drop the brush. I saw crimson paint splash on the yellow carpet. I stared at the stranger in front of me.

Unrecognizable in her shock, my grandmother stood in the doorway to my room. Her face contorted with terror while her body spasmed in a series of tics. Her mouth was frozen open, and what emerged was never-ending.

What was wrong?

I turned away from her and looked at what she was staring at. Saw it all as if for the first time. But how was that possible? I must have been the one responsible for the mural. My fingers were paint-stained. I still held the palette. And yet I didn't remember having painted what I saw.

The walls were ablaze with colors. I'd used bold strokes and painted better than I ever had before. As frightened as I was, for a moment I thought of Monsieur Moreau and how proud he would be that I had given voice to what was inside of me. Maybe I could bring him here to show him what I'd done. I was certain he would respond.

But what had I done? How had I done it? Fleeting memories of the last hours came to me as I concentrated. I began to remember how I'd felt while I'd painted, as if I were in the audience watching a drama unfold and simply illustrating the story.

What power had taken over me? From whence came what my brushes had painted? I had no answers but was certain the tale I'd told contained information that was crucial for me to know and understand.

"See, Grand-mère." I pointed to the walls. "I found our history."

She grimaced. It made me strangely pleased that I was causing her some distress. She had held this story back from me. She'd been at fault in doing that.

"I didn't need you to tell me after all. Cherubino met La Lune when he came to Paris to paint for the king. They lived in the bell tower that belonged to a church on rue du Dragon, and that's part of your house."

"But how did you learn all of this?" She was staring at the walls.

"He came to the salon, a painter from Italy, looking for a model and a muse, and he found La Lune," I continued.

My grandmother came to me, took me by both

hands. Her eyes flitted from mine to the ruby necklace around my neck and then back to my eyes.

"You don't know what you are opening yourself up to, Sandrine. Please let me help you. Take off the necklace." Her voice was anxious and hoarse from the scream.

I wrangled out of her grip, put my hands up to my neck reflexively, and protected my treasure.

She pried my fingers away and grabbed for the necklace.

I jerked back and moved away from her before she could touch me. "Leave it alone."

She came after me. My beautiful grandmother who entertained dukes and counts and Paris's elite looked half mad as she lurched at me and the necklace, preparing to rip it off my neck. Maybe I should take it off? Maybe she knew something I didn't? I reached up to help her. Found the clasp.

Suddenly, sickening nausea overwhelmed me. I wanted desperately to throw up, to get rid of something poisonous inside of me.

My grandmother was still pulling. The necklace dug even deeper into my flesh—it was choking me, it was going to break apart, it had to, it couldn't hold under all her pressure—but miraculously, the necklace remained intact.

The nausea came again. I started to cry. Part of me wanted to take the necklace off for my grandmother's sake, but instead I pried her fingers away and pushed her.

I watched her stumble and fall backward, landing in a heap on the floor. She only missed hitting her head on a chair by fractions of an inch.

What had I done? Why had I done it? I had shoved my grandmother. Almost hurt her. With shaking fingers I pulled my robe tight and tied it so my neck was covered, so she couldn't see the rubies.

"What were you doing to me? You could have choked me. What are you trying to stop?"

She was still on the floor, staring up at me. Her fiery hair had started to come undone, and her own necklace was askew, the string of opals half flung over one shoulder. Her eyes blazed.

"You have to let me help you," she pleaded, and gestured to the walls. "You can't have guessed at this story. How did you discover it?"

"It came to me."

"Yes, yes, it did. Don't you understand what that means? Do you think it came unbidden? This should be all the proof you need that you aren't yourself. The witch has taken you over. You need help. This isn't your story, Sandrine. Don't you see?"

"Not my story? Of course it is. Cherubino came to Paris to paint for the king and found the most important muse of his career. Because of him, the king gave her so many jewels and so much land she never had to lay with anyone who didn't please her again. Not the way you do. If they are stinking or fat or ugly, you still have to open your legs for them to keep yourself in style. But not La Lune."

"Stop!" she cried.

"Why? You don't like the truth? You want to pretend that she didn't exist? But she did. And Cherubino did. He chose her for his model, and he taught her to paint. To paint like a man. It was all she'd ever wanted. And when he went to Prague to paint for the emperor, they went together."

My grandmother put her hands over her ears.

"No, you have to listen," I said. "You need to hear all of it. Cherubino fell under Rudolf's spell, or perhaps it was the other way around. But either way La Lune was of little interest to Cherubino any more as a lover. Yes, he still painted her, still needed her to pose for his sensual paintings . . . and she obliged, so he was able to create painting after painting of the most depraved acts. The more disturbing the sex act, the more Rudolf adored the painting. Cherubino posed her with other women, with other men, with several at once in orgies. Using myths, he painted her as Europa with the bull, Leda with the swan . . . He painted her debauched and conquered. And while he painted her, she would look at her lover and long for him to touch her again. To come to her bed. She asked him once why he stayed away, and he

307

turned on her, railing and shouting and asking her if all that he was giving her wasn't enough. She was living in a palace, had no want for anything. There were treasure chests of silks to dress in and expensive jewels to wear.

"But he never admitted the reason he'd left her bed, never told her what she suspected and then finally proved. He never came to her any more because Cherubino had become Rudolf's lover."

My grandmother talked softly as you would to a child. "You have to let me get you help, Sandrine. You desperately need help."

I pushed her arm away. Took her by the wrist and pulled her over to the wall, pointing at the painting. "Why are you afraid of this story? It's our story. Look at her. She'd learned from her mother that pining away for a man, giving your heart to a man, was to invite disaster and risk sorrow. Pain was not for her. No, never. Not for La Lune! Never for La Lune. But there she was in Prague, pining away for Cherubino, and he was lost to her.

"And so she went to the gold maker's lane." I pointed to the next section of the mural on the wall. "You can see it here. A winding road just behind the castle. Here in these eleven small shops all of Emperor Rudolf's alchemists lived and engaged in a darker art than the making of trinkets. Rudolf was convinced that if he brought the finest minds to Prague—mathematicians, astrologers, mystics, scientists—together they would discover the secrets of the universe. These men all engaged in the search for the philosopher's stone, the Elixir of Life, that fabled and elusive preserver of souls. There, on the golden street, magick was for sale. And La Lune had the money to pay for it—"

"Don't you realize that you could not have found this out on your own? There is no way you could have learned this any other way?" my grandmother interrupted.

"La Lune visited the street every day for one month, working with the astrologer's wife, Hertwig, whose magick was rumored to be the strongest of anyone's in the city. First Hertwig made brews to mend La Lune's heart so she would start eating again and regain some of her beauty. Sadness had robbed her of her appetite, and she no longer interested Cherubino even as a model. Too thin, she no longer fit the image of the lusty woman in the paintings."

My grandmother had been standing, but now she sat down on the edge of the bed. She looked pale and pained, and part of me wanted to soothe her, but the other part of me didn't care about anything but the story.

"Hertwig's teas and infusions helped. La Lune's appetite returned and with it the luster to her hair and the glow to her cheeks. Cherubino began to paint her again, but not to make love to her. She was determined to have him back. They had to be as one, the way they had been before they'd come to Prague. And to do that she needed to be more than a moist nest for him when he wanted a female vessel. She had to be irresistible.

"She told Hertwig she would give her anything she wanted if she would just help her win Cherubino back and make him sick at the thought of laying with anyone else, be it woman or man.

"And so began her education. Day after day, when Cherubino was with the emperor, La Lune was with the crone, learning her secrets, memorizing her spells. In exchange Hertwig wanted beautiful things, and La Lune had them to trade. Pearls, emeralds, sapphires. Hertwig's lust for jewels was as strong as La Lune's was for Cherubino. She traded one fortune for another. A lustrous pearl necklace for the secret to making brews that ensured health. A bracelet of moonstones for the spell to fell your enemy. An emerald ring for the spell to make you see in the dark. It was Hertwig who told La Lune about the legend of the rubies. Inside of each one, she said, was a drop of blood that contained the secret to immortality. She showed La Lune her own necklace. Five ruby flowers strung together on a platinum chain with an Ouroboros clasp. She said that each ruby had been made of blood. How she had come to own it, La Lune could guess. Hertwig was a good trader. She had probably sold someone the secret to poisoning an enemy in order to get that necklace.

"And so the time came for La Lune to finally learn how to mix the potion to make Cherubino love her again. First, Hertwig needed items that took weeks to gather. Strands of his hair. Clippings from his fingernails. And six drops of his blood. But how could she draw and collect his blood?

"Hertwig taught her to make a draught to make him sleep more deeply so that while he slumbered she could prick his finger without waking him up and then capture his blood droplets into a glass tube.

"Sitting at Hertwig's hearth, by the fire where the herbs and flowers hung drying, among the bottles of strange, wonderful, and foul-smelling liquids, La Lune took instructions on how to prepare the final brew, the one the old witch promised would return her lover to her."

I was exhausted, but I couldn't stop telling the story. Not yet. Not until I was finished. For the last few minutes my grandmother had not moved, but sat still, frozen, staring at me.

" 'There is so much blood here—perhaps you would like your own ruby necklace,' Hertwig offered. 'Rubies would look good around your neck.'

"La Lune said yes, she would, and Hertwig promised she would have it waiting for her when

311

the brew was ready. In payment, La Lune gave her two goblets made of gold encrusted with pearls that had been left on a tray in Cherubino's room along with an empty bottle of wine.

"A week later Hertwig was waiting with the necklace and a small bottle of a rose-colored liquid.

"La Lune did everything that she had been taught. She poured Cherubino his wine and whispered the spell over it as she dropped in the proper amount of potion. It worked. Cherubino was seeing her anew. He wanted her as he had when they'd first become lovers. And after they were both satiated, he drifted off to sleep. But he did not wake up. He didn't die, but neither was he alive. He remained in that state for days. Rudolf himself came to see Cherubino and sent his own physicians, but nothing could wake the painter.

"Since La Lune had been seen going to Hertwig's shop on the golden lane, she was accused of being in cahoots with the witch and casting a spell on Cherubino, and Rudolf's henchmen imprisoned her.

"While La Lune languished in that chamber of horrors attached to the castle, she could think only of Cherubino. When the inquisitors came and asked what she had done, she didn't know what to say. If she admitted the truth, they could go to Hertwig to try and reverse the spell. Yes, La Lune would burn for being a witch, but

Cherubino would have a chance to survive. If she didn't tell Rudolf's men, no one would be able to ask Hertwig to help, and Cherubino would certainly die.

"Finally La Lune agreed to tell them what she'd done, but only if she could talk to the emperor himself.

"When he arrived, she offered Rudolf a deal. She would tell him what she had done and who could save Cherubino, but only if he would promise not to have her or Hertwig killed. Rudolf acquiesced with the stipulation that La Lune return to France immediately. That very night, before Hertwig could be summoned to brew an antidote, Cherubino died."

Tears dripped down my cheeks. My mind was a jumble of feelings and images and words.

My grandmother's face was a mask of fear. She stood still and frozen to the spot. Then slowly she raised her hand, pointed at the empty space behind me, and shouted into the air: "Get away! Get away from my granddaughter! Get out of my house!"

Her face was florid. Her expression crazed. Who was she screaming at? I turned. There was no one there. I followed her finger. My grandmother was indicating La Lune in the mural.

"She's laughing at me," my grandmother said. "She's laughing at me because I tried to keep you safe. But you had to seek her out. You had to disobey me. Now she has what she wants. You're under her influence, and I don't know how to fight her. I don't . . ." She collapsed on my bed, crying.

My grandmother's shouts had echoed through the house and brought the housekeeper. Together we managed to subdue my grandmother and take her to her own bedroom, where her maid gave her a draught of laudanum to quiet her. We then went to summon the doctor.

By the time the doctor arrived, I had cleaned myself up and redressed, and I met him at the door. I showed him to my grandmother's boudoir, where he spent a half hour with her before coming out to speak to me.

"She is talking about many very strange things, Mademoiselle Verlaine. Can you tell me what happened?"

"Not really, no. She went to a funeral for our cousin Jacob . . . Rabbi Richter, and returned quite disturbed."

"I suggest you keep her sedated for the rest of today and this evening. I'll check in with you tomorrow. She should be better by then."

But when he returned the next day, she wasn't better. And after three days of keeping her quiet and sedated, there was still no progress. In fact, she was becoming even more incoherent.

"She can only talk about her fear that you are being taken over by the moon. Sometimes she says the moon is a ghost, other times a witch. I think a stay in a sanatorium might be our best hope."

I didn't explain. Perhaps I should have, but it wouldn't have helped her.

And so I signed the appropriate papers and sat and waited in the parlor for her maid to dress her and then watched as the doctor escorted my grandmother out. She seemed to leave willingly, but I knew that she was still under the thrall of the drugs and not herself. She didn't even look like herself. My grandmother had aged years in days. Her vibrant red hair looked dull. Her glowing complexion was pasty. Her flaming eyes had lost all their luster.

"I will come and see you tomorrow," I said to her as I kissed her good-bye at the door. I felt both sick and elated, as if I had impossibly succeeded and failed at the same time.

There were tears streaming down her cheeks. Her lips were pale, and there were hollows in her cheeks. Her voice trembled, and she sounded as scared as a child caught up in a nightmare. As she spoke, her eyes widened as if she were seeing the ghost right there in the room beside me.

"Only if you don't bring her with you. If you do, if you bring that creature with you, I won't let you in."

Chapter 21

With my grandmother in the sanatorium, there was no reason for me to remain in the apartment, and I moved into Maison de la Lune on rue des Saints-Pères, bringing the maids and the cook with me. In addition to wanting to be there, I was comforted by the thought that if Benjamin's detectives had discovered the rue de la Chaise apartment and were watching it, this move would throw them off.

It was a bittersweet homecoming because we all were worried about my grandmother. I fervently hoped she would get better quickly so she could join me there. Was sure that once she saw how happy I was at the maison and how glad the house was to have me back, she would stop being so afraid for me.

I painted for hours that first day. While in the studio, brush in hand, brilliant colors swirling, my mind was focused on the canvas, and I felt nothing but joy. But as soon as I left the tower, I was overwhelmed with concern for Grand-mère and haunted by what she'd said about the spirit taking over me.

The only person I could think of talking to who might understand was Julien's client Monsieur Dujols. As a student of the esoteric and occult, surely he would not be surprised by what my grandmother claimed and would be able to explain it to me. Perhaps he would even have some advice.

It took me most of the next day to work up the courage to go to the Librairie du Merveilleux. Even though I knew Julien didn't approve of Dujols's beliefs I wished he were available to go with me. Something about the store and its owner intimidated me, but Julien had gone back to the furniture factory in Nancy, and I was on my own.

Finally, late that afternoon, I walked over to the shop, being careful to make sure no one followed me. I now habitually watched the reflections in store windows, looking for any suspicious behavior of people lagging behind me.

The latest telegram from Mr. Lissauer had reported that Benjamin had fired his first detective agency, hired a new one, and put forward a reward that was more money than most people made in a year.

Since Benjamin was unaware of just how much I knew about his scheming, the size of the offer made sense. He had to be wondering if my father had confided in me and shown me enough incriminating evidence to destroy Benjamin's reputation.

The largesse was also fueled by pride. In disappearing, I'd outsmarted him and Benjamin couldn't abide being shown up. Why wasn't it enough that, without suffering any consequences, he'd driven my father to suicide and taken over the bank, our residences in New York and Newport, and all our valuable collections?

I turned the corner and arrived at my destination. Dujols's store was so dark I thought it was closed and was about to leave when I noticed shadows moving inside. Trying the door, I found it open and entered.

More than a dozen people milled about, and the furniture was arranged with all the chairs in three rows, as if a lecture was about to begin. The air was thick with the scent of heady incense and sweet tobacco. Open bottles of wine and absinthe were lined up on a sideboard.

A petite woman, wearing a dark caftan embroidered with silver symbols like those on the wall, eyed me suspiciously and asked who had brought me. When I said no one, she arched her eyebrows and looked at me askance.

"I wanted to see Monsieur Dujols," I told her.

She nodded and slithered off, going, I hoped, to find the publisher.

"Mademoiselle Sandrine," Dujols greeted me by taking both my hands in his. "How did you know about our lecture? Did Julien tell you? No matter, you're here."

"I didn't know about it. I came to talk to you because—" I broke off, unsure how to broach the subject that was the reason for my visit with so many people around.

"It's all right, Mademoiselle. I know why you came," he said. "There are things happening that you don't understand, and you need help, don't you?"

There was so much sympathy in his voice that my eyes filled with tears. Taking me by the arm, he ushered me into a small alcove.

"How do you know?"

"I'm acquainted with your grandmother. And as you know, your family's legends are familiar to me. I've studied them and researched them. First for her, then for my own edification. I can help you. Explain what is happening to you. I have an idea of what you are suffering. I have some books . . ." He pulled one book and then another off a shelf. "I think if you start by reading these it will give you a foundation. And then we can delve a bit deeper and contact La Lune."

"Contact her?" I felt the now familiar nausea.

"We often have séances here to reach out to spirits beyond our dimension."

"Has my grandmother attended these séances?"

"No, we met privately," he said without further explanation. "Here, take these."

He handed me the two slim volumes. Their leather covers were worn, and they smelled of old paper, musty and waxy. It was a scent that reminded me of my father and our library at home.

A scent that was both comforting and exciting. My father would have relished poking around in Dujols's collection.

"I am at your service, Mademoiselle. Once you have read what is in these books, come back and I will do my best to explain it all to you. Then we can gather some kindred evolved folks together to reach out to La Lune. Trust me, Mademoiselle, I can guide you through this."

I stayed up late that night reading the first book and began the second the following day. I never left the house but read continuously, even during my dinner of a simple bouillon, roast chicken with braised endives, and a dry white wine. I read without stopping, my mind bursting with questions about the theories exposed by Dujols's contemporaries. The concepts were strange, disturbing, and seductive. Were there spirits trapped between this life and the next? Could they haunt their old habitats? Did they need our help to set them free? Was it possible to summon them through séances? Was what my grandmother believed even possible? Was I being inhabited by La Lune? Was that where my passion to paint had come from? Was she changing me?

And if she was, how could I get rid of her?

A sudden and violent stomachache and nausea chased away all thoughts except of how to alleviate the pain. No doubt my condition had been brought on by my lack of sleep and concentrated reading. I called for Alice and requested she prepare a powder remedy and to make it extra strong.

Despite her doing so, relief was slow to come, but finally, sometime past midnight, I fell asleep.

The next morning at ten, Alice came to my room to tell me that Monsieur Duplessi had arrived and was confused to find her there. I told her I'd see him and hurried downstairs, relieved that he'd come back to Paris, hopeful that, now that he was back, he could help me make sense of what was happening.

I greeted him downstairs, still in my peignoir instead of a day dress. "Welcome to my home," I said.

"*Your* home? Has something happened to your grandmother?"

"Yes, she is unwell. She's been taken to Dr. Blanche's for care."

"The sanatorium?"

"Yes, she had an episode. It was horrible. She is convinced . . . It's so absurd . . . She thought she saw a ghost . . . and couldn't cope with the shock of it."

"How terrible," he said.

"Yes, I've spent the last four nights crying myself to sleep."

And I had. I was a mess of emotions. Elation and horror living inside of me at the same time.

Torn by terribly missing my grandmother and fearing for her and simultaneously delighted that now that I'd moved into Maison de la Lune I would be able to devote much more time to painting and being with Julien.

"Monsieur le Docteur assured me that it is only temporary and that Grand-mère will recover and be able to come home in a week or two. A few weeks at the most."

"How did this happen?"

I didn't know what to say. I didn't know if Julien would be sympathetic or think us all mad. "She went to my cousin's funeral, and when she returned became hysterical."

"Were they very close?"

"I think they were."

"But she's a very strong woman. To become undone to the extent that she has had to be hospitalized? Surely something else occured."

I desperately wanted to confide in him. I kept seeing my grandmother's eyes staring at me with horror and fear. If I told Julien, would he look at me the same way? Surely not. He'd taken me to the occult bookshop, but he didn't believe in Dujols's mystical and occult world. He'd made that clear.

"Sandrine? What really happened?"

"Why do you think something else happened?"

"I can see how nervous you are." He picked up my hand. "Look at your fingernails. You've picked at them to the point that they are bleeding. There are deep circles beneath your eyes."

"My grandmother is in a sanatorium!"

"Yes, but you told me that the doctor believes it is just a short stay and that she will be fine."

Julien pulled me toward him and held me, whispering: "What aren't you telling me? There's no need to be afraid. What is it?"

I insisted there was nothing.

"Why don't you get dressed? We can take a walk. The fresh air," he said, "will be good for you."

It was chilly out, but he was right. The bracing air did clear my head. We walked to Ladurée, where he procured a table for us, and we sat among the lush tropical murals, on scarlet and green cushioned seats and sipped strong tea. He ordered us macarons, but I wasn't hungry, and the pastel-colored cookies sat on the china plate untouched while he held my hands and I recounted the story.

I told him how I'd met our cousin the rabbi and his reaction to me. Then about my grandmother's efforts to have what she and Cousin Jacob believed was a demon exorcised. How my cousin died and how my grandmother had tricked me and locked me in the bedroom to keep me from going to his funeral, and how I'd occupied myself while she'd been gone. By the time I got to the description of the paintings I'd done on the walls, he was biting his bottom lip. I finished by telling him how my grandmother had reacted when she'd seen the mural.

"She was convinced I was being taken over by the ghost of a witch from the 1600s who had returned from the dead to claim my soul."

"What made you paint that story on the wall? What were you thinking? Where *did* the images come from?"

"Ever since you and I found the paintings in the tower, I've been dreaming about La Lune and Cherubino Cellini. They're in my head, Julien, that's all. There's nothing going on except that my imagination has been stirred."

He nodded thoughtfully. Neither of us spoke for a few minutes.

"Does the house feel different to you?" I asked.

"I don't know what you mean."

"Well, what if my grandmother is right? What if La Lune *is* in the house? What if she'd been waiting for me and is glad I'm back?" I whispered. "It would explain why the house seems happier now."

Julien turned my hand over and looked down at my palm as if he was going to find the answers there.

"There's no good to come of this line of thinking."

"So you don't believe it's possible?"

"I most emphatically do not! I do not believe

in ghosts or hauntings or any of that mystical nonsense." The anger was bubbling out of him.

"Then why are you so scared of it?" I didn't know how, but I knew that he was.

He shook his head. "I'm not. It can be seductive, but it's not real, Sandrine. There's too much of this talk going on in Paris. People are losing their reason. Taking you into Dujols's store was a mistake. It put ideas in your head."

I laughed. "Don't be ridiculous. I knew all about those ideas from my father." I took a breath. "I went back there, Julien. Monsieur Dujols is a wonderful teacher. He's given me books to read and is helping me to understand."

"That's not wise."

"Why are you reacting this way?"

He lifted my hand and kissed my palm. I reached out and smoothed down his hair with my other hand.

"I don't want you to become entangled in that dark mess. So many of Dujols's disciples start off like you, merely interested, but . . ."

"What?"

"It's dangerous, Sandrine. That's all. It just is."

I wanted to argue but sensed that it wasn't the right time. No one—not my grandmother and not Julien—could convince me that what was happening to me was something to be afraid of. I was painting. I was alive in a way I had never known before. Yes, I was terribly sad about my grandmother, but she was simply frightened. She'd come to understand that I was flourishing, not being *taken over*. And Julien? I smiled at him. He was just being caring and protective.

We walked back to the house, and he came inside with me. We sat on the sofa in the parlor.

"I have a favor to ask. Monsieur Dujols thinks we should have a séance and see if we can talk to La Lune. Find out what it is she wants. I need you to come with me. I need you to say yes."

He opened his mouth to say no, but before he could answer, I put my finger across his lips. "Don't answer yet. Just think about it. We don't have to speak of it now." I leaned into him and inhaled the scent of his skin mixed with his cologne. I smiled up at him. He seemed to relax a bit. What had I stirred? What secret did he hold so close and tight? "I have to go to class in a little while. We don't have that much time together today to waste it arguing."

"No? What should we waste our time doing?"

Since moving in, I examined the house and all of its rooms. And so I took him to my favorite of the "fantasy bedrooms," as my grandmother called them. Each one uniquely decorated to evoke its own dream.

There was a boudoir that recalled a room in the palace of Marie Antoinette, in which all walls were mirrors; there was a monk's chamber with a narrow bed and straw rug and religious frescoes on the wall; there was an Egyptian room as well as a Chinese pagoda; and there was a Persian garden room.

I chose the last, with its fanciful walls painted with trees and flowering bushes against a midnight blue sky, with stars and a perfect crescent moon and the onion-shaped minarets of the city in the distance. Expensive rugs in deep blues, reds, and greens were piled on one another. Tall vases of peacock feathers filled the corners. Red, turquoise, and gold silken curtains hung around the bed.

I pulled him onto the bed and then knelt before him.

"I'm your servant girl, your slave." I shivered with excitement. I'd never been this bold before, and it was thrilling. "Here to do your bidding, to fulfill your desire. Would you like me to undress you and draw your bath?"

Not waiting for a response, I began, first taking off one boot and then another. His pants. His shirt. His stockings. I never took my eyes off of his, and in them I could see not only my own reflection but also his enjoyment.

"I never knew a man could be beautiful before, but you are. Because of how your collarbones come together here." I touched the spot. "Because of these muscles in your arm." I put my hand on his biceps. "When you finally let me paint you, this will be my favorite part to paint." I put my hand on his broad chest. "Or maybe this will be." I ran my fingers across his shoulders.

He closed his eyes. I felt a clench of intense pleasure inside me.

"When I paint you, this is one place where my brush will dwell." I ran my finger down the thin line of dark hair that traveled from his belly button to his groin. "And here." I moved my hand across his hip bone. "And here." I put one hand on each of his thighs. "And here." I continued down his calves and then back up them, up his hips, his chest, and found his hands pressing down on the bed, clenched.

"When I paint you," I said, "you will be naked and hard and wanting like you are now . . ." I ran a single finger inside and out of each of his fingers, making his hand as sensitive to my touch as the rest of him. "And it will be so difficult for me to keep painting without stopping to touch you."

He arched his back. I wanted to watch his pleasure and know I was causing it. I wanted him to know what he did to me. "When I paint you," I said, "when I get here . . ." I bent to kiss between his legs and inhaled. I could smell the deepest part of the forest. Pleasure throbbed inside of me. This was where I wanted to be, here with Julien. With him unable to look away from me. With him willing to be swallowed up by me.

"When I get here . . . ," I whispered into his

flesh, "I will have to stop so I can do this . . ." And then I took him into my mouth. His head was thrown back. He was lost to me. Lost in the pleasure. All around me was the dark scent of him. The air was ripe with it.

I raised myself off the rug. I would give him his pleasure, but first, I would do something I had never done before. I would claim my own. I pulled up my skirt and swayed above him.

"Hold back for me, Julien. Yes?" I whispered. "I promise you more than you've ever felt if you can just hold back." I reached down, in between his legs, and squeezed him in a way sure to prevent release. How had I known? My husband had surely never told me. Before that moment I'd never even wondered at such a thing.

I lowered myself down on him slowly. All of the world centered on that one amazing sensation. It was all colors and sounds and smells, all that had been denied me for so very long. It didn't matter if Julien was betrothed to someone else; it would only be a matter of time before he would be mine and I would be his. The feelings coursing through me were the ones I was due. This was where I belonged. On the tip of him, on the edge of this exquisite madness.

He moaned.

"Not yet," I whispered as I rode him.

The pleasure . . . how could I ever give up this pleasure? I was supposed to be here, to have this.

Supposed to be with this man beneath me, in me, giving and taking and taking and giving.

I lifted myself up so we were no longer touching. He was panting and ready. "Don't stop," he said in a hoarse whisper.

But still I held back, swaying above him.

"Will you come with me?" I asked him the same question I had asked before all this began. "Yes?" I was offering what he wanted in exchange for what I wanted. "Yes?" I lowered myself just enough so that we were touching, but barely. Enough so that I could feel the heat of him.

"Please," he begged as he tried to push up, but I held back.

"Yes?"

"Yes, Sandrine, yes," he said, and I wasn't sure in that moment what pleased me more, the physical explosion or knowing that he was going to go with me to Dujols's.

Chapter 22

Dr. Blanche, the alienist, had a private asylum in Passy. It was quite a ride from the house on rue des Saints-Pères. As I traveled there the next morning, I was apprehensive. Even though my grandmother's doctor had assured me otherwise, I anticipated a home for the insane: disgusting and dirty and frightening. Especially since the building was the domicile of the Princess de Lamballe during the revolution and the scene of her gruesome end. Certainly it had been renovated since then. After all, Guy de Maupassant had spent the last two years of his life at Dr. Blanche's. Others like Theo van Gogh, the artist's brother, and the writer Gérard de Nerval had also been residents for a time. And yet I was still nervous.

As we got closer, the fashionable neighborhood suggested the clinic was not the horror I'd imagined, and when we pulled up to a beautiful eighteenth-century mansion surrounded by gardens, I was quite surprised.

I entered through grand front doors and was led from the elegant front hall to the doctor's office, I was pleased. Lined with book-filled shelves, it was a warm, welcoming room with tall windows looking out onto the park. Despite the chilly air, the parade of nurses strolling past with patients soothed me.

The doctor introduced himself. He was a man of about seventy-two or -three. Robust and quite healthy-looking, with intelligent eyes and a wide forehead.

"I'm sorry to have to tell you, but your grandmother is not as well as I had hoped she would be by now," the doctor said, shattering my becalmed state. "She is not yet showing any signs of improving. I wouldn't allow the visit except I'm hoping that if she sees you are all right, it might help us in our effort. You *are* all right, aren't you?"

For a moment he examined me as if it might be possible to see my mental health on my face.

"I most certainly am. Except for worrying about her, that is."

"Is there any reason at all that you know of that would cause your grandmother to believe you are in mortal danger?"

"No, nothing that I can think of."

"Well, she told me quite a tale about you and why she believes you are in danger."

I didn't realize I was clenching and unclenching my hands until I saw the doctor staring at my actions. What was I frightened of? What could Grand-mère have told him? About my husband bankrupting my father? About Papa's suicide?

About my running away from Benjamin and taking an assumed name so he couldn't find me? Taking art lessons? Even wearing comfortable clothes to paint in?

"Your grandmother told me that you are possessed by a demon."

I laughed, but from the expression on the doctor's face I grasped that had been a mistake. He appeared disturbed by my response.

"Do you find that funny?"

"I find it absurd, don't you?"

"She believes it. And she told me her cousin Rabbi Jacob Richter believed it, too. She said she took you to him, and he performed an exorcism on you in a mikvah, and that he not only saw the ghost who haunts you but that the ghost killed him on the spot. She also believes she saw the ghost in your bedroom."

"Yes, she believes those things. But more to the point, do you believe in ghosts, Doctor? I cannot allow her to reside in any asylum run by someone who would fuel her deranged fantasies."

"No, Mademoiselle Verlaine, I don't, but at the same time I do very much believe the mind needs a seed to grow a story like this. I would venture a guess that something very real is in fact wrong and that your grandmother has lost perspective on it. Can you tell me more about the days leading up to her breakdown as well as the inciting incident?"

"I'd like to see her first," I said. Tired of the conversation, I wanted to bring it to a close.

"And you will. But in order to treat her, it's imperative that I understand the patient's frame of mind before the onset of the episode. Can you indulge me and fill me in a bit on what happened in the days leading up to her hysteria?"

"There were three deaths close together. Too much death. Too much talk of dying. First there was my father, then her uncle the doctor, and then Cousin Jacob. It left my grandmother emotionally distraught."

"And that day? What happened that day?"

"It was very strange. We were going to go to Cousin Jacob's funeral together, but then Grand-mère had a fit about my hat, insisting I change it to a more sedate one. While I was doing that, she locked me in my bedroom, like a child, and went to the funeral without me."

"Do you know why she did that?"

"I'm afraid I don't."

"She didn't explain?"

"She didn't."

"And when she returned?"

"She came upstairs to see me."

"What were you doing when she entered your room?"

"Reading," I lied.

"What book?"

I searched for a title and came up with that one book, the only book I had read in the last month. *The Picture of Dorian Gray.*

"She told me you were painting on the walls and that the mural was pornographic."

"She is a courtesan well-versed in the ways of the world and she used that word?" I asked.

"I believe she did."

I tried to picture those paintings on the pale yellow walls . . . to see them as someone would if they were to enter the room unprepared. Even someone as comfortable with sexual conduct and sexual pleasures as my grandmother. The sexual liaisons between the painter and his muse were erotic and arousing, but pornographic? I shook my head.

"What is it?" the doctor asked.

"I . . . I'm afraid I don't paint. Oh, the occasional watercolor when I was in finishing school. But murals?" I laughed.

"You don't dress up in gentleman's clothes and study painting at Les Beaux-Arts?"

"Monsieur le Docteur, my grandmother is clearly not only hysterical, she is also delusional. Might I see her now?"

"Do you know who La Lune is?" he asked.

I shivered and tried to keep my voice steady. "Yes, an ancestor of ours. A courtesan who became a legend and started a legacy. Our family home is named after her."

"Your grandmother is convinced that her ghost is taking you over. I'm afraid it's a most disturbing story that she's concocted and is quite obsessed by."

I leaned across the desk toward the doctor, aware that I'd learned the seductive movement from none other than the woman we were discussing. "What would cause such a thing?" I asked, laden with concern.

"There are many possible causes. That's why I was asking you what happened before the doctor was called."

"Deaths . . . wouldn't they make her think of ghosts? Her son. Then her uncle. Then her cousin. Isn't that enough to explain her preoccupation?"

"I don't think so." He stood. "Let us go see your grandmother."

I followed him down a long hallway, past well-lit offices, and then into the living quarters. I glimpsed a simple combination bedroom/sitting room where a woman in a dressing gown sat in a rocking chair by the window. A few doors down, a nurse exited another such room, and I saw two men sitting on a couch, sipping what appeared to be coffee or tea.

"It's very nice here. I'm afraid I was picturing something quite different."

"Thank you. We have the funds needed to ensure we can keep the clinic up to the highest standards. Nothing like the city madhouses."

We'd reached the end of the hall. The doctor pointed to the door on the left.

"This is your grandmother's room. She doesn't yet have all her privileges, so she is restrained. I want you to be prepared."

He opened the door and gestured for me to walk in.

Despite his warning, I gasped.

My beautiful Grand-mère was lying on top of a bed, her arms tied to the bedposts. Her hair was stringy and dull. Her naked face looked drawn and ravaged. Her eyes went wide when she saw me, and something wild filled them. My lovely Grand-mère, who never had looked her age, who entertained some of the wealthiest men in Europe, whose jewels rivaled those of princesses, was wearing a white shift stained with something red—not blood, I hoped—looked right at me and started to scream.

"La Lune, La Lune!" she cried. "Save Sandrine from La Lune!" She began to sob. Then gagged. Then vomited.

The nurse, whom I hadn't even noticed, rose from her chair in the corner and attended to her.

I stood, shocked, disgusted, and saddened. The doctor helped the nurse, then spoke soothing words to my grandmother that seemed to actually quiet her.

He turned to me. "Why don't you try to talk to

her and tell her you're all right? As you can see, she's quite worried about you."

"Can she hear me?"

"Yes."

I walked toward the bed and stepped into my grandmother's line of sight.

"Grand-mère, please, don't worry about me. I'm fine. I love you. I want you to get better."

"I didn't think you loved your husband," she said.

I hadn't known what to expect her to say . . . but that certainly wasn't it.

"I don't. I never have."

"When you first came to Paris, you weren't in love. I was so happy. You were safe. But you've met someone, haven't you?"

"No," I lied. "Why are you asking me this?"

"This is what she does, waits for a woman in love and then inhabits her. Have you taken a lover? You mustn't. She's why I never wanted you to come back to Paris. She waits in her house for someone to fall in love . . . and then she drives our women mad."

This sounded like a version of the legend that my father had alluded to so many years ago. Surely no one could believe this? A woman dead for more than two hundred and fifty years could not somehow live on in Verlaine daughters, sisters, and nieces.

My grandmother turned to the doctor.

"Sandrine is beautiful, isn't she? So strong. So like her father. But she's too curious. Curiosity is dangerous for Verlaines, and—oh! No!" My grandmother screamed and pointed. "Doctor, do you see her? Look behind Sandrine. See the shadow tied to her? That's the witch. That's La Lune."

"Now, now, Madame Verlaine," the doctor began to soothe.

"Don't try to placate me. Look at Sandrine. The witch is right behind her. Do you see the shadow? She's desperate for love." She turned her head to me. "Sandrine, you have to cast her out. Are you listening? Cast her out!"

I turned and run from the room and was soon careening down the corridor. At the end of the hall, out of breath, I stopped. I put my hand on the windowsill and looked out into the garden. Watching a robin picking at a twig, probably about to steal it away for nest building, I tried to stifle my sobs, but I was crying too hard.

A few moments later, the doctor joined me by the window.

"Are you all right, Mademoiselle?"

"My grandmother is really very ill, isn't she?"

He handed me a handkerchief. "She's had a severe break from reality. And it is serious, but I have seen far more serious situations resolve in time. If you would indulge me, though, I'd like to ask you to help me so I can help treat her."

"Of course," I said.

"Would you go back to your grandmother and ask her how you can get rid of La Lune?"

The thought of seeing her again filled me with dread. She wanted to destroy me. The person I was becoming. The painter. Julien's lover. Was she jealous of my youth and my life? Yes, I could see now that had been happening since I came to Paris. My grandmother was aging, and my vitality was a threat to her.

"But you said you don't believe in ghosts."

"No. I don't believe you are any more inhabited by a demon ghost than I am," the doctor said. "But she believes you are, and perhaps if you enacted the ritual that she believes will rid you of the demon, we can convince her that you are safe again. It might be the first step to restoring her vitality."

I didn't respond.

"I'll be with you. The nurse will be there. You don't need to be afraid. You do want to help her, don't you?"

No, a voice I could hear inside of me said. *No, don't help her.*

A wave of nausea rocked me. I pressed my forehead against the cool window glass. What was happening? I was hearing— What was I hearing? The doctor was trying to soothe me and so was the voice inside of me—I couldn't tell which was which—I had to get away—I was so frightened.

I took off, running away from her, from him, from the nurse, from the old lady who had once been my beautiful grandmother. As I ran, I heard the doctor's footsteps behind me as he called out.

"Mademoiselle Verlaine? Please, don't be afraid."

I got lost in the maze of corridors and wound up in a large room filled with eucalyptus-scented mist so thick that at first I couldn't make out where I was. Odd sounds echoed in the space: steam hissing, wind gusts, then a shriek, then a laugh. And under it all was the sound of water, dripping, dripping.

As I stumbled through the space, my eyes adjusted to the condensations, and I could make out copper tubs outfitted with strange metal tubing. In one of the tubs a man wearing a white dressing gown soaked and sang a schoolchild's rhyme in a high-pitched, squeaky voice. In the next tub another man sat upright, his eyes half shut.

"Pretty lady, will you bathe me?" he asked, his voice heavy with sexual innuendo.

I kept running. Past another bather whose head was down, forehead touching the water. The nurse who sat beside him was speaking to him in a low, soothing tone, but the man seemed unresponsive.

Other patients were crying, shrieking, or giggling. Mixed together, it was the song of souls trapped in hell. No matter which way I turned, I saw yet another tub. Some patients, noticing me, became distressed by my presence and reacted. They rocked in their tubs, sprayed, and splashed water everywhere. It sloshed on the floor. I slipped in it. The smell of salts mixed with the mint and stale body odor made me gag. Here was the asylum I'd been afraid to see. And then a hand grabbed me by the elbow.

"Mademoiselle." It was the doctor, and he sounded annoyed. "Please, do come this way. This disturbance is not good for my patients."

Out in the hallway he took one look at me and then added an addendum to his last thought: "Or for you. Perhaps a walk outside would be a good idea."

Julien had said the same thing to me, and it had in fact made me feel better. More myself. I agreed, and we stepped outside.

It was a warm day for early February, warmer than any day had been since I'd arrived in Paris. We entered the heavily wooded park and took a path that led us around a still, calm pond. As we strolled, the doctor extracted a silver case, took out a cigarette, then offered me one. I accepted it. He lit them both.

"I know how upsetting it can be to see someone you love in this state."

I didn't smoke often, but I welcomed the distraction. "Yes, very upsetting." I rolled the cigarette between my gloved fingers.

"But it would really help me to find out more about your grandmother's history—has anything like this happened before?"

"Not that I am aware of. But I've been only been here since January. I saw her infrequently before that, only once every few years."

"Is there anyone else in your family whom we might talk to in order to find out if this has happened before? Someone who lives here in Paris?"

"I'm not sure there is anyone who knew her well other than her uncle and Cousin Jacob, and they are both dead."

"Might I come to the house and talk to the servants?"

"I've already asked and no, none of them have seen any evidence of a disturbance before." It wasn't true, but I was worried that any conversation the doctor might have with the staff would reveal the lies I'd told him.

The doctor dropped his cigarette on the stone path and stomped on it with his shoe. I did the same.

"Are you cold, or shall we keep walking?" he asked.

"I'm not at all cold. I'd like to keep walking." It had been days since I'd felt the weather. Paris's winters were much warmer than New York's, and this was a particularly warm day.

"I once had a patient who was as sane as you

or I, and yet every night at ten PM he went into paroxysms of panic and fear and began to scream and tried to harm himself. Every night. It took me a full year to find out that he had watched his wife be attacked and killed in front of his eyes at ten PM and was reliving it daily."

A pigeon flew past us and alighted on a branch of a chestnut tree. A squirrel darted from behind a holly bush, grabbed an acorn, and ran up the trunk of one of the plane trees.

"If only I could find the trigger to this episode, you see, I could help your grandmother."

"Fine then, yes, come and talk to the servants. Please, talk to anyone you wish to."

"Thank you. Now, I need you to return to the clinic with me and ask your grandmother how you can get rid of the ghost."

I shook my head. "I can't see her again like that."

"Do you love her?"

"Of course!"

"Then you must help me to help her."

I began to shake at the thought of going back inside her room and hearing her spew vitriol again. Her words were like vicious black slime suffocating me. "I just can't."

"Mademoiselle, I am afraid that if we don't allow your grandmother to say what she is so desperate to tell you, we may lose her."

"Do you mean she could die?" I clasped my

hands together to stop the acute trembling. "She is the only family I have."

"No, she's not physically ill. I don't fear for her corporeal body. But her mind is ill, and sometimes a patient can become lost to us inside the pathways of their thoughts. Sometimes they go so far into their terror we can't pull them back."

I would be free. The thought sprang up, unbidden. Like a green shoot, breaking through the last frost. Free to live at La Lune and paint and be with Julien. But at that cost? No, of course not.

"I'll try," I said.

We walked back into the sanatorium, down the main hallway, and stopped in front of my grandmother's room. The door was ajar. Dr. Blanche put his fingers to his lips and motioned me to be quiet and listen.

My grandmother was speaking to her nurse in a very normal voice about a book they had both read and found enjoyable.

"The way the author described the character's hairstyle would look very good on you," my grandmother said. "It would accentuate your cheekbones. You have excellent cheekbones, you know."

She sounded exactly like her old self. A wave of relief flooded over me. The doctor gestured to me that we were going to go in. He opened the door wider for me.

"I'm so happy you're better," I said as I walked toward her bed and then bent down to embrace her.

She leaned toward me. I felt her lips on my neck, and I thought she meant to kiss me on the cheek but missed. Before I understood what was happening, she bit into my flesh, grabbing the ruby necklace with her teeth and trying to pull it off.

I pushed her away, but she was still working her jaw and accidentally bit down on my index finger. Drops of dark red blood popped out on the surface of my skin.

I backed up, massaging my neck, looking from her to my finger.

My grandmother shrieked: "Get her out of here. She has La Lune with her."

The doctor spoke to my grandmother: "Madame Verlaine, listen to me, this is very important. How can Sandrine get rid of La Lune?"

A drop of blood dripped down my hand and fell onto the white marble floor.

"You can't wear the rubies, Sandrine," my grandmother continued. "Take them off. All the women in the portraits are wearing them. Every one of them. You need to take off the rubies, or what happened to them will happen to you. Every one of them witnessed their lovers' lives manipulated so they were free to be with them . . . but it always went wrong . . . In the end every one went mad . . . or died. Some, by their own hand."

"You are making this up."

"No."

"How do you know it then?"

"I know all the stories. They have been passed from mother to daughter. Passed from my mother to me. Warnings. Dire, dire warnings. None of the women were strong enough for La Lune. Every one of them dead. Now I have to warn you."

I was so cold. Her voice was so desperate. Her words seemed to be echoing in my head. Warnings . . . warnings . . . My neck throbbed. So did my finger. And it was still dripping blood. I looked down and noticed the blood had formed a shape. A familiar shape. I twisted my head. It couldn't be. I must have stepped in it and smeared it. It just was not possible that the blood had formed a perfect ruby crescent moon. Nothing that was happening was possible. With the toe of my boot, I turned the shape into an unrecognizable mess. If I couldn't see it anymore I wouldn't have to accept that the symbol that was all over our house had somehow, mysteriously, appeared here too.

Chapter 23

The glitter and the gold, the lights and the sparkle, the rarest marbles, the shine and the spectacle, the overall glow from all the opulence at the opera house stunned my senses. Even living in New York City, I had never seen anything as grand and ornate as the Palais Garnier. There was not one surface that was not filled with sculptures or painted with gods and goddesses and cherubs, or gilded, or mirrored and gleaming.

As we were shown to my grandmother's box, I saw my reflection in a gold-framed mirror. During the day I now only wore men's clothes; tonight I'd taken to borrowing finery from her closet, and the ruby velvet gown I was wearing belonged to her. Cut low across the bosom, it showed off my skin to its best advantage. Around my neck, the necklace that I had not taken off since I'd first put it on glowed, even from a distance. The only blemish was the small welt below the third ruby: I'd had to apply a layer of my grandmother's makeup there to hide the bite marks her teeth had left on my skin.

Grand-mère's seats at the opera had remained empty since I'd arrived in Paris, but I had reason to be sitting in them on this night, especially with the important gentleman on my arm. Monsieur

Garnier, architect of this grand palace and one of the loyal attendees at my grandmother's salon, whom I'd met in the apartment on rue de la Chaise, had been only too happy to attend the gala first night performance of *Cupid and Psyche* with me.

What a coup it would be when Julien noticed me here with Garnier. How jealous he would be that I was being escorted by another man—and a rival at that, the most famous architect in Paris. I had imagined the scene so many times since asking my grandmother's *old friend* to accompany me that I almost believed the scenario I'd sketched out had happened already.

Julien spotting me. Recognizing Garnier. Taking umbrage. Declaring his feelings for me. Promising to end things with Charlotte.

I'd gone to my grandmother's lawyer when the majordomo had come to me needing money to run the household the very day that Dr. Blanche presented me with the first week's rather costly clinic bill. Monsieur Tissot explained that while my grandmother's investments were secure and she was very well off, the extra rent she'd been paying on the rue de la Chaise apartment had depleted her cash on hand.

"I can of course sell some of her stock, but it's all doing so nicely, so I'd rather not," Monsieur Tissot said. "Why don't you reopen the salon? We all miss it, and we always gave her lavish gifts in exchange for the entertainment, food, and drink she provided. Those gifts could help pay your bills."

"No, I think I'd rather if you did sell some stock."

Even if Grand-mère's staff was adept at supplying the champagne, cigars, and delicacies, I had no interest in playing hostess; all I wanted to do at night was paint and spend time with Julien.

Despite my lack of interest, three evenings later, several of my grandmother's callers arrived without invitation. Someone had seen the lights on in the mansion, and a rumor had spread that my grandmother's doors were open once again.

Alice came to find me and explain what had happened, and I came down from the studio, half undressed in a silk kimono, to greet the handful of gentlemen and explain the mistake.

When I entered the parlor, they were relaxed and quite at home, smoking cigars, drinking champagne, and nibbling on the trays of fruit, cheese, and chocolates that Alice had put out.

Instead of finding the evening distasteful, as I'd imagined I would, I enjoyed flirting and being flirted with. The men seemed responsive to my style, which they told me was even a soupçon more ribald that Grand-mère's. More of her manner must have rubbed off on me than I'd noticed.

But it was how Julien reacted that pleased me the most. He'd arrived to find me surrounded by men in formal evening attire lounging in the parlor, drinking, smoking, laughing, and all hovering around me like flies to honey.

"Who are all these men? What are they doing here?" He'd pulled me into the hallway. "And what are you wearing?" He fingered my pale peach silk kimono.

It wasn't the coloring that he objected to, I knew, but how provocative it was. The fabric was so sheer and of such a color to suggest I was naked beneath the silk, even though I was wearing a chemise.

"You look like . . ." He hesitated.

"Yes?"

"What are you thinking, Sandrine?"

"I wasn't thinking. This is an accident. But now that it's happened, maybe I should open the salon again. The clinic is expensive. Running this house is expensive. My grandmother's estate is tied up. It might be a perfect solution. And I rather enjoy the role of libertine."

He didn't say anything for a moment but looked from me to the men and then back to me with an unspoken question in his eyes.

"No, I would not entertain the men in my bedroom."

"Not at first!"

I slapped him. He didn't say a word or put his hand up to his cheek, which I was sure was smarting.

"I'm sorry, I don't know what's come over me. I don't have any right to question you," he said.

"These men have always given my grandmother gifts. Not only for her favors but for her hospitality. For serving the finest food and drink and cigars in Paris and for allowing them use of her bedrooms *fantastique* when they have a special friend they want to entertain. The doctor thinks that with a few more weeks rest my grandmother will be able to come home, and I want her to come home so much. What would be so terrible to go on accepting those gifts in order to keep my grandmother at Dr. Blanche's clinic?"

"Do I need to explain?"

"Julien, please, either stay and enjoy yourself or leave, but don't make a scene."

"I'm sorry. I wish I could solve your financial problems for you." Julien was quite contrite.

"It's all right. Would you like to have some champagne?"

His mouth pursed, and he glanced away for a brief second. The expression was one I had come to recognize. He had plans with his fiancée and was torn between his obligations and his desires.

"If you are already spoken for this evening," I asked, "why are you here?"

"I came to bring you these." He handed me a bouquet of violets he'd been holding that I hadn't even noticed.

"And to spend a little time with me before your dinner?"

"Would that be so unusual?" His smile was self-effacing. "I missed our *cinq à sept* today."

"They are lovely." I leaned up and kissed him lightly on the lips.

He pulled me to him. "That dress," he whispered. "If no one was here, I'd rip it off you right now."

"Stay then, Julien. No one will notice if we disappear for a while."

His evergreen eyes clouded. "I would, but . . ."

"Go to your dinner then," I said. Looked down at the flowers. Back up at him. "Thank you for these." I sniffed the bouquet. "I'll take them with me . . . to bed."

I turned and left him standing in the hall and returned to my guests.

I'd discovered something. Julien didn't mind that I was surrounded by men at the École. There I was in masculine garb and treated like just another student. But when I was dressed as a femme fatale, with other men looking at me, talking to me, flirting with me, he was inflamed with jealousy.

First the salon and next the opera. How much would Julien be able to take?

The orchestra warmed up. Lights dimmed. The crowd quieted. The overture filled the opera house with beautiful, resonant music, and the show began.

I raised my grandmother's jeweled opera glasses to my eye. Charlotte, playing Psyche, appeared on stage and burst into song. Her voice rang out like bells. My heart sank. How to compete with her? She was a magician, enchanting her listeners. They were just notes on a sheet of music and Italian words, but she transmuted them into ambrosia. I felt defeated. I could only imagine the pride Julien felt watching his songbird, listening to her. This couldn't be a marriage of convenience. He had to be in love with her. Who could listen to her and not be a little in love with her?

In person, Charlotte was lovely, but there was nothing striking about her. There was no exceptional light in her eyes, no fetching tilt to her head, no nuance that turned a woman into a true beauty. But now, listening to her, no one could take his eyes off of her.

No one except for me. Moving the glasses, I scanned the boxes for the one I was looking for. Julien and Charlotte's father were seated almost opposite to us, both of them riveted to the action onstage.

I watched Julien as he watched Charlotte sing of her longing to see her lover in the light.

Julien did not like to talk about Charlotte, but I'd been able to surmise that her celebrity opened doors for him. In the last two years, he'd built several nightclubs and residences for people in the theatrical world who were more amenable to his avant-garde style than the staid upper-class clientele who typically hired Cingal's firm. Julien's reputation had grown because of these commissions. Her star shone on him.

On the stage, Cupid made a dramatic entrance, flying in from above, his iridescent, wide, wondrous wings spread. Along with the rest of the audience, I gasped as this beautiful creature came down to earth to make love to a human who was doomed never to set eyes on him.

It was painful to watch the scene on the stage, impossible not to imagine Julien making love to Charlotte. How did they embrace? What did her kisses taste like? Did he become as aroused as quickly with her or more quickly than with me? What secret touches and tricks did they share?

I was staring at the stage when it happened. Staring at the woman who I was certain came between me and real happiness. My resentment toward her was building. My fury at having to deal with and accept these conventions was growing. So what that Julien had given his word? How could he throw away what we had for her? The opera glasses in my hand warmed, my anger heating them. The gold burned my cheek where the rim rested on my skin. I yanked them away lest they leave a mark on my flesh. The heat they were generating through my gloves was almost intolerable. What was wrong?

In the audience, the theatergoers were murmuring appreciation for what was happening on the stage. What theatrical event was this? Cupid's wings were shining with a peculiar vermilion and crimson light—what was it?

Suddenly, Cupid began to move in a furious, hysterical way that didn't fit the part. He was pulling his wings off. They were smoking. The wings were burning.

Charlotte pulled off her mantle. A ring of fire around the hem crept up the garment. The music stopped. For one moment the theater was silent. For that single second the fire held everyone mesmerized, and then the crowd erupted in shouts.

"Fire!"

Panic began to build.

"Fire!"

Beside me Monsieur Garnier took my arm. "Come, Mademoiselle Sandrine. In events like this the panic can be more dangerous than the actual fire. The stagehands are prepared, but the crowd . . . that's where the real risk is. Quickly as you can . . . I'll get you to a safe place and then come back and help them."

I knew he was right, but Julien was in this melee. We had to find him. If Garnier was going to save me, he had to save Julien, too.

"I have a friend here. Can we just find—"

"There's no time, just come with me. Your

grandmother would never forgive me if I didn't keep you safe."

On the stage, a line of men passed buckets of water to those closest to the fire, but as they put out one blaze, it seemed another area of the stage burst into flames. The conflagration traveled from fabric to prop, prop to fabric, faster than they could extinguish it.

"You said they'd contain the fire," I said.

"They will"—but he didn't sound confident. "No matter what happens, though, you will be safe if you do as I say."

He pulled me away from the direction of the main staircase and the lobby, the front doors and Julien, and instead toward the back and into a darkened, unadorned hallway.

At the far end, he opened the very last door with a key he pulled from his vest pocket and pointed.

"Three flights down are stone caverns and a lake. Fire cannot work its way through stone. Wait for me. There are candles and matches inside small hollows as you descend. Use them to light your way. Be careful."

And then he disappeared, shutting the door after him.

I was engulfed by profound darkness. There simply was no light. I tried the door behind me. He'd locked it, or it had self-locked when he'd shut it, I couldn't open it.

Where was Julien? Had he been hurt in the

crush? What if the fire spread before everyone got out? I had only just found him . . . I couldn't lose him. What if he and Monsieur Cingal had rushed the stage to save Charlotte? What if they were trapped? I could smell the inferno now. The acrid scent filled the air.

I had no choice; the door was locked, and there was no going back. I felt to my right for the niche, found it. Groped for the candle and matches. I found the matches, but instead of a candle, there was only a stub of wax, far too small to light. Whoever had used it last had forgotten to replace it.

There were candles in niches all along the way, Garnier had said. But what if they were all like this one?

Somewhere beyond this door, behind me, I could hear the shouts of the operagoers and stagehands.

I took a deep breath, grabbed hold of the hand railing. How could there be a lake? I vaguely remembered a story about a lake and a frightening phantom who lived below the opera, but that was a legend in a novel.

But if Garnier said it would be safe, it would be. If anyone knew about this place, it would be the man responsible for building it.

At the base of that first flight, I felt around and indeed found a second niche . . . and in it a small candle, this one was big enough to ignite. With an unsteady hand, I struck the match. The flame was so terribly bright after the last few minutes I'd spent in pitch-blackness that I blinked back tears.

With a light, the second staircase was less frightening until I reached the third set of stairs. Greeted with the clammy scent of fungus and an eerie silence punctuated by a slow drip, as steady as a heart beating, I panicked. Everything in front of me was a mystery.

Cautiously, I stepped off the last step, walked forward. In the distance I saw a glimmer of water. I had reached the lake. It was just as Garnier said. A lantern hung from a hook drilled into the stone. Blankets were stacked in a niche in a rock wall.

Garnier had told me to wait for him, and I had every intention of obeying him. Venturing deeper into this underground maze without a guide would be suicidal. There was a very small boat tied up to a stake in the lake. It appeared to be silver and black, but I couldn't be sure since my candle gave off only a meager beacon. Where would it take me? I was too frightened to find out. Instead I found a rock that could function as a bench
and sat. How long would it be before Garnier returned? And what if he didn't? What if the fire got worse and worse and everyone was—

Becoming alarmed would not help me. I'd brought a small tin of crystallized violets with me and fished inside my reticule to find it. To do so, I had to first take out the opera glasses that I had been holding when the fire broke out.

As I removed them, I noticed something strange.

I had been nowhere near the blaze, and yet the pearls were blackened and soot covered the rubies. A film of it lay over the lenses. As I examined the small binoculars, I saw that the fingertips of my gloves were singed.

Do you understand now?

The echo slid across the lake and was lost in the gloom.

Who had said that? Had Garnier come back so soon? I turned, but no one was there.

I can help you.

It was a woman's voice. Not a man's. And perhaps the saddest voice I'd ever heard, as if tears had been turned into sound.

I searched the darkness but couldn't see anyone, not by the shore, not in the shadows. There really was no one there. I knew there wouldn't be. Just as I knew the last several weeks in Paris had been leading to this moment. What was happening? I got up and ran for the stairs. Halfway, I remembered that the door at the top of the last staircase would be locked. I turned around.

Back at ground level, I ran toward the boat. I would get away from her by way of the water.

Don't run from me. I'm here to help. We both want the same thing, for you to be with Julien.

I took what I thought was my first step into madness. I responded to the voice.

"The soot on the glasses, the burn marks on my gloves . . . You used me to start the fire?"

I thought this would work . . . The voice was fainter now, and I had to strain to hear her. *But the fire didn't spread fast enough. She got away. Now we have to find another way to be rid of her . . .*

I spun around and around. Searching for the trickster. There was no one in that cavern with me. But there was *something* there with me. And I saw her ghostly image in a glint of moonlight on the lake as she finished her whispered promise.

. . . We will find another way.

Moonlight? It was impossible. We were hundreds of feet underground.

Chapter 24

The morning newspapers were full of the story from the night before. There had been a fire at the opera house, but it was extinguished without incident and little damage except to some curtains and stage props. No one had perished. No one was even hurt.

I was relieved that Charlotte had survived, I thought as I walked to school. The evening had been terrifying and confusing. My mind was swimming with unanswered questions. Painting class with Monsieur Moreau would be a welcome diversion.

Inside, I greeted my fellow students and set up my easel. The model took her position. Monsieur Moreau walked around, tilting his head, asking her to move a little this way and a little that way until he was happy with her pose.

I looked from her to the empty canvas. Taking up my brush, I daubed it into the cobalt swirl, the most magical color on my palette. I changed the white robe slipping down the model's back to a lovely deep-azure shawl. For a moment I closed my eyes and, as if in a dream, saw the depths of the sky in the folds of the fabric, saw the moon and stars shining through its very blueness.

"Yes," Monsieur Moreau said as he looked over my shoulder at my canvas. "You are right to think through color, use it with imagination. If you don't have imagination, your color will never be beautiful. Color must be dreamed."

It was not the first time my teacher had spoken to me as if he could look inside my mind and hear what I was thinking.

"I would like you to stay for a short time after the session. Would that be all right, Mademoiselle?" Moreau asked me.

We were at his atelier at 14 rue de la Rochefoucauld, where he also lived. It was perhaps my favorite place in all of Paris. On the second floor, in the grand parlor, was a nautilus iron staircase. At the top was the painter's rich universe. His stunning paintings, drawings, and watercolors crowded every wall, crammed tightly together, giving the eye no respite. His love of colors was displayed in the gem-like canvases, each sparkling with ruby, vermilion, royal purple, emerald, and gold. His visionary illustrations of tales from the Bible and mythology were inundated with fantastical winged creatures from angels to dragons. Imagery rife with magic and crowded with symbolism.

Once everyone had left, we ventured downstairs for tea. Sitting in a formal and old-fashioned dusty room, we were served by a middle-aged maid who didn't linger or say very much.

"Is it possible you are holding back, Mademoiselle?"

I was surprised by his question. "I'm not sure what you mean."

"I've watched how quickly you pick up on my suggestions and, at the same time, noticed a hesitancy that implies you know exactly what to do but are reluctant to do it. Does this make any sense to you?"

What to tell him? What to admit? Of course I was doing exactly that, afraid that if he saw how fast I was capable of progressing he would become suspicious. It even frightened me. I was making leaps overnight that would take anyone else weeks or months. Perhaps years.

Wouldn't he think I was mad if I told him? I was already considered strange enough for my costume and commitment, but he was interested in the esoteric. Hadn't Gaston told me he'd belonged to a society that summoned angels to help artists? Maybe he was the one person who would understand, who could help me.

"What is it, Mademoiselle Verlaine?"

"Nothing," I lied. "I don't know what you mean."

"Some artists are concerned with expressing the words of the soul. That's all fine, but I'm more interested in rendering visible, so to speak, the inner flashes of intuition. Those have something divine in their apparent insignificance. And transposed by the marvelous effects of pure visual art, they reveal truly magical, I would say even sublime, horizons."

He waited for a moment. I remained silent. Then he stood.

"Wait there. I should like to show you something."

Moreau left the room, and while he was gone, I studied the paintings on the walls. Each of a series of small paintings had a brass plaque on its lower arm naming its subject: Andromeda, Diana, Leda, Cleopatra, Salome, and Bathsheba. Each woman shone like a piece of jewelry encrusted with lapis, emeralds, gold, turquoise, sapphires, and rubies. Each solemn and soulful woman looked secretive, contemplating the murder or sacrilege or sacrifice or torture she had inflicted or endured. The extravagant plant life in each painting was as alive as the women; thin tendrils wove around strong verdant leaves; fanning palms shadowed flowers that suggested religious vessels.

I thought of a passage in À Rebours, a decade-old book that all of Moreau's students had read and quoted by heart, which was considered the bible of decadents. The main character spoke of Moreau's art as "despairing erudite works, which emanate a singular spell, a fascination that is deeply, intimately disturbing." These paintings were prime examples of those spells.

Moreau returned several moments later, holding a maroon leather sketchbook.

"People say I am a *peintre d'histoire* because of my subject matter. But I believe neither in that which I touch nor in that which I see. I believe only in that which I do *not* see. I believe uniquely in that which I *sense,* Mademoiselle."

He opened the book to a fantastical drawing of a whole bevy of angels with elaborate wings of different shapes and sizes. Was the story true? Did he call on angels to help him?

Turning the page, he showed me a Salome dancing before the head of John the Baptist. And the next page, another version of the same tale.

"This is where I record my dreams of kings and queens, witches, unicorns, and strange jewels with unearthly powers. My dreams, you see, are mythical gates that allow me to meet with gods and goddesses and creatures of other realms. The critics write I have *poetic hallucinations . . .*" He paused. "It is a good description of what comes over me. I hesitate to discuss it even with my closest companions, even more so with a student, but something compelled me to share this with you. And I never deny such strong impulse. Have you ever experienced anything like my *poetic hallucinations,* Mademoiselle?"

I nodded, afraid to speak, to admit to him what I hadn't even told Julien.

"You see visions? Hear voices?"

"I have once heard a voice, yes."

"Don't be afraid, Mademoiselle. You are gifted, and such talent comes with manifestations we don't always understand. They say demons are not real, but we know differently, don't we?"

"Aren't demons evil?"

"In our sphere, the way we are taught, they could be classified as evil, but is our way of seeing things always correct? We are viewing it from inside our circle. What if we stepped into the spirit's sphere and looked at us from that same distance. Perhaps we would be evil and they would be goodness. Don't judge, Mademoiselle. Live to paint. Paint to live. It may be the only path open to you."

I took in his words, not sure I even understood them.

"And please don't pretend anymore with me in class, at the Louvre or here. Even if we cannot explain how or why your talent is exploding, you must not dam it up. Mallarmé, the poet, wrote, 'Let the window be the art, the mystical experience.' I want you to show me what you see through the window, Mademoiselle. You must be brave and you must be dark, or you will never be great."

I left Moreau's atelier in a fever. I'd been shown what few had seen and been taken into his confidence. If Moreau believed in the realm beyond this one, then there must be some others I could trust who might also. Would I find them that night at the séance that Monsieur Dujols had arranged for me?

Chapter 25

We were seated at a round wooden table in the Librairie du Merveilleux. The doors had been locked and the shades drawn. As usual, books were piled everywhere; maps were laid out on the floor; alembics and jars filled the shelves— nothing was actually different than when I'd visited before, but the atmosphere was almost sinister without the gas lamps turned on, and only the light from candles illuminating Dujols's cave of wonders. In the dim atmosphere, the undulating wall looked like it might be moving. Or was I just a little drunk from breathing the resinous air rich with burning incense? Or was it the chalk drawing of a pentagram in the center of the table affecting me so?

Dujols shook out a large white cloth and placed it over the symbol. The alphabet was spelled out in four rows of block letters.

Next to the cloth he placed a glass cup, turned upside down.

"Let's be seated," he said.

The six of us, including Julien, who had kept his promise to me and come, took our places at the table. He was still wearing the grim expression he'd greeted me with at my house when he arrived to escort me here. During the carriage ride over he was quiet, and I chose not to press him. He was so against this experiment I'd been afraid he would refuse to accompany me. I didn't want to chase him away by saying the wrong thing.

In addition to us and Dujols, the well-known avant-garde composer Debussy was present. He'd brought the opera singer Emma Calvé, who, while Dujols had been setting up, had talked incessantly of the château in the Aveyron region that she'd just purchased. The sixth person was a friend of hers.

"We should have had this event at my château," she said. "There's far more likelihood of summoning spirits there since it was built by the magician and alchemist Nicolas Flamel."

I wondered if Julien's black mood, which only intensified as the evening got started, was aggravated by someone from Charlotte's world being present. Did Calvé know Julien's fiancée? Was he worried that she might tell the young woman she'd run into him at a séance? Would that disturb Charlotte? My head ached with all these questions.

What happened next is not quite clear, even now.

Dujols began the event by giving instructions that we each were to put one finger on the top of the glass cup and not break contact with it no matter what happened.

He explained he would call the spirit forth and then ask her, or him, certain questions that pertained to my dilemma, which no one but he and Julien knew anything about. The secrecy was important, he said, so that the authenticity of the communication could be preserved.

"If a spirit does communicate, he or she will use us as conduits and push the cup around the cloth, spelling out an answer. I will record the letters since sometimes they move too fast to figure out in the moment. But first, I'd like us to take hands."

We took one another's hands. Dujols was seated to my right. His hand was dry, his pulse even. But Julien's hand was moist with perspiration. I glanced at him, but he wouldn't make eye contact. I thought he looked pale.

"Julien?" I whispered, trying to get his attention. "Are you all right?"

He nodded but didn't say anything.

"And now we begin," said Dujols, preventing me from asking Julien anything else. "Everyone please close your eyes and concentrate on welcoming the spirit into our midst."

A surge of excitement mixed with anticipation pulsed through me. Maybe now I was finally going to find out what had been going on for the last few weeks. Discover if the spirit of La Lune really had survived and truly was connected to me in some way.

"Yes, yes, fingers on the glass, please, ladies and gentlemen," Dujols said.

We all placed our forefingers on the small crystal tumbler. Mine trembled.

Dujols waited a moment and then asked: "Are you with us, dear spirit?"

The glass sped off to the corner of the cloth where *OUI* was spelled out on the board.

Who was moving it? Not I, certainly. I was sure it was not Julien. Who here had any reason to prove a spirit was visiting? This séance was not being held for a price. This was a favor Dujols was granting me in exchange for me promising to show him the grimoire I'd found in the bell tower.

"Mademoiselle Verlaine would like to know what it is you need from her," Dujols asked.

There was a hesitation, and I wondered if the previous answer had been an accident of the wind. Or one of the members of the assembly was playing a trick on us.

And then the cup spelled out one word.

Nothing.

"Then is there something you need to tell her?"

The cup moved and spelled out Julien's name. Beside me, his body tensed.

"You are here for Julien?

Yes.

"What is it you want to tell Julien?"

The board spelled out: *My death not accident.*

I heard Julien gasp.

Then there was a moment's pause, and the cup continued.

Forgive yourself.

A pause.

She loosened wheels . . .

A pause

. . . for money.

Julien stood and pushed himself away from the table with such force that his chair fell backward.

"Enough of this." He looked around at our faces as if he was searching for someone to accuse. His green eyes were clouded, his features set in an anguished expression. After a second he turned and ran to the door, unlocked it, pulled it open with great force, and rushed out into the street.

I ran after him, hurrying to keep up. He was on a tear and going faster than I could. He reached the corner but didn't stop. From the opposite direction a carriage was coming, but he didn't seem to see it. I screamed out: "Julien, stop!" For some reason he didn't stop but just went barreling into the street straight into the oncoming horse and carriage.

He was going to be trampled, and I was not going to be able to get to him in time. I shouted again, but he kept going. Why wasn't he stopping? It was almost as if he were throwing himself in front of the carriage on purpose. As if he *wanted* something terrible to happen to him.

There is no question about what happened next, though it seemed impossible then and impossible now as I recall this.

Everything became very quiet. The street noises abated. I sensed rather than heard a whoosh of words, almost like a breeze was speaking to me in a manner different than how we humans normally communicate. The air itself told me Julien would be all right. That I needn't panic. As I was being given that strange but comforting communiqué, just as the collision appeared inevitable, a wind came up out of nowhere, for it was not a rough-weathered night, picked up Julien—yes, picked him up like a mother lifting a babe—and blew him backward. He sailed two or three feet in the air, just enough to remove him from the path of the oncoming carriage, and landed in a heap on the sidewalk.

I ran to him.

He'd straightened himself out and was sitting on the curb, watching the carriage as it continued on down the street as if nothing strange had occurred at all. But it had. I had seen it.

"Are you all right?"

"Yes," but he clearly wasn't. His eyes were troubled, and his face was drawn.

"Julien, what just happened?"

"I wasn't watching where I was going."

"But just now, it looked as if someone threw you backward."

"Someone? There was no one here. I understood almost too late what was happening and jumped *backward.*"

I stared at him. That was not what had happened. Did he believe it or just want *me* to believe it? I was about to question him further, but he was standing, brushing himself off, speaking to me.

"It's getting late. Let me walk you home."

"What went on at Dujols's? Why did you run out like that?" I asked.

"I told you I didn't want to go. All that mumbo jumbo makes me nervous. I don't believe it. Dujols probably was moving that glass himself."

"Why would he do that?"

"To impress you so that you'll give him what he wants."

"You mean the grimoire?"

"Yes, the grimoire and anything else he can get you to share with him."

"Julien, what was the spirit talking about when he or she said that about it not being your fault—"

Julien interrupted. "It wasn't a spirit; it was Dujols."

"Fine. What accident did he reference?"

"Nothing that matters anymore."

Julien's whole demeanor was different. He'd retreated. Around him was an aura darker than the night sky. When he started walking again, I had to hurry to keep up.

"Something is bothering you. I'd like to know what it is."

"All right. Today of all days is the anniversary of my father's death."

"I'm sorry. So sorry. Do you think that was the accident the spirit referred to?"

"Yes, and I was responsible. I was responsible for my father's death . . ." He had slowed down. His voice had softened. I could see his face, and the expression he wore was crushing. I couldn't bear to hear the pain in his voice. And the longing. And the love.

"The accident was my fault. We were in the carriage. I had the reins—" He broke off.

"And it haunts you."

"Of course, wouldn't it haunt you, too, if you were responsible for someone you loved dying?" His voice was bitter.

"The spirit said it wasn't an accident."

"*Dujols* said. Believe me, I know what transpired. I was driving the carriage. We were arguing. I wanted to come to Paris and study architecture. He wanted me to stay in Nancy and work with him and his brother in the family firm. I loved my father. I loved making furniture, but . . ."

"You know that was your father tonight. He was telling you it wasn't your fault."

"Losing him was more pain than I'd ever known. I can't even entertain what you are suggesting. My sister put us through all this already. Organizing séances, visiting charlatans who claimed to see visions in crystal balls . . . My brother and I had to stop her."

"But what if it isn't nonsense? What if it was your father's spirit tonight? He said it wasn't your fault. Was there someone who benefitted? Who was the 'she' he referred to who loosened the wheels?"

Julien started walking faster again, as if he were racing to the answer. "The only 'she' would have been my stepmother." He shook his head. "My brother and sister and I hated her. She was obsessed with money, with having the best dresses, the finest china, the biggest house . . ."

"Did she love your father?"

He stopped midstep. Turned to me. He was thinking, hard.

"Yes . . ."

"Did she inherit money upon his death?"

"Yes, there was a will that he'd made when we were young that he'd never changed. It left everything to his wife when his wife was my mother. He never actually named her in the document, just referenced *his wife*."

"And your stepmother, what happened to her after your father died?

"Nothing unusual. She continued taking care of my brother and sister. I moved to Paris to study with Cingal."

"Did she remarry?"

"About two years after my father's death."

"Is it possible she'd had the man she married as a lover when she was with your father? That they plotted the accident? That she didn't love your father as much as you all thought?"

"I don't know . . . I suppose so . . ."

He spoke slowly as he put it together in his mind. "You know . . . I did just remember something. I wasn't supposed to be in the carriage with him that afternoon. He was going to meet with a client at the factory. At the last minute I asked him if I could get a ride into the city. I seem to remember my stepmother tried to get me to stay home with her and help her do something, and my father telling her it was fine . . . that I could come."

"You never wondered about that?"

"I was just seventeen years old . . . None of us ever suspected it was anything but an accident . . . I'd been badly hurt . . . Everything about the incident was a blur."

"Except your guilt. And these years later you still haven't forgiven yourself."

Julien had pulled out his watch fob and was fingering the ring that hung on the chain. I'd seen him do this many times but had never questioned him about it.

"What is that?"

He showed me. In the moonlight, I examined the heavy gold ring with the initials inscribed.

" 'AJD'?"

"My father, Alain Jerome Duplessi."

I undid the chain and pulled off the ring. Then I took Julien's right hand and put it on his finger.

"That's where it belongs. He'd want you to wear his ring. He'd be proud."

For a moment Julien didn't speak.

"Thank you," he said in a gruff voice as he tried to swallow his emotion.

We walked on for half a block in silence.

"I still don't believe any so-called spirit sent me messages. Don't you see that this was some kind of sham to impress you so that you would give Dujols the grimoire."

Before I could argue, he continued.

"The accident was well reported in the newspapers. So, I'm sure, was her remarriage. Dujols could have done some research, put it all together, and come up with a theory. He is a publisher after all."

"Perhaps," I said. But I didn't think it was a set up.

From what my grandmother had explained about the legend of La Lune, I was beginning to understand. Somehow Julien's guilt had been keeping him from trusting his emotions. La Lune needed Julien to be free of guilt so that he would be able to love someone again fully . . . love *me,* I thought. That was what she was waiting for, wasn't it?

But would loving me be enough? What exactly did she require?—because there were still other obstacles. Charlotte here in Paris. My husband in New York. I shivered and pulled my coat tighter around me. La Lune had just hauled Julien out of the path of danger. Certainly, if she could do that, she could do the opposite, too.

Chapter 26

For the next few days, when I wasn't at school or at the Louvre copying paintings or at Moreau's atelier, I played detective and followed Julien.

When we were together, I'd ask about his plans, meetings, and appointments so whenever possible I could observe him with Charlotte. I needed to know more about her and about them together.

I spied on them. I watched them. Oh, how I hated the sight of her blond curls next to his dark ones. How I hated the way she put her hand on his arm when they sat in restaurants, as if she owned him. And that flirtatious way she looked up at him from under her lashes. Every action waiting for a reaction, every tease waiting for a response.

He showed all the signs of a man in love. He was attentive and responsive. He laughed with her and was affectionate. When she whispered in his ear, he smiled.

I had never been jealous when my husband interacted with other women at dinner parties or the theater or when we visited with friends. Never taken more than a cursory interest when he paid attention to a female other than myself.

But I had never loved my husband. And I did love Julien. Not just with my mind but also with my lips, my fingers, my skin. When he was not with me at the mansion, I was painting him from memory in my studio or imagining being with him. Julien was my fever. The idea of him burned inside of me. When I went a day without him, I felt actual pain, like the hunger pangs you can suffer when you've gone too long without food. While this kind of feeling was new and marvelous, it was also terrifying to be in its grip.

Wednesday evening, Julien and I were together for *le cinq à sept*, an accepted time when all over Paris, husbands saw their mistresses, wives their paramours, lovers delighted in one another and guilt took the evening off. Hedonism was an indulgence that didn't require complicated justifications, remorse, or blame. There was the institution of marriage, and there were one's sensual needs. When the two weren't compatible, society accepted the alternatives. One didn't reveal one's affairs to a wife, so I didn't expect Charlotte knew about Julien's dalliances, but according to the custom of the day, if she did know, she would try to turn the other cheek.

I had been painting at the Louvre that afternoon, and when I returned, I found Julien waiting for me. He'd brought a fragrant Bordeaux, a creamy soft wheel of Saint André, a little wooden crate of figs, and a fresh baguette. We drank and feasted on the food and then on each other. Afterward, while we lay in between the fine cotton sheets in the Persian bedroom, I asked him what he was doing that evening.

"Why do you ask me if you know the answer is going to make you pout?" he asked.

"I don't pout." I waved my hand as if dismissing the issue like a piece of dust.

"You do pout, darling, you do." He leaned down and kissed me. "I can't just call off my engagement with Charlotte. And we couldn't marry even if I was free. You're not divorced yet. We need time to figure out how to do what we want to do."

"Yes, yes, I know, you're right." I forced a smile. "So tomorrow?" I asked as he got dressed. "I don't have class. Would you like to go to the Bois de Boulogne for luncheon?"

"I would, but I am having lunch with a potential client at the Eiffel Tower. The gentleman, a businessman from Germany and a great patron of the opera, is going to build a new department store in the 5th arrondissement. He's in the process of choosing an architect, and Charlotte has arranged the meeting. It could be my largest commission to date."

"How wonderful," I said, and truly meant it, already envisioning the marvelous sinewy, curling, twisting building that Julien was capable of designing.

Thursday turned out to be the kind of day that I thought showed off Paris in the best light. Others waxed euphoric over sunshine, but for me the magic of the city shone brightest when the skies were moody and melodramatic. That afternoon, charcoal clouds threatened rain, and the air had a slightly metallic scent that added an edge of excitement to the atmosphere. As if a storm was not all that the city was waiting for.

As always, there was a crowd at *la Tour Eiffel*. Only open for four years, the iron latticework structure drew tourists and Parisians alike. It was a constant source of discussion—people debated whether the metal sculpture fascinated or repelled. No one was neutral.

Because of how jammed the tower might be, I had arrived early so I could be there when they arrived and not miss them. After waiting twenty minutes or so, I saw Julien alight from a cab, help Charlotte out, and then lend a hand to a portly gentleman who sported a twisting mustache and extremely tall top hat.

Hiding in the shadows among the crowd, dressed in my masculine garb, I watched as the trio made their way to the elevator.

Charlotte, wearing a fetching verdant-green silk dress and hat that set off her blond hair, was leaning on the gentleman's arm, flirting with him, while Julien walked alone. I felt a secret pleasure that not only did he not seem to be paying attention, he also didn't look annoyed with her. Although even if he was jealous, he couldn't very well show it, could he? She was helping him procure a commission; it wouldn't do for him to make the gentleman uncomfortable.

All three entered the elevator. I watched the cabin rise, keeping sight of Charlotte's emerald-green hat, which sparkled brightly like a bird's wings as they ascended.

I thought of the last thing that Julien had said to me before he'd departed the previous evening . . .

"I will be at dinner tonight, thinking of you here, in bed, naked, like this."

"Don't go then. Stay with me here, naked, like this."

"I am obligated."

"Yes, you are obligated."

But do you love her? I wanted to ask so I could understand. Love, or the lack of it, I wanted to tell him, was not a frivolous reason for making a decision about marriage. It was the only reason. Love, I wanted to shout, was the only reason to do anything. The only value worth living for. A goal truly worth making any sacrifice for.

But I just fingered the rubies around my neck and kept silent.

As the elevator worked its way up the tower, I climbed the stairs, my sensible boots making it easy to keep up a steady pace. In fact, I was able to outdistance the lift. When I reached the restaurant level and stepped off, I looked down and watched the emerald-green feathers rising, flying up.

Would they look around first or go straight to the restaurant? I had made a reservation and would simply wait and let them be seated first and then tip the maître d' to make sure I wasn't in Julien's line of sight.

I positioned myself so I could observe them get off the elevator without them seeing me.

After emerging from the lift, they walked to the right, away from the restaurant and out onto the observation deck. Using the crowd to conceal myself, I followed. With all the people around, it was unlikely Julien would notice me, especially in my drab black pants and jacket and hat pulled down to cast my face in shadow.

The trio stood at the railing. Charlotte put down the straw basket she was carrying, bent over, and opened it. Withdrawing three champagne flutes, she handed one to the German and two to Julien. As she did so, she leaned close to him, brushing his arm with her breast. I bristled. No matter what he had told me, he was betrothed to her, not to me. She had the right to be this way with him in public. To lean on him. To touch him. And I did not.

Next she pulled a bottle of champagne out of the basket and with great ceremony proceeded to open it. At the end, she lost control of the cork, either by accident or on purpose to make the moment even more exciting. As it went sailing over the edge, she gave a shriek I could hear despite the crowd's murmuring. It was a lovely sound—she was a singer after all—but at the same time it had an ominous tone to it, like one of the broken bells in the tower.

I caught sight of the cork as it arched over the crowd and then dropped. Peering down, I followed its trajectory. Would it hurt someone when it landed? There were a lot of trees below; most likely it would be caught in the branches of a chestnut or plane tree.

The dizzying view made me uncomfortable, and I stepped back from the edge. As I did, I bumped into someone. Turning around to apologize, I came face-to-face with my husband.

No. That was impossible. He was in New York. It was the dizziness. It was the shadows from the clouds. Indeed, he was similar in height and coloring, but his features were not the same and his eyes were kind. My husband's eyes were intelligent and shrewd but never kind.

"Excuse me," I said to the stranger.

He smiled and told me it wasn't a problem, but he stared. It took me a moment to realize why. The juxtaposition of the feminine voice and masculine clothing had caught his attention.

I resumed watching the trio by the railing. Charlotte filled the glasses. The three of them clinked the flutes with a toast I was too far away to hear, and then they drank.

Keeping at Julien's back so that he didn't spot me, I inched closer. I wanted to listen to what they were saying.

The German was pointing out over the rooftops of Paris. "That is the street. Right there will be the finest store in all of this fine city. I want to be able to stand here and look out over Paris and see my store. Will you be able to do that, Monsieur Duplessi?"

They were all leaning over the railing now, looking far into the distance, toward the 5th arrondissement.

"Of course! The tallest, most fantastic store in the city!" Charlotte cried, answering for him.

The wind picked up, and I felt the first few drops of rain. But no one seemed to notice, or if they did, it didn't dampen their spirits.

Charlotte pointed. "Is it right there? Next to the church? Will you sell hats? I love hats," she sounded as if the champagne had gone to her head already.

"No," the German said. He took her hand and moved to the right. "That street. Do you see it? There is a long row of uneven rooftops, like bad teeth."

The wind grew stronger, but no more rain fell. It seemed to me that the tower was swaying. Some of the crowd noticed it, too. I heard comments of concern and surprise.

Another stronger gust caused a more obvious

swaying that was disturbing enough for a surge of people to rush to the elevator. In the crush someone shoved me. I began to fall into the man in front of me. The stranger whom I'd thought looked like Benjamin. But at the last minute he moved, opening up a direct path between me and Charlotte. I was going to fall right into her as she leaned over the edge. I might throw her off balance.

I twisted to the right, falling instead into a middle-aged woman holding a child's hand who was beside me and nowhere near the ledge.

"Be careful!" she shouted as she pulled her child closer.

I stood, turned around, looked for whoever had jostled me to complain. But no one around acted in the slightest way responsible. I had no idea who it had been.

At the railing, Charlotte, Julien, and the German were still looking out over the city, oblivious to my mishap and how close we'd come to disaster. Neither the strong winds nor the tower's tremble seemed to be troubling them. Charlotte, still leaning, was now using her champagne glass as a pointer and swaying in rhythm with the tower, as if the wind were her dancing partner.

Julien pulled a notebook from his pocket and sketched rapidly, while the German looked on, lavishing praise.

Fat, cold raindrops began to fall then, enough so

that the two men inched away from the railing and moved closer to the restaurant and shelter so Julien could keep drawing.

Charlotte, however, remained, still leaning over, still looking out, as focused on the city as the men were on the sketch.

A woman struggling to open her scarlet umbrella asked me to help. Taking the frilly contraption from her, I tried to release the catch while a squall pushed against my efforts.

Just as I was about to give up, the wind moved direction. At my back now, the gusts helped and the umbrella opened quickly. Suddenly, with a force that took me by surprise, the wind flew into the open canopy and stole the whole umbrella from me.

It flew, like some odd bird, through the air, right toward Charlotte, as if aiming for her specifically.

"Watch out," I shouted over the rain.

I'm not sure what she heard, but she turned, saw the umbrella, moved to the right, giggled, and, following its trajectory, tried to grab it. What was she thinking? It was just some stranger's red umbrella.

Teasing, the wind blew the elusive silk parasol back to her and then away in the other direction. Charlotte laughed, making me think of a kitten playing with a ball of string.

The sky blackened. In the distance thunder rumbled. The wind blew the umbrella back toward

Charlotte, who, reaching for the wayward instrument, stretched out her hand and leaned all the way forward.

Too far forward.

I rushed toward her, reaching out to help her, to stop her, because I could see what was going to happen and I couldn't allow it. To my horror my fingers grasped only air. Impossibly, in one quick and terrible instant, she'd gone over the tower's railing. The parasol along with her, winging its way through the charcoal sky, picked up by drafts of air, dancing still. But Charlotte did not dance. She fell straight down, hurtling toward the crowd and the hard pavement below us. She fell fast, becoming smaller and smaller, while all I could do was watch.

A scream rent the air. At first I thought it was Charlotte but then realized I was the one screaming. She was laughing, drunkenly, hysterically, pathetically, and the sound of it rose up on the wind and splashed my face along with the cold, cold rain.

Chapter 27

I arrived at the bottom of the tower, shaking and disoriented. I looked around, trying to figure out which direction to take to leave, to make my way to the road, to find a carriage, to go home.

There were so many people milling around I couldn't see any street signs.

To the right, at least a dozen uniformed officers had formed a barricade and were blocking off a section of the plaza. Was that where Charlotte had fallen? Was her body there on the pavement? I tried to see through their legs, but they had formed too solid a wall. Standing on my tiptoes, I searched for a glimpse of Julien between their starched caps. I didn't see him, but I did catch sight of the German.

Then one of the policemen shifted position and nothing but uniforms were visible.

Not knowing which way to go, I decided just to walk in the opposite direction from the disaster site. I would be able to find a carriage on any street. It didn't matter if it was in the opposite direction from La Lune. Heading a few blocks out of the way was of no importance now. I needed to get home. Everything would be all right once I got home.

I began to walk, two terrible words going around

and around in my head, in some crazy rhythm that wouldn't abate.

Fire, fall . . . fire, fall . . . fire, fall . . .

There was no avoiding the awful truth. The fire had been her first attempt. This had been her second.

My legs were shaking so badly each step seemed to take forever.

I began to notice more police had arrived. Or had they been there all along? Dozens of them, their hats standing out like white caps on a stormy sea. It appeared the gendarmes were stopping random people and asking them questions.

What would happen if they interrogated me?

Nothing, I reassured myself. I had nothing to hide. No reason to be so nervous, to be *this* nervous.

Trying not to attract any attention, I continued moving through the crowd, heading toward the street. Despite my efforts, one of the gendarmes focused on me. I bent to pick up an imaginary something from the ground.

How was I going to answer his questions? I didn't even understand what I'd seen. I was only sure of what I'd felt—someone in the crowd had shoved me; the wind had pushed me. Such a strong wind. It was the wind that had picked up the umbrella. Why had Charlotte been determined to grab it? Had she drunk too much champagne?

"Monsieur?" The policeman blocked my path.

I stood up and looked at him, meeting his glance, at the same time pretending to put whatever I'd picked up from the ground into my pocket.

"Oh, excuse me, Mademoiselle." He was embarrassed to have gotten my sex wrong.

"That's all right."

"Were you up on the terrace?"

I nodded.

"You are aware of what happened?"

"It's so terrible," I said, my voice breaking.

He gave me a sympathetic nod. "It is. Did you witness the accident?"

"No, I didn't. I was on the other side of the balcony."

He was trained to know when people were telling the truth. Would he know that I was lying?

"And so how is it you know what happened?"

"On the steps . . . it's a long way down . . . there were people who saw it and were talking about it . . . Is it true what they said? A woman fell to her death?"

Was he looking at me strangely? Had he guessed? Did he think I had been involved? Had I somehow implicated myself? But I hadn't been involved. There was no way I could be found guilty. It was not me. I had not touched Charlotte. I had nothing to do with her accident.

"So then, you didn't actually see anything?"

"No, nothing but the crowd surging toward that side of the terrace."

"Thank you then."

I turned.

"One more thing."

My heartbeat quickened.

"Yes?"

"May I have your name?" He had taken out a pad and a pencil.

"My name?"

"We need to keep a record of the eye-witnesses."

"But I didn't actually see anything," I insisted.

"A record of people on the platform." His pencil was poised; he was waiting.

"Of course. My name is Eloise Bedford," I said, giving him the name of the same girl I'd gone to school with whom I'd used in another lie the day I'd applied to the École des Beaux-Arts.

Closing his notebook, he moved on.

I tried to keep my pace calm and not hurry as I kept walking. *Fire, fall. Fire, fall.* I wanted to run. I could barely breathe. My clothes were drenched in sweat. I was shivering. And still I had to keep going at an even gait. *Fire, fall. Fire, fall.*

Chapter 28

It was the accident, not my grandmother, I thought of during the carriage ride from rue des Saints-Pères to Dr. Blanche's clinic in Passy. I could think of nothing else. I kept seeing Charlotte falling. Kept remembering the policeman questioning me. Kept wondering how Julien was.

I had not heard from him that night. Or the next day. Of course I hadn't. He would have been in shock. Then plunged into mourning. Any strength he had he would need to devote to helping Charlotte's father cope. As the cab traversed the city, I wished I were on my way to him. How was he faring? How was he enduring the solemn ceremony of his fiancée's funeral? I'd thought about attending, to be with him, to offer support, but he had not come to me, and under these circumstances I did not think I should go to him unasked.

This was the fourth death that had touched my life in so very few months. My father, my grandmother's uncle the doctor, our cousin Jacob Richter, and now Charlotte. Too many deaths. Too close together.

As I alighted from the carriage, I noticed Dr. Blanche was coming down the street, and we reached the front door at the same moment.

Greeting me warmly, he said, "Your grandmother is doing so well, Mademoiselle. I think you'll be delighted."

As we walked down the hallways toward her room, he explained some of the treatment she'd been getting and how responsive she was. "She's even started flirting with the male patients, which is a very good sign." He smiled.

When I entered Grand-mère's room, her face did indeed light up. No longer confined to her bed, she was sitting at the table set for tea, presumably for my visit. I was delighted and relieved to see she appeared rested and much better groomed. Her hair was clean and up in a twist, and she had on rouge and lipstick and was dressed in a salmon silk morning dress I'd brought from home the last time I visited. The change in her since then was astonishing. This was my grandmother again, not a deranged stranger. Tears filled her eyes as she looked at me.

Had I ever been as happy to see anyone?

I took her hands and leaned down. She kissed me. I wasn't sure if it was her tears or mine that wet my cheeks.

"Your perfume smells wonderful, Sandrine. I don't have any perfume here. Can you bring me some? And my tortoiseshell combs."

"Of course."

"Sit down, *mon ange*. They have made a tea for us."

She poured with a hand that trembled only a bit, and I relaxed seeing how much herself she was.

"Dr. Blanche said that I might be able to go home in another two weeks or so."

"Not soon enough," I said.

"Is the apartment all right? Is everything running smoothly?"

"Of course," I lied. I wasn't ready to tell her I'd moved back into the house for fear I'd set her off. It was too good to have her back, sane and calm. "I've even been keeping the salon afloat."

She smiled.

"All your beaus miss you and wish you well." From the bag I'd brought, I pulled out a box of chocolates from Debauve and Gallais, the oldest chocolatier in Paris, which was just a few doors down from La Lune. "Monsieur St. Simone sent you these."

"How very thoughtful." She took the beautiful cream-colored box with its gold-and-navy insignia and gazed at it like a fine jewel. The ribbon was ornate, navy satin embroidered with gold fleurs-de-lis, and she traced the decoration with her forefinger, for the moment lost in thought.

"Dr. Blanche said that I might be able to go home in another two weeks or so." She repeated what she'd said before but whispered it this time, and I wondered how many times a day she soothed herself with that single thought.

"Would you like a chocolate?" I asked.

"Perhaps later." She placed the box on the table, picked up her teacup, and took a sip. She turned back to me, watching me carefully, as if searching for something in my eyes. She frowned. Shook her head. "I am worried for you."

"No need, I'm fine."

"But you are lying to me. You moved into the house." Her voice quivered.

"How did you know?"

"Alice came to visit me yesterday."

Of course her maid would have come to visit—she was devoted to my grandmother.

"I miss you less there. I even miss Papa less when I am there." All that was true. It was also true that I felt more welcomed there than anywhere I'd ever lived.

"But you can't live in that house. You're in danger there."

"No, no, I'm not. There's nothing wrong with your beautiful house. The pipes and the plumbing are all fine."

She shook her head impatiently. "That's not what I mean, and you know it. Don't try to fool me. Something has changed, hasn't it?"

"What do you mean?"

"I don't know exactly. But I can see it in your eyes. Something terrible has transpired since the last time you were here. What is it, Sandrine, what is it?" She had become highly agitated.

What to tell her? Some version of the truth? "I was at *la Tour Eiffel* yesterday and saw an accident."

"You saw the opera singer fall?"

I nodded.

"I know her fiancé," my grandmother said. "He has been doing work for me, and when I read about the accident in the newspaper, I was so upset for him. It's very tragic. They had a photograph of her . . . so young and lovely. And you were there? It must have been horrible. But what were you doing there?"

"I hadn't been to see the tower. All this time in Paris and I hadn't yet gone up." Too late, I remembered that was the wrong lie.

"No, not so," Grand-mère said. "We visited the tower your first week. We had a lovely luncheon there. Surely you have not forgotten that. Why are you lying to me about this, too?"

I didn't know what else to say. "Yes, you're right, we did."

"So then why were you there?" She was examining my face and thinking out loud. "The article said she was there with a German business-man who is building a department store in the 5th and her fiancé and . . ." She put it all together and let out a small scream. "Oh no! It was La Lune. She caused the accident? This is how it begins."

Fall, fire. Fall, fire. I could not hear what my

grandmother was saying anymore. I was seeing my burnt gloves, the blackened pearls. Hearing Charlotte's laugh as she sailed over the balcony railing. I put my head in my hands. Dug my fingers into my forehead. Wanted to feel pain. Searing stings. Anything to stop thinking what I was thinking. Accepting this horrible reality. *Fire, fall.*

I heard a noise. Glass breaking. My grandmother was reaching across the table. She'd knocked over one china cup, now was knocking over the teapot, which spilled onto the cloth and her dress, grabbed my hands and pulled them to her. She was holding them so tightly I worried she might break my bones, and then how would I paint?

"This is what she does. She wants her passions fulfilled, Sandrine. At any price. She craves it. And she uses us to do it."

"Tell me," I whispered, needing to hear the story. I had seen a woman die. I had felt the push at my back, and it hadn't been the wind.

My grandmother leaned forward conspiratorially, as if she were afraid for anyone but me to hear. "She incubates in a host in order to relive her past. That is what my mother told me. What I told your father. She incubates. Always trying to re-create her time in Paris when she was painting, when she was with Cherubino, being in love and being loved back, before her jealousy cost her lover his life. None of the women she's infested have been strong enough to withstand La Lune's spirit and stay sane or talented enough to become the artist she was. Marguerite, Camille, Eugenie, Clothilde, Simone . . ."

My grandmother was naming all the women in the portraits on the stairs.

"Marguerite claimed that within days of becoming betrothed to her lover, she began to see La Lune when she looked in the mirror. A month later, she threw herself off of the Pont Neuf in the dead of winter and froze to death in the swirling, black waters.

"Under La Lune's influence, Simone became so passionate, so hungry for her lover, that she drove him away. Her beau was so frightened by her appetite that he left her the night before they were to announce their betrothal. She painted over a hundred portraits of him—all terrible—and, when she completed the last, took poison and died."

And then my grandmother's voice changed and became a hoarse whisper with a heavier accent. Completely and totally unrecognizable.

"Don't be afraid, Sandrine. I've learned from my mistakes. From each woman I learned a little bit more. I know better how to control my appetites. I won't force all my desperation onto you. I won't overwhelm you with my appetites. I will just show you the life that you can have and

400

you will want it enough . . . want it so much . . . that you will invite me to stay. And then we will both have what we want. What we need."

"Grand-mère? Grand-mère?"

She didn't say anything more, just sat frozen like one of Rodin's marbles, sightless eyes staring straight ahead, not speaking, not acknowledging that she could even hear me.

"Grand-mère? Grand-mère?"

Finally she blinked, and then her eyes widened in horror. She knew, as did I, what had happened.

My grandmother rose, came around the table to me. Reaching out, she grabbed the neck of my dress and jerked it open. Buttons flew. Fabric ripped. I pushed her hand away. She stumbled and fell against the bed.

My grandmother looked so helpless then, sprawled half on and half off, clutching at the comforter for balance. She was breathing heavily, sweat on her forehead, her eyes glazed.

"Are you all right?" I asked.

"She got inside me. She made me talk to you for her." She lunged at me again. "You have to take her necklace off," she yelled as she pulled at the rubies around my neck. "Off . . . off . . ."

Alerted by the noise, the nurse ran into the room. "Madame Verlaine, please, please. It's not good for you to become overexcited."

The nurse tried to disengage my grandmother from me, but she resisted.

"Let go of your granddaughter, Madame, or you will not be able to see her again."

My grandmother pushed her off. The nurse fell. Grabbing hold of me, my grandmother gripped my arms. Her fingers dug, like talons, into my skin. Her hair had come undone, and tears had melted her mascara. The charming coquette had disappeared. My grandmother was gone, and once again I was facing a madwoman I did not know.

The nurse, who'd gone out to get help, returned now with two orderlies who rushed in and dragged my grandmother off me, but not before she'd ripped the sleeve of my gown and scratched the skin beneath the fabric.

I backed up, away from her, and stood against the wall, watching the scene.

"She's a succubus . . . She sucks us dry like a whore sucking a cock . . . like a bitch in heat . . ."

While my grandmother continued ranting, the two orderlies held her down and the nurse administered the sedative. That done, the male helpers tied my grandmother to her bed, first her wrists and then her ankles.

My grandmother, who wore the most expensive silks and satins, who slept on the finest Egyptian cotton, was bound by coarse hemp, fabric too rough for her skin.

And all I could do was watch in terror.

"If you keep this up, Madame, the doctor isn't

going to let you go home. And you want to go home, don't you?" the nurse said soothingly, trying to calm my grandmother.

"La Lune needs a host, Sandrine. You think I'm mad, but I'm not. I'm as sane as anyone around me. You need to believe me. Go home. Look at the portraits . . ." She was slowing down. The sedative was taking effect. "They are all wearing the rubies . . . Look at the women . . ." She was falling asleep as she spoke. Now her voice was just a whisper, and I had to move forward to hear what she was saying.

"Look at the women . . . in their eyes . . . the same . . ."

And then she was asleep.

At rest, she looked once again like my grandmother. I reached out and touched her cheek, wanting so much to relieve her suffering.

The nurse put her arm around me. "I know it's very hard to see her like this, but it's just a little setback. She didn't have an incident all week. She's been just wonderful."

I nodded but didn't say anything. Would it do any good to tell the nurse that it was me? That my grandmother couldn't be around me for any length of time without becoming deranged and spouting lunatic theories that were all ridiculous?

My fingers moved up to my neck, and I touched the rubies. I'd been careful to wear a dress that would cover the carved stones lest she see them and try to take them off me again. I wouldn't allow that to happen. No one would ever remove them from my throat but me. They'd been hidden in the house for me to find, and I had. Good things had happened since I'd put them on. Hadn't Julien become my lover since I'd found them? Hadn't I begun painting? Wasn't I becoming exactly who I was meant to be?

Chapter 29

I returned to Maison de la Lune with a purpose. I told Alice that no, I didn't want coffee or *chocolat chaud*, and yes, I'd call her later if I changed my mind.

"Do you want the telegram that arrived?" she asked, holding out a silver tray with a single slim envelope in its center.

I took it with trepidation. Mr. Lissauer's communiqués never contained good news.

The lawyer wrote that the longer the search to find me continued, the more Benjamin became convinced I was in hiding because I had information that could destroy him. In addition, rumors were now circulating in the business community that my husband had become so obsessed with the fruitless efforts, he was becoming unhinged.

Benjamin believing I was dangerous to him was the worst possible news I could have received. I ripped the offending correspondence in half and then in quarters, and finally ripped each of those sections to shreds. When I couldn't rip them into any smaller pieces, I left the mound of paper on the silver tray.

I was halfway up the stairs when I realized I'd come home with a purpose and that I could not allow Benjamin to deter me. That would be giving him power and I was determined never to do that again.

Starting from the bottom of the staircase once more, I walked up slowly, taking the time to examine each of the portraits. A deep-red-and-midnight-blue Persian runner covered the center of the steps. If I kept to the rug, I'd be too far from the paintings to examine them carefully, so I walked on the marble, aware of every footfall ringing out on the stone, like solemn chimes marking time.

I'd been painting at the École for more than two months and knew so much more than I had when I first arrived in Paris, and yet for all this time I'd paid almost no attention to these remarkable paintings that were right here in my own home. They were masterful and evocative, but familiarity, or something more dangerous, had prevented me from really studying them as I did now.

There were six life-size portraits climbing up the stairs, each of a woman sitting in the same room, a room in this very house. My grandmother called the small square room that protruded out into the courtyard the jewel chapel because three of its walls were stained glass. All day long sunlight streamed in and illuminated the glass masterpieces. While it did have the feel of a chapel, there was no religious iconography in the window's illustrations—rather, all the symbolism celebrated the secret and the sensual.

If it was a temple, it was a temple to the senses.

The windows were bordered with mother-of-pearl frames painted with runes, numbers, mystical symbols, and signs that I'd recognized in Dujols's store. Each of the three distinct panels illustrated a different scene. On the left a sun set over a stone circle, the sky suffused with the violets of twilight. In the middle, a midnight-blue night sky shone with stars, the full moon magical and heavy, glowing silver-white. On the far right panel, the sun rose over an idyllic lake, a rustic waterfall in the distance. The pastel rose and peach colors of early morning reflected on the water.

A chandelier of amethyst and ruby glass teardrops hung down over an altar in the center of the room. Instead of a religious icon in its center, there was a row of bronze sculptures of lithe, naked women in suggestive poses. Beside them, silver censers used to burn incense.

There was a divan covered with a chinchilla fur against the far wall. Next to it an Indian hookah sat on the floor, exotic and strange. Deep plush chairs upholstered in violet mohair were scattered on a thick carpet of black and purple flowers on green verdant stems heavy with leaves.

Each portrait had been painted in that room, the light streaming in from the windows creating an aura of incandescent color behind the women. Mysterious studies, all of them were truly masterpieces. And puzzles.

Puzzles that I now knew also contained clues.

After examining all of them for their similarities, I began to study each one for its differences. Every painting had a painted trompe l'oeil scroll on the lower arm of the frame. Only one did not have an end date next to her name.

Lunette	1580
Eugenie	1664–1694
Marguerite	1705–1728
Simone	1734–1777
Camille	1782–1814
Clothilde	1800–1832

It appeared the hand that had painted the names and dates was the same.

When I'd stayed here the summer I was fifteen, I'd asked my grandmother about these women who didn't have last names and stared out at me as if trying to tell me a secret.

Grand-mère had told me they were all my ancestors, women who had lived in this house during the last three centuries.

And there was a family resemblance. They all had fiery red in their hair—some extreme like my grandmother's, others subtle like mine. They all had almond-shaped topaz eyes, too, some with more golden-orange flecks than others. Haunting eyes, I thought as I considered them. They all had hands like mine with very long fingers and tapering nails. Piano fingers, my father used to call them.

But there were other things to notice now that I was really scrutinizing them. Odd things.

Since they each stood at a different angle in the little temple, the focus was on different symbols in the stained glass behind them. I wondered if the symbols appeared in some kind of specific order? Was there a message here? The choice of where to place the woman couldn't have been an accident. I'd need to get a piece of paper and make some notes.

Each woman was wearing the same beautiful burnt-orange silk robe, embroidered with russet and cream flowers and green dragons. The dark coral was the color of embers burning in a grate. Of fall leaves when they are at their most colorful. A sensual, suggestive color—too strong and too powerful for it to be anything but a promise. Each woman held a rose, not in full bloom but just a day past, when its lush scent was at its most provocative. Beautiful, but too heavy. When the scent wasn't any longer a perfume but a drug.

I could smell it so strongly that I looked around for a vase of the flowers, but there was none there. When I turned back to the portraits, I noticed something I'd certainly been aware of but had never thought much about. None of the women's full, almost pouting lips were finished. The color wasn't quite filled in, and the shading hadn't been completed. Unlike the gowns, the roses, the stained glass, the hair, the fingers, and the evocative eyes . . . the mouths were still in progress. I'd told Julien I used to think they'd been kissed too many times.

Now, it seemed to me that the artist had somehow, magically, let the viewer know that each woman had a story to tell, but the time had not yet come for her to tell it.

I studied the color of their lips. I could mix that specific red on my palette. Use a tiny bit of cobalt with cadmium to create that color . . . the color of blood. The same red in the stained glass behind each women and in the stones of the ruby necklace that each wore. The identical necklace that hung around my neck.

I heard my father's voice telling me about the ring he had given my husband to use as my engagement ring.

"Inside of every ruby is a drop of blood, suspended, petrified, and if we could but learn how to release it, it would lead us to the secret of immortality," my father had said.

I walked back down the stairs, found my sketchbook in my reticule, returned to the portraits, and copied down the strange letters and symbols. It was time to go back to the Librairie du Merveilleux and ask Dujols for another favor.

Chapter 30

I walked the short distance to rue de Rennes and, as I approached number 76, felt my stomach begin to flutter. Every time I'd gone to the mysterious shop, I'd grown apprehensive. But fear wouldn't help me work through my puzzle. I pulled open the door. As I touched the twisting vine handle, I thought of Julien. The burial service would be over by now. Julien and Charlotte's father would have returned to their apartment house. Was Julien all right? How badly was he suffering? Was he taking care of himself?

It was wrong of me, but even as I worried about him, I was jealous, jealous that even dead Charlotte could keep him away from me.

The store, which was often crowded with men and women searching for information about the psychic and spiritual worlds, was empty, and that pleased me. I preferred privacy for the questions I'd brought. Monsieur Dujols was inside, seated at a round table, marking up what appeared to be a manuscript.

"Monsieur Dujols," I said, "I'm hope you're not busy, but—"

"Of course not, Mademoiselle Verlaine," he interrupted as he capped his bottle of ink and rose to greet me. "I was so upset about how the séance ended and hoped you would return. The art of influencing events and using hidden forces is a temperamental one. I asked Julien if he would bring you back, and he said he would, but . . ." He shrugged and then gestured for me to have a seat in one of the alcoves. He sat down also.

I wondered why Julien had not told me about Monsieur Dujols's request. How long would it be before I would even see him to ask? I pictured him and Cingal sitting sadly in a parlor, surrounded by friends and family.

"Did you have a specific reason for asking me to return? Other than wanting the grimoire, of course?" I asked.

"Did you bring it?"

"I'm not comfortable taking it out of the house in inclement weather." The truth was I couldn't actually move it out of the tower and didn't want to admit it. Twice I'd picked it up and carried it to the door. Normally heavy and cumbersome, once I reached the bell tower threshold, it became suddenly and impossibly weighty. When I'd turned back to return it to its hiding place, it was manageable again.

"The Secret Witch of rue du Dragon is an enigma." There was a long, low table in front of us covered with maps, and as Dujols spoke, he piled them up and moved them to one side. "I have studied her for years. Through you, we may be able to learn more about her secrets. Will you bring it soon?"

"Of course I will." Another lie. "But how can you be sure she wasn't just an ordinary seductress? Perhaps a bit more intuitive and sensitive to the people around her, but cast unfairly in the role of a witch?"

"Alchemy, witchcraft, casting spells, understanding the occult . . . captures our imagination. We sense that there are secrets beyond our grasp; we are sure there are powers greater than us, some benevolent, others malevolent. Religion has tried to explain the mysteries of the universe, but man does not just strive to understand; he needs to harness them. Through time, those of us who have had just a soupçon more of the ability to access the mysterious have been feared, revered, thwarted, maligned. Almost never elevated as deserved. No, I don't think La Lune was an ordinary seductress." Dujols studied my face. "And neither do you, so why do you suggest it?"

I was caught off guard by his forthrightness and for a moment wasn't sure how to even respond. As it turned out, I didn't have to.

"I'm sorry, that was quite rude," he said. "I didn't mean to challenge you. You came here to see me today, so how can I help you?"

I regained my composure and took the paper out of my silk reticule. "I was at the flea market last weekend and saw a painting that had some curious symbols on it. Some were a bit familiar and I thought they might intrigue you, so I copied them down. Since you know so much about symbols, you might know what they mean."

I was pleased with my story. It made sense without suggesting that my interest was any more than curiosity or that the painting was something I owned or had access to.

"Yes, yes, this is quite interesting," he said as he peered at the paper.

"Why is that?"

"Let me show you something." He got up and walked over to a large, low file cabinet, the kind that oversize prints and drawings were kept in, and began to riffle through one of the drawers.

I was thinking about what he'd said about La Lune. I know he'd called her a witch before, but this time it terrified me to hear it. The word coming from his lips was harsh and ugly, and La Lune, while desperate and determined, was none of those things.

But what else was there to make of all the strange phenomena that had occurred?

A necklace with a clasp that sometimes refused to open? I knew it was not the result of an old hinge.

And the paintings I was creating? It was impossible they were only a latent talent blooming out of tragedy, stirred by my surroundings and nurtured by one of Paris's best teachers.

The horrible accident at the Eiffel Tower? A woman who'd drunk too much champagne? An errant umbrella carried away by a gust of wind at just the right moment?

"Yes, yes. Here it is," Dujols said as he withdrew a sheet the size of a frontispiece to a large book.

Gingerly, he placed it in front of me.

Judging by the ragged edge of the yellowed paper, the page had been ripped from an ancient book. The printing was not refined, and the quality of the ink was uneven in spots. The type was fairly small and hard to read, but I could make out enough to know it was archaic French.

Painted over the printing, in an oddly familiar style, was a woman scantily clad in a dress made of cobwebs. Bugs and insects nested inside her long reddish-brown hair. Around her was a laboratory with shelves of alembics and beakers. I recognized the position of the windows and beams—this was my bell tower.

And the painting was done in the same style as the illustrations I'd discovered in the grimoire in the ancient studio. La Lune's paintings. La Lune's grimoire.

"What is this?" I asked.

"A page from a book called the *Malleus Maleficarum* in Latin, which, translated, is *The Witches' Hammer*. It was written in 1486 by Heinrich Kramer, a German Catholic clergyman. It's a treatise on the prosecution of witches."

I shivered, as if the door had opened and a frigid wind had blown in, embracing me in its chill.

"The goal of the manifesto was to prove that witchcraft existed and to educate other members of the church and government on how to hunt and prosecute them, since sorcery was condemned by religious and secular institutions. The papal bull instituting the first inquisition was included in the preface of this book. The rest is broken into three main sections. The first is an argument against critics who denied the existence of witches and the reality of witchcraft. The second lists and explains all the forms of witchcraft and what witches are capable of, including how they recruited other witches. Usually something would go awry in the life of a younger woman, causing her to seek out the wisdom and guidance and help of a witch."

My shivering increased. I had painted that very scene in my bedroom on rue de la Chaise the morning my grandmother went mad. I'd painted La Lune going to the old crone in Prague for help in seducing Cherubino.

Dujols noticed my discomfort. "You are cold— let me throw some more coal into the heater."

While he was gone, I examined the page. It appeared to be the very one that had been ripped out of the front of my book in the tower.

Dujols came back and picked up where he'd left off: "The book describes rituals and explains how witches cast spells. It includes remedies to prevent young women from falling victim to those spells." He stopped. He was staring at me.

"And the last section?" I prompted.

"Yes, yes. The last section is for those who are given the power to judge and confront the witches and witchcraft. What to look for, how to determine if someone is a witch, how to test her. It's quite horrific. The tests were set up so that no one could survive. For instance, a suspected witch was submerged in the water. If she drowned, she was not a witch, but she was dead. If she didn't drown, she was a witch, but then she was killed."

"What about the painting?" I asked in a voice that surprised me with its strength since I felt quite weak. "Why do the letters and symbols match the ones I've brought you?"

"The legend is that the woman who painted this was herself a witch, and it was said that she had a formula that not only gave a witch immunity from harm but also allowed her to keep herself alive forever."

"The formula for immortality."

"Yes."

"And you think the symbols and letters I copied down are part of that formula?"

"Yes."

"Why do you think that?"

"Because of the instances where it's turned up."

"So there are alchemists who have tried out this formula?" I asked.

"Yes, but what's survived is incomplete. We only have the first step in what must have been a long and complicated set of steps."

"And what does all this have to do with La Lune?" I asked, even though I was sure I already knew the answer.

"It's believed La Lune is the witch who was given the formula, who painted this."

"Believed? Doesn't anyone know?"

"No, no, not for sure. It's an ancient legend that dates back to the 1600s. Just one grain of sand in a search for hidden knowledge that goes back to the beginning of time. It is a labyrinthine journey, Mademoiselle Verlaine. Sometimes we are searching in the dark; other times we have but a single candle to shine on the walls of the caves as we crawl through them, hunting for clues."

For a moment neither of us spoke. I was glad I hadn't told Dujols the symbols I'd written down came from paintings in our house. But had showing him even this much put me in jeopardy? How insatiable was Dujols's hunger for more information?

"Well, it's very fascinating," I said, "but like all legends, I'm certain it's become more fantastical over time." I waved my hand as if dismissing the possibility that it had any basis in reality.

"Perhaps or perhaps not," he said in a voice that sounded as if he were still wandering those dark passages in his mind. "Certainly your grandmother has told you how the legend was passed down to her? Surely she's given you details."

I shook my head and lied again. "Nothing like what you told me, no. I know of La Lune of course, but only that she was a courtesan and an artist's muse. Bewitching for sure but not a witch."

Dujols smiled.

"That's odd. Your grandmother and I have talked about it at length. She discussed you with me, too, a long time ago, before I met you. She told me how much she feared for you."

I was stunned.

"You didn't tell me that before. Not when you met me. Not when I came back and you offered to set up the séance. Why?"

"She's always been so concerned that La Lune would one day try to possess you, I assumed it was she who had sent you back here."

I was angry that my grandmother had talked to a stranger about me and confided her fears in him. But anger now was a wasted emotion. We were far past that. There was still more information I needed, and I couldn't afford to alienate Dujols. He was my only ally now, even if it was an uneasy alliance. We both wanted the same thing. The question was, how far would he go to get it? How much did I have to fear him?

"So these symbols"—I pointed to the edge of the page ripped from the book—"what exactly do they stand for? Do you know?"

"Yes. The first is the symbol for blood. This second is for salt, and the third is for night."

"Blood?"

"Blood, herbs and flowers, chemicals, human hair, excrement, skin, parts of animals . . . they were all used by alchemists." He shrugged his shoulders. "I believe that there are more mysteries that we will never solve than those that we will."

Dujols picked up the paper I'd brought and placed it next to the ripped page. "But to return to your question and what brought you here today, the symbols and letters are out of order in the painting you saw. The way they are written there, they spell out nothing . . . but if you rearrange them to go backward, not forward, they say . . . 'Make of the blood, a stone. Make of a stone, a powder. Make of a powder, life everlasting.' "

"That phrase. You know the first time you said it, I was sure I'd heard it before."

"And had you?"

"I didn't think so, but now . . . I think I might have dreamed it."

I was remembering. Yes, these were the words I'd heard in the recurring dream I'd had as a child. I was certain of it.

"A stone? Powder? What do you think it means?" I asked.

"It's the first part of the formula, Mademoiselle Verlaine."

He looked from me to the page he had shown me and then back to me again.

"When you are ready to tell me where you really found those letters and symbols, I will be here to help you. In the meantime, it's best to be careful. It's called darkness because there is no light. And without light it is easy to trip and fall."

He was scaring me. Hadn't Julien warned me that the men involved and invested in the search for hidden knowledge were determined? I felt something shudder under my feet. Almost as if the earth was warning me as well.

I got up.

"There is so much to explore . . . and I *can* help you. But you have to let me help you." Dujols took my hand, bent over it, and kissed it. When he straightened up, he looked right into my eyes. "You do resemble her, you know. In fact the likeness is extraordinary."

"Resemble who?" I asked, feigning ignorance.

But he didn't answer; he just walked to the door and opened it for me.

I stepped out into the evening. The temperature had dropped, and it was chilly again. I pulled my coat around me and looked for a carriage. There was none in sight. No matter, it was only a few blocks and the fresh air would invigorate me. Blow away the miasma that had settled over me.

I'd gone several blocks, preoccupied by the phrase at the heart of the mystery.

Make of the blood, a stone. Make of a stone, a powder. Make of a powder, life everlasting.

What did it mean?

I'd come to a corner. Crossed the street. Walked half a block more and then, in a shop window's reflection, glimpsed a figure that I thought I'd seen before. I had been so preoccupied since I left Dujols that I hadn't stopped to check to see if I was being followed. How could I have been so careless? Continuing on, I willed myself not to turn around and give myself away.

A few yards farther on, I glanced in another window and saw the same man reflected there. He was small, hunched slightly; he wore a tall hat and a long coat. And he didn't walk as much as he crept.

Did this man work for Benjamin, or was he just a passerby going in the same direction I was?

I hailed a carriage and had the driver follow a circuitous route across the Seine, through the Tuileries, and then, when I was one hundred percent certain no one was following us, had him take me to rue des Saints-Pères. All I could do was pray Benjamin's men hadn't found me and vow to be ever more vigilant.

Chapter 31

Make of the blood, a stone. Make of a stone, a powder. Make of a powder, life everlasting.

It meant nothing to me, and yet it stayed with me, a recurring thought I ruminated on that night and all the next day, even at the École. There was no question it was what the woman in my dream had said to me so long ago. The same words she'd said to my father.

I was trying to do what Moreau had taught me and use my consternation and fear as I painted the female model. She was lying on the podium on a chaise longue in need of new springs, but I had placed her in my bell tower, on the daybed, surrounded by ornate pillows, cast in shadows, lit by candles. Moonlight from the windows illuminating her eyes.

"This style of yours intrigues me, Mademoiselle," he said when he came up to me. "The loving way you render the skin so that I can almost touch it, the ability that you have to caress it with your brush and make it come alive . . . it's almost alchemical."

I felt pinpricks of shivers. That word again. It seemed to be following me.

"The opulence and the sensuality is powerful, but I still think you can go further to claim it.

Our job," he said, continuing, "is to see the world in all its storied wonder and synthesize it through our personal vision and then give it back to others on canvas. Look at Matisse, with his bold colors and the way he flattens out the figure. Or Rouault—" He was pointing across the room to his two favorite students. "They are painting their version of reality. Just as you are. What I am saying is that I want you to make this even more your own version. Exaggerate the things that interest you. Make the blacks blacker. Make the skin more luminous. Exploit the sensuality."

After all those weeks of studying with Moreau, I suddenly completely and totally understood what he meant, as if a switch had been turned on in my head, and for the next four hours I painted in a wild frenzy.

At the end of the day, Moreau stopped by to see my progress. He stood watching me for several minutes. Then nodded. Once and again. Finally, he said just four words, and it felt as if I'd waited a lifetime to hear them.

"You have found yourself."

I bowed my head.

"Now you are ready to give some thought to what you are going to submit to the Salon," Moreau said.

"I didn't think I was ready."

"You might not have been before, but you are

now. Your improvement has been remarkable. Truly remarkable."

A few easels away, I saw Serge Mouton glance over at us.

"Do you have a suggestion?" I asked Moreau.

"I would never suggest a subject. This is one of the steps you must take on your own on your path to becoming the artist you are meant to be. Your choices at every juncture make a statement, and it is through those choices you will speak to us. Make a woman look like a statue, or make her look like a harlot. Paint the light as if it were healing and holy, or paint it as if it were flat and damning. Use the paint as harsh reality or as fantasy. Make red violent or as generous as a rose. Every choice speaks of who you are."

I looked at the painting I was working on. What did it say about who I was?

Moreau seemed to be looking, too.

"Choose wisely and paint a sketch this week for us to consider. Many of my students work on the Salon submission all year . . . but your best work, Mademoiselle Sandrine, is not labored. Use your darks and your lights and your feelings, and paint me something. Make me some magic this week."

"Don't you think there is something curious about Mademoiselle's work, Maître?" Serge asked. He'd walked over and was standing to the right of Moreau. "Suspicious perhaps?"

Our teacher looked surprised by the interruption.

"Suspicious? What an odd choice of words. By all means, Monsieur, what do you think is suspicious?"

"These paintings are nothing at all like the paintings that Mademoiselle showed in order to be admitted to your classes. I saw those—we all saw them. These paintings, this style, everything she has created since she's been with us has been markedly different. While she uses the same Renaissance-era chiaroscuro, the new paintings are looser and more contemporary."

"Her style has changed, of course." Moreau frowned.

"It's more than just change," he countered.

"What are you suggesting? And be careful, lest you make an accusation you can't back up," Moreau said.

Several of the students had stopped what they were doing and gathered around. The silence in the large high-ceilinged room was extreme. I was afraid they would all be able to hear my heart beating so loudly in my chest as my fear escalated as I waited to hear Serge's accusation.

"I charge Mademoiselle Verlaine with using paintings that weren't hers to gain entry to the École."

Moreau looked from Serge to my canvas. He cocked his head. Studied my work.

"You are right in that her style is markedly different," Moreau said.

I had just been invited to enter a painting into the 1894 Salon. Was that honor to be snatched from me so quickly? "Yes, different," I said. "I've studied and grown under your tutelage, Monsieur Moreau." My voice trembled—did they all notice?

"All that matters to me is this work—the painting you are doing now," Moreau said.

I held my breath. Was it going to be all right? Was he dismissing Serge's charge?

"But would you be so kind as to bring your admission paintings with you next week so that I can take a look. I don't expect a problem. I have a feeling about you. I have faith in you. But an accusation has been made, and as distasteful as this is, investigate I must."

Chapter 32

I walked home in tears, overwhelmed by a combination of exhaustion from what I'd painted that day, the excitement of the praise Moreau had heaped on me, and then the devastating allegation.

I was waiting at the corner to cross Boulevard Saint-Germain when a carriage stopped in front of me. There were two passengers in the back seat. Both men. One turned, looked right at me. He was backlit, his features indistinct, but . . . Was it Benjamin? Could it be? It had to be, didn't it? The man next to him, even in profile, looked like William Lenox, his business associate, who I'd seen on the ship from New York to Southampton two and a half months ago.

I stepped back into the shadow of a storefront.

I hadn't heard from Mr. Lissauer in days. Wouldn't he have telegraphed if Benjamin had left New York? Yes, if he knew he'd left, but why would he? Mr. Lissauer didn't work for the bank. He wasn't privy to Benjamin's whereabouts.

There was always the possibility that Benjamin's presence in Paris, if it was Benjamin, might be a coincidence. Perhaps he was here on business.

I was grasping at straws, and I knew it. The most

likely scenario was that, if this was Benjamin, his efforts to find me had succeeded at long last. Had there been papers revealing my grandmother's identity in my father's study? Or a record of a bank account with her name on it in one of his desk drawers? There had been no one to prevent Benjamin from searching through my father's personal effects. He'd had months to sift through every file and slip of paper. If he was here, it was my fault for not being more vigilant before I left.

I strained to see into the carriage. Someone walking down the street passed in front of me, blocking my view. And then the horse trotted on. I remained frozen to the spot.

Had that been my husband? Had he recognized me? The man had not seemed to do more than give me a cursory glance. Why should he? I was wearing a man's pants, coat, hat. My hair was short, and my face was hidden in shadows.

As I continued on, I convinced myself that the man in the carriage had not been my husband. It was my overactive imagination again. Hadn't I thought I'd seen him at the Eiffel Tower? Hadn't I been wrong that time? Benjamin was haunting me the way a problem you've put off confronting keeps creeping into your mind given any opportunity. Like the problem I'd brought home with me from class. One that I was not over-thinking or exaggerating. Would Moreau be able to tell I wasn't the artist who'd painted the works in my admissions portfolio? Was there something in those lines and brushstrokes to give me away? And if there was, what would the ramifications be? Was there anything I could do to prevent being found out?

I didn't usually stay in my art-school attire when I got home. Not wanting to be late for my *cinq à sept* with Julien, I always hurried to my bedroom, undressed, bathed, and then, after attending to my toilette, dressed for my lover. But my lover was mourning his fiancée, and I had nothing to dress for that afternoon.

I climbed the stairs slowly, studying the gallery of ladies who seemed to be watching my progress. The longing in their eyes spoke to me. What had they wanted? Love? Passion? Did any of them have a desire to create? How many of my ancestors had stood here and faced their futures with the same dread I was feeling at that moment?

Their eyes locked on mine as I passed each one. Their unfinished lips mocked me. For what? For caring so much about my paintings? For caring so much for Julien? Like Charlotte, Julien's father had died in a terrible accident, and Julien had never stopped blaming himself. Would he do the same now? After all, Charlotte had been on that tower in order to introduce a potential client to him.

As I soaked in my bath, I tried to plan how I should deal with Moreau's request. If only I could ask Julien. He always had a solution. I tried to imagine what he'd suggest, but I couldn't think the way he did.

A radical idea occurred to me. Maybe I didn't have to bring the paintings in at all. I was an accomplished liar. I would claim they had been damaged. Perhaps burned in a fire? Or what if I said I'd destroyed them because they were so inferior to the kind of work I was doing now? Would that work?

"Mademoiselle?"

I opened my eyes.

"Monsieur Duplessi is downstairs," my maid said.

Julien was here?

"Thank you. Help me get dressed, Alice."

I stepped out of the bath into waiting, warmed towels and watched in the mirror as my grandmother's maid rubbed my skin. I felt blood rushing to the surface. Around my neck the ruby rosettes that I wore even when I was naked glinted in the setting sunlight.

Make of the blood, a stone. Make of a stone, a powder. Make of a powder, life everlasting.

What did it mean? Julien was back now. He would help me figure it out. And he'd help me come up with a solution to my problem with Moreau. Everything would be all right now that he was here.

"I'm so glad you've come. I wanted to see you but didn't want to interfere," I said as I stepped into the salon where he was waiting.

He came over to me and took my hands. For a moment he just looked at me, as if he'd never seen me before, as if he was learning my face. Then he bent and kissed me chastely on the lips.

"It's only been days, but it feels as if I haven't seen you for so very long . . ." He hesitated. "Sandrine, there are some things I must tell you."

Oh no. I imagined his confession. He felt guilty that he had been seeing me when he was betrothed, and now that Charlotte was dead and he was in mourning, he was going to call off our affair.

I felt a sudden breath of hot air behind me. Turned around. No, no one was there. Beads of perspiration gathered at my hairline.

"Let's sit, we'll have some wine." I called out to the maid to see to some refreshments.

There was a chill in the room. I glanced over at the mantel. Yes, the fire had been laid in anticipation of the evening's soiree. Approaching, I lit the paper fan and watched it blaze. Once I was sure the fire had caught, I returned to Julien, who was on the couch.

"I'm so very sorry for your loss," I said.

He bowed his head. "Thank you."

My grandmother's manservant came in with a decanter of Julien's favorite Bordeaux and goblets. I poured two glasses and handed one to my lover, who took one sip and then another. He was so dark, so gathered into himself. His green eyes were a deeper shade than I'd ever seen.

"How is Charlotte's father?"

"Inconsolable. Since his wife died three years ago, he'd become dependent on Charlotte. Now I can't get him to eat . . . He barely sleeps." Another sip of wine. "I didn't expect him to rebound quickly, but I'm actually worried that he might try to take his own life. I've been staying with him all day and all night. That's why I haven't been here sooner and—"

"You don't need to explain. I understand. You're both devastated. Mourning has its own timetable, I know."

He nodded. "I saw her fall, Sandrine. It was terrible. You do know that she fell from the Eiffel Tower, don't you?"

"Yes, I heard," I said. I wasn't lying. I'd heard her laughter echoing as she fell, as her body tumbled, buffeted in the wind, becoming smaller and smaller the closer she came to the sidewalk.

"It was a freak accident. The railings are too low. She was reaching for an umbrella. *An umbrella.*"

"I'm sorry you had to see it."

"The worst part was telling Olivier. Seeing his

face. As he listened, as he absorbed what I said, and I saw something in him die."

My eyes filled with tears. If my grandmother was right and La Lune chose which women to inhabit, then she had chosen unwisely with me. I was not strong enough to withstand this. "I can't . . ." I stood up.

He reached out and grabbed my hand. "Where are you going? What's wrong?"

"You loved Charlotte. She was going to be your wife. I understand how upset you are, but I can't be the one to hear this."

Holding on to my hand, he stared at me. His eyes were so troubled.

"Sandrine, do you think that I loved her?"

Now it was my turn to stare at him. "Of course."

"But I told you it was a marriage of convenience."

"Yes, but I assumed you told me that so that I would feel sorry for you and take you as a lover."

He laughed a long, bitter laugh. "Sit down, Sandrine." He pulled me to him on the couch.

I sat.

Julien took a deep breath.

"Charlotte had an image of the life she wanted to live. She planned to sing opera for two more years while using her access to wealthy patrons of the arts to help me get important commissions. When I had the kind of prominence she envisioned, we'd marry and build a mansion on

Parc Monceau, where she'd entertain as the wife of the important architect Julien Duplessi."

"It's hard to blame her for wanting to help you. You are a brilliant artist. I would want to help you, too."

"But you wouldn't want to cage me, and she did."

"What do you mean?"

"Our very engagement was a trick. She told her father I proposed when I had done no such thing, and he was so delighted that I . . . Stupidly, I let it go. Cingal's wife had just died, and I couldn't cause him more grief right away. But it was a mistake, and I told Charlotte so. She refused to call it off, and when I insisted, she turned on me and said she would tell her father that I'd gotten her with child and taken her to a charlatan doctor for an abortion. We both knew that he'd believe her, lose all respect for me, and probably let me go. My reputation would be tarnished. If word got out that Cingal had fired me, it would be difficult for me to get other employment. Paris is a town of gossips. Again I let it go. Blamed her inability to be reasonable on her mother's death. I planned to wait a time and then approach her again. But it became intolerable to keep up the charade. She was a shallow and conniving woman. Finally I called her bluff and said I would tell her father the engagement had been a misunderstanding and take my chances; that if she did tell him her preposterous story, he would believe me.

"Before I had a chance to speak to Cingal, a fire broke out in one of the nightclubs I had designed that was under construction. One of the workers was badly burned. Within days a potential client canceled a commission because he'd heard the fire was the result of us using substandard material in order to save money. Then a second client queried our practices. Cingal was vexed and upset. Where was this gossip coming from? His reputation was stellar, as was mine.

"Charlotte came to my apartment after the rumors had been circulating for a week. We already had three jobs in jeopardy. She confessed, with a sly smile, that she'd been responsible for both the fire and the talk, and if I ended the engagement, she would stage more accidents.

"I couldn't put the firm or my mentor at risk. Once again, I allowed the engagement to stand."

Julien stopped speaking and drank some more wine. "So you see, Sandrine? I am not racked with guilt. My mourning is dishonest. She was a spoiled woman determined to plot out her life to her own specifications regardless of my wants and desires. The question I never understood, though, was, why me? I am not wealthy. I have no pedigree. I'm just the son of a furniture builder from Nancy. There are many better catches in Paris."

I smiled. "Did it never occur to you that she loved you?"

"How could she love me and threaten to ruin me like that?"

"Whoever told you that love was pretty?" I was picturing the paintings on the staircase. The terrible stories my grandmother had told me. Atrocities committed in the name of love, by a woman who could still, after almost three hundred years, yearn for a man who had spurned her.

That night was the first since we had become lovers that we were together without making love. But Julien was clearly exhausted and emotionally drained and needed rest.

I put him to bed in the royal bedroom, which I'd appropriated as my own. As he slept in the goose-down bed, under its gilt headboard of fat cherubic putti and garlands of roses, I watched him. In the silver moonlight illuminating the room, I could see that all the tension had left his face. When his eyes were open, their intensity was commanding. You didn't notice the rest of his features. But with his eyes closed, and his lashes dusting his cheeks, he looked quite different. Younger and, even though he was not classically handsome, beautiful. Like the aristocrat in the Agnolo Bronzino portrait of Lodovico Capponi hanging in Mr. Frick's mansion in New York.

Pulling back the covers, ever so slowly, I gazed

at Julien's naked body. I ran one finger down his long sinuous arm, across his chest. His muscles were like marble, carved by a master but miraculously covered by warm flesh. Leaning down, I burrowed my face in his neck and inhaled. It was easier to get drunk on his scent than on absinthe or wine.

Between my legs I felt the first stirrings of desire gathering . . . growing . . . as if my want was picking flowers . . . adding one and then another, until all the single stems were one huge fragrant bouquet of lust.

Innocently, unaware of me, Julien slept on.

I gazed at his stomach, his thighs, his shoulders. The wonder of his body in rest. I was unsure which I wanted more, to paint him or make love to him.

Why, I wondered, were there so few sensual portraits of men? None of the female artists had tackled this subject. Not Mary Cassatt or Berthe Morisot or Suzanne Valadon. They kept to mothers and daughters, female nudes.

Why were women afraid to paint a man the way Courbet or Titian or Rubens or Klimt or Renoir painted a woman? As creatures desired, as creatures of passion?

The needs to make love to Julien and to paint him merged in my mind. To do one *would* be to do the other. I would take him both ways, inside of me and on canvas.

Stealthily I crept out of the bedroom. It took two trips to gather my paints and a canvas and an easel, and while I set up everything in my bedroom, Julien slept on, undisturbed.

Once my palette was ready, the satiny paint glinting in the moonlight, I began, first sketching out Julien's form with a medium round and a thinned wash of burnt umber. I filled the foreground with him, in slumber, satiated, at rest and at peace. I painted his arms, his legs, his long neck . . . and behind him, his beautiful wings extended in all their glory.

He was my model for the mythological god Cupid. And in the shadows, approaching the bed, I painted Psyche, coming forward with her candle, expecting to see a monster. I shivered to think of how she must have felt when light fell on her husband and she beheld his beauty.

All night I painted with my heart and all of my desire. Painted Julien until the canvas was filled with a picture of a dark bedroom, slivers of moon glow illuminating the god's glorious iridescent feathers and luminous skin.

Here was Cupid as no one had yet painted him. Full of desire and passion for his Psyche, dreaming of laying with her again and again. And Psyche acting out the dangerous curiosity that would almost destroy her. Here was a story of tests and punishment and divine favors and redemption. A story that resonated in me, for was it not so like my own? So like La Lune's? Except hadn't she found her lover *was* a monster? Wasn't she still searching for redemption?

All through the night, the twin desires—to keep painting Julien and to make love to him—did battle. Finally, at daybreak, I put down the palette and brush and went to him. Lightly, I kissed his neck. I didn't want to wake him, not yet. But I needed to feel him, to touch him. I wanted to become Julien's dream. Wanted to be deep in his darkness, where he could not resist me. Certain that once I was there, he'd be mine.

Ours.

Had I just heard that? Or had I just imagined what La Lune might have said if the stories were true? But they were not. She was a tale. A myth. A legend. I had heard a door creak, the wind outside the window. I had heard a cat in the courtyard scampering up a tree. Only in my imagination was it a three-hundred-year-old woman's voice.

I ran my hand down Julien's thigh. His skin was so warm. I inhaled the smoky maleness of him and wondered if she had smelled it, too.

What was I thinking? Why did I care what she had seen, smelled, thought, wanted? She was gone. I was not.

Careful not to move too abruptly so as not to jiggle the bed, I inched down until my face was even with Julien's hips and took him into my mouth. I held him like that, barely moving, only putting a little pressure on him with my lips. Not enough to wake him. Just enough to arouse him in his sleep.

Was I in his dream now? Was he dreaming of me as he grew and then grew some more? In his sleep—or was he even still fully asleep?—he began to thrust. I matched his rhythm, letting some of him slip out, then taking him back in deeper. Looking up, I saw his eyes flutter open. A smile played on his lips.

I let go of him. Climbed up and lowered myself down on top of him, all the while watching his beautiful face, thinking that it was a miracle I had found him, that I could open my body to a man, that I could find and experience pleasure after all.

I lifted my hips. Slid down and then again up. My body was one motion of agonizing pleasure. One motion of sliding and rising, sliding and rising. Feeling full, filled . . . I was on fire. Burning up. He was burning me up. He was allowing me to stay in control; he asked for nothing. I ground myself into him, rubbing myself on him. Years of being taken roughly, thoughtlessly, dissolving. Anger at having someone move in me and inflict pain, dissolving. Centuries of waiting, of failing, of longing, dissolving. I was taking him. Grinding, sliding, squeezing, holding, going slow, slower, sliding, rising, slow, slower, sliding, rising. There was no sound but of our skin rubbing. No smells but the fragrant secret scent of my sex and his, mixed with the faint scent of paints. No feeling but those of great, gigantic swells gathering. My world had shrunk to the two of us in this bed in this one room, and I never wanted it to end, yet I urgently wanted to find the end so that I could feel the explosion, find the release, let the gathering go, because the pressure was too great to hold onto for much longer. For any longer. For any longer.

Beneath me Julien began to thrust up harder, with more intensity.

"No," I whispered. "Not yet."

I did not want him to change the pace. This was my velvet and silk bejeweled pleasure. This was my streaming light, my diamond-encrusted treasure. My blood, hot and thick, rushed. His was heated to the temperature of a furnace. We were melting metals, and together we would make gold and solve the search for the elusive Elixir of Life.

I had visions that were not mine as I moved on top of Julien. I saw a man who was not him and a woman who was not me. I began to smell their scents, which were not ours, and hear their whispers in voices other than his and mine. What I felt was what she felt. And what Julien felt? I couldn't be sure.

"No," I whispered, this time to her. "I don't want you here. This is mine. I am Sandrine. This is Julien."

Slide, rise, want, wait, then slow, slowly, slide, rise, want, and wait.

His eyes opened wider. The smile faded from his lips. Whispering, he said my name urgently, like a prayer: "Sandrine."

"I want you, just you. Just you," I said.

"You have me." He knew more than I'd thought he did. "And I want just you"—and as he said it he reached up and grabbed my necklace. He forced his fingers under the rubies and pulled.

"Help me take it off, Sandrine."

I was sliding up and down on him. The pressure was building. "I can't."

"I will."

He pulled at it harder. The necklace bit into my skin. The way it had when my grandmother had tried to pull it off. It hadn't come off for her. He pulled harder.

"It won't come off!" he hissed, frustrated.

But I barely understood what he was saying anymore. And what I did understand didn't matter to me. I was exploding on top of him. It was a slow-rolling opening. A heated agony of longing. Of yearning. An explosion of promises and possibilities.

And in the midst of it, I knew two things:

Julien had never experienced anything like this with Charlotte, and he was becoming mine in a way that he had never been before.

And I knew that La Lune had found yet one more foothold to help her step into the present and into me.

Chapter 33

I was examining the canvas I had painted the night before. I'd just decided that yes, once finished, this would be my entry to the Salon. I was thinking about what improvements I needed to make when Julien awoke.

I called for the maid to bring us café au lait, and as I sat with him on the bed and ate flaky croissants and drank the scalding coffee, I thought everything was all right. He was studying the painting.

"It seems almost impossible for you to have learned so much so quickly and become so proficient."

"It seems so to me, too."

He continued to study the painting.

"You didn't paint it, did you?"

"What are you suggesting? Someone snuck into the bedroom last night and painted you?" I laughed.

"Isn't that what you believe?"

"What do you mean?"

"I think you believe you are becoming someone else. Taking on a role. Being unduly influenced by a myth. I spoke to Dujols. He came to see me during the week, to pay his respects."

"What does that have to do with this?"

"He told me you had gone back to see him and what you talked about. They are a dangerous group, Sandrine. They know how to stimulate people's thoughts. There are rumors of black masses and witches' covens and—"

"I still don't understand what this has to do with me and the painting."

"Dujols told me about the legend . . . about La Lune spending eternity searching for a woman to . . . What did he call it? Oh yes, a woman she can merge with so that she can relive her thwarted love affair and make it turn out all right this time."

I nodded.

"I reminded him that I'm a rationalist. An atheist. I don't believe in a god above or a devil below. But he told me there was a way I could prove it. He said La Lune would need to be physically tethered to you in some way for her to incubate. And that no one but you could loosen her grip."

His eyes moved to my ruby necklace. I put my hands up and hid it from his gaze.

"Is that why you tried to take this off last night?"

He'd failed, though. Did that mean he believed in La Lune now? Would he accept her? Or would he run from me if he thought me possessed? I held my breath, waiting to hear what he was going to say next.

"But you fought me. You wouldn't let me remove it. Why?"

I let out a breath. So he didn't believe what Dujols had told him.

"You were hurting me. I pushed you away."

Julien threw back the sheets. He was naked underneath but didn't seem to care. He stood, walked over to the window, looked out for a moment, and then turned back to me.

"I love you, Sandrine. All your passions and your aspirations. But you are becoming invested in this myth. You believe this ancestor of yours is helping you with your painting. It's very understandable. You arrived in Paris aggrieved over your father's death and your unstable marriage. You were ripe to be influenced. But now it's time to detach yourself from the fantasy."

I didn't know what to say. He'd told me he loved me. But at the same time it sounded as if his affection came with demands.

"You believe that you're communing with a ghost, don't you?"

"I'm not certain."

"I do not believe in ghosts. Or witches. Or demons," he said.

"I never did either."

"Before."

"Before," I echoed.

"I can't accept that you are haunted and that there is a force pushing you to do things you wouldn't ordinarily do. That would mean that I wasn't in love with you but with your demon. That the things about you that make you special are not you but rather attributes of some spirit who has given you these abilities, and at the same time caused havoc around you."

I reached up and touched the necklace around my neck.

Make of the blood, a stone . . .

What was I supposed to do? All the things Julien was saying he loved about me were her gifts to me. Would he really care for that woman who had come to Paris? She was untalented. Timid. Frigid. But if I didn't exorcise La Lune, would he stay with me?

"You are who you are. You have talent. It was there all along, but being in Paris triggered it. Yes, it seemed to spring forth miraculously, but it didn't. It couldn't. You've been working night and day, learning more and more. Your progress is *your* accomplishment. It's not some supernatural power changing you."

"What are you saying?"

"I can help you, but you have to be willing to let go of this fantasy."

"It's not a fantasy."

"There are doctors."

I shook my head. "I'm not ill."

But he was looking at me as if I was.

In desperation I offered the only solution I

447

could think of. "I can work with Dujols and the others. There must be methods they can teach me to control—" I was about to say *her*. Instead I said: "—control what is happening."

"Dujols is part of the problem. He's filling your head with this nonsense." Julien was angry.

"It's not nonsense. People have died. Things have happened we can't explain. You are right that I need help, but help from people who understand this for what it is."

"It is irrational," he said.

"It is as old as the Bible," I responded.

"It is fearmongering and mythology."

I went to him and put my hands in his. He lifted my hands to his cheeks and kept them there for a minute. He was so tender with me that it hurt my heart.

"Let me take you to Dr. Blanche," he said softly.

I pulled my hand away. "You think I'm crazy?"

"I told you, I think you need help."

"I can't go back to the way I was."

"There is nothing wrong with the way you were. You *are* the way you were. This is you. The other thing is only in your mind."

I felt La Lune there with me, trying to help. After all, she had a stake in this, too. She had done so much to get Julien and me to this point. My grandmother was in an asylum. Cousin Jacob and Charlotte were dead.

For the first time since I'd come to Paris, I wished I were not there. Not faced with this untenable conundrum: accept Julien's help, banish La Lune, and become someone he might not love, or fight him, hold on to La Lune, and lose myself.

I smelled violets, and the scent nauseated me. Her anger swirled around me, crimson, purple, and stinking of flowers and sulfur.

I was on the verge of losing the very thing she wanted, but the only sure way to keep it was to let her go.

"Please, Sandrine, please let me take you to see Dr. Blanche."

"To be locked up like my grandmother? I said no. I am not mad!"

He let go of my hands, turned from me, and dressed without saying another word.

Before he left, he stood at the door for a moment and gave me the saddest smile I'd ever seen. "When you are ready to be rational and let me help you find a doctor, you know where to find me."

And then he walked out of my bedroom, leaving me alone with the glorious painting of him and a ghost who was, at that moment, as lost as I was.

Chapter 34

I returned to school a day later, bringing Moreau the paintings that he'd requested. He assessed them quickly and said he was satisfied that I'd painted them.

That was because I had.

These weren't the paintings I'd showed him that first day but copies—close enough to the originals to look familiar, but at the same time done in my hand.

Did he know I'd tricked him?

Now, looking back, I think he did, for he assessed them in seconds and seemed relieved to move on and discuss that day's work.

I watched Serge watching Moreau, his eyes narrowed, his lips pursed. Was he that frightened of my talent that he would sabotage me? More than ten thousand artists submitted paintings to the Salon. Thousands competed for a prize. What difference did one more make?

After class, I tried to visit my grandmother but was not allowed in by orders from the doctor. It seemed my visits impeded her improvement too greatly. I went home and spent the rest of the day and night and then the rest of the week miserable, missing Julien, confused as to what to do next, and trying to distract myself by working on my *Sleeping Cupid.*

On Wednesday of the following week, a package with a label from a jeweler on rue Royale awaited me when I came home from school. Opening the fine leather box, I found a single luminous pink pearl hanging from a ruby station necklace.

Sandrine—Are you ready to exchange her necklace for mine? I miss you.—Julien

I fingered the smooth pearl. I wanted him back. Wanted to be with him. Should I submit to seeing a doctor? Would Dr. Blanche even agree to help me?

I put the necklace away and went to Passy.

Sitting across the desk from Dr. Blanche, fully prepared to discuss La Lune with him, I found I couldn't speak. Every time I started to explain what had brought me there, I began to cough. I felt as if La Lune was inside of me, tickling my throat and holding my lips closed. I wondered if they looked bloodless to him, like the lips of the women in the paintings.

They couldn't speak to tell their stories either.

Embarrassed and frustrated, I croaked out a question about my grandmother. I told him I was unhappy at not being able to see her and wanted to know why he was keeping me away. And I was. I had never been so alone in my life. Maison de la Lune echoed with my footsteps, and I felt as empty as the house.

I left Passy dejected and returned to rue des Saints-Pères.

The painting of Julien became the only thing that mattered to me and, other than attending classes, my only interaction with the outside world. I worked almost nonstop preparing my submission for the École. I'd come to believe that if *Sleeping Cupid* was accepted, Julien would come to the opening and see the painting and accept me as I was. Both the dark and the light of me.

The morning of March 1, I awoke from nightmares with a feeling of dread. It was the day submissions were due for the 1894 Salon. After dressing, I went to the studio to prepare *Sleeping Cupid* for the walk to the École.

The bell tower was in shadows. Without any sun shining through the windows, an atmosphere of melancholy clung to the pillows and coverlet on the daybed. It seemed to be sitting in the chairs, adhering to the walls. The only light came from the portrait sitting on the easel in the middle of the space.

Julien Duplessi depicted as an adult male Cupid. Julien's body, his face, but with an angel's iridescent feather wings. An erotic otherworldly creature. Luminous and shining. Long torso, longer legs, and between them, the partially erect proof of his arousing dream.

A nude painted of lust, painted in lust. It was

provocative, to be sure. Too much so? Moreau would be surprised. I had brought a sketch of Leda and the Swan to his atelier, and he'd approved that. But I knew she didn't have the chance that Cupid did. More than ten thousand paintings would be submitted, and only three thousand would be chosen. Of those, only a handful would be anointed. To be one of them, a painting not only had to be superlative; it had to stand out.

The entrance to the school was crowded with throngs of painters all dropping off their paintings on this one day. I stood on line, not seeing any of my classmates until I made my way inside. A group of them had already been through the line and were watching the goings-on from the sidelines.

Gaston saw me first, came over and told me that after I was done they'd be at La Palette if I wanted to join them.

"All year leading up to one day," he said, shaking his head. "We deserve to get good and drunk."

He cocked his head toward my covered canvas. "Are you pleased with how Leda turned out?"

"I'm too nervous to know."

"That's how I felt, too," he said. "May I see?"

Before I could refuse, he lifted up the cloth and after a moment emitted a long slow whistle. "Now, what's this? Not the painting you've been working on."

"No, I thought this would have more of a chance."

I was too nervous to ask him what he thought of it. But I didn't have to. He told me.

"Are you out of your mind?" Gaston asked.

"I'd say far more clever than mad." Serge had come over to see my painting and eyed it with disdain. "Played a trick on all of us, didn't you, Sandrine? Pretended you were doing something tame and cautious while all the while planning a shock like this." He paused as he stepped back to examine it from a greater distance. Other students noticed what was going on and gathered round, all examining my submission, talking and whispering among themselves.

"It's perverse and decadent. And they will reject it," Serge predicted. "Women are not allowed to paint male nudes. Not one has ever been accepted. And being Moreau's darling won't make any difference. You wasted your chance."

I thought I detected a smile.

"Unless the committee is in the mood to prove one century is ending and the future is upon us," Gaston said hopefully.

Other students came and went, reacting with shock and scorn. Other than Gaston, no one had a kind word to say.

Had I made a mistake? Would the committee reject my painting without even judging it simply based on its subject matter? No matter, it was too late to do anything about it.

I'd reached the head of the line. Marching into the auditorium, painting in hand, I held my head up and tried to prepare myself for what was about to happen.

Monsieur Moreau and four other teachers sat at a long wooden table at the far end of the room. They appeared weary, which was not unexpected since they'd been looking at submissions since early that morning. Judging from the lines, they would work late into the night and probably have to return the next day.

"Mademoiselle Sandrine Verlaine," I said for the benefit of the clerk who logged in each painting and gave it a number.

"Mademoiselle Sandrine Verlaine, one thousand five hundred and eighty," he called out.

I shuddered involuntarily at the coincidence that the number I'd been assigned was the same as the year of La Lune's birth.

I put the canvas on the easel facing the judges and pulled off the cloth.

There was a moment of silence, then an intake of breath, and then Monsieur Moreau spoke.

"A surprise indeed, but well done, Sandrine." He had used my first name for the first time. "Very well done." He smiled at me, and I could see that he was proud. "Brave and bold. Very well done."

The other professors were not as forthcoming. One was frowning. Two had implacable faces that I couldn't read.

"Thank you, Mademoiselle," said the clerk who was recording all the entries, and I was dismissed. At least Moreau had been impressed.

Outside my classmates were waiting.

"How did it go?" Gaston asked.

"Moreau seemed pleased."

"Now that you've committed your first brazen act of defiance, you must be ready for a drink," Serge said.

And I was.

Six of us traipsed off to La Palette, where Gaston ordered a bottle of champagne and we drank to our luck.

It seemed the café was filled with nothing but art students that afternoon. Nervous, hopeful, excited, and depressed. Bottles came out full and quickly went back empty. Everyone had delivered his best, and now the wait began. The hours and days and weeks before we found out if we had been accepted loomed.

My thoughts were a jumble. I was exhausted. I'd slept so very little for the last two weeks. I'd been lonely without Julien, worried about my grandmother, and obsessed with my painting.

But there was another reason for my fatigue. I was carrying not only my own emotional burdens but also La Lune's. Where did she end? Where did I begin? Again the smell of violets permeated the air; I felt waves of nausea rise in me.

As much as I missed Julien, so did this creature

inside of me. As much as I wanted to paint something worthy of acceptance and worried about my ability, so did she. The double dose of emotions, aspirations, and expectations had exhausted and depleted me.

We had just finished our champagne when Heloise, Adele, and Stephanie, three models who posed for us in Maître Moreau's class, arrived to celebrate our accomplishment. Gaston ordered another bottle, and after we toasted with that one, we moved on to our next stop, the popular Café du Bagne.

Themed bohemian cafés and cabarets were all the rage. Built around exotic concepts, they were much more than eating and drinking establishments; their very atmosphere was entertaining, and the stranger the environment, the more popular the venue.

One of the oldest, the Château d'If, had opened its faux-drawbridge door in the early 1880s. Designed to mimic the prison of the same name made famous by Dumas's *The Count of Monte Cristo*, it boasted cells and dungeons.

L'Abbaye de Thélème dressed its waitstaff as monks and nuns, and patrons could hide away in medieval confessionals to sip their absinthe in private.

When we arrived at the Café du Bagne, there were queues of Parisians waiting outside, but Serge knew one of the managers, and we trooped into the club en masse. Decorated to resemble a penitentiary eating hall, the café featured gray and somber walls covered with graffiti of the kind inmates would leave behind. The long wooden tables were etched with more of the same. The waiters, dressed as convicts, dragged papier-mâché balls and chains as they brought our drinks.

Serge and Gaston ordered absinthe, but I stayed with wine, not ready to succumb to the smoky depths the powerful liquor offered.

At about ten o'clock we all decided that we were hungry and went to Au Lapin Agile, where we gorged on onion soup with a thick crust of melted Gruyère cheese, spicy sausages, and crisp *pommes frites*.

Heloise and Stephanie and Adele were still with us, and somewhere along the way we had picked up two more models whose names I didn't know. We were a group of eleven now. Noisy and boisterous and wanting the night to last forever.

It was there, for the third time since I'd arrived in Paris, that I thought I saw Benjamin. But this time it was certainly him. He'd arrived with two other men. One was absolutely William Lenox.

I'd been mistaken when I believed I'd spotted him on the observation deck of the Eiffel Tower, so I had assumed I'd been wrong about the man in the carriage on the Boulevard Saint-Germain, too. But I hadn't been wrong. Benjamin was here and he was walking right toward me.

Chapter 35

My husband looked directly at me but didn't recognize me. His eyes barely rested on my face. He was too busy looking first at Heloise and then Stephanie.

Of course he didn't recognize me. I was wearing a man's jacket, shirt and cravat, and hat. I was sitting with half-nude models and bohemian artists. No New York society matron was at our table. The woman he knew wasn't there.

What was he doing in the restaurant? Had he tracked me to Paris, or was his being here a coincidence? Certainly, now that my father was dead and Benjamin was running the bank, he would have reason to be in Paris. The branch in New York was still tied to the French branch.

"Sandrine." Heloise squeezed my arm. "Where did you go? You look like you saw a ghost."

"I did," I said, trying for levity but not sure I'd managed to keep my voice light enough.

"But there are no such thing as ghosts," she said. "Am I right, Gaston? Serge? Are there such things as ghosts?" she called out.

"Of course there are." Gaston laughed. "Let's go to Hell. You can see ghosts and more there! Everyone in agreement then? Hell will be our next stop?"

The facade of Cabaret de l'Enfer screamed at us from across the street, trying to terrify and attract us at the same time. Sandwiched between ordinary buildings, the monstrous dark gray plaster face with wild eyes and Medusa-like hair opened its mouth wide and invited us in. The frightening face's lines were sinuous and artful, and reminded me of—yes! This was the club Monsieur Dujols and his friends owned and that Julien had designed. Although he'd told me about it and promised to bring me here, he never had.

And as soon as I walked through the open mouth and over the threshold, I understood why Julien hadn't wanted me to see this. The darkened rooms were cooler than they should have been. The lights were red and orange. It was a tour de force of horror. The walls were sculpted bas-reliefs of guillotines in action, skulls and bones, winged dragons fighting with devils, and snakes wrapped about skeletons. I felt as if I'd stepped into one of Hieronymus Bosch's visions of hell. Dark corners dripped with stalactites; there were coffins instead of couches.

"Enter and be damned. The Evil One awaits you!" the maître d' snarled as he welcomed us.

Music from the opera *Faust* emanated from a giant cauldron hanging over a fire. The mammoth brass container was filled with male and female musicians all dressed as devils and playing various stringed instruments painted red. Incense burned coal-red inside of brass censers. The club smelled like a Roman Catholic church.

It was a magical, terrifying atmosphere, at once dangerous and tempting. The end of the world, the end of a century, and a vision of what awaited us in the next.

"I don't I like it," Heloise said. "It's full of ghouls. It's scary."

"It's all make-believe," I said, and laughed.

"Don't you mind the smell?"

I sniffed again, taking more of it in. "No, it's wonderful."

Heloise looked at me strangely. "It's blasphemous."

"To you perhaps, but I'm not a Christian. To me it's exotic and foreign."

We all sat down on a long coffin couch. The tables were tombstones. Everywhere you looked you were reminded of death and carnage, from the murals to the black hangings painted with sayings about mortality. An imp somersaulted across the floor. Another approached to take our orders. Serge and Gaston ordered absinthe again, and I followed now, craving its soothing warmth.

Our drinks came, and we sipped the green liquor and watched the ever-moving, ever-changing hellish scene around us. The corners of the room were sculpted into caverns lit by fires issuing thick, acrid smoke. Bursts of thunder erupted at intervals. Flames darted out from crevices in rocks.

Gaston asked Heloise to dance. Serge asked me. I refused at first, but he took my hands and pulled me up. "You're too serious for your own good. You need to have some fun."

The surprise of how his body moved against mine in time to the music exhilarated me. His hostility and familiarity confused me and excited me. The drink—the whole night of drinks—was catching up with me. I was dizzy with wild thoughts. When he leaned down and kissed me, I kissed him back, hard. He pulled me closer, reached down, and wildly, blatantly, stroked me between the legs. For a moment I forgot everything but the sensation, and then I jumped back, shocked.

"I have to find a lavatory," I said, and ran from the dance floor.

It wasn't just a convenient response. I had thought I was going to be sick. How could I have let Serge touch me? Even worse, what part of me was so corrupt that I had responded?

What happened next remains clear in my mind, even though I'd had a lot to drink, including that devil's water, absinthe. But I don't believe that my being inebriated contributed to what I remember.

I found a waiter and asked for directions to the lavatory and listened carefully to his instructions to turn this way and then that way. They were just long enough for me to get confused, and I probably made a left when I should have made a right. Or made two lefts in a row instead of two rights. But I found myself in a hallway that seemed to go on for a long time. When I reached the end, there was no visible door or exit of any kind that I could see.

I turned in a slow circle.

On my second rotation I saw a faint outline on the wall. I must have missed it before. There was an indentation suggesting a door but no handle or obvious way to open it. So I pushed on it and found myself peering into a closet. Devil, imp, and ghoul costumes hung from hooks. Horns and tails were piled on top of a long shelf. A storage room for Satan's followers.

I could hear distant singing. Was it coming from the cabaret? It didn't seem to be coming from behind me but from below me.

I got down on my knees and put my ear to the wooden floor. The song was amplified. There *were* revelers down below. As I knelt, I felt chilled air on my face. Coming from the floor? I felt around with my finger and found a crack. Following its circular contour, I came to an iron handle.

I lifted it. A large trap door opened up, and with it a gust of cool, perfumed air. I peered down.

Like at the opera house, a staircase cut out of

rough-hewn stone descended into the earth. It was dark and impossible to see past a certain point, but I could hear, even more distinctly now, human voices chanting.

I remembered what Monsieur Dujols had told me: "If you ever decide that you want us to help you, you can find us in hell."

I had assumed he'd been speaking metaphorically. But now I realize he hadn't been. This must be the very spot that he had been telling me about.

These were the people who could help me. People who had the answers. Who knew what La Lune was and how I could control her—or rid myself of her, perhaps, without losing the powers she had imbued in me. Because I knew now, if I wanted Julien back, I had no other choice.

And so I descended into the depths of hell.

A half dozen men and women, all wearing dark robes with hoods that obscured their faces, sat on the ground, encircling a pentagram drawn in the dirt. In its center, a small fire burned, the smoke emitting a rich, resinous, and salty fragrance. Torches in iron holders flickered on the stone walls and cast shadows over the complex drawing. I recognized symbols, numbers, and creatures I'd seen in the grimoire in the bell tower and in the etchings in Dujols's library.

There were white candles arranged in a circle

around the pentagram. To the right and left of the circle were deer or antelope antlers, at least four feet wide. Propped against the wall was a tall mirror with the outline of a circle painted on it, framed with a border of Jewish stars and alchemical symbols. Some I recognized; others I didn't.

One of the men threw something into the fire. It was the color of rubies and the size of a fist. The scent of pepper, musk, and saffron filled the air, and as the object burned, they chanted:

"We evoke and conjure thee, O spirit Vauael, by the Supreme Majesty, the true God who is known by the names of Yod Heh Vav Heh Adonai, Eheieh, and Agla, to appear before us in this mirror in a fair and comely shape. We evoke and conjure thee . . ."

One of the members of the group noticed me and held up his hand to stop the others from chanting. He pointed at me. Everyone looked. Then the whispering began again, and while I couldn't make out the words, I could tell I wasn't welcome.

"Who are you?" one of the hooded figures asked. "How did you find us? Who told you to come?"

"I did," a male voice rang out. The speaker pushed his hood back, and Monsieur Dujols revealed himself. "Ladies and gentlemen, this is Mademoiselle Verlaine."

Murmurs of approval now.

A woman with long, white wavy hair came up to me and took my hand. She must have been in her seventies, but her skin had a youthful glow. She smiled. "I'm Alexandra. Thank you for coming, and for bringing her with you."

"I'm alone."

"No, the woman known as the Secret Witch is with you," Alexandra said.

She was the first person other than my grandmother who could see La Lune.

"Would you like to see her?" she asked me.

I nodded.

"Come look." She took me by the hand and led me to the mirror leaning against the wall. They all had stood and now crowded around me. Alexandra pointed. I stared into the mirror.

I shook my head. "I don't see her."

"You're not ready," Alexandra said. "How can we help you?"

I undid the top button of my shirt and showed her the rubies. The fragrance of violets seemed to be filling the dank air. I braced myself for the nausea that followed and then forced myself to ignore it.

"I can't take the necklace off."

"May I try?" Alexandra asked.

I nodded.

She went behind me and tried, as Julien had, to work the clasp. When her fingers touched my skin, they were cool and soothing. After a few moments, she gave up.

Alexandra turned to Dujols. "It's attached. La Lune is melded to her."

"Is she harming you?" The man who asked was wearing a long purple robe with the zodiac embroidered all over it.

"Not me, no. Others."

"Who has she harmed?" Dujols asked.

I clasped my hands together, my fingernails digging into the skin of my palms. It took enormous effort not to scream out at the pain I was causing. The effort it took to answer Dujols's question was even greater. "My grandmother," I whispered.

"What did you say?" Alexandra asked.

I tried to speak more loudly, but my voice wouldn't comply. They all had to lean closer.

"My grandmother. A rabbi. An opera singer who was affianced to a man I know."

"She's very powerful. She had to be to survive this long," Alexandra said.

"Who are you?" I asked her. "Who are all of you?"

"We study and try and decipher the past and uncover the secrets that have been lost over time," she said.

I remembered what Julien had told me about Dujols and his followers.

"Is this black magick?"

"We don't use terms like that," said Alexandra. "We are students of ancient traditions and hidden knowledge. You can help us."

"And we can help you," said Dujols.

"How?"

"The book, the grimoire you found, is important, Sandrine. We can learn from it. Not only to help you but to unlock mysteries we have been trying to uncover for decades . . . for centuries."

"And if I give it to you, you'll help me?"

"Yes, but in order for you to turn it over to us, for us to be able to accept it, you must be initiated," Alexandra said.

"Then initiate me." The stench of the violets intensified. So did my need to vomit. I swallowed.

She laughed. "It takes time. You'll need to study and learn so you understand our goals and our efforts."

"But I don't have time. Julien has left me. Benjamin is here in Paris, and I'm afraid of what he can do to me. My grandmother goes mad when I come near her . . ."

I stopped explaining. I was distracted by something in the distance. The cellar was more beautiful now that my eyes had adjusted to it. Mica rocks shimmered in the firelight. Two crystal monoliths glowed as if lit from inside. They were what I had noticed. And they seemed to be pulling me. I walked to them. I found myself at the beginning of a labyrinth created with round black stones embedded in the dirt.

Alexandra pulled me back. "You can't, not yet. It's part of the rites and rituals, and you aren't ready."

"But she seems to know her way," Dujols said.

"It's too dangerous," Alexandra argued.

Dujols put his hand on hers. "Let her go," he said.

I had stopped listening to them. I was walking the path. Was making all the right turns. I could feel energy pulling me forward.

Soon their voices were far in the distance and no more intrusive than a bee's buzzing. Reaching the center, I discovered a spiral staircase descending below.

I climbed down. The cavern was even darker. It smelled of earth. Of fungus and moss. Of fecund leaves rotting. The scent of violets followed me in.

A wooden slab with a brass handle was set into the floor. Lifting it, I looked down into a coffin-shaped hole in the ground, just big enough for a body. Dirt floor. Dirt sides.

The wooden slab had a handle on the inside, too.

"Sandrine?"

Startled, I turned.

The beautiful white-haired woman had followed me.

"You need to come back up with me."

"What is this place?"

"Our initiation chamber."

"What happens in the initiation?"

"You're not ready. Before you even attempt it, we need to teach you how to manipulate your breathing so, like the ancients, you can slow your body down, gain power over your heart, your lungs, and the flow of your blood. It's the first step to learning many forms of restraint."

"So that I can control La Lune's coming and going?"

"Yes."

"What would happen down here once I'd learned to slow my body?"

"You would pass a certain amount of time in this chamber of illumination. Once you proved you could withstand that, we would know you were ready to learn the rest."

I knew what I had to do. If I didn't stop La Lune, I was going to lose everything that mattered to me. I had to banish her. Then Julien would return. There was no other choice.

I crawled into the earthen box and, before the woman could object, pulled the lid closed. Heavier than I thought, it slammed with a loud bang I hadn't expected.

"No!"

Alexandra's scream was followed by the sound of rain. But it couldn't be raining, not down here.

For what seemed like several minutes I listened to pings, chinks, and dings falling against the wooden lid.

When silence fell again, I took hold of the handle and pushed up. The lid did not budge. I put both hands against the plank and pushed.

Nothing.

"Can you hear me?" Alexandra's voice was muffled.

"Yes."

"I'm going to tell you how to slow your breath. And then I am going to get help."

Her voice was too far away.

"What happened?"

"The wall partially caved in, and the door is covered with stones and dirt. Listen to me and don't talk. You need to conserve your energy. Get control of your breath. Feel it. Breathe in to the count of four with me . . . one . . . two . . . three . . . four . . . Now hold it just as long . . . one . . . two . . . three . . . four . . . Now out . . . one . . . two . . . three . . . four . . . Now hold . . . counting two . . . three . . . four . . . Keep that rhythm. Breathe slowly. Slowly. Now give your breath a color. A light color that floats. Pale blue or rose . . . pastel green. Imagine that you can see each breath as you expel it and hold it and take more in. Now slow down even more. Count to ten as you take it in . . . five . . . six . . . seven . . . eight . . . nine . . . ten . . . and then count to ten as you let it out. Watch the breath. Watch it as you exhale it and as you hold it.

My panic abated as I followed her instructions and saw and counted the pastel green breaths.

"Now count to fifteen for each inhalation, each hold, and each exhalation. And then twenty. Allow the color to become lighter and lighter as you breathe more and more slowly."

I focused. I saw Julien's face in the green miasma. I didn't want to leave him. I counted to twenty. Was I breathing slow enough? Something was going wrong. The air grew thinner. Too thin. I could feel La Lune in the coffin with me. Nervous, not for herself but for me. For her best chance in generations. I almost felt sorry for her. Lost, wandering, waiting. We wanted the same things, she and I, but they could not be taken by manipulation as she had done through all these years. She was going to lose. I would not go mad like Marguerite, Eugenie, Clothilde or Simone. My portrait would be added to the wall, but the story they would tell about me would not be of a woman who succumbed.

Until that moment, I'd thought I needed La Lune in order to be the woman whom Julien had fallen in love with. To be a painter. To be a sensualist. To be brave. But it wasn't that way at all, was it? I didn't need her. She needed me. Without me she was just vapor. Just wind. If La Lune wanted to feel love, she needed me.

I was going to die, here in a dirt coffin in hell. And she would continue her wait . . . searching for someone to infiltrate. Poor La Lune, forever restless, forever hungering for just one thing, to love again, to be loved and be set free.

But I didn't want to die!

My breath was labored. As slow as it was, it wasn't slow enough. I couldn't see the pastel breaths anymore. Only a viscous oily blackness that seeped in through the cracks in the wood, dripping onto me. Skinny snakes of disgusting filthy air that I could not take in. Poisonous vapors. Overtaking me. And there then was a blinding long last burst, and I knew I could stop trying. That it was the end. That I had lost.

Chapter 36

Hands pulled me out. Lifted me up. Carried me up the stairs. Coughing, I gasped the fresher air. Gulped it down.

They took me to a room in the back of the club. Laid me on a cot.

"No one has ever been in the box that long," Alexandra said as she wiped my face with a cool cloth.

"Drink this," Dujols said, and held a glass of water up to my lips.

I took several sips. Then several more.

"How long was I there?" My voice sounded hoarse.

"Over two hours," Dujols answered. "When you closed the lid, it slammed, and the vibrations set off an avalanche of small rocks. A part of the wall caved in. We had to dig you out. We were worried the whole time that you wouldn't make it."

"And only two of us at a time fit in that small space. Without any real tools. We had to use our hands and cups," Alexandra said. "Did you sleep?"

"I don't think so. But then again it didn't seem like I was there more than a few minutes. I just did what you said and slowed my breath."

I sat up. I knew I could no longer pretend—or hope—that La Lune was a manifestation of my guilt. A figment of my imagination. She was not a response to my father's suicide. My grandmother was right. La Lune was a malevolent force, and she needed to be evicted from my soul.

"I'm under a spell, aren't I?" I asked Dujols.

"Yes, yes, that's why you can't take off the necklace. Why you can't send her away," he said. "She doesn't want you here. Doesn't want you to see us. She may not let you come to us again."

I nodded. I could feel a fight coming from La Lune. I didn't know how she was going to manage it, but I was sure she was getting ready.

"I think you're right. Around you all, it seems as if she has less strength. Everything seems a little more clear to me. Can you tell me how I can end this? How I can break her spell?"

"The ritual would be written in La Lune's grimoire," Dujols said.

"Why would she write it down? Wouldn't that be risking someone doing just what I plan to do?"

"Spells are complicated and dangerous. They must be followed exactly, and so they are almost always committed to paper. There are too many steps to remember with exactitude. I would guess that the magick she's used all these years to stay contained, to merge, to get what she wants, is recorded on the pages of her book."

"What do I need to do?"

I knew what he was going to say before he said it from the way his eyes were shining.

"Bring me the book. I will help you figure it out."

"And what do you want from me?" I asked.

"What I've told you all along. To study the book. To find the secret. To learn the formula."

"The formula?"

" 'Make of the blood, a stone' . . ."

Chapter 37

Dujols and Alexandra escorted me home. It was four o'clock in the morning, but my grand-mother's maid had been worried and was up and waiting. Alice was shocked to see me so dirty and disheveled and fussed over me, making me a draught of tea, honey, and brandy. After I'd drunk it down, she helped me bathe and put me to bed.

I slept all through that day and night and woke up the second morning feeling restored. And resolved.

A note had come from Dr. Blanche the afternoon before, and Alice brought it to me in bed along with my café au lait and croissants.

My grandmother was asking for me, the note said. She'd had nightmares that I was in danger, and nothing they said settled her down. The doctor felt that if I visited, even if my visit upset her, that angst would be preferable to the panic that she was experiencing now.

I dressed for painting at the Louvre later that day, then went to see my grandmother. When I arrived, the doctor wasn't at the clinic, but the head nurse met me and told me that my grandmother had a guest. And then she gave me a coy smile. Some of the men who were salon regulars had taken to visiting her, and I wasn't surprised one was here.

"The doctor left word that when you arrived, it was fine for you to go in right away. She's anxious to see you."

The door was partially open. I put out my hand to open it wider, but what I heard my grandmother say made me stop.

"I don't understand, Benjamin. Are you saying that you aren't responsible for my son's death?"

I felt a wave of dizziness. Benjamin? With my grandmother? How had he found his way here? What would happen if he saw me? Would the nurses and doctors at the clinic help me or deliver me to him?

I wanted to run, but I needed to hear what he was going to say, what lies he was going to tell. I had to know how to fight him.

Taking a step back into the shadows behind the door, I held my breath and listened.

"Of course I'm not. That's Sandrine's delusion." His voice was kind and concerned. "Philippe was a second father to me. I owe him everything."

"What happened then?" my grandmother asked. Did she believe him? Was she goading him into revealing his motives? Before she'd become ill, she'd certainly been capable of matching wits with him, but was she still?

"Philippe was racked with guilt that so many clients' savings had been lost due to his poor investments. He couldn't face his *own* actions.

Not mine. I hate that he took the coward's way out—but that is what he did. And now Sandrine is suffering because of *his* actions. I came here to help her. You want that, too, don't you? To help her?"

"Yes, of course. We have to help Sandrine. The best way to do that is to get her away from Paris. Away from Paris and back home," Grand-mère said.

What? Did she really believe La Lune was that much a threat to me that I would be safer with the man responsible for her son's death?

"That's what I want, too. Just tell me where to find her," Benjamin said.

"The doctor told me he tried to reach her yesterday but without luck. Perhaps Julien would know."

"Julien?"

"Julien Duplessi, the architect I hired to— That doesn't matter now. Julien is mostly likely at his office. I'll write down the address for you."

"Why would he know where she is if you don't?"

There was a silence. My grandmother never should have mentioned Julien to Benjamin. I stepped farther behind the door, deeper into the shadows.

She was silent.

"I see," Benjamin said. "I do hope you recover your health, Madame. Thank you for your help.

You needn't worry about Sandrine anymore. I'll take good care of her."

Benjamin walked out of the room and down the hall, never for a moment sensing I was there, behind the door to my grandmother's room, holding my breath.

I waited until I could no longer see him and the echo of his footsteps was long gone. I pushed open the door to my grandmother's room.

"Sandrine, I have been so worried." She clasped her hands together. She looked so much better. Almost like herself.

"Oh, why did you tell him about Julien?" I asked her.

"You need to go home. You have to leave Paris. And Julien."

"But Benjamin was lying to you! He's the one who stole the money, gambled it away. Put Papa in debt and shamed the firm. Why would you throw me into his arms? He only wants me back for the shares of the bank that Papa put in my name years ago."

"Divorce him once you return to New York. Just get away from Paris now. Away from La Lune. She feeds off of love. If you give it up, you can protect yourself and protect Julien. If you love him, you'll do that. Don't you see? You'll save him and you'll be safe."

Tears filled my eyes. I went to my grandmother and put my arms around her. She felt so solid and strong. She believed I was haunted by the ghost of a sixteenth-century witch, and now so did I.

I straightened up.

"Sandrine?" My grandmother's voice sounded surprised, lighter.

"Yes."

"Where is she?" Grand-mère asked. "I don't see her shadow. What's happened?"

"I don't know."

"Has something changed? How are things between you and Julien?"

"Terrible. I haven't seen him for more than two weeks. He's broken it off with me."

"Thank God."

"But I love him."

"You can't, Sandrine. That's why I don't see her shadow. She's losing some of her power."

I sighed. What did I believe? One of us was crazy. Or we both were. Did it even matter anymore?

"The doctor said that once I could be with you without getting upset I would be able to go home. It will only be a few days now, *mon ange*. I'll go home, and you can go back to America with your husband. You'll be safe, and I can rest easy."

"No. I belong here. Painting. Being an artist. Being with Julien. I won't go back."

And with that my grandmother let out a shriek and pointed to my right. I didn't have to look. I knew there would be nothing I could see.

My determination had strengthened her hold. My grandmother was seeing La Lune again.

The nurse came running. As she attended to my grandmother, who had collapsed onto the bed, I walked out of her room, down the hall and outside, into the carriage I'd had wait for me.

I would go to the Louvre. Moreau would be expecting me, and I could paint with him and try to settle my mind. No, there was something bothering me—something my grandmother had said. Grand-mère had told Benjamin about Julien.

I gave the driver Julien's office address and asked him to take me there instead. I needed to warn him that Benjamin was here in Paris and that my grandmother had told him about our affair.

The young woman who sat in the foyer of the architectural concern knew me by now and smiled when she saw me.

"Is Monsieur Duplessi in?" I asked.

"He is, yes, but—"

So intent was I on seeing Julien, I didn't let her finish, didn't in fact realize she was still talking. I knew that nothing would have changed for Julien; he had made it clear that until I gave up the reality or the idea of La Lune, he could not be with me, but I had to at least warn him.

The door to his office was closed. I knocked as I opened it, afraid if I said who I was that he would tell me to go away.

I stepped into the room. Julien's eyes took me in and then shifted to my left. I twisted around and saw Benjamin.

My husband had turned to see who had come in. His face registered surprise but no recognition. For a moment I was confused and then looked down. I was still dressed in my student's garb: man's pants, day coat, hat pulled low on my forehead, casting my features in shadow.

"Who is this?" Benjamin asked Julien.

Julien ordered me out of the room without answering. "Please leave us. This is none of your affair."

"It's exactly my affair," I said.

Benjamin frowned. Had recognized my voice. He walked closer to me. Reached out and yanked the hat off my head. Stared at my hair, then my clothes.

I grabbed my hat back.

"You have no right to be here, Benjamin. And no reason. I know what you did and the lie you are using to cover it up. I'm not going back to America with you, and you aren't going to get your hands on my share of the bank's stock or my father's estate."

Benjamin laughed and turned from me.

"As I was saying, Monsieur Duplessi, I am told these events take place in the Bois de Boulogne. Tomorrow in the morning? Is dawn still the fashionable hour for a duel?"

"No," I cried out to Julien. "Benjamin won't fight fairly. He's not to be trusted."

But Julien ignored me. "Yes," he said to my husband, "at dawn."

Chapter 38

The afternoon had been fraught with emotion. Seeing Benjamin, confronting him, then trying to talk Julien out of dueling with my husband had exhausted me.

Of course Julien had refused me. It was a matter of honor, he said, and it wasn't up to me or really about me.

He'd pointed to my neck. "You're still wearing that?" His voice was sad, his expression grim.

"Julien, I went to Dr. Blanche . . . I tried. I do want to take it off." I saw a glimmer of hope lighten his evergreen eyes. "I've decided to take the grimoire to Dujols and have him help me find a way to rid myself of her."

"What about your painting?"

"I believe I will still be able to paint. I have to believe that. And if I can't . . ." I shrugged.

He took my hand, bent low over it, and kissed it. "Stay away from the Bois in the morning, all right? I'm a very good shot—there's no reason to worry. I'll come to the house after it's done. And then we'll work everything out. You'll be free, and I'll be free, and we can be together."

Exactly what La Lune wanted, I thought, but didn't say.

At home I wrote a note to Monsieur Dujols,

asking him if he would stay at the store later that evening. I was going to bring the grimoire, and I needed his help. I got a response an hour later that he would wait.

As I wrapped the book, I cut off a sheath of paper and nicked my finger. The blood wouldn't be stanched, and I bled over the book and onto the paper. Grabbing a towel, I wrapped it tightly around my finger and held it. It still had not stopped after ten minutes. Not after twenty. Finally, after almost forty minutes, the blood abated but my finger throbbed.

And it had looked like such a small and insignificant cut.

I finished packaging the grimoire and strained to pick it up, surprised at how very heavy it was. So much more burdensome than it had been when I'd taken it from the cabinet a half hour ago. Leaving the bell tower, I struggled down the narrow steps. Halfway I tripped and went tumbling. Hitting my shoulder on a sharp riser, I felt a pain shoot through me, tears filling my eyes.

On its own, the book continued falling. Down, down the steps. As if it had a destination and was on its way there.

Standing, I discovered I'd also sprained my ankle, badly. I couldn't put any weight on it and sat back down. I stared below me at the book. Alone in the bell tower with my foot swelling and my shoulder throbbing, I began to panic. How would I get help? Was I stuck there until I was able to get up?

This was La Lune's doing. She'd engineered this series of calamities. She knew what I planned to do with the book, and she didn't want me to do it.

"I have to understand who you are and what your powers are and how to protect myself from you," I said into the empty stairwell. The gray stone wall absorbed my words and threw them back at me in a mocking echo. *From you . . . from you.*

"I can't get Julien back if you're still attached to me. Don't you see that?"

I listened to the silence. I was so sure that she was going to answer me, but she didn't. She'd caused the cut, the fall, the ankle sprain, but now she had disappeared.

I hobbled down the steps, managing by putting almost all my weight on my left foot. At the bottom of the stairs, I picked up the weighty book and somehow got back to the main part of the house, where I engaged Alice to come with me to the bookstore and help with the book.

Even though it was close by, we took a carriage because of my injury. Only a block from our house, something spooked the horse, and he reared up. When he came back down, one of the wheels broke, and the carriage almost tipped over. Thanks to the driver's fast thinking and a very responsive horse, we avoided a much more damaging accident.

There were no other cabs on the street, and we were forced to walk, which was anything but easy on my badly hurt foot. And then it began to rain. Heavy winds accompanied a cold downpour, and fearing for the book, I found us refuge in a café. When the rain stopped, we found another carriage. Finally arriving at the bookshop, we found the door locked.

I peered inside. It was dark. No, I was not going to give up. I wouldn't go back without getting the information I needed.

Using my fists, I beat upon the door until they were sore. Finally Monsieur Dujols appeared. Slightly out of breath and red in the face, he ushered me inside.

"I thought you were not coming. I was just going to leave."

"Why would you think that?"

"Your note very clearly stated that you wouldn't be coming."

"I sent no such note."

He turned away from me, went to the very cluttered desk, picked up a sheet of expensive cream-colored paper, and handed it to me.

It was my grandmother's stationery, imprinted with the insignia of the house, the hand of fate, and under it the address in fine black copperplate. I read the handwriting.

Monsieur Dujols,

Please excuse my canceling at such late notice, but I will not be able to keep our appointment this evening,

Thank you,
Sandrine Verlaine

Everything was correct. It even appeared to be in my hand. But I had no recollection of writing it. What had happened? Had La Lune taken me over somehow and used me to write this? Just how powerful was she?

"Did you bring it? Is that it?" Dujols, always so serious and dour, was almost dancing as he circled the book. Reaching out, he touched it gingerly.

"May I unwrap it?"

I nodded, knowing that he would be even more careful than I. He was the expert in dealing with antique manuscripts.

As he discarded the paper, he noticed the streak of red and looked up at me.

I held up my hand. "I cut myself while I was wrapping it."

"Very dangerous," he said.

"I know, the knife slipped."

"No, I mean getting blood on a grimoire. Blood is often called for in instructions on casting spells and preparing talismans and amulets to summon angels and demons and other super-natural creatures. The book itself—" He touched the leather cover. "The book itself is magical and has properties that can be activated with blood."

I stared at the ancient volume and knew it had been wrong for me to take it out of its hiding place. For almost three hundred years it had been stored away, protected, and I had been the one to bring it out into the light. If anything happened to it, it would be my fault and my problem.

Monsieur Dujols opened the book, and I heard him give a little gasp. He had recognized the rip on the frontispiece. He knew his page would be the missing puzzle piece.

I watched as he turned and looked at the first two pages, foxed and yellowed, overpainted with the complicated and bizarre drawing of the drowning witch. He peered at the faint handwriting in the margins.

Carefully he turned to the next two pages. And then the next two. He barely seemed to breathe.

"This is amazing," he said. "I've only seen one or two volumes in my life that come close to being this important."

"The handwritten notes are her spells, aren't they?" I asked.

"Yes. Legend has it that these are the spells that La Lune learned in Prague. She probably wrote them down, here in this book, to protect them. Where better to hide spells and magical incantations than in a book that told inquisitors how to rid their states of witches and their influences?"

"Can you find the spell that I need to control her?"

"I'm sure in time I will be able to."

"There's no time."

"I'm afraid there has to be time," Dujols said.

"What do you mean?"

"Now that I have this, I need to study it. I am going to have to keep it here for a time."

"No. That wasn't our agreement. You said you wanted to see it. Not keep it. I agreed to show it to you in exchange for you helping me."

"And I will. In time."

Chapter 39

One of the shuttered windows flew open. Wind, rain, and leaves blew in. There was no dramatic magick that followed. Dujols, as much as he wished, was no conjurer. He was just a man devoted to and interested in the occult. To shut the window he had no choice but to leave the book on the table. Taking that as my one chance, I picked up La Lune's grimoire. Wrapped it up in my cloak and, without saying a word, walked out of his library.

I could hear him shouting as I headed down the street.

"Mademoiselle Verlaine, I want to help you. You need me to help you. You're in terrible danger . . ."

I spent the rest of the day working my way through my ancestor's grimoire. Reading the ancient French, trying to figure out the words I didn't understand from their Latin roots, looking for the spells I was searching for. I needed one to protect Julien in the duel. Another to banish La Lune.

I managed to isolate two potential enchantments by the time midnight fell. I lit the gas lamps and kept reading. La Lune's handwriting was so faded there were times I took more than an hour to work out just one paragraph.

By two hours past midnight I had found another three spells that might be what I was looking for, but I still had a hundred pages unread, and dawn was approaching fast. I needed to be at the Bois before Benjamin and Julien and prepared for their confrontation. Even if I was right about which of the hexes might work, and had translated the ingredients correctly, where was I going to get these odd things during the night?

I settled on one that suggested it would work as a magick charm against harm.

> The recipe for Abramelin Oil is as follows:
> Take of Myrrh in tears, one part; of fine Cinnamon, two parts; of Calamus, half a part; and the half of the total weight of these drugs of the best Olive Oil. To which aromatics you shall mix together according unto the art of the apothecary, and shall make thereof a balsam.

I fell asleep at my grandmother's kitchen table, the ancient grimoire a hard and unforgiving pillow.

When I woke, I had no time to bathe or dress if I was to get to the Bois before Benjamin and Julien arrived. The duel had been set for dawn, and so I had hired a carriage to arrive at five thirty, and the driver was waiting for me when I emerged from the house.

We set off for the large park on the outskirts of the city. My ankle hurt, and I was nervous and scared. Certain only of what I had to do and how dangerous it was going to be. It had been years since my father and I had practiced, and while I'd proved adequate, I never became the skilled marksman he was.

The driver could only take me so far, and I had to go the rest of the way on foot.

Being in the ancient oak forest in the semi-darkness made me apprehensive. The shadows were heavy, and too many noises were unidentifiable. How easy it was to imagine nefarious criminals lurking in the gloom. Rapists skulking behind giant boulders in wait for unsuspecting maidens. But in my pants and coat and hat, with the aura of masculinity around me, I had at least some protection, and I tried to take solace in that.

What was a fashionable meeting place during the day, filled with carriages, horseback riders, and men and women on bicycles, was empty and desolate at dawn. There were no families picnicking on any of the lawns. The lakes had no boaters idyllically rowing past.

I continued through the last allées of pines, the scent rich and sharp, and came to the clearing where the men were to meet. Looking around, I found a perfect hiding place and secreted myself there to wait.

Less than a half hour later, Julien arrived along

with his second, an architect I recognized from his office, and within five minutes Benjamin arrived with his friend William. The group spoke a few words to one another, gestured to the surrounding area, appearing to set up the rules.

Overhead, a crow cawed loudly, a ribald noise that shattered the silence. Julien looked up. Benjamin didn't. He was examining his pistol.

My nervousness was making me shake. That wouldn't do. I had to steady my nerves. Prepare myself. I would have only seconds to shoot my father's gun and prevent Benjamin from killing Julien. Was I capable? Did I have any choice?

The two men turned from each other and walked their forty paces. My hiding place put me equi-distant between them. When Benjamin raised his weapon, I had to be ready that instant.

I rested my hand on a boulder.

The next seconds passed at once achingly slowly and terribly quickly.

Benjamin lifted his arm before Julien did. My finger was on the trigger. All I had to do was pull, but I couldn't stop trembling. As much I hated my husband, as much as I despised him for what he had done to my father and was about to do to Julien, I couldn't pull the trigger.

But I had to save Julien!

Then I felt a hand cover mine. La Lune trying to help. As much as I wanted to save him, so did she. And in that moment, just as she must have known what I was thinking, I knew what she was thinking. We each were in love with Julien, and together we had to protect him.

Except even with her help, I couldn't pull the trigger. There was only one choice left to me, to us. And so as Benjamin's finger curled around the trigger, early, too early, cheating, I ran out into the clearing.

I heard that first shot, then a second. And then a third shot. A cry from Benjamin and a shout from Julien. A third shot? Who had broken the rules of the duel? Had one of the seconds come with a weapon? Had Benjamin brought another pistol so he could fire off two shots in succession?

I think I blacked out for a moment because the next thing I knew I was on the ground, my head pounding, my vision blurry. With a great effort I turned to my left and saw Benjamin lying in the dirt, clutching his chest. I turned the other way and saw Julien sitting up, his man attending to him.

"The American has been hit," a man shouted. "The woman, too. That's blood on her hand. Get help."

My hand, the man had said. My right hand? That I painted with? Had I deflected Benjamin's first shot with my hand? But it didn't hurt. All the pain was wrapped around my head, squeezing my skull. A few moments passed. I must have closed my eyes again.

"Sandrine?" It was Julien. Beside me. Sitting at an awkward angle, his arms crossed over his chest. "You little fool, why did you take such a risk? He could have killed you."

"I knew he was going to cheat. He brought a second pistol, didn't he?"

"You saved my life."

"It was my fault you were even here. I couldn't let him—" I broke off, suddenly noticing what Julien had been trying to hide from me. A crimson stain was spreading across his white shirt. "You're bleeding? You're bleeding. Are you all right?"

Julien's shirt was soaked through with blood. It leached out and soaked into the ground. It saturated my clothes, its warmth reaching my flesh, its sweet smell permeating the air.

"The bullet just grazed my side. I'll be fine," he tried to reassure me through labored breaths. "But Benjamin isn't going to make it, Sandrine. He's not ever going to bother you again," he said, and then he collapsed.

Chapter 40

They brought Julien back to Maison de la Lune with me in my carriage and summoned the doctor. As it turned out, he wasn't fine. As it turned out, the butt of my father's gun had deflected Benjamin's first shot, but he used his second pistol to shoot Julien in the stomach before Julien shot him. No major organs appeared to have been damaged, but Julien was losing too much blood too quickly, and the doctor told me that he was afraid if he couldn't stop the bleeding soon, Julien was not going to make it.

I was bruised, but none of my injuries were serious. I'd fallen on a rocky patch of earth. I'd cut my hand on a sharp stone. Hit my head on another. And a third had shattered one of the rosettes on the ruby necklace.

As I sat in the sickroom by Julien's side, watching him losing all that blood, I knew it was time. He'd asked me to do this weeks ago. I hadn't been strong enough then, I still wasn't now, but I needed to show him how much I cared even if it was too late.

"Look, Julien, look." I reached up and around the back for the clasp and found the Ouroboros waiting. The dragon allowed me to take his tail out of his mouth this time.

I took off the antique I'd been wearing for more than three months. Now it sat on my lap. I stared at the odd piece of jewelry that had encircled the neck of so many of my ancestors, tethering them to La Lune. Connecting them to the witch who had done everything to love again.

The dragon's ruby eyes flashed at me in the light. As if he were winking. I examined the rubies, all intact except for the one floret that had been damaged. How odd. I could see that the floret wasn't a ruby at all but two halves of a crystal casket filled with some red substance. I examined the other flowers and found a slight indentation on the rim of each. All of them opened. Every crystal was filled with the same red-caked substance.

Suddenly I heard the words that Dujols had said to me, but heard them spoken in a whisper, by a woman in a dream, words mixed with tears.

Make of the blood, a stone. Make of a stone, a powder. Make of a powder, life everlasting. Save him, Sandrine, save him.

I tilted the necklace toward the light. The red-caked interior had no glitter and no gloss. I ran my finger over it. It was dry. Dry? Almost powdery. Almost like . . .

No, it wasn't possible. But it did feel like solid pigment. Like a brick of watercolor that you drew your wet brush across to access.

I licked my finger and touched the cake, and it

came away red. The same color of the unfinished lips of the women in the painting. Pigment this color was in the studio. Bottles and bottles of it. I'd seen it.

What kind of necklace was this? What kind of special precious paint did it contain?

La Lune didn't speak to me with words, but her thoughts were inside my head. She knew the spells. She could save Julien.

"I have to do this," I whispered to him. "I have to allow her in. Please forgive me."

He shook his head. "No. Let me go. Let me go. Please, Sandrine. She's evil. She'll taint you."

He was still talking, his voice weak and faint, when I left the room.

As I climbed the steps to the bell tower, I knew that I would never again attempt to pretend that La Lune was a figment of my imagination born out my depressed state over my father's death . . . my reading that Oscar Wilde book at the wrong time . . . or my grandmother's fear of a family curse.

La Lune was real, and I had known that for a long time even if I wasn't always able to admit it. It was La Lune who had brought Julien to me —or me to Julien—and she could take him away just as easily. She might have already taken him away, just to prove to me that she could.

I opened the door to the ancient studio, put the necklace down on the table, and gathered the materials I needed: a knife, a bottle of linseed oil, my palette.

"Don't make me do this," I shouted to her. "There must be some other way to save him."

I listened for her answer, but she was silent.

"He's in love with me. That happened because of who *I* am. It had nothing to do with you."

Still she did not answer.

"I won't let you bully me. I am alive—you aren't." But in the end that didn't matter.

As I scraped the cake from inside the necklace, the bells in the tower began to chime. Slowly. Marking the occasion. I felt La Lune's excitement flowing through *my* blood in *my* veins. She was going to achieve what she wanted after all, despite all my best intentions. But what good would my resolve be if Julien died?

I wasn't the one with the power to keep Julien alive. She was.

Even if it was wrong, even if it meant opening myself up to all the darkness in her soul, I had no choice but to do everything I could to try and save Julien.

When I had enough powder, I poured out the oil and blended the concoction, watching the pigment metamorphose into a mound of silken, sensuous, ruby paint. The exact color, I thought, of the lips of the women in the portraits. The lips that looked as if they had been kissed too often.

After I'd mixed up the paint, I chose a fine sable brush. The best one I had. Closing the door on the tolling bells, I climbed down the narrow staircase from the rue du Dragon tower and made my way back to the main part of the house.

Chapter 41

Palette and brush in hand, I stood on the main staircase and examined the portraits that had hung there for as long as the house had belonged to my family. I turned up all the gas lamps so the hallway was flooded with light. I dipped the sable tip into the vermilion paint.

How dare I touch one of these masterpieces? It was blasphemy. All around me, the house seemed to be waiting, almost holding its breath. This was no time to be hesitant. Julien was fading.

The portrait was only a two-dimensional painting. It had no value compared to a human life. What difference did it make to anyone if I finished one of these paintings after all this time? Who was there to object?

I lifted the brush to the portrait of Lunette Lumière, and as I did, I heard Dujols warning me that there was no way to know what La Lune would do to her host when finally given a firm foothold.

How much of me, if any, would survive?

I thought of my grandmother, whom I loved so very much. Who was going to be released from the sanatorium soon. Could I bring her back here if La Lune inhabited my body? And Julien? If I saved him this way, would he ever forgive me?

Did that matter? Even if he never spoke to me again, he would be somewhere on this earth, alive, and that would be enough. To know that his talent would thrive, that his heart would love, that he would survive would be enough. And I— At least I would not spend the rest of my days feeling guilty that he had died defending my honor, which deserved no such sacrifice.

I touched the brush to the centuries-old canvas, and I painted in La Lune's unfinished lips. Stroke by stroke, adding the silky paint to the full, petulant lips that had been waiting for this for so many hundreds of years. I was meticulous. I lifted the brush. Applied the dab of paint. Repeated the process. One dab and then another.

I saw I'd smeared paint on my middle finger, and the sight of it frightened me. Paint made out of blood. Blood that would bring the painting to life and bind her to the painter.

It had to be this way. From the moment I stepped into this house when I was fifteen and again this January, I was not strong enough to withstand La Lune any more than the women in these other portraits had been. I was at her mercy. A force more powerful than time.

I thought about my own journey.

Coming here. Meeting Julien. The beginning of loving him. Meeting Cousin Jacob and his death. Then my grandmother's illness. My anger at seeing Charlotte singing at the opera. The fire. The horrible incident on the Eiffel Tower. Benjamin finding me in Paris and the terrible duel. All these events orchestrated by La Lune so Julien and I would both be free to be with each other. This was what she needed. To find a host who, unlike the other women in these portraits, was talented enough to paint, capable of love, and strong enough to withstand the witch's presence. A woman who would allow La Lune to incubate and live out her needs, to be an artist, to love and be loved back. With Julien—or, if he walked away, with someone new.

My brushstrokes were so fine they were invisible, and as I painted, I saw the lips become fresh, red, living lips. When I finished, I stood there on the steps, holding the palette and the brush and listened as La Lune began to speak and give me the instructions that I needed to bring her to life so she could save Julien.

Chapter 42

And so we come to end of the story. I survived that night, and so I will finish the tale.

Weeks had passed. My grandmother was living in the apartment on rue de la Chaise, I was living in Maison de la Lune. It was the end of May. Is there any more beautiful season in Paris than the spring? Julien and I were strolling by the Seine, on our way to celebrate a new commission he'd just received to build a hotel on Boulevard Raspail. As we passed a newspaper kiosk, something caught my lover's attention.

"Look," he said, pointing to the journal devoted to the arts: *Chronique des Arts et de la Curiosité.*

On the front page near the bottom was a headline:

CONTROVERSY AT THE SALON
BY ROGER MARX

Julien picked up the paper, threw some coins down on the vendor's tray, and pointed to an illustration beside the headline. It was a drawing of my painting. Standing side by side, our shoulders touching, we read the article together.

Sleeping Cupid, painted by a heretofore unknown young artist from America who has been studying at the École des Beaux-Arts and atelier of Gustave Moreau, has raised temperatures and excited tempers at this year's Salon. The provocative painting, which many call pornographic, has won a second prize in a jury headed by Monsieur Moreau himself, who defended his student's painting by saying it was no more graphic or disturbing than a hundred paintings of nude women that are admitted to the Salon every year.

"Why is a man's nudity more lewd than a woman's? This is a mythological god, in love with his wife, executed in a marvelous style by an up-and-coming artist of whom we all expect great things. That the artist is a woman, and the academy's first female student, just makes this prize all the more important."

"There are laws over this kind of salacious art," said Hector Previn, one of the judges who resigned in protest during the juried show. "Look at the lust on the sleeping god's face. That's not art. This painting is pornography."

The painting went on to . . .

Julien had raced ahead of me, and I hadn't caught up when he grabbed me by the hands.

"Darling, you have been awarded a second prize

by the Salon." He swung me around. "How marvelous." And then he grabbed me and kissed me, lifting me up.

"You will be hailed as the finest woman painter in Paris. The first to attend the École. The bravest. The first to win a prize. Your paintings will be sold in galleries. All of Paris will want to buy one. In parlors and boudoirs your creations will hang on the walls, and people will marvel and ask, *Who is this woman? Who is Sandrine Verlaine?*"

I kissed him. Full on the lips, there on the Quai. I could smell the amber and honey and apple scent that was his alone. His arms were so strong. Was *he* as strong?

"No," I said.

I was watching his clear, evergreen eyes now, watching to see how he was going to feel about what I had to tell him. For it was time to tell him. I had no excuse to wait any longer.

Julien loved me and I him. My confession would not, could not, change that. We were bound to each other in a deep and abiding way because of what we had gone through and what we were willing to go through for each other. Our appetites, our passions, our goals were in harmony, and we were solidly on the same path toward the future.

"No, *mon cher* Julien. They will not be asking about Sandrine Verlaine. They will be asking about *me*. The woman who signed that painting. The woman who painted it. La Lune."

Author's Note

As with most of my work, there is a lot of fact mixed in with this fictional tale.

Belle Époque Paris is painted as close to the truth as the story allowed. There was in fact a very strong occult moment in France during the time, and there is a large body of literature written about the sometimes frightening and wild cults, believers, and experimenters. The nightclubs all existed as I describe them, as did the streets, restaurants, cafés, sights, Dr. Blanche's clinic in Passy, and all the stores, including the fabulous Sennelier art supply store, and the Librairie du Merveilleux, owned and run by Pierre Dujols. The École des Beaux-Arts is still one of the finest art and architecture schools in the world, and women were not allowed to attend until 1897—though in my novel I move that date forward three years. The painter Gustave Moreau was a teacher there in 1894, and Henri Matisse was one of his prize pupils. The art world and anecdotes about now famous painters and the École's salon are all based on source materials. Last but not least, Jews, especially Kabalists, do hold exorcisms to banish dybbukim and various kinds of demons, and the ceremony portrayed in this novel follows the ancient laws.

I am especially indebted to my researcher, Alexis Clark, who saved me from hours of going down the wrong path and gave me insights and facts into the world of Belle Époque Paris and her artists, which allowed me to spend more time in my imagination than in the library and online.

Acknowledgments

For the fourth time and with even more gratitude, huge thanks to my terrific editor, Sarah Durand, who helped me bring this novel to life. And to Sarah Branham, who so graciously inherited it and gave it such a thoughtful polish.

To my wonderful publisher and dear friend Judith Curr, whose faith in me is not only reassuring but always inspiring.

To Lisa Sciambra, Hillary Tisman, Ben Lee, Daniella Wexler, Andrea Smith, and everyone at Atria whose hands this book passed through—your hard work and creative thinking does not go unnoticed. And to Alan Dingman, whose artistry graces my covers and always takes my breath away.

To my agent, Dan Conaway, my forever knight in shining armor, whose insight and caring shore me up and make me a better writer. And to the team at Writers House, whose help is invaluable. A special thank-you to my first reader, Marjorie Braman, who is more than worth her weight in gold, and to my last, Nancy MacDonald, for her precision and thoughtfulness.

To the amazing Meryl Moss and Deb Zipf—the best publicists in the biz.

To my friends who make me laugh, make me think, keep me sane, and give me invaluable advice—Liz and Steve Berry, Douglas Clegg, Randy Susan Meyers, Lee Child, C. W. Gortner, Alyson Richman, Jenn Risko, Linda Francis Lee, and Pauline Hubert. And a special thank-you to everyone at ITW and the Fiction and Historical Fiction Writers Co-opers for all your support and camaraderie.

I also want to thank readers everywhere who make all the work worthwhile (please visit MJEmail.me for a signed bookplate). And to all the wonderful booksellers and librarians without whom the world would be a sadder place.

And as always, I'm very grateful to my family, especially my father and Ellie, the Kulicks, Mara Gleckel. And most of all, Doug.

Center Point Large Print
600 Brooks Road / PO Box 1
Thorndike, ME 04986-0001 USA

(207) 568-3717

US & Canada:
1 800 929-9108
www.centerpointlargeprint.com